Arroga...
so...
Del......us, innocent yet
tempting brides…
Each destined to delight the other

**Two marvellous bestselling novels
from favourite authors
Lucy Monroe and Alexandra Sellers**

100 Reasons to Celebrate

We invite you to join us in celebrating
Mills & Boon's centenary. Gerald Mills and
Charles Boon founded Mills & Boon Limited
in 1908 and opened offices in London's Covent
Garden. Since then, Mills & Boon has become
a hallmark for romantic fiction, recognised
around the world.

We're proud of our 100 years of publishing
excellence, which wouldn't have been achieved
without the loyalty and enthusiasm of our
authors and readers.

Thank you!

Each month throughout the year there will
be something new and exciting to mark the
centenary, so watch for your favourite authors,
captivating new stories, special limited
edition collections…and more!

THE DESERT

Sheikh's

BRIDE

LUCY MONROE &
ALEXANDRA SELLERS

*M&B™ and M&B™ with the Rose Device
are trademarks of the publisher.
Harlequin Mills & Boon Limited, Eton House,
18-24 Paradise Road, Richmond, Surrey TW9 1SR*

THE DESERT SHEIKH'S BRIDE
© by Harlequin Books SA 2008

The Sheikh's Bartered Bride © Lucy Monroe 2004
Sheikh's Honour © Alexandra Sellers 2000

The Sheikh's Bartered Bride and Sheikh's Honour were first
published in Great Britain by Harlequin Mills & Boon Limited
in separate, single volumes.

ISBN: 978 0 263 86683 4

10-1008

*Printed and bound in Spain
by Litografia Rosés S.A., Barcelona*

The Sheikh's Bartered Bride

LUCY MONROE

The Desert Sheikhs
COLLECTION

August 2008
THE DESERT SHEIKH'S VIRGIN
Penny Jordan

September 2008
THE DESERT SHEIKH'S PASSION
Sharon Kendrick & Susan Mallery

October 2008
THE DESERT SHEIKH'S BRIDE
Lucy Monroe & Alexandra Sellers

November 2008
THE DESERT SHEIKH'S MARRIAGE
Jane Porter & Sarah Morgan

Lucy Monroe started reading at age four. After she'd gone through the children's books at home, her mother caught her reading adult novels pilfered from the higher shelves on the book case...alas, it was nine years before she got her hands on a Mills & Boon® romance her older sister had brought home. She loves to create the strong alpha males and independent women that people Mills & Boon® books. When she's not immersed in a romance novel (whether reading or writing it) she enjoys travel with her family, having tea with the neighbours, gardening and visits from her numerous nieces and nephews. Lucy loves to hear from readers: e-mail Lucymonroe@Lucymonroe.com or visit www.LucyMonroe.com

Don't miss Lucy Monroe's exciting new novels coming to you soon from Mills & Boon® Modern™

To Isabelle...
You are more precious to me than words can ever
express and I thank God daily for giving you to me
as a very special gift. With love, Lucy

CHAPTER ONE

"MISS BENNING."

She wasn't Miss Benning. She was Catherine Marie, captive of The Hawk, a sheikh who still lived by the code of the desert, where only the strongest survived.

He was coming now. She could hear his deep, masculine voice as he spoke in a tongue she did not understand to someone outside her tent. She struggled against the cords that bound her hands, but it was useless. The silk scarves were soft, but strong and she could not get her hands free.

If she did, what would she do? Run?

Where?

She was in the middle of the desert. The sun beat against the tent, heating up the cavernous interior. She wouldn't last a day in the vast wasteland on her own.

Then he was there, standing in the entrance to the room in which she was held. His features were cast in shadow. All she could see was his big body encased in the white pants and tunic typical of his people. A black robe, his *abaya*, fell from his massive shoulders to mid-calf and his head was covered with the red and white *smagh* that denoted his position as sheikh. The headband holding it in place was made of twisted black leather.

He was less than fifteen feet away, but still his face was hidden from her by the shadows. Only the strong line of his jaw denoting his arrogance was discernable.

"Miss Benning!"

Catherine Marie Benning's head snapped up from where it had been resting against her fist and her eyes slowly focused on her surroundings. Tent walls hung with faded silks, to be replaced by cool gray cement, relieved only by the posters advertising the upcoming book drive and literacy event. They were the walls of the break room in the Whitehaven Public Library, much closer to a cold and wet Seattle, Washington than the blistering hot deserts of the Sahara.

Fluorescent light cast a harsh glow over the pointed features of the woman standing in front of her.

"Yes, Mrs. Camden?"

Straightening her double-knit polyester blazer, almost identical in color to the library's walls, Mrs. Camden, Catherine's superior, sniffed. "Your head was off in the clouds again, Miss Benning."

The disapproval in the older woman's voice grated against Catherine's usually limitless patience. Perhaps if the man in her fantasies would ever show his face, she wouldn't be feeling so frustrated, but he did not. This time had been no different. The Hawk was as elusive to her imagination as he was in it.

"I'm still on break," she gently reminded the older woman.

"Yes, well, we all do what we must."

Recognizing the beginnings of a familiar lecture, Catherine stifled a sigh at the knowledge her lunch break was to be cut short. Again.

Hakim bin Omar al Kadar walked into the library and scanned the reference area for sight of Catherine Marie Benning. Her picture was indelibly printed on his mind. His future wife. While arranged marriages were not uncommon in the royal family of Jawhar, his was unique.

Catherine Marie Benning was unaware that she was to become his wife. Her father wanted it that way.

One of the stipulations of the deal between Hakim's uncle and Harold Benning was that Hakim convince Catherine to become his wife without telling her about the arrangement between her father and the King of Jawhar. Hakim had not asked why. Having been educated in the West, Hakim knew that American women did not view arranged marriages with the same equanimity the women of his family did.

He would have to court Catherine, but that would be no hardship. Even in an arranged marriage, a royal prince of Jawhar was expected to court his intended bride. This marriage would be no different. He would give her a month.

Ten weeks ago, his uncle had been apprised by Harold Benning of the probable deposits of a rare mineral in the mountains of Jawhar. The American had suggested a partnership between Benning Excavations and the royal family of Jawhar.

The two men had still been negotiating terms when Hakim had been attacked while out riding in the desert in the early hours of the morning. Investigations had revealed that the assassination attempt had been made by the same group of dissidents responsible for his parents' deaths twenty years before.

Hakim was unclear how marriage for Catherine had become part of the deal. He knew only that his uncle considered it convenient. Should the need for long-term living visas arise for the royal family, Hakim would be in a position to sponsor them as the spouse of an American. There would be no need to go through regular diplomatic channels, thus preserving the privacy and pride of his family.

The royal family of Jawhar had not sought political asylum from another country in the three centuries of its reign and they never would. Already overseeing the family's interests in America, Hakim had been the logical choice for the alliance.

Harold Benning also saw the marriage as beneficial. His concern over the continued single state of his twenty-four-year old daughter had been obvious. According to him, she never even dated.

The result of the older men's negations had been a Royal Decree: Hakim was to marry Catherine Benning.

He spotted his quarry helping a small boy on the other side of the room. She stretched to pull a book from the shelf and the button-up black sweater she wore above a long, straight skirt caught his attention. Molding her breasts, it revealed a surprisingly lush feminine form and he felt himself stir.

This was unexpected. Her picture had revealed a pretty woman, but nothing like the exotic beauties he had bedded in the past. That he should react so readily to such an innocent sight made him stop in his journey toward her.

What had so aroused him? Her skin was pale, but not alabaster. Her hair was blond, but a dark blond and twisted up on the back of her head as it was, it looked drab. Her eyes were a shock, a gentian-blue that had startled him with their intensity in the picture and were even more unusual in person.

Aside from the eyes, nothing about her stood out and yet his body's response could not be denied. He wanted her. While he had experienced this sort of instant physical attraction before, it had been with a lot more provocation. A certain way of walking, dressing or an alluring look. Catherine Benning exhibited none of these.

It was a puzzling, but not unpleasant surprise. A genuine physical attraction on his part would make the job of her seduction that much easier. He had been prepared to do his duty regardless of personal attraction. Country came first. Family came second. His own needs and desires last of all.

He walked forward, stopping a little to her left. As the boy walked away, her dark sapphire gaze did a quick survey of the room, skimming over him, and then settled back on a man who had come to stand in front of the desk.

But even as she pointed to something on her computer monitor, her gaze flicked back to Hakim. And stayed. He met her eyes, noting peripherally the man she had been helping walk away. The next person in line went unnoticed as her attention remained on him.

She appeared poleaxed and he smiled.

Her entire body went taut and her cheeks pinkened, but she did not look away.

His smile went up a notch. Fulfilling his duty would be a simple matter of turning that attraction into a desire to wed.

''Miss Benning! Pay attention. You have patrons to serve.''

The martinet haranguing Catherine was no doubt the dragon of a boss Harold Benning had mentioned when briefing Hakim on his daughter.

Catherine's head snapped around and her blush intensified, but she did not stammer as she answered the older woman. ''I'm sorry. My mind wandered.'' She turned to the next person in line, repeated her apology and asked how she could help them, effectively dismissing her superior.

The older woman harrumphed and marched away like a petty general deprived of his battle spoils.

He waited until the last of the line had walked away before greeting Catherine. "Good afternoon."

She smiled, her eyes even more startling up close. The blush was back. "Hi. What can I do for you?"

"I am interested in antique telescopes and the history of stargazing. Perhaps you can direct me to a good reference."

Her eyes lit with interest. "Is this a new hobby for you?"

"Fairly new." As recent as the discussion Hakim had had with her father. Although Hakim's own father had shared Catherine's passionate interest in ancient stargazing, since his death, his books had remained unused in the observatory in the Kadar Palace.

"It's one of my personal interests. If you've got a few minutes I'll show you the right section and point out a few books that I think are particularly good."

"I would like that very much."

Catherine sucked in air, trying to calm her racing heart as she led the handsome and rather imposing man to the proper nonfiction area of her library. The aura of barely leashed power surrounding him was enough to send her pulse rocketing, but the fact that he physically embodied every characteristic of her ideal fantasy tipped her senses into dangerous territory.

At least a couple of inches over six feet, his muscle-honed body towered above her own five foot seven in a way that made her feel small beside him. Even knowing she was not. The silky black hair on his head was only a shade darker than the color of his eyes and if he didn't speak with such impeccable English, she would think he was the sheikh of her fantasies.

A wave of totally unfamiliar desire swept over her, leaving her even more breathless and confused.

He hadn't touched her and somehow she had always believed this level of sexual awareness could only accompany touch. She'd been wrong.

They stopped in front of a row of books. She pulled one off the shelf and handed it to him. "This is my favorite. I have my own first-edition copy at home."

He took the book and his fingers briefly brushed hers. She jumped back, shocked by the contact. Her body throbbed in a way she hadn't experienced before, but she desperately tried to look unaffected by his nearness.

"I am sorry." His black gaze probed her own, leaving her even more unsettled.

She shook her head, but could feel that infernal blush crawling along her skin again. "It's nothing." Less than nothing. Or at least it should have been.

He flipped open the book and looked at it. She knew she should go, but she couldn't make her legs move in the direction of the reference desk.

The book shut with a snap and his dark gaze settled on her again. "Do you recommend anything else?"

"Yes." She spent another ten minutes pointing out different books and suggesting a couple of periodicals he might be interested in ordering.

"Thank you very much, Miss…"

"Benning, but please call me Catherine."

"I am Hakim."

"That's an Arabic name."

His mouth twitched. "Yes."

"But your English is perfect." What an inane thing

to say. Lots of Arabic people lived in the Seattle area, many of them second or third generation Americans.

"So it should be," he drawled in a voice programmed to melt her insides. "The royal tutor would be most displeased if one of his pupils should speak with anything less than complete mastery."

"Royal?" The word came out sounding choked.

"Forgive me. I am Hakim bin Omar al Kadar, prince in the royal family of Jawhar."

She was breathing, but her lungs felt starved of oxygen. A prince? She'd been talking to a prince for more than ten minutes. Lusting after him! Heavens. Her half-formed idea of inviting him to attend the next meeting of the Antique Telescope Society died a swift death. Unfortunately the attraction he held for her did not.

She swallowed. "Can I help you with anything else?"

"I have taken up enough of your time."

"There's a society for people interested in antique telescopes in Seattle," she found herself blurting out, unable to let it go at that. She wouldn't invite him to meet her there, but she could tell him about the meeting.

"Yes?"

"They meet tonight." She named the time and place.

"Will I see you there?" he asked.

"Probably not." She would be there, but she sat in the back of the room and he was not the sort of man content to enjoy anything from the sidelines.

She wasn't wholly content, either, but she didn't know how to break a lifetime of conditioning.

"You will not attend?" He actually looked disappointed.

"I always go."

"Then I shall see you."

She shrugged. "It's a big group."

"I will look for you, Catherine."

She barely stopped herself from blurting out the question, "Why?" Instead she smiled. "Then maybe we *will* run into each other."

"I do not leave such matters to fate."

No doubt. He was much too decisive. "Until tonight then."

She turned to go and was only marginally disappointed he did not call her back. After all, he'd said he would look for her.

He checked the books out she had recommended and left the library a few minutes later.

Catherine watched him go, certain of one thing. The sheikh of her fantasies would no longer be faceless.

He would have the features of Hakim.

CHAPTER TWO

CATHERINE walked into the meeting room in one of Seattle's posh downtown hotels. Though she was early, over half of the seats were already taken. She scanned the crowd for Hakim while butterflies with hobnail boots danced an Irish jig on the inside of her stomach.

Would he be here?

Would he really be looking for her?

It was hard to believe. Even harder to accept the sensations she felt at the mere thought of his presence.

A scar-riddled face and subsequent laser treatments had meant she'd missed out on dating in both high school and college. Her shyness had been so ingrained by then that the *late blooming* her parents had expected never materialized. She thought she'd come to terms with the fact she would most likely die a maiden aunt in the best tradition of little old ladies with white hair and homes filled with other people's memories. She was too shy to pursue men and too ordinary to be pursued. Yet something about Hakim compelled her to step outside her comfort zone.

And that scared her.

No way would a guy like that return her interest.

"Catherine. You have arrived."

She knew the owner of the deeply masculine voice, even as she turned. "Good evening, Hakim."

"Will you sit with me?"

She nodded, unable to immediately voice her acceptance.

14

He led her to a chair in the middle of the room, much closer to the front than she usually sat. Taking her arm, he helped her into the seat with a courtesy that was both captivating and alarming. Alarming because it meant he touched her and the feel of his warm fingers on her arm was enough to send her senses reeling.

Several pairs of eyes turned to watch them take their seats, the curiosity of the onlookers palpable. She smiled slightly at an elderly woman whose stare was filled with avid interest. Catherine remembered talking to her at the last meeting. She was nice, but a bit nosy.

Catherine moved her own gaze to the front of the room where tonight's speaker stood talking to the president of the society.

The speaker was the leading authority on George Lee and Sons telescopes. He was supposed to bring along one from his collection for the society members to look at up close. She couldn't wait to see it and thought the red silk covered shape in the front of the room must be it.

She was proved right forty minutes later when the silk cover was removed and the general assembly was invited to come forward and take a look.

"You wish to see it?" Hakim asked her.

She shrugged.

"What does this shrug mean?"

She turned her head, allowing herself the luxury of a full-on look. The impact was that of a bomb exploding in her brain and she almost gasped, but held back the revealing sound.

She smiled wryly, knowing herself. "The shrug means I'll probably forego the pleasure."

"I will accompany you."

Like a security blanket? "It's not that," she denied,

even though it was exactly that. "I'd just rather not wait in line. Do you see how many people are already waiting to look at it?"

Hakim looked toward the line of society members and then back at her. "Are you quite certain you do not wish to see it?"

Even a George Lee and Sons telescope could not compete with Hakim for her interest, she admitted to herself. "Very sure."

"Then, perhaps you would consent to dinner with me this evening and we could discuss my new hobby. You appear highly knowledgeable in the subject."

"Dinner?" she parroted.

"Are you concerned about sharing a meal with a stranger?"

The quite justifiable concern had never entered her mind, but then she'd never been in a sheikh's company before, nor had she ever experienced the debilitating cocktail of feelings being near him elicited in her body.

"No," she said, shocking herself and making his eyes widen fractionally.

"Then you will allow me to buy you dinner this evening?"

"I don't know…"

"Please." The word sounded much more like a command than any sort of pleading, yet it affected her just the same.

"I suppose I could follow you to the restaurant in my car." She should show at least a rudimentary level of self-protection.

"Very well. Is seafood to your liking?"

Her mouth watered at the thought. "I adore it."

"There is a beautiful restaurant not a block from here. We could walk."

"I think it's just starting to rain," she said.

His lips tilted in a sardonic smile. "If so, I will lend you my raincoat."

She laughed at the instant picture she had of herself in a raincoat several sizes too big. "That won't be necessary. I just thought you probably wouldn't like to walk if it was wet out."

"I would not have suggested it otherwise."

"Of course."

It was a short walk and though the gray clouds were heavy with moisture, it did not rain.

They spent dinner discussing her favorite hobby. She was surprised at his knowledge and said so.

"I read the books you gave me this afternoon."

"Already?"

It was his turn to shrug. "Most of them."

"Wow. I guess you didn't have to go back to work."

"We all must have our priorities," he said with a smile.

"I wouldn't have pegged you as someone who put his hobbies above his work."

"There are times when the unexpected takes precedence in our lives."

She wondered at the mysterious statement, but did not know him well enough to ask about it.

They both declined dessert and he walked her back to her car. He took her keys from her and unlocked it. Opening the door, he indicated she should get inside.

She stopped before bending down to get into the driver's seat. "Thank you for dinner."

"It was my pleasure, Catherine."

Two days later, Hakim invited her to attend a Saturday showing of a journey among the stars at the theater. It required spending the whole day together as well as a three-hour drive to Portland. The prospect of all that time with just her and Hakim in the enclosed space of a car had her nerves completely on edge. She jumped when the security buzzer rang to announce his arrival.

She pressed the button on the small black communications box. "I'll be right down."

"I'll be waiting." His short reply came; his voice even sounded exotic and sexy over the apartment building's tinny intercom system. She was still finding it difficult to believe that such a gorgeous man had a serious interest in her. Grabbing her hold-all and purse, she left the apartment.

When she got downstairs, she found him waiting in the lobby.

"Good morning, Catherine. Are you ready to go?"

She nodded, while her eyes devoured the sight of him. Wearing a snug-fitting black sweater and tan trousers that managed to emphasize his well-developed muscles, he made her mouth go dry with desire.

She licked her lips and swallowed. "I've got everything I need."

"Then, let's go." He took her arm and led her outside where a long, black limousine waited.

"I thought you were driving."

"I wanted to be able to focus my attention on you. There is a privacy window. We will be as secluded as we desire."

The way he said it made totally inappropriate images swirl through her head and her nipples tightened almost painfully. It was such an unexpected sensation, she gasped.

"Are you well?"

"F-fine," she stuttered before practically diving into the backseat of the limousine.

As a tactic to hide her discomposure from him, it was no doubt a dismal failure. Most of his escorts probably waited for him to help them into the car. Of course, these same escorts most likely had a love life outside of their fantasies and could handle the close proximity of such a sexy man with equanimity.

Not so her.

She was in over her head and the man had never even kissed her. When he took the seat opposite her, her breasts swelled at his nearness.

And his smile was positively lethal to her self-control.

"Would you like some refreshments?" He flipped open a small door in the side console of the car to reveal a fully stocked fridge.

"Some juice would be nice." She was really proud of herself when her voice came out fairly normal.

He poured her a glass of cranberry juice and handed it to her. "So, are antique telescopes your only hobby?"

"Oh, no. I'm an avid reader. I guess that makes sense, me working in a library."

"I think I expected that, yes."

She returned the droll smile. "Right, but I also love hiking nature trails."

His brows rose at that and she couldn't help a rueful shrug of acknowledgment to his surprise.

"Maybe I should have said ambling through the woods."

"Ah." He sipped at his mineral water. "And do you daydream as you walk, I wonder."

She could not hide her own surprise that he had guessed something so private about her quite accurately.

"Yes. Being outside and away from people is sort of magical."

"I too like the outdoors, but prefer the desert to the woods."

"Please tell me about it."

And he did, but he deftly directed the conversation back to her on several occasions and they spent the long drive talking about subjects she rarely discussed with anyone but her sister. Hakim seemed to understand her shyness and was not bothered by it, which made it easier for her to be open with him.

He also never dismissed her views as her father was so adept at doing. Hakim listened and as he listened, Catherine found herself falling under the spell of his personality.

He took her to lunch at a restaurant that overlooked the Willamette River. The food was superb, the view of the river amazing and his company overwhelming to her heart and her senses. She was very much afraid that she was falling deeply and irrevocably in love with a man that was far out of her league.

When they'd settled into their seats at the theater, Hakim slipped his arm over Catherine's shoulders, smiling to himself when she stiffened, but did not pull away. She was not used to a man's touch, but her body gave all the signals of being ready for a sexual awakening. The latent and untapped passion he sensed in her would play to his advantage, making it easy for him to seduce her into marriage and fulfill his duty.

His specialized training had made it possible to save himself from the recent assassination attempt, but his parents had not been so lucky. He had been unable to save them and the knowledge still haunted him.

The fact that he had been ten years old at the time did nothing to assuage his need to protect his family now, whatever the cost.

He could still remember the sound of his mother's scream as she watched her husband shot before her eyes, a scream cut short by another gunshot. His little sister had whimpered beside him and he'd taken her hand, leading her out of the palace via the secret passage known only to members of the royal family and their most trusted servants.

Days of grueling heat in the desert sun had followed as Hakim had used the knowledge taught him by his Bedouin grandfather to seek shelter in the wild for him and his small sister. He had eventually found his grandfather's tribe. He and his sister had survived, but Hakim would never forget the cost.

A small sound from Catherine brought him back to the present. He realized he had been caressing her neck with his thumb. Her eyes were fixed on the huge screen, but her body was wholly attuned to him and hummed with sexual excitement.

A month of seducing her toward marriage might very well be overkill.

Catherine reveled in the feel of Hakim's arms around her and pretended it meant more than it did. It was only natural that he ask her to dance with him. After all, he was her escort for the evening and everyone else was dancing.

The black-tie charity ball was to raise money for St. Jude's Children's Hospital. She'd invited Hakim to be her escort, half expecting him to say no, but he hadn't. He'd agreed to bring her and even to have dinner with her family beforehand.

Her mother and sister were completely charmed by his exotic charisma and enigmatic presence. Even in a business suit and tie, the man exuded sheikhness.

"Your sister is very kind."

She let her body move infinitesimally closer to his and fought the urge to lay her head on his shoulder and just breathe in his essence. "Yes. She and I are very close."

"This is good."

"I think so." She smiled up at him.

His expression remained serious. "Family is very important."

"Yes, it is."

She wasn't sure where this was headed.

"Having children, passing one's heritage from one generation to the next is also important."

"I agree. I can't imagine a married couple not wanting children."

Finally he smiled. "Perhaps there are those that have their reasons, but you would never be one of them."

She thought longingly of marriage and family, specifically with this man and it was all she could do to keep her smile pasted in place. "No, I'd never be one of them."

She was unlikely ever to be married at all, but why bring up that depressing thought?

His thumb started a caressing rotation in the small of her back and her thoughts scattered, even the depressing ones.

Closing her eyes, she gave into the urge to let her cheek rest against his chest. He'd probably never ask her to dance again, but she just couldn't help herself.

Instead of acting offended by her forwardness, Hakim

settled her more fully against him and danced with her until the music changed to a faster beat.

He didn't ask her to dance again that evening, but he didn't neglect her, either. Using his easy sophistication to deflect the interest of other women who approached them with the intention of flirting with him, he kept his interest fixed firmly on her and her heart gave up the battle.

She was in love.

Hopelessly.

Helplessly.

Completely.

Catherine opened the card attached to the flowers. It read, "For a woman whose inner beauty blooms with more loveliness than a rose."

Tears filled her eyes and it was all she could do not to cry. She and Hakim had spent the night before at a benefit concert. Catherine had gotten up and spoken on behalf of the children and their hopes and dreams. She'd been shaking with nerves, but she'd felt compelled to make a plea on the foundation's behalf.

Afterward, Hakim had told her that her obvious love of children and compassion for them had shown through even her nervousness. She'd been warmed by the compliment, but the long-stemmed red roses totally overwhelmed her.

She put the vase on the corner of her desk where both she and the rest of the librarians could see them easily.

Picking up a pile of papers that needed filing, she contemplated the crimson blooms. He made her feel so special, even if they were just friends. Sometimes it felt like more than friendship and her hopes would soar, but

what else could it be when he never so much as kissed her?

They spent a lot of time together and her attraction
for him grew with each occasion, but he appeared unaffected on a physical level by her.

She wasn't surprised.

She was hardly the type to inspire unbridled lust in
a man like Hakim, but her desire for him continued
unabated. Growing with each successive meeting, both
it and the desire to be in his company became gnawing
needs within her.

Her thoughts stilled along with the rest of her as
Hakim walked into the library. She should be used to
his arrival by now, it happened often enough and every
time since the first, he'd made it clear he had come
specifically to see her.

He walked toward her with an unconscious arrogance
that she found rather endearing. He was just so sure of
himself, but then he was rich, gorgeous and had been
raised a prince. Why wouldn't he be?

She remembered the papers in her hand just as he
reached her desk and leaned over to put them away
quickly.

Hakim stopped in front of Catherine's desk, just as she
bent to put something away in the lowest drawer.

"Catherine…"

Her body straightened and her intense blue gaze met
with his, her mouth twisted in a rueful grimace. "Sorry,
I just remembered I had to file these—" she waved a
sheaf of papers in her hand "—when I saw you."

"And it could not wait until you had greeted me?"
he asked with some amusement.

"I might have forgotten easily."

Did she realize what she was giving away with that admission? He already knew he had a definite impact on her ability to concentrate, but a more sophisticated woman would not have admitted it.

"Then I shall have to content myself conversing with the top of your head while you finish."

"Sometimes, you sound so formal. Is that because the Arabic language is a more formal language, or is it because English is your second language and therefore you don't slip into slang as easily?"

Not for the first time, her rapid change in topic left him slightly disorientated. "French is my second language," he said in answer to her question, "I did not learn English until I had mastered it."

She tilted her head to one side. "Oh. I've always thought French would be a lovely language to learn. I studied German and Spanish in school, but I have to admit I don't have a facility for it."

"I did not come to discuss my fluency in other languages."

"Of course you didn't." She smiled. "Why did you come?"

"To see my friend."

Something flickered in her eyes at the word "friend", but was gone too quickly for him to interpret.

"Oh," she said again. "How many are you?"

"How many what, little kitten?"

Her face heated to rose red as he knew it would at the small endearment. Such words were common in his culture between a man and the woman he intended to marry. They were nothing more than an admission of his intent, but they flustered Catherine a great deal.

"How many languages are you fluent in?" Her voice

was breathless and he had the not so shocking urge to steal her breath completely with a kiss.

He could not do it of course. Not here and not yet, but soon. He smiled in anticipation, causing her eyes to widen.

"I'm fluent in French, English, Arabic and all the dialects of my people, little kitten." He repeated the phrase on purpose just to watch the effect it had on her, which was perhaps unfair of him.

It was startling. She sucked in air, grimaced and then whispered, "Hardly little."

While she was maybe an inch above average in height for a woman, she often made comments as if she saw herself as some kind of Amazon. He stepped toward her until he stood only a few inches from her and reached out to brush the smooth curve of her neck with one fingertip. "To me, very little."

She trembled and he smiled.

Very soon she would be his.

Her head tilted back and she eyed his six-foot two-inch frame with unmistakable longing. "I suppose so."

He wanted to kiss her. It took every bit of the self-discipline developed in his training with the elite guard to step back and drop his hand.

"I came to see if you would like to join me for dinner tonight."

Her mouth opened and closed with no sound issuing forth. They had known each other for three weeks now and eaten numerous meals together, as well as attending several formal functions. Yet she acted shocked every time he asked her out.

"Come, this is not such a surprise. We had lunch together only yesterday."

She smiled whimsically. "That's why I'm surprised. I thought you'd want to spend time with..."

Her voice trailed off, but her eyes told him what she had been about to say. *Other women.* She had so little concept of her own value. While he should be relieved his duty would be so easy to see through, it made him angry she dismissed herself so easily.

"I want to spend time with no other woman."

He had no difficulty reading her expression now. Her eyes were filled with both joy and hope. Yes. She was ready. He had courted her long enough.

"I would love to have dinner with you."

"Then I shall see you this evening." He turned to go.

"Hakim."

He stopped.

"You could have called. It would have saved you an hour of driving here and back to Seattle."

"Then I would have foregone the pleasure of seeing you."

She looked ready to melt at that assurance and he smiled before walking away. His duty would be fulfilled very soon.

CHAPTER THREE

HAKIM took Catherine to his favorite restaurant on the waterfront for dinner. The ambiance was quiet and elegant. Perfect for proposing to his future wife.

He'd thought about taking her to the restaurant at the top of the Space Needle. He'd been told it was considered the height of romance, but sharing a noisy elevator with tourists on the way up held no appeal. At least not for tonight.

She smiled at him as he held her chair for her at the table. She'd worn a black dress with long sleeves, a peasant neckline and gathered waist. The full skirt swirled around her legs as she sat down. He let his fingers trail along the exposed skin of her shoulders above the wide neckline and she shivered. Satisfaction that his mission would soon be accomplished settled over him as he dropped his hand, moved around the table and took his own seat.

Even in the dim light of the restaurant, he could tell she was blushing again.

"Surely such a small touch is not cause for embarrassment?"

She smoothed her already perfectly coiffed hair. She'd worn it up again. Though he liked the view it gave him of her slender neck, one day soon, he would remove the clip and see what the dark honey strands looked like tumbling against her shoulders.

"I'm not embarrassed. Not exactly." Her sigh lifted

her breasts against the soft fabric of her bodice, revealing the source of her blush.

His little virgin was excited. Two unmistakable ridges under the black material gave her away. They also apprised Hakim of the fact she was not wearing a bra. The knowledge had a by now predictable effect on him.

"What are you exactly?" he asked, wondering if she would admit anywhere close to the truth.

"Stupid."

He shook his head. Little did she know, but her desire for him would soon be fulfilled. "Jewel of my heart, you must not say such things."

She dropped her focus to her lap, where she straightened her burgundy napkin against the black fabric of her skirt. "You shouldn't call me things like that. I know you're just saying it because it's the way you talk, but…"

He reached across the table to tip her chin up with his finger. "It is not merely the way I speak. Do I use such terms with other women in your hearing?"

Her bottom lip disappeared between her teeth and her eyes reflected confusion. "No." It was a bare whisper.

He wanted to kiss those trembling lips. Her vulnerability called to primitive instincts inside him.

"They are words meant for you alone."

It was as if she stopped breathing and she went utterly still, the look in her eyes a revelation of emotions so volatile he was shocked by them. Then her eyelashes lowered and she sucked in air too quickly, choking.

He offered her a glass of water as she sought to get the small coughing fit under control.

"Thank you." She drank the water and he watched as her throat convulsed gracefully with each swallow.

"You have a beautiful neck."

The water glass tumbled and only the quick action of a nearby waiter saved her dress from a drenching. Considering her reaction to his last statement, Hakim decided it would be best to wait until after dinner to propose.

By the time Hakim pulled his black car to a halt in the parking garage of her apartment building, Catherine's nerves were stretched tighter than an overtuned violin string. They wound one notch tighter when he insisted on seeing her inside.

She watched his dark hands as they unlocked her door and turned the knob to open it. Such masculine hands and yet so fluid in their movement, she desperately wanted them on her.

He pushed the door open and ushered her inside, one of the hands she found so fascinating secured around her waist. Her lungs stopped working while her heart went into overdrive. He closed the door and locked it, indicating he wasn't leaving any time soon and her already racing heart went turbocharged.

He led her toward the living room and she was surprised when her legs were able to move. She felt like her bones had all melted to jelly.

When they reached her bright yellow couch, he gently pushed her down onto the overstuffed cushions and then sat beside her. So close beside her that her shoulder was pressed against the hard wall of his chest. "I wish to speak with you."

"Oh," she squeaked.

He laid the hand that was not attached to her waist on her thigh, succeeding in surrounding her completely with his body and putting her on the verge of hyper-ventilating.

What would he do if she turned to him and did what she'd been longing to do for so long, touch the black silkiness of his hair and kiss the sensual line of his mouth? She clasped her hands firmly together in her lap to stop them from taking liberties that might end in her humiliated rejection.

For several seconds, neither of them spoke, the rush of air going in and out of her lungs at such a rapid rate the only sound in the room. He started to draw small circles on her thigh with his forefinger, sending aware-ness arcing up her leg and to the center of her being. She stifled a gasp of pleasure. She couldn't move. Nor could she look at him. Her attention was firmly fixed on that darkly tanned hand as it moved lazily against the black knit of her skirt.

Still he said nothing.

The quiet became unbearable. ''Hakim?''

His silence beat against her and she sensed he wanted something from her, but she did not know what. Finally, when she could not tolerate one more second of the tortuous anticipation, she raised her head and tilted it backward to look at his face.

It was what he'd been waiting for. Eye contact.

Dark ebony bored into her. ''You have enjoyed these past weeks in my company, have you not?''

''Yes.''

''Am I a fool to believe you would like our associ-ation to continue?''

''No.'' She had to clear her throat before she could get more words out. Necessary words. ''You could never be a fool.''

"Then I would also not be out of bounds to hope you might want to deepen our relationship?"

He wanted to be her boyfriend? Her mind couldn't quite grasp the concept, but she nodded her head in agreement anyway.

"Yes, I would be out of bounds, or yes you want to deepen our relationship?"

"I want…" She forced her halted lungs to pull in a breath of air. "I want to deepen our relationship."

Would he kiss her now? The mere thought sent her pulse on a ride like a runaway stagecoach.

"Marry me."

She was daydreaming. She had to be.

But there was something wrong with the fantasy. "But you've never even kissed me."

"I have not had the right."

"What do you mean? Were you… Were you attached to someone else?"

"No, not that, but I was not as you put it *attached to you*, either. It would not have been right for me to kiss you before formal declarations were made."

Did he mean declarations of love? No. He'd said formal declarations. "Do you mean you have to be engaged in your country to kiss?"

His hand moved from her thigh to her cheek and he cupped it, his expression almost tender. "To kiss a virgin, yes."

Was her lack of experience so obvious? She supposed it was. "But this is not Jawhar."

"Nevertheless, I will treat you with the respect due you."

That was nice. "If I say I'll marry you, will you kiss me then?" This was by far the strangest daydream she had ever indulged in, only she knew on some level it was all too real.

A distinctly predatory light entered his obsidian eyes. "Yes."

"Yes," she repeated, not ready for the fantasy to end.

"You will marry me?"

"Yes." He couldn't really mean it and she would say just about anything to experience his mouth on hers. "Now you can kiss me."

He lowered his head, until his lips were centimeters from hers. "I can?"

"Yes." When he didn't close the gap, she said, "Please."

The kiss was as soft and fleeting as a butterfly flitting from one flower to another, but he did not move his head away and their breath continued to mingle.

The scent of his cologne mixed with a fragrance that could only be him. Male. It called to the primordial woman in her. She wanted to claim this man.

"Are you teasing me?" she asked, wondering why he had not kissed her again, more thoroughly.

"I am teasing myself."

His admission was flint to the gunpowder of her self-control. To say such a thing implied he wanted her and that was as exciting as having his body so close she could feel his heartbeat. She closed the gap of those few centimeters, her mouth locking to his with enthusiasm, if not skill.

He didn't seem to mind. His grip on her tightened and he took control of the kiss almost immediately. His mouth moved against hers, his tongue running along the seam of her lips. She opened her mouth on a small rush of air and he took possession of the interior. She'd thought of kissing like this before of course, but it had seemed messy.

It felt wonderful.

He tasted like the tiramisu he'd had for dessert at the restaurant. He also tasted like Hakim and it was a flavor she could not get enough of.

She moaned and sucked on his tongue.

He growled, his grip on her going painfully tight now and she found herself in his lap, her breasts pressed against his chest.

She wanted to touch him. She had to touch him. Her hands landed against his shoulders and stayed there for a full five seconds while the kiss went on and on. But just feeling the heat of him under her fingers was not enough. She wanted to explore.

First she let her fingers trail through his hair. It felt soft, almost like silk and she explored the shape of his head through it. He was so male, even his head felt a particularly masculine way to her searching fingers.

A sense of desperation, laced with fear that this would end soon and she would miss having touched the rest of his body, she brought her hands down on either side of his face, slowly sliding them toward his neck, then shoulders. With each centimeter of movement, she memorized the feel of his warm skin against the pads of her fingertips.

Sliding her hands down the polished cotton of his shirt, under his jacket, she outlined each muscle, each ridge and valley on the masculine torso so close to her own.

He shuddered and she rejoiced that she could affect him.

His hands were kneading her backside and she could feel a growing ridge of hardness under her hip.

In the back of her mind, she registered that meant he was getting excited which sent her emotions careening out of control and the impossible feelings she harbored for this magnificent man poured out through her lips and fingertips.

As if the release of her emotions had freed something in him, his ardor increased and the kiss went nuclear.

His tongue dueled with hers, demanding a submission she was only too willing to give. While he conquered her mouth, she tore at the buttons on his shirt, getting enough undone to slip her hand inside and feel the smooth, hot flesh of his naked chest. It was at that point that she accepted this was not a waking dream. No fantasy could possibly be this good.

And somehow because it was real, it was more. More intense. More feeling. More excitement. Almost too much.

She broke her mouth from his and sucked in air, trying to breath as her world spun around her in a kaleidoscope of feelings she had never experienced, but nonetheless recognized.

She wanted him.

Desperately.

"Do engaged people get to make love?" Her own boldness shocked her, but she waited tensely for his answer.

The kneading action on her bottom stopped and his forehead fell against hers. "No."

"Is it because I'm a virgin?" she asked, feeling tears of frustration already burning at the back of her eyes.

Hakim was going to wake up to whatever insanity had prompted his proposal and withdraw. And she would *still* be a virgin. Life was so unfair.

"It is true. This is part of it."

"But I don't want to be a virgin," she wailed and then felt mortified color drench her face, neck and even the breasts achingly aware of the proximity of his body.

He didn't laugh. He didn't even smile. He kissed her, hard and quick against her mouth. "We must wait."

"I can't."

He groaned like a drowning man going under for the last time. The hardness under her thigh twitched and his mouth locked with hers again, this time not waiting for her to open her lips, but forcing them apart for the entrance of his tongue.

His hand came up and cupped her breast, his thumb brushing over her achingly erect nipple. She arched into his touch while squirming her backside against his hard maleness. She loved him so much. Loved what he was doing to her. Loved the anticipation of more. For the first time in her life Catherine was glad she had never been with another man.

She wanted Hakim to be her first.

He kissed his way down her neck, stopping to suckle her rapid pulse beat. Arrows of pleasure shot through her limbs and she cried out at the wonder of it all.

Then his mouth was on her collarbone, his tongue caressing her in a way she had not expected. She went completely still when he pulled the stretch neckline of her dress down to expose her braless breasts.

He stopped moving, too, pulling back until he had an unfettered view of her exposed flesh. There was a lot on display. Her figure in no way resembled the boyish shapes so popular in today's media.

She felt another blush crawl up her skin as her senses prickled with heat and heady excitement.

Dark fingers caressed her pinkened flesh, making her moan and shake in response.

"So beautiful. So perfect." His words registered with the same sensual impact as his touch had done.

"I'm—" She'd meant to say something about how she was not exactly cover model slender, but he forestalled her with a finger against her lips.

"Exquisite. You are exquisite."

Then his head lowered, his lips touched her sensitized flesh and she lost her sense of place and time. He tasted her. All of her, covering each square centimeter of her naked curves with tantalizing attention. By the time he took one of her nipples into his mouth, she was shaking and inexplicable tears were running hotly down her temples and into her hair.

It was too much. The pleasure was too great.

"Hakim, darling, please!"

She didn't know what she was begging for, but he seemed to as his hand trailed down her body until it reached the hem of her skirt. His fingers brushed against her stocking clad leg and moved upward, slowly, ever so slowly.

Combined with his tasting of her breast, this tormenting slowness was driving her mad. But then his hot fingers were on the skin above the top of her stocking, curving toward her feminine center. His fingertip brushed against the silk of her panties where it covered her most tender flesh and sensation exploded inside her like a nuclear reactor.

Her body bowed. She screamed. She thought Hakim cursed, but she couldn't be sure. Nothing but the agonizing pleasure of her body was registering completely.

His hand slipped inside the waistband of her panties, down to flesh that had never, ever felt a man's touch and she cried out in an overload of sensation as he touched that bit of feminine flesh that other women talked about, but she had never even experimented with finding.

She went rigid and then shook in convulsions that were so strong, her muscles ached from supporting them.

He continued his ministrations until her entire body went limp from the strain.

He pulled her close to his chest, wrapping her in his embrace with strong, sure arms. The tears that had been a trickle became a torrent and she sobbed against his chest with as much abandon as she had given to her pleasure.

He comforted her, whispering soothing sounding words in a language she did not recognize. It didn't matter that she couldn't understand the words, their tone was what she needed.

"That was too much," she said between hiccuping sobs.

"It was more beautiful than the desert at sunrise," was his response.

"I love you," she confessed, her heart left unprotected by the amazing experience she had just gone through.

She was hopelessly in love with a man who could have any woman he wanted and that scared her. Refusing to admit it did not change it and there was a certain amount of relief in letting the truth out.

His hands caressed her back and she shivered with another convulsion. If it had been an earthquake, she would have called it an aftershock. It had been close enough.

He picked her up, carrying her as if she weighed no more than one of the throw pillows off the sofa. When they came into her bedroom, he flipped on the small light by her bed, casting a warm glow in the room.

Stopping beside the bed, he bent to lay her down, but she clung to his neck. "Please, don't leave."

She couldn't bear being alone after *that*.

He tensed.

"Please," she begged again.

"Do not plead. If you want me to stay, I will stay."

She let go of his neck and let him lay her down on the bed. He straightened to stand beside her. "Prepare yourself for bed and I will return to hold you."

"Aren't we going to make love?" she asked, not at all sure she could stand another dose of pleasure like what she had just gone through, but willing to try.

"Not until we are married."

She still didn't believe for a minute they were actually going to end up married. "But…" She could see the hard ridge still pressing against his slacks.

He shook his head decisively. "We will wait."

She couldn't expect him to hold her all night in that condition.

"I could…" She blushed without completing the offer, knowing he was a smart enough guy to figure it out.

"I'll take a shower."

"You're going to take a cold shower?" The thought of a sexy man like Hakim having to take a cold shower over her was somehow very appealing.

He smiled as if he could read her thoughts. "As you say. Prepare yourself for bed. I will return in but a moment."

She nodded and silently watched him walk into the en suite. It was only when she looked down that she realized her chest was still exposed. Her nipples were still hard and wet from his mouth. Oh my. The sight paralyzed her for a full minute before she was able to get up and find a nightgown to wear to bed.

Hakim stood under the warm jets of water, his body buffeted by the pain of unrequited passion, his mind filled with pleasure at how successfully his campaign had gone.

Catherine had agreed to be his wife.

His uncle would be pleased. Her father would be pleased. Hakim was pleased.

Marriage to Catherine would be no hardship.

Under the shy exterior, she was so passionate, so beautifully sensual. It had been harder than he ever would have thought possible to pull back from making love to her completely.

She'd liked that. His sweet little wallflower had liked thinking he was in here taking a cold shower because of his desire for her. The shower wasn't cold, but only because he'd never found that an effective deterrent to desire. He had found that warm water could sometimes soothe the physical ache of wanting what he could not yet have.

It wasn't working right now though. His sex was so hard, he was in pain.

He could not banish the image from his head of how she had looked with her dress pulled down, her breasts swollen and quivering with her desire. And the way she had exploded...her entire body bowing with such strong contractions, he had found it most difficult to keep his jewel on the couch. He groaned as his male member throbbed at the memories.

Maybe a cold shower would help.

Turning the knob all the way to the right, he was

soon blasted with an icy spray. He gritted his teeth,
practicing a self-discipline technique he had learned
while training with elite guard in his uncle's palace.

Catherine would have to marry him very soon.

She would not demur at a simple civil ceremony, he
was certain. She was too happy to be marrying him.

She loved him.

Though it was not necessary, it pleased him, it
pleased his pride that his future wife loved him.

Her shock at his proposal underscored the reality that
she had reached the age of twenty-four without once
having had a serious relationship, or even a steady date.
Or so her father had asserted and Hakim had no reason
to disbelieve him.

Her virginity had been an important issue to Hakim's
uncle. According to the old man, no royal prince of
Jawhar could marry a woman of uncertain morals.
Hakim felt a certain primitive satisfaction in Catherine's
untouched state, but he hardly placed the importance on
it that his uncle did.

After all, he'd been prepared to marry once before
and the woman had not been a virgin. Undoubtedly his
uncle would not have approved.

And right now, when he wanted very much to bury
himself in the silken wetness of Catherine's body, her
innocence was more barrier to pleasure than benefit.

Reentering the bedroom, he found Catherine sitting up
in the bed wearing a virginal, almost Victorian gown in
white and her dark honey hair hanging over one shoulder in a thick braid. He smiled at her innocence.

As he got closer to the bed however, his smile
slipped. He doubted very much that she realized it, but
the gown was borderline sheer and the dark aureoles of

her nipples were visible as well as the outline of her gorgeous breasts. He wished he'd left his slacks on as the benefits of the cold shower disappeared and the silk of his boxers shifted with his growing erection.

Catherine didn't seem to notice. Her blue eyes were unfocused as she stared at something beyond his right shoulder. Her lips were slightly parted and he could see the sweet, pink, enticing interior of her mouth.

As he climbed into the bed beside her, she jumped as if startled.

"Hakim!"

"You were not expecting me?"

Soft color flooded her cheeks and she scooted down into the bed so that the quilted spread covered her to her neck. "I was thinking about something."

"And was I this something?"

Expecting a shy affirmative, he was surprised and chagrined to see her shake her head in a jerky motion.

"What were you thinking of?"

She started. "Just, just a story that's all."

"A story?"

"Sometimes I like to tell stories in my head."

"Our lovemaking was not enough to keep your mind occupied?" The fact his innocent fiancée had been able to dismiss their lovemaking from her thoughts when he had not, irritated him.

"I didn't want to think about it."

Offended, he demanded, "Why not?"

And only realized as she pulled back that he was leaning over her in a most intimidating fashion. He did not move back however. He wanted an explanation.

"You said we couldn't make love until we're married."

"Yes. This is true."

"Well, then what would be the point of letting myself get all worked up if you aren't going to let anything happen?"

It was a good question. One he wished he could answer, but he had not been so successful in tamping down his own desires. He was rock hard and the only thing saving his pride were the blankets covering them both. Even so, had he not had his body tilted toward her, his erection would have tented the covers and given him away.

It shamed and frustrated him that his usual ice-cool restraint was letting him down. With all his training, she had more control over her desires than he did his. He did not like weakness, even that of a purely sexual nature.

"So you told a story in your head?" What sort of story would have been sufficient to take her mind off of the pleasure of their lovemaking?

"Yes."

"And it was not about me." He felt his irritation turn to irrational anger at the thought.

"That would defeat the purpose, wouldn't it?" Her tone said her words should be obvious to even the simplest of minds.

He glared at her. "I thought you wanted me to stay with you tonight."

Suddenly the pragmatic tilt to her mouth disappeared and searing vulnerability beamed at him from the startling blue of her eyes. "Yes. Are you going to leave because I was daydreaming?"

She had much to learn about him. "I made a commitment to stay. I will stay."

She chewed on her bottom lip, still red and full from his kisses. "Do you always keep your promises?"

"Always." He repeated the word in his mind, reminding himself he had given her his word to wait until their marriage to receive the gift of her purity.

CHAPTER FOUR

"IN OUR marriage, you will always know that when I promise a thing, it will be done."

Catherine stared at him. Their marriage? This joke had gone far enough. "Stop teasing. We're not really going to be married."

Hakim's black eyes snapped at her and the darkly dangerous side to his nature she had first suspected became all too real. "When you promise me something I expect the same from you. We will be married."

"But why?" It had to be obvious to him that he didn't have to marry her in order to make love to her. She was way too vulnerable to her desire for him and after what had happened on the couch, he had to know it.

He tapped the end of her nose with his forefinger. "Are you so uncertain of your own appeal you must ask this question?"

"But you're a sheikh for goodness' sake. Don't you have to marry a princess or something?"

"We are not quite so medieval in the royal family of Jawhar. Catherine, it is my desire to marry you."

A twenty-four-year-old children's librarian who had never even been kissed by a man before that night? "I don't think so."

The gentle touch of his palm against her cheek mesmerized her. "I want you, Catherine. I thought that was obvious."

Was it true? Felicity had told Catherine many times

that she was no longer the girl too tall for her age or whose face was pockmarked with severe acne. But Catherine had never stopped feeling like that girl.

He tilted her head toward him. "Accept that it pleases me very much to make you my wife."

But why did it please him? The only logical answer that she could think of was so beyond the realm of reality, she felt shock thrill through her even contemplating it. Yet, she could think of only one reason for a man like Hakim to marry a woman like her. She had no diplomatic pull, could not increase his cache with his people and while her father was wealthy, Hakim was wealthier.

Love.

He had to love her. It was the only thing that made any sense of their situation. He'd never said the words, but maybe that was a cultural thing. Or an alpha guy, totally in charge and too cool to admit to really tender emotions kind of thing. Whatever.

When she remained silent, stunned by the thoughts racing through her mind, he sighed and rolled onto his back. "The time has come for me to marry. It is my uncle's wish I marry now."

"And you picked me."

"You are my chosen bride, yes."

She thought of the years since her laser treatments during which her father had thrown men at her head, men interested only in what they would gain materially from the marriage. Men who had not stirred her emotions or her senses as Hakim did. Not only did he stir her emotions, he returned them.

A glorious smile broke over her face. "I want children." Family who would love her and accept her love unconditionally.

"As do I."

Then a sudden thought assailed her, one she could not dismiss. Not when he'd withheld the words of love so there was this little niggle of doubt way down, deep inside. "You have to be faithful. No mistresses. No other wives."

He didn't smile, didn't make a joke of it as some men would have. In fact, his expression turned even more serious, his mouth set grimly. "Polygamy is not practiced in Jawhar and to take a mistress would be to compromise my own honor as a prince among my people."

"Then I will marry you." Even as she said the words, she had a hard time believing them.

"Then I am content."

The words were a little disappointing. *I am content* did not sound nearly as romantic as *I love you*, but what did she expect with a sophisticated guy like Hakim? A brass band?

"It is time we slept." He kissed her briefly and it was all she could do not to follow his lips as they pulled away from hers.

"All right."

Although, he did not pull her into his body, he did lay one arm across her stomach and it felt so nice, she wasn't even tempted to slip into fantasizing herself to sleep. For once, reality outshone anything her imagination could conjure.

A featherlight touch on his cheek woke Hakim. He waited to open his eyes to see what she would do.

Her small hand settled on his chest, her fingertips touching his collarbone. And then nothing. No movement of any kind, but he could feel her gaze as if it were an electric current directed at him. Opening his eyes, he found her looking not at his face, but at her hand against his chest.

"Good morning."

Her gaze rose to his and the wonder in the blue depths of her eyes did strange things to him. "Good morning, Hakim."

She was closer than she had been last night, her warm, womanly body pressed against his length and his morning erection tightened to urgent need in the space of a heartbeat. She could not help but notice, the small gasp and perfect "O" of her lips confirming she had indeed felt his body's response to her nearness.

He needed to move away. Immediately.

This was much too dangerous.

"Do you…"

He waited for her to finish her question, but she didn't. Instead, her hand, which had been immobile for several minutes, now started a slow slide down his chest.

He should stop her. He knew he should stop her, but that hesitant little hand turned him on as no woman performing the *raqs sharqi* after years training in belly dancing had ever done. He waited with heart-stopping impatience for her hand to reach its destination. She stopped when her fingertips reached the top of his boxer shorts. He would not ask her to continue, but waiting to see if she did so was driving him wild.

One tentative fingertip outlined the hard ridge. His sex twitched. Her exclamation drowned out his moan. She yanked her hand back and rolled away from him. Her breath was coming out in little pants.

She stared up at the ceiling, her fingers gripping the blankets with white-knuckle intensity. "I've read romance novels, you know? Some of them have pretty steamy love scenes.''

"And?''

"Experiencing it is different than reading about it.'' She sounded so perplexed, he smiled.

"Yes.''

"I mean, I didn't expect to be so nervous.''

"You are a virgin, little kitten.''

Her head turned and gentian blue eyes pinned him. "Why do you call me that?''

"Your name.''

"My name?''

"Catherine. Cat. Only you do not act like a cat. You are more like a kitten. Inquisitive. Sometimes shy. Innocent.''

"Oh. Are all virgins so jumpy about touching male flesh?''

He did not know. He had never bedded one. "You did not touch my flesh.''

Catherine whipped over to face him fully.

Her braid landed heavily against her unfettered breast and he found his attention riveted by the hardened nipples pressing against the almost transparent fabric of her nightgown. So he did not catch her words at first. His brain had to play them back for him to make sense of them.

She had said, "I did touch you.''

He reached out and brushed the back of his fingers against the nipple that tantalized him so. "This is touching you through your gown.'' Then he untied the ribbon holding the neckline of her gown together, slowly pulling the ends until the bow unraveled.

She stopped breathing.

He parted the edges of the gown and gently cupped her naked breast, palming the excited peak.

"Oh, my gosh!"

He could not quite smile. He was in too much pain from his need, but he felt the smile inside. She was so responsive to him. So perfect. "This is touching your flesh."

Her, "Oh," came out choked.

He knew he was teasing them both because he did not believe he could give her completion without taking her. His control was too close to the edge. Yet, he tormented himself playing with her nipples and caressing the swollen skin around them.

"Can I… Can I…" She repeated the phrase with each rotation of his hand, but did not complete her thought.

"Can you what?"

"Touch your flesh." The word *flesh* came out a long, soft moan.

He wanted it. He wanted it very much, but if she did, they would consummate their marriage before the wedding. This would be wrong. He had made a promise. He must keep it. His mind knew the truth, but his libido argued that this was America, not Jawhar. She did not care about the standards to be adhered to by a sheikh of his people, would not care if he broke his word on this.

"It would not be wise."

"*Hakim.*" Her tortured cry was loud in the silent room.

He reluctantly pulled his hand from her soft curve, moving to lie on his back. He felt as if he had been hiking in the desert under the noonday sun.

"You go to my head." He should not admit such a

thing. It gave her power over him. Her innocence and eager response to him was too much of a temptation.

Her soft laugh had him turning his head to look at her. Her smile was that of an imp. "I was under the impression I *went to* other parts of your body."

"That too."

She looked so happy with herself, he was tempted to kiss the lips curved so sweetly. Then a wrinkle formed between her eyebrows and she frowned as if in thought. "Are you sure it's me?"

"I see no one else in the room."

She bit her bottom lip. "I mean, I read that men wake up feeling that way. Maybe it was just your normal morning reaction, you know?"

He couldn't help it. He burst out laughing.

The uncertainty in her gaze contained his mirth. He reached out to brush her cheek because he could not prevent himself. "You know book knowledge, but as you said earlier, the reality is quite different. I want you, Catherine, I am throbbing with need, I assure you."

That had her smiling again. "Good."

Hakim had been gratifyingly complimentary over the Belgian waffles and scrambled eggs seasoned with her own special combination of spices that Catherine had made for breakfast. It was the first time she'd made breakfast for a man. The entire morning had been filled with firsts for her. The first time waking up beside a man. The first time she had to share a toothbrush. She'd been surprised when the fastidious Hakim had so calmly asked to use hers.

It had seemed like such an intimate thing to do.

Like what they'd done on the sofa and then in her bed hadn't been, she chided herself.

She finished putting the dishes in the apartment's small dishwasher while Hakim wiped down the counters and table.

"You're awfully domesticated for a sheikh."

"I lived alone for most of my university years."

"You said most, does that mean you had a roommate for a while?" Her mind boggled at the thought of rooming with a sheikh. Of course she would be doing that soon. As his wife.

His expression closed. "Yes. I had a roommate for a while." He tossed the dishcloth in the sink.

She rinsed it, wrung it out and hung it over the sink divider. "It didn't work out, huh?"

She could remember horror stories from friends at college who had shared their dorm rooms with impossible people.

"No. It did not work out."

Something in his voice alerted her that he wasn't talking about getting rid of a roommate because he was a slob.

"Was it a woman?" she asked before thinking better of it.

Hakim's face tightened. "Yes."

She had to know more. "Were you a couple?"

"Yes," he said again, but offered nothing more.

She swallowed an inexplicable lump in her throat. "Was it serious?"

"We considered marriage."

"But you broke up."

"She did not fancy life in a backwater like Jawhar." The way he said the words, Catherine got the impression he was quoting the faceless woman he had once considered marrying verbatim.

"But you live in Seattle."

"At the time, my plans were to return to my homeland."

"She refused to go with you?" Catherine was incredulous. How could any woman who loved him turn
down a lifetime with Hakim, no matter where they
lived?

"Yes. When do you plan to tell your parents of our
engagement?"

Knowing he had loved another woman enough to
want marriage hurt, even though she knew it shouldn't
and she was more than willing to go along with his
abrupt change in conversation.

Nevertheless, his question caught her unawares. Tell
her parents? What would happen if he backed out? She
still couldn't quite believe Hakim wanted her, wanted
to marry her.

Stop it right there, she firmly told herself.

She wasn't going to live in fear of rejection for the
rest of her life. She had to stop reacting like the emo-
tionally scarred preadolescent or physically scarred
teenager she had been and start acting like the future
wife of a sheikh.

"I can tell my mother this morning."

A strange expression crossed his face. "What of your
father?"

That would concern Hakim. Parental approval was a
big thing in his culture…in hers too, really. They just
went about different ways of getting it. He asked beforehand while she'd learned it was easier to get her
parents blessing on a project than their permission before starting it.

She looked at the clock which read seven-thirty.
"He's already at work, but Mom will be home for another couple of hours."

"Then let us call her."

They did and Lydia Benning was ecstatic at the news her youngest daughter was finally getting married. Catherine grimaced at the phone. *Twenty-four was not that old.*

"You'll have to bring him for dinner tonight. I'll call right now and invite Felicity and Vance," she said, naming Catherine's sister and brother-in-law. "I can't wait to welcome the man who wants to marry my little girl. He's a sheikh—that's just so romantic."

After gushing for another full five minutes, she cut the connection.

Catherine smiled at Hakim. "I hope you don't mind, but I've agreed to dinner at my parents' house tonight."

"So I gathered. I will pick you up here."

"We could just meet there. They don't live all that far from your penthouse building."

"I'll be here at six-thirty to escort you."

"So, she's agreed has she?" Harold Benning made no effort to disguise the satisfaction he felt at the news Hakim had recently imparted. His brown eyes fairly sparked with it.

"Yes."

Harold's hands rubbed together. Of average height, he had the look of one of his miners. Even his suit, made by an exclusive London tailor, did little to hide the raw musculature of Hakim's soon-to-be father-in-law. He looked like what he was, an extremely wealthy self-made man.

He never apologized for that fact, either. At no time during negotiations with the King of Jawhar had Harold Benning showed the least discomfiture at the prospect of his daughter married to the Sheikh of Kadar.

Hakim wondered briefly how such a self-assured man could have raised Catherine, who was so insecure.

"You haven't told her about our little arrangement, have you?"

"No."

"Good." Harold's graying red head bobbed twice in acknowledgment. "She wouldn't understand. Her mother and I have been concerned about her lack of a social life for quite a while. Sure, it was understandable when she was younger, but since the laser treatments, she's been as reclusive as ever. And she balks at every attempt Lydia and I make to introduce her to men."

Laser treatment? He would have to ask Catherine about that. "She sets great store by her independence." Something that would naturally change with their marriage.

"Yes, that she does. She can be stubborn."

Hakim could not picture the shy Catherine being willful, but did not bother to disagree with her father. "Is your wife aware of the arrangement between my uncle and your company?"

Tugging at his collar, Harold grimaced. "Not exactly. I told her I was looking to fix a husband up for Catherine, but she wouldn't understand the business side of it any better than my daughter. Women are romantics at heart, the lot of them."

"You would know your family best." His sister knew to the coin how much dowry money had exchanged hands upon her marriage to a prince in their mother's father's Bedouin tribe.

Yet, she had been brilliantly happy on her wedding day. He wanted his bride to be equally pleased and if keeping certain details from her was conducive to such happiness, that was what he would do.

CHAPTER FIVE

HAKIM approved of the understated décor and Queen Anne furnishings in the Benning's Seattle mansion. Catherine's mother, Lydia, had excellent taste and it showed from the gloss black grand piano in the living room to the subdued upholstery on the dining room chairs.

They were in the dining room now, just finishing dessert. The evening had been illuminating. Catherine's mother and sister could have been twins with their petite builds, pale blond hair and gray eyes. And while Catherine and her sister were obviously close, there was a distance between mother and daughter he found disturbing.

Despite this, Lydia Benning appeared genuinely pleased her daughter was happy. *And Catherine was happy.* It radiated off her in waves, her enticing lips constantly curving in one sexy smile after another.

He watched as she took a bite of her crème brûlée, his temperature spiking when she closed her eyes and licked the spoon.

There was a small bit of burnt sugar on the corner of her lips and he reached out to gently wipe it away with his fingertip. She went still at his touch and suddenly what had been simple became complicated as her eyes reflected the desire he felt.

Laughter around them broke the sensual link.

''The wedding had better take place soon, if that

look means anything.'' Vance's voice was full of amusement.

Hakim agreed with the sentiment completely. "I believe the waiting period in the state of Washington is one week."

"Actually it's three days." Catherine's voice was husky. "But what difference does that make? It will take at least six weeks to put together a church wedding."

Hakim turned to face his fiancée. Their eyes met again, hers had gone the color of the night sky in the desert. "Do you really want a formal wedding?"

She was much too shy to desire to be the center of attention at such a gathering.

"Why not?"

Her question shocked him. "Have you forgotten the meeting of the Antique Telescope Society we attended together?"

She looked puzzled. "What does that have to do with our wedding?"

"You refused to examine the telescope because it required going up in front of the others to do so." She had denied that was the case, but it had been obvious her shyness had held her back. "You shook like you'd been standing in the cold when you gave that small speech at the charity reception. You would be a nervous wreck put on display in front of several hundred wedding guests."

The glow of happiness surrounding her dimmed a little. "You want to marry in a civil ceremony?"

Perhaps the thought of being wed by a judge did not sit well with her. "We can arrange a midweek ceremony with a clergyman if you prefer."

Her eyes flickered, but she did not smile in gratitude as he expected. In fact, her smile disappeared altogether.

"You don't mind being married in a church?" Vance asked.

Hakim looked away from Catherine reluctantly, disturbed by her sudden lack of animation.

"My grandfather's tribe is one of the many Bedouin tribes converted to Christianity centuries ago."

"But I thought all the Bedouins had converted to Islam," Felicity remarked.

"Not all." Hakim didn't really want to get into a discussion of religious history among the Bedouin people. He wanted Catherine to smile again. "You are all right with a small ceremony?" he asked her.

Catherine thought a certain amount of arrogance must be bred into men like Hakim. Even his question came out like a command.

What could she say? That she had dreamt of her wedding since she was a little girl? That those dreams had not included a poky wedding held in the middle of the day in the middle of the week with only family as guests?

He was right. Considering the way she reacted to being the center of attention, there was no reason for him to have suspected she wanted anything more than a few words spoken in a judge's chamber.

But her dreams were not limited by her fears and knowing that Hakim wanted to marry her had given her confidence. He was a special guy. Sexy. Gorgeous. He was a sheikh, for Heaven's sake. And he loved her. That knowledge had given her a desire to fulfill the secret dreams of her heart.

Before she could answer, he reached out and touched

her. His look was intimate and full of promise. "I want to make you my wife."

The unspoken message was clear. He wanted to make love to her and he'd already said that would have to wait until after the ceremony.

She wanted him, too, even more than the fairytale wedding trappings. She forced a smile. "All right."

"Catherine!" Felicity's voice registered shock and a certain amount of disappointment.

Felicity would have fought for the flowers. In fact, she had. Not that Vance had even hinted at anything less than a full production when they'd gotten married, but then he had loved her sister. He had not even balked at Felicity's insistence on having her sister for a bridesmaid. At the time, Catherine's face had looked like she had a perpetual case of severe chicken pox.

In the end, it had been Catherine who begged her sister to allow her to be the candle lighter instead. She hadn't wanted to stand in front of a church full of people during the ceremony or be in any of the wedding photos. Her mother had been more than willing to give instructions to that effect to the photographer.

Shaking off the painful memories, Catherine smiled reassuringly at her older sister. "You can help me put it together."

Felicity's mouth opened and shut, her porcelain fine features drawn in lines of rejection. "Sweetie, you wanted a horse drawn carriage, oodles of flowers, music—"

Catherine cut in before her sister exposed her childish fantasies completely. "That was when I was nine years old." A year before she'd become *Amazon Girl*, growing five inches in one summer and towering above her classmates the following September. Boys and girls alike. For one reason or another, the next ten years had been hell on Catherine's self-confidence.

"But—"

"Do you want to go shopping with me tomorrow? I need a wedding dress."

That caught her sister's attention. "Of course, but don't you have to work at the library?"

"I'll take a personal day." She'd never taken one. She was due the concession.

"What about a honeymoon?" Vance asked.

Catherine shook her head decisively. "Not possible."

"Why not?" Hakim asked. He had planned to take her to Jawhar immediately to meet his family.

"I can't leave the library in the lurch like that. We don't have enough time to schedule someone to cover all of my shifts."

"That's ridiculous. I'll hire a temp if that's what you need," Harold inserted, his first contribution to the wedding plans.

Catherine shook her head. "Reference Desk librarians don't generally hire out through temporary agencies, Dad."

"You could always quit your job." Lydia smiled tentatively at her daughter. "Hakim will need your attention once you are married. You'll want to establish a firmer social footing."

Hakim agreed with Lydia. Not necessarily about the social scene, but he wanted to come first in his wife's priorities. The narrowing of Catherine's eyes and straight line of her mouth said she did not think much of her mother's suggestion.

"I'm not quitting my job," she said tightly, "I like it."

"And if I told you that was what I wanted?" Hakim

asked, testing how much in common his fiancée had with his former live-in lover in regard to the importance they placed on their careers.

"Is that what you want?" she asked, turning the tables back on him and giving nothing away with her expression.

"I would like to know you are available to travel with me when the need arises."

"With sufficient notice, I can travel with you now."

And one week was not sufficient notice. "Then we will have to plan a trip to Jawhar after you've given proper notification for your vacation time at the library. I want you to meet my family."

"Won't they be coming for the wedding?" Felicity accepted a fresh glass of wine from her husband. "Surely your parents would not want to miss it."

"There is only my sister. She and her husband will be delighted to meet my new wife when we travel to the desert of Kadar."

"Don't you have any other family?" Felicity asked.

"Some. There is my mother's father. He is the sheikh of a Bedouin tribe." He paused. "There is also my father's brother, the King of Jawhar, as well, and his family."

"Your uncle is a king?" Felicity demanded, her eyes round.

"Yes." He caught Catherine's hand to his mouth and kissed the small circle of her palm. "Grandfather will be pleased. He has been encouraging me to marry since I graduated from university."

Of course the old man had thought marriage would bring Hakim home to the desert and it would not.

"Why can't your family come?" Felicity asked, clearly unwilling to drop the subject.

Grimness settled over him. "There is a faction of dissidents in Jawhar that oppose my uncle's leadership. He fears to leave the country now would be to put it at risk from this group of rebels."

"But I thought your family had been the ruling sheikhs for generations." Catherine's expression was clouded with confusion. "It seems odd there would be serious opposition after all these years. Your uncle is loved among the people of Jawhar."

She had been studying his country. The knowledge pleased him. "This is true. Nevertheless, dissension arises from time to time. Twenty years ago, there was an attempted coup. It failed, but many were left dead." Like his parents he thought bitterly.

"What does that have to do with today?" she asked.

"The remnant which survived that attempt have been gathering forces outside Jawhar for the past five years. My uncle is concerned they will once again attempt a removal of our family from power. He cannot risk leaving the country, nor can my cousins."

"What about your sister?"

"She is married to the man that will one day succeed my grandfather as sheikh of his tribe and will meet you when we travel to the desert for our Bedouin marriage ceremony."

Catherine's eyes widened. "We're going to be married a second time in Jawhar?"

"Yes." It would be necessary to fulfill his obligation of respect toward his grandfather.

Catherine was quiet in the car on the way to her apartment. She and Hakim were to go for the wedding license the first thing the next morning. She was still finding it difficult to assimilate that bit of information.

And her mind continued to play with images of long

ago dreams. Lights flickered over the dark interior of the car as Hakim passed a semitruck on the freeway, but it barely registered as Catherine's thoughts slipped into a fantasy of the perfect wedding.

She was standing at the altar in a gown of the most exquisite lace and Hakim looked at her the way a man in love gazed at the woman he was about to marry. That was definitely a dream. They were surrounded by candles and flowers. Bunches and bunches of flowers, all white, all in perfect bloom.

A soft sound escaped her lips.

"What are you thinking, Catherine?"

She was so lost in her daydream, she answered without thought. "Flowers. Lots and lots of flowers."

Then she realized what she'd said and felt the warmth steal into her cheeks. At least he would not notice in the dim interior of the car.

Hakim sighed. "Tell me about the horse drawn carriage and oodles of flowers your sister mentioned."

"It was just something we used to talk about when we were little."

"And something you were thinking about just now." He sounded resigned. "Tell me, Catherine. I want to hear."

Why not? He'd asked. It wasn't as if she was demanding they go through with her long ago plans. "Felicity and I used to talk about what our dream weddings would be like. I think a lot of little girls imagine themselves in a beautiful gown, riding in a carriage with Prince Charming at their side. It was all just silly fantasy, nothing that applies to this marriage."

"Am I not your Prince Charming?"

She couldn't help smiling at the question as she was sure she was meant to. "Well. You are a prince in

Jawhar and you are charming, so I suppose it would be appropriate to call you my Prince Charming.''

''So, it is only the fantasy wedding you find impossible.''

''It's not something you can throw together in a week.'' She couldn't help the slight wistfulness in her tone.

''It is something that takes a minimum of six weeks?''

He had remembered her comment from dinner.

''I don't know.'' She'd never planned one and Felicity's wedding had been organized over several months.

''With sufficient financial and manpower resources at your disposal, do you think you could put together this dream wedding in less than six weeks?''

''How much less?'' What was he getting at?

''Could you do it in under a month?''

''Are you saying you're willing to wait?''

''It pleases me to make your dreams come true.'' He sounded so arrogant, but could she blame him?

He *was* making her dreams come true.

''Three weeks?'' she asked, as if she were bartering a deal.

''You will take sufficient time off after the wedding to visit Jawhar?''

With three weeks' notice, she could arrange it...just. ''Yes.''

His smile flashed. ''Then it is a deal.''

The engagement dinner was more like a party. Her mother had invited a hundred of her nearest and dearest, arranging for the meal to take place in an upscale Seattle restaurant with a live orchestra and dance floor.

Catherine circled the floor in her father's arms and listened while he listed off Hakim's attributes.

"Boy's got a good head for business on his shoulders."

She wondered how her sheikh would feel being referred to as a boy. Suppressing a smile, she nodded her agreement.

"He's considerate. Look at how he changed his mind about the wedding."

Finally her amusement found vent in a small laugh. "Dad, you don't have to sell Hakim to me. He's not one of your matchmaking attempts." *Thankfully.* "I chose him and he chose me. I want to marry him."

Satisfaction coursed through her at the knowledge that her father had had nothing to do with her and Hakim meeting. She wasn't a pity date, or being eyed as a possible way into her father's good graces. Hakim wanted nothing from her father, needed nothing from Benning Mining and Excavations. His desire for her might be physical, but at least it was for her. He wanted her, Catherine Marie Benning, and nothing else.

Hakim waited for his bride at the front of the church. Organ music swelled and he turned to face the massive oak doors at the back of the church. They swung wide and Catherine's sister came into view. Hakim felt shock lance through him. The filmy fabric of her dress was the color of a robin's egg, but that was not what held Hakim motionless. It was the *al-firdous* style of the dress. It had been embroidered and beaded in traditional Middle Eastern patterns with thread and beads the same color as the dress. Felicity wore the matching sheer scarf looped over her pale blond hair much the same way his own sister would have done.

Hakim felt his pulse increase as he waited to see his bride. He barely noticed the flower girl as she came forward, dropping rose petals along the white runner, or the small boy wearing a traditional tuxedo bearing the rings.

Each of the attendants had taken their place when the music halted for the count of several seconds. When it began again, the organ played the strains of the "Wedding March." And then she was there, framed by the open portal of the two massive doors. Hakim's mouth went dry. She had brought together east and west with mind-numbing effect.

The traditional white wedding gown fit snuggly against her body, accentuating the feminine curves to her hips and then flared out in a skirt that rustled as she made the slow march toward him. But the hem, the edges of the medieval sleeves and the off the shoulder neckline had all been embroidered with gold geometric patterns. The semitransparent veil had matching embroidery around its edges, a veil worn in the tradition of his homeland covering all but the exquisite gentian blue of her eyes. Which as she came closer he could see had been outlined with kohl, giving his shy little flower a look of mystery.

Her lips were curved in a smile behind the soft white chiffon covering her face. She reached his side and her father put her hand into Hakim's. He curled his fingers around hers. Her skin was cold and the hand holding her white bouquet was shaking. He squeezed, offering the assurance of his presence. She had wanted this large wedding, but that did not mean a lifetime of shyness had dissolved in a fortnight.

They spoke their vows, he in a firm steady voice, she almost in a whisper. Then he was sliding a white gold band to accompany the large ruby in a Bedouin setting he had given her after she agreed to marry him. The ring had belonged to his mother.

The pastor gave Hakim permission to kiss his bride and everything around them faded to nothing as he reached out to unhook her veil and expose her face. He did it slowly, wanting to savor the moment of unveiling. Then he lowered his head until their lips barely brushed.

He liked this particular Western wedding custom. Her mouth parted slightly and he pulled her to him for a kiss that staked his claim on the beautiful woman before him for all the wedding guests to see.

When Hakim lifted his head, he knew his sense of satisfaction and accomplishment radiated off of him.

He had fulfilled his duty and had for a wife a woman who would satisfy his passions.

He was content.

"What are you thinking about, Catherine?"

Catherine turned from the window whose only view was a night-darkened sky and smiled at Hakim. "Nothing."

She'd been thinking about the night ahead, but could not have said so to save her life.

He'd been in the cockpit with the pilot for takeoff which had given her some much needed moments to herself. Ever since he had informed her there was a bedroom on the plane, with the implication they would make use of it, she had been vacillating between fear and anticipation.

She wasn't sure which one she was feeling now. "Tell me, will you insist on overseeing the landing as well?" she asked to avoid the probing look in his dark as night eyes.

He shrugged broad shoulders. "Probably."

"Your uncle's pilots must love flying you."

He flashed her a smile. "They have made no complaints in the past, but then I had been content to remain in the cabin for takeoffs and landings."

"So, what's so special about this flight?"

"You need to ask? My wife is on the plane. I must always see to her safety."

Emotion caught in her throat and she had to take a deep breath before speaking. Sometimes she forgot he didn't love her and basked in the feelings his naturally protective nature caused. "Your wife is a lucky woman to be so well looked after."

His hand cupped her cheek and anticipation overwhelmed fear in the space of a heartbeat.

"I am hoping she thinks this is so."

"She does." Involuntarily her head turned and her lips kissed the center of his palm. The scent of his skin and the warmth of it against her lips tantalized her senses. "I do."

He leaned across her and unbuckled her seat belt. Taking her hand, he pulled gently until she stood. "Come little kitten, we have a bed that awaits our pleasure."

Was it just her, or did his speech become more eastern when his passion was engaged?

She nodded, her throat too tight to speak. It was time.

It occurred to her that she should have gone to the bedroom earlier, so she could greet him in the sensuous white satin nightgown Felicity had given her to wear tonight, but that was not to be. Catherine wasn't sure how she felt about that. Part of her was a bundle of nerves at the thought of parading herself in front of him in something so revealing. Another part of her did not wish to miss out on any of the traditional aspects to her wedding night.

Which was a silly response probably, so she said nothing.

He led her into the small bedroom at the back of the plane and she stopped, stock still, unable to believe her eyes. The bed was the first thing to arrest her interest. It was covered with quilted silks and tasseled pillows. There were flowers everywhere, all white and red. A silver ice bucket with a bottle of champagne stood beside the bed and red silk scarves covered the wall-mounted lights, giving a warm but subdued glow to the room.

"It is to your liking?"

Her eyes misted over. "Oh, yes. It's just beautiful." She turned to face him.

Heat radiated from his eyes. "I am glad to have pleased you. For today you have given me great delight."

"You liked the dress." She smiled. She'd known he would.

His hands settled on the shoulders of her bright blue suit jacket. "I loved the dress, but right now I would like very much to see you without even this most charming outfit you chose for traveling in."

She looked down at the suit and then back at Hakim. "You want me to take it off?" Somehow she had pictured him doing that for her.

"You have something else you would like to change into?" He sounded like he wouldn't mind seeing that nightgown Felicity bought her after all.

She looked around the small room uncertainly. Did he expect her to disrobe in front of him?

"There is a bathroom through there." He indicated

a door in the wall of the bedroom. "However, you would be more comfortable changing in here, I think. I will make use of it to undress."

He'd seen her practically naked, but her nerves didn't recognize that salient fact and she smiled her gratitude at him.

CHAPTER SIX

HAKIM came out of the tiny bathroom, having given his bride time to prepare for him.

Catherine sat in the middle of the bed surrounded by several Turkish pillows. Her glorious hair was unbound for the first time of their acquaintance and its dark honey strands cascaded over her shoulders.

She had her arms locked around her drawn up knees and the expression on her face was rueful. "I didn't know if I should be standing or lying down. So, I compromised and sat."

"Are you embarrassed for me to see your body?"

She shook her head causing her hair to ripple and he felt an instant reaction coursing through his body.

"Yet you are curled up like a small kitten."

"Small?" She laughed. "Perhaps you haven't noticed, but I'm a good deal taller than most women."

"Surely not. You are perhaps a shade above average in height, but to me, you are quite small." He wished he understood this tendency she had to refer to herself as if she were a giant.

"Yes, well, you are pretty tall aren't you?" The fact seemed to please her.

He shrugged. "Truthfully, among my people I am considered so." He had not thought to spend any portion of his wedding night discussing their relative heights, but if it relaxed her, he was willing to be tolerant.

"Kids used to tease me when I was little. They called me Amazon Girl, beanpole and other horrible names."

He sat down on the bed and laid one hand over her clasped ones. "Talk to me."

"I don't want to ruin tonight with bad memories."

He wanted to banish the remembered torment in her eyes. "Share these memories and I will help you dispel them."

"You're so confident."

So she had said before, or rather that he was arrogant. He shrugged. "I am a man."

She shook her head.

"I assure you this is true."

She laughed softly. "I'm not doubting you."

Unable to resist, he reached out and let a swath of her hair slip through his fingers. "Tell me." He waited in silence while she made up her mind to do so.

"When I was a little girl, I grew five inches in one summer. I didn't stop growing until I was taller than all the other children at school. I was thirteen then and some of the boys were beginning to catch up, but I remained taller than most of them for at least another year."

"It happens to many girls, it's not so bad."

"*It was.* I suppose it's hard for you to understand, but I went to co-ed school. The boys teased me about being a giant and the girls pitied me. I was shy and didn't make friends easily anyway, my sudden height just made everything worse."

"But as you say, the boys grew taller and the girls— many of them—would have caught up."

She shut her eyes. "I don't want to talk about this anymore."

There was something else. Something she did not

want to share, but he had a need to know everything about this woman he had married. A memory teased his conscious. "Your father said something about laser treatments. What were they for?"

She looked confused and not at all happy. "When did he mention them?"

Remembering the conversation, Hakim considered how best to answer without revealing his secret and could see no way of doing so and speak only the truth. There was a proverb among his people, *lying in its proper place is equal to worship*. It applied now. "We were discussing the upcoming wedding."

His lie was one of omission only.

"Oh." A look of profound sadness crossed her features. "When I was thirteen, I started to get acne."

"This is not unusual for an adolescent."

"No, but mine was horrible. The doctors tried antibiotics, acne skin treatments...the works. Nothing helped. My face was discolored with the purple scars from acne and fresh breakouts for five long years. The fresh breakouts finally cleared up when I was eighteen and I started the laser treatments on the scarring when I was nineteen."

He rubbed his thumbs along the perfect smoothness of her cheeks. "You are beautiful."

She grimaced. "Hardly that, but I'm no longer a social embarrassment to my parents and an object of pity to my peers."

Tension snaked through him at her words. "Surely your parents were not concerned about your looks to that extent."

She shrugged, but it was anything but a casual gesture. "They couldn't make it better, so they ignored the problem."

He sensed there was more to it than that and remained silent, hoping she would share it with him.

She looked into his eyes for several seconds, hers glazed with memories he could not see. But he could feel the pain of their impact in her.

Then she spoke. ''There was only one way for them to close their eyes to the problem and that was to avoid me as much as possible. We didn't take family photos for those five years. They frequently entertained away from home rather than risk having their disfigured daughter the cynosure of all eyes.''

Her eyes shone with tears she blinked away. ''Felicity was the only one who didn't let it matter. She often invited me to stay with her and tried to help me out of the shell I'd crawled into to avoid possible rejection.''

The picture Catherine painted was a chilling one.

''What happened after the laser treatments?''

''They went on a campaign to get me married. I think they believed that once I got a husband it would prove their genes weren't damaged after all.''

''You resisted.'' Harold had said Catherine had refused to consider any of the men he'd brought to her attention.

''I didn't want pity dates or to be married as a means to an end in procuring a rich and influential father-in-law.''

Hakim's body tensed. ''I do not want your father's wealth.''

Her smile was dazzling. ''I know.''

He could never tell her of the plans associated with their marriage. She would not understand. But he could show her what a desirable woman she was now, erasing the painful perceptions shaped by her past.

He stood up beside the bed and looked down at her. She tilted her head back and returned his gaze.

"You said you were not embarrassed for me to see you."

"I'm not."

He put his hand out to her. "Then come."

She hesitated only a fraction of a second before placing her small hand trustingly in his and allowing him to pull her up from the bed.

Sleek, shimmering white satin settled around the generous curves of her body, accentuating each dip and hollow in a way that sent his thoughts scattering to the four winds.

Forcing himself into movement, he turned and poured a glass of champagne. He took a sip of the bubbling wine and then grasped her shoulder, pulling her body into his so that the gentle roundness of her bottom pressed against his thighs. He placed the glass against her lips at the exact spot from which he had sipped.

"Share with me."

She allowed him to pour the champagne onto her tongue and then she swallowed. His hand drifted from her shoulder to cup her left breast. The nipple beaded against his palm, straining against the silky fabric and she let out a small moan.

He fed her another sip of champagne while squeezing the soft flesh in his hand. He continued the sensual torment until her head tipped back on his shoulder and her breath was coming out fast and strong. He transferred the glass to his other hand and began the same kneading motion on her right breast. He put the champagne to her lips, smiling as she drank mindlessly while her body writhed to his touch.

By the time the glass was empty, her moans were

loud and her tender peaks were hard like pebbles. He dropped the glass to the carpet and cupped her creamy fullness with both hands, drawing his fingertips together until both her nipples rested between a thumb and forefinger. He pinched, gently.

She screamed, arching her body into his touch.

He rotated the excited flesh, ignoring her pleas to desist, to do it harder, and finally to make love to her. He wanted to draw this out, to give her more pleasure than she could imagine. His own body ached for a release he refused to give it.

"Please, Hakim. Please... Please... Oh, you have to stop. No. Do it harder." Her head thrashed from side to side against his shoulder. "I can't stand it!"

"But you can. Your body is capable of great pleasure." He whispered the words into her ear, knowing the warmth of his breath would add to her passionate enjoyment.

"Then please me," she implored.

Without warning, he dropped one hand down to her thigh and discovered something he had not noticed before. Her gown was slit all the way up her hip. Primitive satisfaction flowed through him as he delved beneath the satin to tangle in the dewy curls at the juncture of her thighs.

"Oh!" She tipped her pelvis toward his hand and his forefinger slipped onto the slick bud of her femininity.

He circled it once. Twice. And she came apart, her scream echoing in the room as her body shuddered in ecstasy against his own. He continued to touch her until she convulsed again and then shook with each light stroke of his finger.

"Oh, Hakim, it's too much." Her tormented whisper came just before her entire body went limp in his arms.

She would have fallen but for the intimate hold he had on her. He just held her, his sex hard and hurting, but the satisfaction in giving her pleasure so deep, he had no real desire to let go.

Her head turned and her lips pressed against his neck. "I love you." Her whisper against his flesh was finally too much for his control.

"I want to make you my wife." Hakim's growl against her temple barely registered in Catherine's pleasure sated state.

But being spun around and kissed to within an inch of her life did.

Unbelievably his passion sparked renewed life in the erogenous centers of her body, causing extremely sensitive nipples to tighten almost painfully and swollen flesh to throb. She opened her lips, wanting his tongue. He did not disappoint her. He conquered her mouth with a sensual invasion that took the strength from her limbs and she sagged against him.

He swept her high against his chest and soon she found herself being lowered to the silk covered bed. Breaking the kiss, he loomed above her, his expression sending jolts of pure adrenalin through her body.

"You belong to me."

Tears of intense emotion burned her eyelids. "Yes."

This time when his lips touched hers, the passion was laced with a sense of purpose. He peeled off the silk robe he'd worn out of the bathroom and laid his completely naked body along hers. Hot satin skin inundated her senses everywhere their bodies collided. She started to tremble as if she'd been playing in the snow too long, uncontrollable shivers of sensation wracking her body.

Her reaction did not seem to concern him. Warm

masculine lips never parted from her own while talented fingers skimmed the sleek smoothness of her night-gown. She felt as if the air she was taking in was devoid of oxygen.

Breaking the kiss, she tossed her head against the pillows. *"Hakim."* She could not form another word, just his name.

He reared up above her, gloriously naked, gloriously male. "It is time."

The words were ominous. Her eyes widened as he leant forward and began the process of pulling her nightgown up her body. She was glad for the subdued lighting as the sudden memory of her physical imper-fections rose up to taunt her.

He sensed her miniscule withdrawal immediately. "What is it?"

He'd see soon enough anyway. Perhaps if she told him, the scars would not come as such an unpleasant shock.

"I have marks." She couldn't bring herself to say the ugly word *scars*. "From the summer I grew so fast."

She could tell nothing from his expression as he fin-ished removing her white satin covering. He then did something that took her completely by surprise. He rose, moving until one foot rested on the floor and one knee on the bed. Then he reached out and pulled one of the scarves from a wall sconce increasing the light in the room by almost tenfold.

Flinching, she felt the desire drain from her like water draining from an unplugged cistern to be replaced by dismay.

"Hakim, please…"

But then her gaze settled on his fully naked, fully aroused body and she forgot to worry about his reaction to her scars in the new and more gripping concern over making love for the first time. Was he as big as he looked or was that her inexperience showing? She wasn't about to ask him.

That would be mortifying.

New brides did not ask questions like that of their husbands but she had to.

"Are you oversized, or am I just worried?" The words blurted out of her mouth, halting the tan hand reaching toward her.

His head snapped up and she could tell she'd surprised him. That was fine with her. She'd downright shocked herself. Could she have gotten more gauche?

He gestured with both hands toward his erect flesh, a rueful expression on his face. "I am what I am. I do not measure myself against other men." He sounded deeply offended by the very thought.

Well, good on him, but that didn't answer her question, did it? And anxiety ridden or not, she was beginning to have deep misgivings about proportionate sizes. For the first time since she was ten years old, she felt very small and fragile. It was not an entirely pleasant feeling.

Her gaze skittered to his face. He didn't look like one iota of his desire had deserted him. In fact, he was looking at her like a ravenous wolf ready for its first meal after a long, hungry stretch. The shaking she had experienced earlier came back, but this time it was liberally laced with anxiety.

Despite his apparent hunger, when he touched her it was with a featherlight fingertip.

He brushed along the thin ridge of raised flesh at the juncture between her arm and body, then reached across her and traced the matching one on her other side.

"They are barely an inch long and very narrow. From your concern, I thought they would be much bigger."

"They're ugly."

"No, they are not."

There was no arguing with such an implacable tone and she didn't really want to. Was it possible the blemishes truly didn't bother him?

"I have some on the sides of my knees as well." She never wore short dresses because of them.

His attention was no longer on the old flaw. It had strayed along with his hands to the generous curves of her breasts. She felt them swell and tighten in response and a small moan escaped her. He bent down, lowering his head until she had no doubt of his intention.

Her breath froze in her chest as she waited for the incredible pleasure of his mouth on her. Only when it came, it landed first on one of the scars. His tongue traced where his fingertip had before and her moan this time was much louder. His mouth swiftly braced over her body until he closed it over one now turgid peak and her body involuntarily bowed off the bed, pushing her excited flesh more firmly into his mouth. Her eyes closed on the exquisite pleasure. She cried out when his hands grasped her rib cage, keeping her pressed against his mouth while he kissed, nibbled and sucked in an ever increasing circular pattern over first one breast and then the other. He was very thorough, giving every centimeter of sensitized flesh erotic attention.

He lifted his head and she gasped in protest at the loss of his pleasurable ministrations.

"You said your knees have these small marks as well?"

"What?" She got no further as his fingers began a comprehensive inspection of the area around her knees, pressing her legs apart so he could touch the stretch marks on her inner knees as well.

"I must admit, when I am here, such tiny scratches cannot hold my attention. I find other things of far more interest."

Catherine knew exactly what he meant as his fingertips started a slow glide up her inner thigh and she had to admit her stretch marks had stopped mattering to her with the first stroke of his tongue several minutes ago. Just remembering what it had felt like when he had touched her between her legs before had her aching, burning and squirming against the silk coverlet.

"Hakim?"

"Hmm?" His fingertips were on the hypersensitive flesh just before the juncture to her thighs.

"Could you put the scarf back on the lamp?"

She felt vulnerable, open and naked to his gaze and the harsh light only increased that feeling.

"Is that what you really want?" As he asked the question his fingers trespassed her most intimate flesh, finding tissues wet and swollen in preparation for their joining.

"Oh…my…gosh…" she panted as one masculine digit slid inside her untried body.

He pressed forward until she flinched with pain. He did not draw all the way out, only far enough that the discomfort left. "You are very responsive."

He delighted her too, but she couldn't get the words past the constriction in her throat.

"I want you so very much, but you must be made ready." There was no mistaking the sincerity of his statement. His voice sounded tortured.

"I'm ready now," she fairly screamed as he began

moving that one finger in and out, stretching her, exciting her.

"No, but you will be. It is my responsibility as your husband and your lover to make it so."

She would have answered, but his thumb had found her sweet spot and her vocal chords were only capable of moans.

"There is an ancient tradition among my grandfather's people for the women to prepare the bride for her husband by dispensing with the maidenhead. Thus there is no pain on the wedding night." His deep voice mesmerized her. "However, I must admit to a primitive satisfaction in knowing you have left this privilege to me."

"You're not going to do it so long as it's only your hand on me." It had been a struggle to get the words out.

His laughter was low and rich. "Ah, little kitten, you are so innocent. I could indeed, but I prefer to wait for my complete possession of you."

"Are we—"

The feel of a second finger joining the first inside her cut off the question of whether he intended to wait all night to make that possession.

She felt full and only slightly uncomfortable as he made the same motions with two fingers he had made with one. Tension built inside her, a now recognizable strain toward fulfillment. Just as she felt the precipice near, he withdrew his hand.

Her eyes, which had been closed in ecstatic pleasure, flew open and she looked at him, but all she saw was the top of his head as he did something she was totally unprepared for. As his mouth settled over intimate flesh she instinctively tried to arch away, but strong fingers held her hips in place.

"Hakim. *Oh, Hakim.* Please… Oh, my gosh! It's too much. Don't stop, please don't stop!"

It was unlike anything she'd known, even in his arms. The intimacy of his action mortified her on one level, but the physical sensations more than conquered her mental misgivings.

Pleasure built. Tension increased. Her body strained against his mouth, her hips against his hands. Her mouth opened on a silent scream. She thrashed. Her hands gripped the quilt. Her heels dug into the bed.

All the while, the sensual torment continued.

Then it all coalesced into a crescendo of delight so intense, she screamed wildly with the joy of it.

It was then, at that moment of intense delight that he moved up her body and slid inside her, breaking through her small barrier with a pain she hardly acknowledged. Her body was too busy dealing with the aftermath of what he had just given her.

She looked into his black eyes, her own swimming with tears and said the words she knew he was thinking. "I'm yours now."

"Yes."

She smiled at that one arrogant word. "You're mine too."

"Can you doubt it?"

And he started to move and incredibly it all began again. This time when her body convulsed, his feral shout joined her feminine whimpers as the overwhelming pleasure ignited a crying jag of monumental proportions.

He was no more affected by this than he had been by her shaking earlier. He hugged her close and whispered to her in a mixture of Arabic and English, every word and caress seemed to be assurance and praise for her femininity and passion.

Her tears finally subsided and he carried her to the bathroom where he showered with her, washing her body with meticulous care and then groaning in delight when she insisted on returning the favor.

She discovered that a soapy hand and curiosity could end in a very male satisfaction.

She was still smiling at her own daring and success when they exited the shower and he began drying her with a towel.

"I can do that."

"But it gives me greater pleasure to do it than to watch."

"Are you going to let me dry you?" she asked, grinning cheekily at him.

He laughed out loud. "You are flushed with your triumph in the shower, are you not?"

She felt herself blushing, but nodded. "It's nice knowing you aren't the only one giving the pleasure around here."

He stood up and placed his hands on her shoulders, his expression terribly serious. "The joy your response gives me is greater than any I have ever known."

Her breath caught in her throat. She could definitely get used to the flowery and extravagant way of talking passion seemed to elicit in him. "Thank you."

They went back into the bedroom and he brought forth that same uninhibited response in her three more times before they fell into exhausted slumber, wrapped tightly in one another's arms.

CHAPTER SEVEN

MYRIAD impressions stamped Catherine's awareness through the tinted windows of the stretch limousine on their way from the airport to the Royal Palace of Jawhar. The gray of the window glass muted the harsh light glinting off the desert sand and roads that seemed to stretch into nothingness. Yet Hakim had assured her that they were quite close to the Royal Palace as well as the capital city of Jawhar.

Both would be found on the other side of the tall sand dunes that appeared to swallow the road on which they traveled.

She was grateful for the air-conditioned car as her skin already prickled with the heat of nerves. She would be sweating if the car matched the heated temperatures outside.

Catherine adjusted the long chiffon scarf draped over her hair for the tenth time in as many minutes and the fragrance of jasmine tickled her senses. This time she crossed the filmy fabric at her neck, letting the excess dangle down her back. She was glad women in Jawhar did not wear veils. Hakim had told her she didn't even have to wear the head covering, but she had wanted to out of respect to his uncle. The King.

The car topped the sand dunes and suddenly her vision was filled with the massive domed structure of the Royal Palace.

Hakim had grown up here since the age of ten. He'd shared that bit of information over breakfast, but had not told her why and she hadn't asked, being too awed by the prospect of meeting the rest of the royal family. What if they didn't like her? How could an American woman be their first choice for Sheikh Hakim bin Omar al Kadar? For here, he was a sheikh, not just an extremely wealthy businessman.

And he looked the part. Her gaze strayed momentarily from the rapidly approaching palace to the man she had married less than twenty-four hours ago.

Hakim in full Arab mode was somewhat intimidating. Dressed much as the sheikh in her fantasies, he wore white, loose-fitting pants, a long white tunic over them, and a black *abaya* that looked like a cross between a robe and a cloak over that. His head covering was the only deviation. It was white like his pants and shirt with a gold *egal* holding it in place, the ends of the golden rope twisted and tucked into the band that circled his head.

She'd seen a red and white checkered head covering in his suitcase and couldn't help wondering if he wore it when he was amidst his grandfather's Bedouin tribe.

Her eyes flicked between him and the home of his youth. Even the gray tinting on the windows could not disguise the bright colors of the domes, walls and revealing archways of the huge complex.

Her heart started to hammer.

She was going to meet a king in less than five minutes.

She smoothed a miniscule wrinkle out of the overdress of the caftan ensemble she was wearing. She'd adored it on sight. The underdress was the simplest component. It was floor length and cream in color with wine roses embroidered around the hem and sleeves. The matching overdress had a V-neck outlined in the roses and was sleeveless. Both sides were slit up to her waist for ease of walking, and to expose more of the underdress's fancy work.

It, along with several other gorgeous things to wear while on their honeymoon in his homeland, had been Hakim's gift to her that morning.

She tugged her sleeves so they fell past her wrists.

"If you don't stop fidgeting, your dress will be in tatters by the time we reach my uncle's palace."

She gave Hakim a wry grimace. "I've never met a king before."

"Now you are married to a sheikh. It is expected."

"Have you noticed that since arriving in your country, you've gotten more arrogant?" And that was saying a lot. She thought he'd been pretty imposingly confident before.

He smiled. "Is that so?"

"Even your voice has changed. You've always had a certain air of authority, but since getting off the plane you just exude power."

"I am considered one of the rulers of my country. I am the only remaining sheikh of Kadar."

"I'm surprised your uncle encourages you to live in the States then."

"There are some duties only family can perform."

Those were the last words between them before the limousine slid to a halt outside the Royal Palace of Jawhar.

Hakim helped her from the car, but then removed his hand from her arm and maintained a distance of at least ten inches between them as they made their way inside the palace.

The incredible splendor, vibrant colors and grandiose size surrounding her, registered even as she kept her eyes fixed firmly on the huge wooden double doors they were headed towards. Just before they reached them, a servant wearing a headdress and flowing garments stepped forward to open the one on the right so that she and Hakim could walk through.

If the entranceway had been impressive, the formal reception room was overwhelming. Mosaic patterns interspersed with ornate carpets dyed a predominant red covered the floor that stretched at least fifty feet in each direction. Her eyes only skimmed the furniture and no doubt original statuary surrounding the room, before they settled on the man sitting in a chair that could only be described as a throne on a raised wooden dais.

"Bring your bride forward, Hakim."

Hakim took her hand then and led her forward until they stood only a foot from his uncle, the King.

The next two hours were a complete haze as she was first presented to King Asad bin Malik al Jawhar and then introduced to Hakim's other relatives on his father's side and expected to converse with them. Where her wedding had been both exciting and terrifying, this was worse. She did not know these people, did not speak their language and every single one of them had their attention fixed firmly on her.

She'd been shy all her life and her first instinct was to hide behind a wall of reserve or a nearby pillar, but she refused to let Hakim down. So, she forced herself to smile and talk to the intimidating strangers.

King Asad came up and hugged Hakim at one point. "Your duty is more pleasing than you at first expected, hmm?"

"Yes, Uncle. I am content."

Since both men were looking at her, Catherine as-

sumed the comment was directed to her in some way
and felt herself blushing at its implications.

''She is charming.'' The King's tendency to speak of
her as if she wasn't there made her want to smile. He
was much more traditionally Arab than Hakim, who had
been educated in France and then America. ''Her fair
skin reveals her blushes and innocence I think.''

''Can you doubt it?''

She felt like melting through the floor. They couldn't
be discussing what she thought they were discussing,
but after the big deal Hakim had made over her virginity
she suspected they were. He'd said it was important to
his family, she remembered.

''No, I do not doubt it. Assurances were made.''

Assurances were made? What the heck did that
mean? She wasn't about to ask in front of his uncle, but
she was going to find out if Hakim had told the older
man that she'd admitted to being a virgin. Just the
thought of them talking about her like that made her
skin heat with a truly mortified blush.

''Hakim.'' Her voice came out strangled and not at
all charming.

Hakim's expression had turned wary, as well it
should be. ''Yes?''

''If you and your uncle are talking about what I think
you are talking about, things could get ugly very
quickly.''

As threats went, it appeared to be very effective because Hakim excused them on the pretext that she was
tired from the long journey.

''Stop by Abdul-Malik's office on your way to your
apartments. He has the final geologist's report for you
to review before Mr. Benning can begin his excavations.''

Catherine stopped walking at the second mention of her father. "My dad's mining company is coming to Jawhar?"

"Yes."

"Why didn't you tell me?"

"It is not important to us, unless you wish to visit him when he is here."

"Yes, women should not concern themselves with business."

She chose to ignore the king's chauvinistic remark. There were still men among her father's generation who agreed with him, not to mention her own mother's willful ignorance of her father's business dealings.

However, she was determined to discuss the issue with Hakim when they made it to their private apartments.

Hakim's seemingly limitless ardor prevented any conversation but that which occurred between lovers from taking place as he made love to her throughout the lazy warm hours of the afternoon.

Several hours later, she was dressed for their official wedding celebration dinner and waiting for Hakim to finish a business call when she noticed the geologist's report again. She wasn't surprised her father had moved quickly to take advantage of his new connection to Hakim's resource rich, if small country.

She picked up the report, wondering what type of mining her father planned to do here. She didn't recognize the named ore, which was nothing new. Geology had not been one of her strong suits in school. Her interest had always been books and teaching children to appreciate and use them to their advantage.

As she scanned the first page, the date of the initial

inquiry caught her eye. At first she wondered if it had
been a typo, but other dates coincided with that being
the initial query. The problem was that it was for a date
significantly *prior* to her meeting Hakim for the first
time at the Whitehaven Library. Her brain scrambled to
understand what her eyes were telling her.

Hakim had known her father before they met.

She shook her head. No. This report was for Jawhar.
His uncle had surely had business dealings with her
father, but that did not mean Hakim had been apprised
of them until later.

It seemed like such a huge coincidence though. Why
hadn't her father or Hakim mentioned it? He obviously
knew now. When had he found out?

The questions were still whirling through her mind
when she looked up to find Hakim's gaze locked firmly
on her. His face was completely expressionless and for
some reason that really worried her.

She laid the report down, feeling an inexplicable need
to make sure it lay in the exact spot from which she
had originally picked it up. "It's dated for some time
before we met."

"That report is confidential." The words were hard,
clipped, unlike any tone she'd heard from him before.

"Even from your wife?"

"I do not expect you to concern yourself with my
business dealings."

"You sound just like your uncle."

Hakim's head cocked arrogantly in acceptance of that
fact.

"I don't believe women are too stupid to understand
business dealings and you'd better accept that I'm not
going to pretend ignorance to feed your male ego."

That made his eyes narrow, but she ignored the reaction.

"Why didn't you tell me you had met my dad?" She made the accusation as a wild stab in the dark, hoping he would deny it. She wanted to believe the original business had been conducted between his uncle and her father.

"Harold thought it would be best."

A mixture of raw emotions swirled through her, but chief among them was confusion. Why would her father suggest keeping their business dealings a secret from her? "Did he think I might reject you once I knew you two were business associates?"

"I believe that was his concern, yes. You had shown that marked tendency for the past several years."

"But *you* had to know my feelings for you were genuine, that I wouldn't turn away from our relationship just because you and my father knew each other." She felt like she was navigating her way through heavy fog without the aid of headlamps.

"It was not a risk I was willing to take."

Because he was falling in love with her and hadn't wanted to risk losing her? For a guy with Hakim's arrogance, such an explanation just did not ring true, no matter how much her whimpering heart wanted it to.

She tried to make sense of everything while her husband watched her, his expression wary. Hakim had known her father before meeting her at the library.

"My father set us up."

Something flickered in his eyes and she had the strangest sense he was going to lie to her.

"If you won't tell me the truth, then don't say anything at all."

He jolted, his black eyes widening fractionally before

the emotional mask once again fell into place. "Not all truth is desirable."

"I don't care. I won't be lied to by my husband."

"Your father arranged for us to meet, yes." The words came out grimly and gave no satisfaction at all.

He was right, some truth was unpalatable.

As unpalatable as having her virginity discussed between her husband and his uncle. Almost as if she were watching a movie screen, the scene in the reception room played over in her mind.

His uncle, looking pompous with a bearded face and white robes of state. *Her fair skin reveals her blushes and innocence I think.*

Hakim's expression sardonic. *Can you doubt it?*

Herself standing there, blushing painfully.

The King taking a deep breath and letting it out with an expression of supreme complacency. *No, I do not doubt it. Assurances were made.*

And suddenly she understood what assurances had been made and by who. "You asked my father if I was a virgin before you asked me to marry you!"

In a very peripheral way, she realized she was yelling. She never yelled. She was the quiet one, the one who stayed in the shadows and was content to do so, but she didn't feel like being quiet. She felt like screaming the place down.

"He volunteered the information."

"Is that supposed to make me feel better?" Why in the world would her dad have felt the need to tell Hakim she'd never had a serious boyfriend? "It's not like you couldn't have made an educated guess on your own."

Her lack of experience around men had to have been obvious.

"I did not know you then."

"Are you telling me that you discussed my virginity with my father before we ever met?" Dread was curling its ugly tentacles around her heart even as she hoped against hope that he would deny the charge.

Hakim's eyes closed as if he was seeking an answer and then he opened them and jet black glittered at her with hard purpose. "This is not something you truly wish to know. It will only upset you to discuss this further and it will serve no good purpose. We are married. That is all that matters now."

No way. "My being able to trust my husband matters."

He drew himself up, his expression going grim. "You have no reason to mistrust me."

"If you've lied to me, I do."

"There is a proverb among my people. *Lying in its proper place is equal to worship.*"

She felt the words like a slap. Was he admitting to lying to her? "Well, there is a proverb among my people. A lying tongue hides a lying heart."

"Your father and my uncle discussed your innocence prior to our meeting the first time." He bit the words out. "Does that please you to know?" The sarcasm hurt.

"You know it doesn't." She wasn't yelling anymore. In fact, she could barely get more than a whisper past the tears now aching for release. "I was just a pity date."

And not even a pity date arranged between her father and Hakim, but one arranged between two old men. Had she not been a virgin, she had the awful feeling even a pity date would not have occurred. It was medieval and felt like the worst kind of betrayal.

"Why didn't you tell me?"

He reached out, following her when she backed up and took both her shoulders in a gentle but firm grip. His thumbs rubbed against her collarbones. "You are my wife. Does the reason we met mean so much?"

Of course it mattered, her mind screamed. "He fixed us up. He even told you I was a virgin! *You don't think that matters?*" she asked, trying not to choke on the words.

"Are you saying you would have been content to give your innocence to another?"

How dare he sound offended?

"Stop trying to sidetrack the issue! You lied to me. My father lied to me. I feel manipulated and it hurts, Hakim. It hurts more than you can imagine."

"It was a lie of omission only." His hands moved to cup her face. "Was this so terrible? If I had told you the truth, you would have rejected me like you rejected all the others. We would not be married now. Is that what you want?"

He wasn't putting it back on her like that. She yanked her face from his grasp. "I love you. I wouldn't have rejected you because of the truth."

"Like you are not rejecting me now?"

"I'm not rejecting you," she screamed, out of control and in emotional pain, "I'm rejecting being lied to, being betrayed by the man I love."

How could he not understand that? "How would you like knowing I had colluded with your family behind your back? How would you like knowing you'd been made a total fool of?"

"How did we make a fool of you? Do you consider it folly to have married me?"

They stood facing each other, two combatants on a battlefield of emotional carnage.

Her shoulders slumped, all energy draining from her as she acknowledged the truth that came from knowing he had been dishonest with her. "Yes, if it meant tying myself to a man I cannot trust."

"You are making more of this than it is," he retorted coolly.

"Am I?" Two words whispered so low, she didn't know if he heard them, but he moved.

"Yes."

She shook her head. Denial? Confusion? She didn't know, but it served to loosen the hot wetness gritting behind her eyes. He pulled her into his body again as she started to cry, great gulping sobs that sounded as awful as they felt. She struggled, but he was too strong and she gave in, letting the grief take over. He didn't try to quiet her, but just held her, seeming to realize she had to have this emotional outburst.

Eventually the tears subsided and he handed her a handkerchief to mop herself up. She stepped away from him to do so.

He watched her broodingly. "How we came together is no longer important. You must believe this. We are husband and wife. Your father's interference has no bearing on our future. We make of our marriage what we choose to make of it."

The crying had calmed her enough to really take in what he was saying and his words made her stop and think.

She'd been rebelling against her dad's interference in her life since reaching adulthood, but could she really regret meeting Hakim just because Harold Benning had a hand in it? Or even his uncle for that matter? Two old men had played matchmaker and discussed private affairs of hers they had no business discussing, but in the end she had married the man she loved. No one had coerced her.

Unlike the other men her father had fixed her up with, Hakim didn't need anything from Harold Benning.

No matter what had brought them together, he had married her for her own sake and he loved her. But a man who loved her would not have lied to her, would he?

"It hurts that you hid this from me, that you didn't trust my love enough to believe I wouldn't let it matter. A-And…a lie by omission is still a lie." She was trying not to cry again and her words came out stuttered.

"It was not my intention to hurt you."

"But you did."

"This I can see. I made a mistake." She could sense this was not easy for him to admit.

"You didn't trust my love."

"I did not see it that way."

If he hadn't seen it that way, then, *"Why did you lie to me?"*

"It was your father's wish."

It was chauvinism at its worse for her dad to think he had the right to ask Hakim to keep the secret and for Hakim to believe he had an obligation to do so. Maybe how they met wasn't so important, but where she stood in his list of priorities was. So was knowing he would never lie to her again.

"My wishes should come first with you. I'm your wife and you made promises to love and cherish me. My father has no place in our relationship."

"That is what I have been saying."

"Then promise me that from now on I come first in your considerations." She meant between her and her father. She knew she could not come first over everything for a man in Hakim's position.

"This I will do."

"Do you *promise*?" He always kept his promises.

He brushed the wetness from under her eyes with his thumbs. "I promise."

"You're big on keeping your promises. I remember you telling me that."

"This is true."

"Then promise me one more thing."

He looked wary. "What?"

"That you will never lie to me again."

He hesitated and she glared at him. "I don't care if you think the truth will upset me. I can't trust you if I believe you'll lie to me, even if it is to protect my feelings."

"Then I promise this also."

She nodded, feeling a sense of relief that he had agreed so easily. If she couldn't trust him, she could not stay with him, no matter how much she loved him. "I need to fix my makeup."

He drew her forward and dropped a soft kiss on her lips. It felt like an apology and she took it as such.

He released her. "Be quick. The dinner will have started without the guests of honor."

CHAPTER EIGHT

LATER, sitting between her husband and the wife of one of his cousins, she thought the dinner would go on forever. It wasn't that the company was not entertaining. They were. Hakim's cousin's wife was sweet and everyone had been very kind to Catherine, but her husband was driving her crazy.

He seemed to have gotten it in his head that she needed reassurance regarding their marriage. Physical reassurance.

Since it was considered unseemly among his people for a husband and wife to touch in public, all of his touches were surreptitious. And dangerous. Under the cover of the table, he caressed her thigh through the black lace overlay of her dress.

He had told her to dress in Western style for the dinner. She'd been glad she'd followed his advice when she arrived to find the other women similarly attired, although the men wore traditional Arab costume.

However, when she felt Hakim's foot brush the inside of her calf under her long skirt, she wished she was wearing more than a pair of sheer stockings. Her body was humming with the excitement only he could generate and no way to appease it. They could not leave the dinner until his uncle excused them.

She turned her head to tell him to stop it and found herself mesmerized by a pair of obsidian eyes.

"Hakim."

"Yes, *aziz*?" His foot moved and sensation arced right up her leg to the very core of her.

She gasped.

He smiled.

She was still smarting a little from their earlier argument, but he had promised never to lie to her again. "If you don't stop it my foot is going to make contact with your leg as well, but it will still have a shoe on and its sharp toe will be the point of impact."

He laughed and popped a grape into her mouth. "Your impact on my body is sharp indeed."

She couldn't help smiling at him.

He removed his foot and winked.

She sighed with exasperation and turned to her other dinner companion, Lila.

The other woman turned to her and smiled warmly. "You and Sheikh Hakim are well matched."

"Thank you."

"It is good to see him find pleasure in a duty that must have been hard to accept."

"Yes." The more time she spent around Hakim in Jawhar, the more she realized how much he had sacrificed of his personal happiness to oversee the family's business interests abroad.

"In my opinion, it was not necessary. It seems reactionary to believe the dissidents could force the family into fleeing the country. And, after all, marriage to an American would be difficult for the more traditional members of our family, but Hakim is content." Lila leaned forward and whispered, "My husband would never approve my having a career."

Considering the fact the woman's husband was the Crown Prince of Jawhar, even Catherine could understand his reasoning. Being a queen would be a full-time job.

Catherine didn't know what her marriage had to do with politics. "Does King Asad really believe a coup could succeed?"

"I do not think so. I believe he assigned Sheikh Hakim his duty to be prepared in case it is so, but not out of real necessity. The dissidents have less support than they did twenty years ago and that uprising failed."

"It's too bad the king will not trust anyone but family to oversee the business interests. Hakim would be happier living here in Jawhar." Catherine was certain of it.

"Perhaps my honored father-in-law could be persuaded to assign a trusted advisor to oversee the business affairs for the family, but he would only trust family to fulfill the duty assigned to Hakim."

Catherine didn't understand. Was the language barrier the problem, or was Lila implying that Hakim had additional duties in the States?

"After all, only a family member could be trusted to sponsor the others for living visas in the United States. I think your government may even require it to be a relation. You would know better than I."

Catherine's confusion at finding the date on the geologist's report was nothing compared to what she felt now. "I don't understand," she admitted.

Lila smiled. "I found it rather complicated when my husband told me about it as well. It pleases me that he shares so much with me. In some ways he is very traditional, but he does not dismiss my intellect."

Catherine would have felt more empathy if she wasn't so puzzled. "Can you explain it to me?"

"Why don't you ask Hakim? I, too, prefer not to

admit to my husband when I don't understand something he has explained. I suppose it is an issue of pride." She sighed, then smiled. "It's quite simple, really. Once Hakim married you, he was then eligible through you to sponsor long-term living visas for members of his family provided he could guarantee their income. Which, of course is no problem."

"Long-term living visas?" Catherine choked out.

Lila nodded and went on. "Then of course there is the mining partnership. King Asad wants to realize the benefit of the geologist's findings. He is convinced your father's company is key to making that happen."

"Mining partnership?" Catherine asked, her voice faint to her own ears.

Lila missed the question and leaned forward confidingly. "My husband thought King Asad would surely bring forth a more distant relation for the marriage alliance until he realized that as usual, his father had other benefits in mind."

"Long-term living visas." The words came out of her subconscious as Catherine dealt on a conscious level with the other things Lila had told her.

Lila nodded. "King Asad is a sharp negotiator."

Catherine's mind was still stuck on the concept that a marriage had been part of the mining deal. *Her marriage?* "You mean Hakim's duty was to marry me?" Catherine whispered in dawning horror.

Lila's brow furrowed. "Well, yes. You could put it like that."

Catherine wondered if there was any other way of putting it. "The further benefits of my marriage to your husband's cousin were the long-term living visas in case political dissidents made them necessary?" she asked, clarifying it in her mind as she spoke.

This time Lila did not answer, seeming to finally latch onto the fact that what she'd been saying was news to Catherine. And not welcome news.

For her part, Catherine was finding it almost impossible to wrap her mind around the idea that her marriage had been arranged as part of a business deal with Benning Excavations. That the man she believed had loved her had lied to her and tricked her. No love there.

Lila looked worried. Really worried.

Catherine felt sick to her stomach and had to swallow down bile as her throat convulsed. Everyone at the dinner probably knew that she was the albatross around Hakim's neck. Necessary for him to fulfill his duty, but *not* a wife he truly wanted and desired. Certainly not a loved wife.

Humiliation lanced through like a jagged edged sword.

"Does the whole family know?" she asked, needing confirmation of the worst.

Lila shook her head vehemently. "No one outside of King Asad, Abdul-Malik, my husband, Hakim and you know of the plan."

Learning that the mortifying truth was known by only a select few did not lessen the pain threatening to engulf her in a tide of black anguish. She'd been betrayed on every level. Her father had lied to her. Her husband had lied to her. She'd been used as a means to an end by a king she'd never even met before today.

She'd been used to fulfill his duty by the man seated next to her. The swine. The no good, double-dealing… She couldn't think of a word bad enough to describe him.

She hated him.

She hated herself more. She'd been such a fool.

Twenty-four-years old and still too stupid to realize when she was being manipulated and used. Hakim did not love her. He didn't even care about her. You didn't use people you cared about. What did that say about her dad?

She felt another wave of sickness wash over her.

Did her mother know?

Did Felicity? No. Felicity would have told her.

"Are you all right? You've turned very pale." Lila's concerned voice barely penetrated the fog of pain surrounding Catherine.

Lila leaned around Catherine. "Sheikh Hakim. I think your wife is ill."

Hakim turned, his duplicitous face cast in a false show of concern. "Is something wrong?"

"You don't have a heart." Venom born from an unbearable pain laced each word. "I hate you."

He reeled back as if she had struck him. Lila's shocked gasp barely registered. Catherine just wanted out of there. She was breaking up, her heart shattering into jagged pieces inside her chest. She went to stand, but Hakim caught her and held her to her chair.

"What is going on?"

"Let me go."

"No. Explain what has you so upset."

"You lied to me."

"We discussed this. You understood." Even now, he wasn't going to admit the full truth.

"I'm the duty. You *had* to marry me." Her voice rose with each successive word until she was practically shouting. "It was part of some mining deal with my father!"

Hakim's gaze slid to Lila. "What did you tell her?"

Catherine answered for the other woman. "She told

me the truth, something my husband and father did not see fit to do.''

She could hear King Asad inquiring about what the problem was. Her husband's answer and his anger both registered in the peripheral of her consciousness. As did Lila's profuse apologies. It was all there, but none of it was real. She couldn't take it in.

She'd felt the pain of rejection many times in her life, but nothing had ever been like this. To know she was nothing more than a commodity to be bartered by her dad and a means to an end to the man she had loved. To know where she had believed herself loved, she had been merely tolerated. It was too much. Too much betrayal. Too much pain to take in.

She tried to stand again, forgetting Hakim's iron grip on her arm. She looked at his hand curled around the black lace sleeve. It hurt to see it, to know he was touching her. She didn't want his hand on her, but her voice would not work to tell him so. So, she looked away, letting her gaze roam over the rest of the room.

Shockingly no one seemed to notice the holocaust of emotion at the head table.

Then she realized that everyone else had kept their voices down, their expressions bland. Even Lila, whose eyes registered remorse wore a plastic smile on her lips. Hakim was no longer talking to King Asad.

He was talking to her, but the words weren't registering over the rushing in her ears.

''I want to go to our room,'' she said, right over the words coming out of her husband's mouth. ''Please tell your uncle I am not feeling well and must go.''

She wondered if he would argue with her.

He didn't.

She watched dispassionately as he turned to his uncle,

spoke a few words in the other man's ear and then turned back to her.

"He will give his official blessing to our marriage and then we will be free to go."

She did not respond.

She simply sat, wishing Hakim would let go of her arm, while the King stood and spoke his official blessing. When he was done, he instructed the newlyweds to retire to their apartments, saying they had better things to do than listen to old men tell jokes well into the night. The room exploded in laughter, but Catherine's sense of humor had vanished.

Hakim pulled her to her feet.

She swayed. Stupid. She refused to let her body be so affected by her emotional devastation. That is what she told her mind, but the woozy feeling persisted.

Suddenly Hakim swept her into his arms, making a comment about following western tradition and carrying his bride over the threshold. That was supposed to happen in their new home, but she didn't correct him. She doubted anyone cared.

They were all too busy cheering her bastard of a husband's seemingly romantic action.

She said nothing all the way down the long hallway, up the ornate staircase, down another hallway and through the door into their apartments. Silence continued to reign as he released her to sit on the gold velvet covered sofa, but when he went to sit beside her, she spoke.

"I don't want you near me."

He ripped his headgear off and tossed it on the desk. It landed smack on the offending mining report.

"What has changed, Catherine? I have not changed. Our marriage has not changed. We discussed this before the dinner. How we met is not important to our future. It is already in the past."

She glared at him, wishing looks really could singe.

He sighed heavily. "There is no need for you to be so upset."

"No way did you just say that."

His jaw went taut, his expression frustrated.

"I find out that I've been manipulated by people I should have been able to trust above anyone else in my life, my husband and my father, and you don't think I should be upset?"

He'd grown up in Jawhar, not another planet...even if he was a sheikh. He couldn't be so dense.

"I did not manipulate you."

"How can you say that?"

"Did I coerce you into marriage?"

"You tricked me."

"How did I trick you?"

"Are you kidding?" She threw her hands in the air and even that hurt, like her muscles were as bruised as her emotions. "You made me believe you were marrying me because you *wanted* to marry me. Whereas in reality it was all some plan your uncle had cooked up with my father." Her jaw ached from biting back the tears. "I thought you loved me."

"I never said I loved you."

Her heart felt like it shattered in her chest. "No. You didn't, but you knew I believed it was me you wanted."

"I did want to marry you, Catherine."

"Because it fulfilled your duty to your uncle and because my father made it part of his filthy mining deal with an opportunistic king."

Hakim tunneled his fingers through his hair and

clasped the back of his neck. "It also fulfilled my desire, little kitten."

"Don't call me that! It doesn't mean anything to you. All those endearments you use. They're just words to you. I thought they were more, but they aren't."

He crossed to her in two strides and fell on his knees before her. "Stop this. You are tearing yourself apart, imagining the worst and it is not true. It pleased me to make you my wife. It pleased you to marry me. Can you not remember that and forget the rest?"

Ebony eyes compelled her to agree.

She wanted to, if only to stop the drumbeat of pain remorselessly pulsing through her. She tried to stifle a whimper, but the broken sound escaped her.

He groaned and pulled her to him. "Why I asked you to marry me is unimportant," he said, speaking into her hair. "The only thing that matters now is that we are married. We can be very happy together."

He was wrong. So wrong. "It is important."

"No." His hand brushed her back. "Many marriages are arranged among my people and they are very happy. It is what we give to our marriage that will determine what it becomes for us. Trust me, jewel of my heart."

She'd been listening right up to that moment, wondering if he was right. Wishing it could be so, but it couldn't.

"I can't trust you." And she wasn't the jewel of his heart. He didn't love her, therefore she had no place in his heart. Rage borne of betrayal welled up in her. She pushed on his chest. *"Get away from me!"*

Again he had that look like she'd smacked him. "I am your husband. You will not speak to me like that."

His arrogance wasn't in the least attractive at that moment.

"You're only my husband until I get home and file for divorce." What that wouldn't do to all his uncle's and her father's machinations.

She supposed that none of them had taken into account the possibility that the worm would turn. They probably thought that she'd stay married to a man who had lied to her and manipulated her. After all, what else did she have to look forward to?

She might not be the kind of woman who haunted men's dreams, but that didn't mean she was willing to live the nightmare of loving someone whose whole purpose in pursuing her had been to use her.

He jumped to his feet and towered over her. "You do not mean that. I will not allow it."

"I don't know how things work in Jawhar," she said with dripping sarcasm, her heart hemorrhaging with grief, "but back home I can file for divorce without the approval of my sheikh husband." Or her deceiving father for that matter.

"You are tired. You are not thinking rationally." He rolled his shoulders as if trying to lessen the tension surrounding them.

She could have told him it wouldn't work. Nothing would work. The tension was born of anguish and it was anguish that had no respite.

"You're wrong. I'm thinking more rationally than I have for the past six weeks."

He shook his head, as if he could negate her words. "You need rest. We will not discuss this further right now."

She crossed her arms over her chest. Was he for real? Okay, maybe that was the way things worked in Jawhar, though she took leave to doubt it. But he'd gone to school in both France and America, both countries hotbeds of feminism. And although she had never considered herself a raving feminist, that didn't mean she was going to let her husband treat her like a child.

"*That's it?* You say we aren't going to talk about it and I'm supposed to shut up and go to bed?"

He rubbed his hand over his face. "That is not what I meant, Catherine. If it pleases you, I am tired, as well. I would be most grateful if we could wait to discuss this further until we have both had a chance to sleep."

As hard as she tried, she could not detect a single note of sarcasm or condensation in his voice. He looked tired, too. Considering how little sleep they'd had the night before and the way they had spent the afternoon, she could even understand why.

But a cynical doubt needled her already agitated brain. Was he just trying to take their battle to a location he had shown his mastery in so well already?

If he was, he had a rude shock coming.

"You're right. I am tired." And heartsick. "I would like to go to bed."

He looked relieved.

"But there is no way on this earth I'm sleeping with you." She said each word as it were its own sentence, spacing them succinctly so there could be no confusion about her intentions.

"You are my wife."

She didn't feel like a wife right now. She felt like a dupe. "I'm your means to an end," she derided.

His body tightened and he pulled himself to his full height, his chilling expression of outrage making him look bigger than his already tall six feet two inches.

"You are my wife," he gritted out between clenched teeth, more angry than she had ever seen him. "Several hundred guests bear witness that this is so. I have legal documents that state you are no longer Miss Catherine Benning, but Catherine bin Hakim al Kadar. Do not ever again say you are not my wife or attempt to deny my name.''

His vehemence shocked her. He looked ready to spit nails. Good. She shouldn't be the only one hurting here. Though, she doubted sincerely he was hurting. Angry more like. Apparently it offended his male ego in a very big way for her to deny the reality of their marriage.

''Legal documents don't make a marriage. They're just paper. They don't prove anything.'' Even in her anger, she doubted her own words. Being married meant something, but not the same thing to her and Hakim evidently.

''The consummation of our marriage is a fact.''

She went hot then cold as his words sank in. ''Are you saying you only made love to me so that I would consider myself married to you?'' she asked wildly, realizing that she was fast approaching the irrational state he'd accused her of earlier. If she wasn't already there.

The question seemed to stun him because his head jerked back and then he stared at her with incredulity in every line of his face. ''You dare ask me such a question?''

''Why not? You married me for reasons I knew nothing about. As far as I'm concerned, all your motives are suspect.''

She watched in a furious kind of fascination as he visibly took control of his anger until his face was a blank mask.

He spun away from her, his hands fisted at his sides the only indication that his emotions were not completely controlled. ''Very well. I will sleep on the divan in here.''

Even in the agony of her devastation, practical considerations asserted themselves. He was way too tall for the smallish divan.

"You can have the bed. I'll sleep out here." She sincerely doubted she'd get much rest anyway.

"Either we share the bed or you sleep in it alone." He still hadn't turned back to face her, but from the sound of his voice, she didn't doubt he meant what he said.

"Fine." If he wanted to suffer, let him suffer. She'd offered a better solution. It was his own fault he was too stubborn to take it, but why he had refused to take it niggled at her conscience. "I'll sleep alone."

A slight inclination of his head was the only indication he had heard her words.

She got up and went into the bedroom. She stopped at the doorway and compulsively looked back at Hakim. There was something incredibly lonely about his stance by the window. He looked as isolated as she felt.

But he'd chosen this path, her mind cried. She hadn't. It had been chosen for her by men who thought she was unworthy of truth and honest consideration. Unworthy of love.

CHAPTER NINE

CATHERINE woke to the smell of coffee.

Her eyelids fluttered, but did not open.

"Good morning. I have brought you breakfast."

The sound of Hakim's voice was a welcome intruder into her slumber until the pain she had escaped for a few short hours in unconsciousness rushed back in a wave so strong she actually moaned.

Masculine fingers tunneled through her hair to cup her scalp. "Are you all right, little kitten?"

The shock of the stupidity of the question brought her eyes wide open and her gaze to the source of her torment.

He was sitting beside her on the bed, wearing a *thob*, but clearly having just woken himself. His hair was mussed, his jaw darkened with morning stubble, his eyes faintly shadowed from what must have been a near sleepless night for him as well. She'd known the divan was too short for him.

How could a man look so very masculine and appealing in something that could be mistaken for full-length robe or dress? Yet, he did. The typical Arabic lounging garment accentuated Hakim's maleness rather than detracting from it. And she didn't want him looking attractive.

She'd come to some very difficult decisions in the long hours of the night. Being reminded of just what she was giving up did not help her resolve or lessen the ache in her heart.

113

Determined to ignore his blatant maleness, she struggled into a sitting position. She tucked the blankets around her, covering the sheer fabric of her nightgown. She didn't want Hakim thinking she was extending any invitations.

His brows rose at the gesture, but he said nothing and laid the rattan breakfast tray across her lap.

There were two croissants on the plate and two demitasse cups of dark, fragrant coffee as well as a small bowl of figs.

She picked up one of the cups of coffee. "Thank you."

"It is my pleasure."

Seeing no reason to put off telling him of her decision, she dove straight in. "I want to go back to Seattle."

He waited to answer until he had finished chewing a bite of his croissant. "We will, inevitably return as planned. My business is there, your job as well."

She placed her cup carefully back on its small white saucer. "I meant today."

The ridge of his jaw became more pronounced. "That is not possible."

"Your jet is broken?"

Rather than respond to the sarcasm in her question, he answered it as if it had not been rhetorical. "No."

"Then I don't see the problem."

"Do you not?" The silky menace in his tone reminded her that this was a man who had been trained since birth to exercise a great deal of authority.

Still, "No," she insisted stubbornly.

"Have you forgotten the wedding ceremony among my grandfather's people?" He asked the question conversationally, as if they were discussing their social schedule rather than the end of one of the shortest marriages on record.

She wasn't about to play the hypocrite. "It would be ridiculous to go through yet another wedding ceremony when I intend to go home and file for divorce, don't you think?"

That elicited a reaction, albeit a subtle one. His entire body tensed as if prepared for battle. "There will be no divorce." So decreed Sheikh Hakim bin Omar al Kadar.

"I don't see how you can stop me." She wasn't one of his subjects.

The expression on his face said she didn't have a very efficient imagination and as much as it shamed her, she shivered. "I mean it, Hakim. I won't stay married to a man who sees me as nothing more than a convenient means to an end."

"You are not a convenience. You are my wife."

"So, you keep saying. Funny, I don't feel like a wife."

Something feral moved in his eyes. "I can take care of that small problem."

She knew just what he meant and she shook her head vehemently. "I'm not going there again."

"Where?" he asked in a honeyed drawl that made her wish she was fully dressed and sitting across a table from him, not a small breakfast tray.

Nevertheless, she refused to let him see how intimidated she felt. "Bed," she said bluntly.

"But we are very compatible in bed." His fingers brushed down the curve of her breast.

She sucked in air, but it didn't help the goose bumps instantly forming on her flesh or the tightening of two erogenous bumps she hoped did not show through the blankets. Her heart felt dead inside her, why didn't her body follow suit?

"That's sex and I'm sure you've been *compatible* with other women before."

"Never like with you."

She wished she could believe him. It would have been some small assuagement for her lacerated pride. But after yesterday, she didn't trust anything he said. "Tell it to the marines."

He laughed at that, though it was a harsh sound. "I have no interest in making love to anyone but you."

"It's not making love when you don't love me."

His superior smile made her want to scream. "Then what is it?"

"Sex, or if you'd rather..." She said a blunt Anglo-Saxon term she had never used before in her life. Then she picked up her croissant and forced herself to take a bite to show she wasn't affected by the conversation.

"Crudeness is unbecoming in you."

She finished chewing her food before speaking. "I'm not interested in what you find becoming. Not anymore."

With a gesture of frustration, he stood up. "Enough."

She glared at him. "You can't order me around like a child."

"Why not? You are behaving like one."

"In what way am I acting childishly?" she demanded.

"You are happy married to me. You love me, yet you threaten to dissolve our marriage on the flimsiest pretext."

"I do not consider betrayal a flimsy excuse!"

"I did not betray you!"

She'd never heard him shout before. She didn't like it.

He took a visible hold on his temper. "When we married, you were so filled with joy, you glowed."

She opened her mouth, but he held his hand up.

"Do not deny it."

"I wasn't going to."

"Good. Finally, we move forward."

"I'm not happy *now*."

"That is apparent, but not something that cannot be changed."

"It will never change," she said with all the despair eating away at her emotions. She'd been happy because she believed the man she loved also loved her. He didn't. End of joy.

He shook his head, the movement decisive. "This I do not believe."

"It may come as a shock to you, but being used by both my father and my husband does not make me happy and since that reality cannot be altered, I don't know how you expect my feelings to change."

Time was supposed to heal all wounds, or so the old saying went, but right at that moment the future stretched forth in one bleak ribbon of pain.

"It is not a matter of being used. I know you resent your father's interference in your life. You have said so, but it is a father's prerogative to find a suitable husband for his daughter. And all the pleasure we found in one another's company awaits only your acceptance of the truth."

"Sex without love is degrading and a father concerned for his daughter's well-being does not sell her in exchange for a mining partnership."

"He did not sell you."

Tears that should be impossible considering how many she had shed in her lonely bed the night before welled and spilled down her cheeks. "Yes, he did. I'm nothing more than a duty wife, bought and paid for."

It hurt so much, she felt as if her heart was being squeezed by a vice.

She turned her face away, not wanting him to witness her grief.

The tray was lifted off her lap. A moment later, she was being pulled into his strength. "Don't cry. Please."

She didn't want him to comfort her. He was the enemy, but there was no one else and the pain was just too heavy to bear alone. His hands rubbed her back, his mouth whispered soothing words while she wept silent tears, soaking the front of his *thob*.

"You are more than a duty wife."

"You don't love me." Her voice broke on each word as the tears competed with her mind for control of her tongue. "You married me because your uncle told you to."

His arms tightened around her, but he did not deny it.

She pressed her face into his chest, wanting to blot out reality. But reality would not be ignored. She was only putting off the inevitable, she realized, allowing Hakim to hold her because she knew it was the last time.

Taking a deep breath, she hiccupped on a sob, but eventually managed to gain control of herself again. She pushed herself from his arms. "I need to get up."

He frowned. "This conversation is not finished."

"I need to get ready to travel."

He searched her face, but she refused to meet his gaze.

Finally, he sighed. "You are right. We need to prepare for our journey to Kadar. We go by helicopter. As
much as it pains me to see your hair bound, you should
braid it."

Hadn't he heard a word she had said? "I'm not going
with you to the desert. I'm going home," she spelled it
out as if to a slow-witted child.

"You are wrong." His expression was carved in
granite. "You will come with me to *our* home in the
desert."

"I won't."

"You will." Standing beside the bed, he looked
every inch the Arab prince, his belief in his own authority absolute.

"You can't make me."

"Can I not?"

Frissons of unease shivered along her spine, but she
defied him with her eyes. "I'm not going through a
second sham of a marriage."

"There is nothing fake about our marriage."

"That's your opinion and you are entitled to it, but
it won't change mine."

"I have had enough of this. We will participate in
the Bedouin ceremony tomorrow as planned. I will not
allow my grandfather to be shamed before his people.
Nor will I allow you to dismiss our marriage."

With that, her even-tempered, civilized husband
stormed out of the room.

Two hours later, Catherine was dressed in a sleeveless
fawn sweater and doeskin pants for traveling. It had a
matching calf-length cardigan that made it perfect for
the transition in weather from Jawhar to Seattle. And

she was going to Seattle, regardless of what her arrogant, deceitful wretch of a husband had decreed.

She checked to make sure her passport was still in her handbag and nodded in satisfaction at the sight of the small blue book. She had cash, her credit cards, everything she needed for departure from Jawhar.

She'd called the airport minutes after Hakim had stormed from their apartments that morning. Then she'd called for a car, reasoning that he was too arrogant to have put a moratorium on her going anywhere. She'd been right. There'd been no problem ordering a car to take her to the airport.

Hakim had assumed she'd wait for him.

That they would continue discussing their marriage.

But there was nothing left to discuss.

She hurt in ways she hadn't known it was possible to hurt and she was not sticking around for more of the same.

She'd come out onto the balcony to wait for a servant to announce her car was ready.

The sights and sounds of Jawhar's capital were open to her as their apartments were on the outer wall of the Royal Palace. While the city was much smaller than Seattle, the cacophonous mixture of voices, beeping horns and tinkling bells that rose to her was more impacting on her senses than Seattle's downtown district. The sun beat against her skin, warming her body while leaving her heart a cold lump in her chest.

A sound in the sitting room alerted her to a servant's arrival.

The trip to the airport was uneventful.

As a member of the royal family, getting a seat on the next flight to a major airline hub was a cinch and within short order she found herself in a first class seat waiting for the plane to take off.

The door closed and then the pilot announced their departure. They taxied to the runway and then stopped, no doubt waiting in line for their takeoff slot.

It seemed a long time coming and other passengers began talking amongst themselves, asking the flight attendant about the delay. Unfortunately, the conversations were in Arabic and she had not yet learned enough to interpret them fully.

But as the minutes ticked on a premonition of dread began to assail her.

When the outer door opened, she watched with almost fatalistic detachment as her husband's form came into view.

His eyes caught hers immediately and the rage she saw in the black depths made her mouth go dry.

He didn't bother to come to her row, but barked out a command to the flight attendant who quickly removed Catherine's bag from the overhead compartment.

Catherine didn't move, but glared her defiance at him.

He could take her bag. She didn't care. She wasn't getting off this plane. "I'm going home."

Hakim did not respond. He spoke again to the flight attendant, this time his voice not so harsh, but the implacability of his tone was apparent even to Catherine, who could not understand what was said.

The flight attendant approached Catherine. "His highness has decreed we cannot take off until you leave the plane, madam."

She didn't need the immediate and quickly escalating grumbling to tell her defeat was staring her in the face. She could not hold everyone back. There was no doubt but that Hakim had the power to ground their plane indefinitely and the hard-faced stranger standing by the open doorway would do it.

She unbuckled her seat and stood up. Hakim turned and left. She followed him off the aircraft, stepping gingerly down the portable stairway that had been transported to the runway for her husband, the sheikh's benefit.

When she reached the bottom, one of the black clad security men led her to a waiting limo.

She climbed into the back seat. She refused to look at her husband. She was both furious and frightened. The level of power he exerted was nothing short of intimidating when she faced the prospect of bucking his will.

Stupid tears burned her throat, but she would not give in to them. Not again.

She'd cried more in the last two days than she had for the past ten years.

Silence reigned for the brief trip in the car.

It stopped and another black clad gentleman opened the door. Hakim climbed out first and then extended his hand to help her out. She ignored it and ignored him.

"You can walk, or I can carry you, but you will come."

"Go to hell." She'd never cursed like that at someone, but she wasn't meekly following Hakim. No way.

A discussion ensued outside the limo.

Then Hakim leaned in, his intent obvious.

She shot to the other side and threw open the door. She scrambled outside only to be caught by manacle-like hands.

"Let me go!" She struggled against the hands and

aimed a kick to her captor's testicles. It never connected.

She was bodily lifted from behind and two arms like steel bands wrapped around her. "Be calm, Catherine."

"Release me right now!"

"I cannot."

She kicked backward and connected with his shin. He grunted, but his hold did not loosen. "Please, *aziz*, do not make this more difficult than it already is."

"You're kidnapping me. I'm not going to make it easy for you!"

"You cannot return to Seattle without me."

"Watch me."

"To do so could very well be to watch you die."

With those startling words, he swung her up into his arms in a hold that immobilized both her legs and arms. He carried her to a waiting helicopter. He lifted her into the helicopter and followed too swiftly for her to jump out again.

"You can't do this." The words were stupid. Patently he could because he was.

With a flick of his hand toward the pilot, the already warming engines revved and then the blades began their rotation. They were in the air within seconds.

There was no hope of conversing over the noise inside the chopper, so she didn't even try.

Trying to talk sense into a madman was difficult enough without having to shout above the sound of the rotor blades.

It was all so unbelievable. Her sheikh, whom she had considered far too civilized for such a thing, was kidnapping her in the best tradition of an Arabian Nights fantasy. Only it wasn't a fantasy. The dark, grim lines of his expression were all too real. So was her anger and the words he'd spoken before bodily carrying her to the helicopter. She might die if she went home without him. What was that all about?

Her thoughts whirled in confusion as the helicopter flew away from the oasis that supported the capital city of Jawhar and toward the region of Kadar.

She looked out the window, straining to see the first glimpse of the mountains bordering Hakim's home.

The helicopter was hovering above an oasis surrounded by tents when Hakim leaned next to Catherine and spoke into her ear so she could hear him. "Put your sweater on."

The desert's evening air was chilly, particularly so far above the ground, so she acquiesced without argument. Besides, even furious with him, her body responded to his nearness in a disastrous way. She didn't want to encourage more of it by arguing and keeping him close to her. She could smell his unique scent, the one her body identified with her lover, her mate and longing that should be as decimated as her heart, but wasn't, went through her.

Using the excuse of pulling her sweater into place, she maneuvered further away from him.

Once the long cardigan was on, he eyed her critically and then leaned forward again until his mouth practically touched her ear. "Can you close the front?"

She shivered as his breath intimately caressed the inside of her ear. He had no right to do this to her. He knew how easily she responded to him. Was he tormenting her on purpose? She shrugged him away with her shoulder.

"It's meant to be worn open." She had raised her voice to a near shout in order to be heard without having to move into his close proximity again. If her traitorous lips got anywhere near his ear, there was no telling what they would do.

The helicopter started to descend.

He said something she couldn't hear. She shook her head to let him know she hadn't gotten it.

He waited to speak again until they were landed and he'd pulled her from the helicopter to stand on the pebbled sand a hundred feet from the oasis and encampment. "It would be better if you could close it. My grandfather is very traditional."

His grandfather? Her attention skittered to the tents within her line of vision. Some were as small as a potting shed and others as large as a cottage with several rooms. They were all cast in a pink glow from the setting sun. One of those dwellings belonged to his grandfather.

"I thought we were going to your palace."

She was in no mood to make nice with more of his family.

"I changed my mind."

"Then change it again. I don't want to meet any more of your relatives."

"That is unfortunate because you are about to."

Who was this man?

He was not the man who had agreed to wait so she could have the wedding of her dreams, nor was he the man who had been so patient with her shyness, who had tempered his passion with gentleness the first time they made love...and every time since.

This man was a stranger.

"I don't know you at all," she whispered.

His body jerked and his eyes narrowed. "I am the man you married."

"But you are not the man I believed you to be. The man I met in Seattle would not have kidnapped me against my will and dropped me in the middle of the desert."

"And yet I am that man. I have been forced to measures I would not have otherwise taken by your irrational behavior."

"That's not true." How dare he say she was not rational?

"Enough of this? You see no perspective but your own. We will talk when you have calmed down."

Judging by the tight reign he had on himself, Hakim had some cooling down to do.

"At least tell me why we're here instead of your palace." They had not planned to come to the Bedouin encampment for another two days.

Her sense of being married to a stranger increased as the shadows cast by the setting sun gave him a hawklike appearance.

He raised his hand and with a flick of his wrist, the helicopter lifted into the air again. His expression was bleak. "There are no phones here."

Her gaze moved from his face to follow the disappearing helicopter. "And no source of transportation?"

But she knew the answer to the question before she asked it. He wasn't taking any chances on her running away.

"Not unless you know how to ride a camel."

She looked away from the sky and back at her husband, expecting dark humor or triumph to be glinting in his eyes after that comment. Neither mood was in evidence in the predator sharp lines of his face.

She licked lips that felt dry. "You know I can't."

"Yes."

"So, in addition to kidnapping me, you intend to make me your prisoner?"

"If that is necessary, yes."

She frowned. "I'd say it is already a fact."

"Only if you choose to see it that way."

"What other way is there to see it?" she asked belligerently.

"You are my wife. You are here to meet my family. It is something we planned days ago. There is nothing sinister in that," said the man who had just sent the only form of escape available to her flying off into the rapidly darkening sky.

"Eventually you will have to take me back to Seattle."

"Yes."

She would have said more, but a shout from behind them silenced her. Hakim raised his hand and called out in Arabic.

"Come, let us go meet my grandfather."

She turned away from him and using the scarf that matched her outfit, she fashioned it like a belt around her waist, pulling one edge of the sweater over the other increasing the modesty of the outfit significantly. "All right."

He surprised her by taking her hand and began leading her toward the largest tent and the delegation that had gathered to meet them. Torches cast light on those assembled. Standing in the center was a man almost as tall as Hakim. The wrinkled leather of his skin and red checked covering on his head worn by sheikhs indicated he could be no other than Hakim's grandfather.

He stepped forward to greet them. "You are welcome among my people." He had spoken in English, clearly for her benefit and she was impressed by the courtesy coming from a man so obviously used to authority.

Hakim stopped a few feet from the other man, released Catherine and then stepped forward to embrace his grandfather. "Father of my mother, I am grateful for your welcome."

He came back to her side, taking her hand in a firm hold once again. "Grandfather, this is my wife, Catherine."

The old man's eyes narrowed. "Your bride, you mean."

Catherine looked to Hakim for an explanation, but he wasn't looking at her. His attention was fixed on his grandfather. A quick dialogue in Arabic commenced. Hakim sounded angry. His grandfather sounded adamant.

It ended with Hakim releasing her hand.

A beautiful woman stepped from behind the man to the old sheikh's right. She wore the traditional dress of a Bedouin woman, the garment black, but embroidered with red, her head and neck covered completely by a black georgette scarf.

She smiled at Catherine. "I am Latifah, wife of Ahmed bin Yusef, sister to Hakim. You are to come with me."

Again Catherine looked at Hakim for understanding.

This time, he was looking at her, his expression grim. "My grandfather does not recognize our marriage because he did not witness it. It has been decreed that you will sleep in my sister's tent tonight. You are no doubt pleased by this turn of events." He inclined his head in acknowledgment of that reality.

"You must go with my sister." His hand reached out as if to touch her, but then dropped back to his side.

"Grandfather has decreed that since I am not yet your husband in the eyes of him and his people, to touch you would dishonor you among them."

The words disconcerted her, but it seemed she had an unwitting ally in the old sheikh.

Still smiling, Latifah touched Catherine's arm. "Come. We have much to do, much to talk about."

CHAPTER TEN

BY LATE afternoon the following day, Catherine thought *much to do* an understatement of monumental proportions.

Evidently a Bedouin wedding was every bit of a production as the one they had already gone through. She wondered when she would see Hakim. She had been cloistered in his sister's tent since her arrival and when Catherine had asked, Latifah had smilingly shrugged. Whenever their grandfather allowed him to visit appeared to be the answer.

She wondered if he arrogantly assumed she was going through with the ceremony, or if he was worried she would follow through on her refusal.

She didn't know her own mind right then. Too much had happened, her emotional wounds too fresh for her to do anything more than try to make it through the day without bursting into tears. Luckily Latifah made it easier, assuming agreement from silence and happiness where there was none.

Throughout the day and while they made preparations for a wedding Catherine was not reconciled to, Latifah talked. She was extremely kind and extremely friendly. She'd told Catherine about growing up in Kadar until she was eight. She had also told Catherine why Hakim had gone to live with King Asad and Latifah had gone to live with her grandfather. Catherine shivered at the memory of what Latifah had told her.

The attempted coup twenty years ago had left their

parents dead. She and Hakim had almost died, too, but the ten-year-old boy had managed to spirit his sister out of the palace under attack and had tracked his grandfather's tribe in the desert. When they had found the Bedouins, both children had been suffering from dehydration and hunger, but they had been alive.

Catherine thought about a small boy who had lost his parents and taken the responsibility of his younger sister's safety. Her heart ached for him. Because from what Latifah said, Hakim had not only lost his parents, but latter arrangements had effectively severed him from his remaining closest relative.

Latifah had been raised Bedouin and Hakim had been raised to be the Sheikh of Kadar, trusted adopted son to King Asad.

His feelings of obligation toward his king stemmed from more than a simple sense of honor, they stemmed from his emotions as well. How could it be otherwise when the King had become the only consistent entity in Hakim's life?

"And these troublemakers, they are the same ones who threaten the royal family now?" she asked Latifah.

Latifah's dark brown eyes snapped with anger. "Yes. Though smaller in number. The sons took over where the fathers left off. It is criminal. They have no popular support and still they attempt these horrendous things. They would have succeeded in their assassination attempt on Hakim had he not been so well trained in combat."

Unwelcome fear jolted through Catherine. "They tried to kill Hakim?"

"Yes. Did he not tell you? Men. They hide these things and believe they are protecting our feelings.

Women can give birth. Do not tell me we are too weak to know the truth.''

Catherine agreed, but right now she wanted to know more about the assassination attempt, not discuss the misconceptions between the sexes. ''When did this happen?''

''On Hakim's last trip home to Kadar. It upset my grandfather very much and for once he did not complain when Hakim returned to America.''

He'd married her, not only out of duty, she now realized, but out of a very real need to protect his family from the horror of the past. For him, these living visas represented an opportunity to protect his family. Something he could do personally, not just pay for with his great wealth.

She understood that.

She also understood that the concept of barter being exchanged at a marriage was not the same for him as it was for her. That had been brought home as Latifah helped Catherine sew several gold coins onto her headdress for the wedding. It was a dowry provided by the old sheikh in order to show her value to his people.

Among these people, such an exchange was not only acceptable, it was expected.

Her father and King Asad's deal that centered on her marriage to Hakim was in no way out of the ordinary.

In one sense, she could truly comprehend his view of their marriage, but understanding did not lessen the pain. She had believed he loved her and he didn't. She felt betrayed by him, by her father and by her own misreading of the situation. She'd talked herself into believing he loved her, but he'd never used the words. It had all been in her own mind and that made a mockery of the wealth of feeling she had for him.

''What about love?'' she asked Latifah as the other woman finished affixing the final coin to the fabric.

Latifah's brows drew together. ''What do you mean?''

''Does love have no place in marriage among your people?''

The other woman's eyes widened in shock. ''Of course. How can you doubt it? I love my husband very much.''

''Does he love you?'' Catherine could not help asking.

Latifah's smile was secretive and all woman. ''Oh, yes.''

''But...''

''Love is very important among our people.'' Latifah lifted the headdress and admired it.

''Yet your marriages are based on economic gain.'' Catherine was trying to understand.

Latifah shrugged. ''It is expected for love and affection to grow after marriage.''

''Does it always?'' Did Hakim expect to come to love her? Was he open to the possibility?

Latifah carefully laid the headdress aside and surveyed Catherine. ''It is the duty of both husband and wife to give their affection to one another. You must not worry about this. It will come in time.''

Catherine met Latifah's exotic eyes with her own. Could a woman so beautiful comprehend her own insecurities? She did not see how. Latifah's husband had probably found it very easy to fall in love with his wife. They shared the same background, the same hopes and expectations and she was stunning to look at.

Hakim, on the other hand, was married to a woman who had been raised very differently from himself. The fact that she was also ordinary and shy only added to the mix of Catherine's insecurities.

That evening, she was allowed to see Hakim under the sharp eyed chaperonage of his grandfather. They had no opportunity to talk about anything of a private nature, which frustrated her. She understood many things about Hakim that had eluded her, but she needed to talk to him before she would commit to going through with the Bedouin marriage.

The fact she was even considering it spoke volumes about the effect his absence from her life for two nights and a day had on her. She missed him and if she missed him this much after such a short absence what would the rest of her life without him be like?

Although the marriage had clearly been a business arrangement, he had made the effort to develop a personal relationship between them. He had shared his time with her, proving to her that they enjoyed one another's company. His friendship was as hard to let go of as his lovemaking.

And that was saying something.

Her body was now permanently addicted to his, the craving he engendered in her a constant pulsing ache in her innermost being. It shamed her she could be so affected by physical need, but when she considered how gloriously he fulfilled those needs, she wanted to weep.

What did she have to look forward to if he let her go? She knew she'd never love another man as she loved Hakim. No matter what he felt for her, the feelings she had for him were too deep, too permanent to ever be repeated with someone else.

When she went to bed that night, it was with a great deal of frustration. The wedding was to take place in two days' time and if those days followed the pattern of this one, she would not get a chance to talk to Hakim.

She lay in the bed of silk quilts and cushions, listening to the sounds of the desert and camp nightlife outside. A group of men walked by and their masculine laughter filtered through the thick wall of the tent. The camels were silent, but not all the animals had gone to sleep.

The air had cooled significantly and she snuggled into the blankets, glad for their layers between her and the cold.

She was on the verge of sleep when a hand closed over her mouth. Adrenaline shot through her system, sending her into fight or flight mode and she jackknifed into a sitting position, only to be trapped in a steel-like grip.

"It is I, Hakim."

As his voice whispered directly into her ear penetrated her terror, she relaxed, her body going almost boneless from relief.

He removed his hand from her mouth.

"What are you doing here?"

"Shh." Again he spoke straight into her ear, his warm breath fanning the always current flicker of desire in her to a small flame. "Do not speak loudly or we will be discovered."

"Okay," she whispered, "but what are you doing here?"

"We must talk."

He helped her to stand and the cold air quickly penetrated her thin nightgown, but he was wrapping her in a cloak that smelled of him before she could voice her discomfort.

He led her outside the tent, via a passageway she had

noticed earlier. It surprised her to discover there was more than one entrance to the outside in the large, but temporary dwelling. Once they were outside, she realized she had forgotten shoes as her tender feet came into contact with sharper objects than sand.

Once again, Hakim seemed to know before she spoke and he swung her up into his arms, carrying her beyond the light cast by the torches of the Bedouin camp.

He stopped and sank gracefully to the ground, keeping her close as he did so. She found herself in her husband's lap and felt the unmistakable evidence of arousal against her hip.

She tried to move away.

He tightened his grip on her. "Relax."

"You're…" She couldn't finish the sentence.

"I know." He sounded disgruntled and angry, but at least she knew his desire for her was real.

She also liked knowing he'd felt the need to talk before the ceremony. It meant he wasn't completely sure of her. His arrogance actually had limits.

She waited for him to talk, but he seemed preoccupied. One hand wrapped in the strands of her hair and his face was averted, as if he was contemplating the stars.

Finally he spoke. "We are to be married by Bedouin ceremony in two days' time."

"So I've been told."

He faced her. "According to Latifah's husband, you have been engaged in preparations all day."

"Yes." If he wanted to know if she planned to go through with it, he could ask.

"Have you considered you might be carrying my child?"

The question was so far from the one she expected

that at first, she did not take it in. When she did, she stopped breathing for several seconds.

Could she be pregnant? With a sinking sensation in the region of her heart, she had to admit it was likely. Their marriage had coincided with the most fertile time in her cycle. It had not been planned that way, but the result could very well be another al Kadar. Her baby. Hakim's baby. *Their* baby.

Her plummeting heart made an unexpected dive for the surface. The thought of carrying Hakim's child was not an unpleasant one, but she could hardly divorce the father of her child before it was even born.

"No."

"No you have not considered it, or no, you are not pregnant?"

"I hadn't considered it."

"That is funny, for I have thought of little else since the first time I planted my seed in your womb."

She went hot all over at his words, becoming even more keenly aware of the hardness under her hip. "You don't know they got planted."

"Considering how frequently we made love, I would say it is very likely."

She couldn't deny it, so she said nothing.

"Is the thought of having my child an unpleasant one?"

She had asked him for truth. She refused to prevaricate herself. "No."

She could feel tension drain from him and only then did she realize how uptight he had really been.

"Will you love my child?"

"How can you ask that?"

"It is not so unreasonable to believe the hatred you hold for the father could be transferred to the child."

"I would never hate my own child." Or any child for that matter. The comment that she hated him, she refused to answer.

"For the sake of our child, will you go through the ceremony in two days' time?"

"We don't know there really is a child." But the thought was a sweet one.

"We do not know there is not."

"It would really shame you if I refused, wouldn't it?" That had become very apparent the more time she spent observing the Bedouin life.

"Yes. It would also cast shame on the child of our union."

He'd latched on to her weakness right away and was obviously intent on making use of it.

"I cannot say vows I don't mean."

"There is no vow of love in the Bedouin ceremony."

He really believed she'd stopped loving him. She wished it was that simple to turn off emotion. It wasn't, but she was not about to share that knowledge with him.

"You married me as part of a business deal."

"I cannot deny this, but that does not negate the reality of the marriage."

She wasn't so sure about that, but she decided to pursue another grievance. "You kidnapped me."

"It was necessary."

"For you to get your way you mean."

"For your safety."

"That doesn't make any sense." How could she be in danger going home to Seattle?

"Threats were made against your life the day after our marriage."

"What? How?"

"A letter to the palace. King Asad showed it to me the day we left."

While she had been making her plans to leave him. No wonder he had had the plane held at the airport.

"It is my duty to protect you. I could not let you go."

"Duty," she said with disgust. She was coming to hate that word.

"Yes, duty. Responsibility. I learned these words very young. I am a sheikh. I cannot dismiss my promises as easily as you do your wedding vows."

That infuriated her and she jumped off his lap to land on her bottom in the cooling desert sand. She scrambled to her feet. "I'm not dismissing them."

He stood, too, casting a dark and ominous shadow in the moonlight. "Are you not? You threaten divorce hours after promising me a lifetime."

Okay, maybe from his perspective she was dismissing those vows, but they didn't count. "I was tricked into them."

"You were wooed."

"How can you say that?"

"It is the truth."

His truth.

She sighed. "I should get back before your sister realizes I've left the tent."

"We are not done talking."

"You mean I haven't agreed to your plans."

"I want your promise you will go through with the ceremony."

"I want some time to think."

"You have two days to think."

"What will you do if I say *no*?"

Instead of answering, he kissed her. Anger pulsated

in that kiss, a fury she had not even realized he was holding in, but there was passion too. Desire. And seduction. When he pulled back, she was limp in his arms and barely standing. "You will go through the ceremony so that you are my wife in my grandfather's eyes. Then I will make love to you and you will forget this talk of divorce."

His complacent belief that he could seduce her utterly to his will made her angry. So she lashed out. "Why not? We've already been through one sham wedding. Why not another?"

She fully expected him to explode, but he didn't. Tension filled his body, but he merely said, "Indeed."

He scooped her up into his arms and then carried her back to the tent, not putting her down again until he reached her bed. He leaned over and spoke with his lips so close, their breath mingled. "Good night, *aziz*."

Then he kissed her. She expected another passionate assault on her senses. More anger. More seduction. She got a gentle caress that left her lips tingling.

Then he was gone.

Catherine wrinkled her nose, both from the sight and the smell of the camel kneeling on all four legs before her.

Latifah had informed Catherine that her husband had ridden this animal to victory in the past three camel races. The knowledge was small comfort as she climbed into the boxlike chair on the camel's back. She'd never even ridden a horse and here she was, getting ready to ride a camel.

She adjusted herself on her seat, gasping as the box swayed with her movements. It was tall enough for her to sit fully erect, but she had to curl her legs under her because there was no place else to put them.

She was supposed to ride in this rather daunting conveyance to her wedding. Evidently this was the Bedouin equivalent to the romantic horse and carriage she'd dreamed of and been forced to discard as impractical in the rainy winter weather of Seattle.

The old sheikh led the camel himself, saying that since her father was not there to do it, he would be pleased at the honor.

She felt as if a thousand eyes were on her as the camel made its sedate pace toward where the ceremony was to be held.

Catherine kept her head down, but peeked through her lashes at the desert people who had gathered to watch her and Hakim marry according to their tradition. Small silver bells on the ornate necklace she wore made a tinkling sound as her body moved with the jarring gait of the camel.

When they reached the site for the marriage, the old sheikh helped Catherine down from the camel and led her to take her place beside Hakim. She didn't look at him during the ceremony, but kept her gaze focused downward as Latifah had instructed.

The ceremony itself didn't take very long, but the Mensaf, a dinner prepared to celebrate their union, did. The men and women ate separately and came together only afterward for the entertainment. They sat in the open air with fires going around them. The wood was so dry, hardly any smoke emitted from the fires, but the scent of burning chicory filled the air. Men played instruments and women sang, their voices beautiful in their Eastern harmony.

Hakim interpreted the words for her, his voice husky in her ear, his fingers curled around her wrist.

She could not ignore the way his touch affected her and the growing desires in her body, not after four nights away from their marriage bed. By the time Latifah led Catherine to Hakim's quarters in his grandfather's tent, it was quite late and she was jittery with pent-up feelings.

Lit with hanging lanterns, the room was surprisingly large. Richly colored silks covered the interior walls of the tent and the floor was made of the beautifully woven rugs the Bedouin women had become famous for. Hakim's bed was in the center of the room.

It was too elaborate to be called a pallet even though the large cushion for sleeping reposed on the floor with no frame under it. A multitude of pillows indicated the head of the bed. They were framed by billowing white silk that draped from a round frame hanging from the tent's ceiling.

It was like a tent within a tent.

Other than the impressive bed, there were few other items in the spacious room. Big Turkish pillows, obviously for sitting, were arranged around a small table.

She opted to sit on one of the pillows rather than the bed to wait for Hakim. Unfamiliar with the customs of his grandfather's people, she had no idea how long her husband would be. She could hear the revelry continuing in the camp and then she heard the unmistakable tenor of her husband's rich voice just outside the wall of the tent.

As her attention fixed on the doorway through which he would come, it struck her how like her fantasy her current predicament was.

She'd been kidnapped by a sheikh and waited for him

to have his way with her, but unlike the daydreams, Hakim was flesh and blood. She could touch him and he would touch her.

She shivered in anticipation at the thought.

Hakim paused outside the entrance to his chamber.

Catherine waited inside. She'd charmed Latifah with her sweetness, impressed his grandfather with her humility and scandalized the women who had helped Latifah prepare Catherine for the wedding by refusing to have her hair hennaed.

However, she had been very quiet throughout the evening's festivities. At least she had not refused to go through with the wedding. He had not been sure until he saw his grandfather leading the camel that she would actually go through with it, but then she considered it a sham. *Another* sham.

He would show her tonight there was nothing fake about their marriage.

He brushed aside the covering over the opening into the room and went inside.

The sight of her sitting on a pillow on the far side of the room stopped him. She had removed her headdress and it rested in her lap. Her hair hung loose, its dark honey strands glistening with sweet smelling oil. He inhaled the fragrance, taking in her distinctly feminine scent as he did so.

"My grandfather is pleased with you."

Her eyes flickered, their blue depths turbulent with emotion. "Does he know why you married me?"

"He does not know of my uncle's arrangement with your father, no."

She lifted the gold laden scarf. "Latifah told me this

is considered quite a dowry for a bride, even the bride of a sheikh.''

Hakim wished he knew what she was thinking. ''Grandfather values you.''

She looked down, her hair falling to shield her face from his gaze. Her small, feminine fingers traced the patterns on the coins for several seconds of silence.

Her hand stilled and her head came up. ''Do you?''

''Do I value you?''

''Yes.''

''Can you doubt it?'' She was his wife. Someday, God willing, she would finally understand what that meant to a man raised as he had been raised.

''If I didn't doubt it, I wouldn't be asking.''

The reminder of her mistrust angered him, but he forced himself to speak in a mild tone, without recriminations. ''On the day we arrived in Jawhar, I made you a promise.''

She frowned, her lovely skin puckering between her brows. ''You promised never to lie to me again.''

''And I have not.''

She nodded, apparently accepting that at last.

''I made a promise before that, little kitten.''

Her face showed her confusion. It was a mark of how impacted she had been by later revelations that she had forgotten something that had been very important to her at the time.

''I promised to always put your needs and desires first from this time forward. Tell me how I could value you more?''

''Are you saying that if it came between something your family wanted and what I wanted, you would choose my wants over theirs?'' Her voice was laden with skepticism.

"Yes. That is what I am saying."

"So, if I said I didn't want you to sponsor their living visas?"

"Could you say that and mean it if their lives were in danger?" he asked instead of answering her question.

Her head dropped, her face hidden from him again. "No."

Her continued refusal to see the good in their marriage and in him, frustrated him. "You are very pessimistic."

She jolted, her head coming up. "What?"

"You see only the negative."

CHAPTER ELEVEN

CATHERINE felt Hakim's words like an arrow piercing her. "I don't see only the negative." But even as she said the words, she wondered at their truth.

His expression told her he didn't have to wonder. He knew she was lying. "You would dismiss our marriage as nothing because of an agreement that has no bearing on our lives together. You seek new evidence at every turn to justify your mistrust of me and your cheapening of our marriage."

"I did not cheapen our marriage!" How dare he say that? She had loved him. It was his and her father's deceit that had cheapened the marriage and she said so.

"I did not dismiss you as nothing and demand divorce the day after we were wed. I did not refuse you the comfort of my body or the affection of my heart. You are angry because *love*," he said the word scathingly, "did not motivate my proposal of marriage. Yet you professed your *love* for me and then rejected me and threatened to dishonor me before my people. What is this love?"

Each charge affected her conscience like a prosecuting attorney's court indictment. He had never said he loved her and yet he had treated her with consideration. She had said she loved him, but then threatened divorce within thirty-six hours of their marriage.

"I..." She didn't know what to say.

His words were true and yet it had not been a weakness in her love that had made her do those things, but

146

the strength of her pain. Of her sense of rejection, but he had never actually rejected her.

"You are no doubt sitting there right now planning to tell me not to touch you. No matter that you are my wife. You do not care if I ache with wanting for you. No doubt you will rejoice in the knowledge I am suffering."

"No, I—"

He rode right over her words. "You can easily spurn the intimacy between us."

"It's not easy," she cried.

He snorted, clearly unimpressed with her response. "I have promised you honesty, do I not deserve the same?"

"I'm not lying."

"Are you saying you plan to share my bed?"

"Yes." She had already decided that for the sake of her pride, she would not fight him on this. She would rather walk back into intimacy with Hakim under her own steam than deny him and be seduced into his bed anyway. She loved and wanted him too much to deny him.

That fast, his eyes heated with a desire that burned her. He started walking toward her, but she put out her hand.

"Wait."

He stopped.

Before another storm of anger could rise between them, she quickly held up the headdress still clutched in her other hand. "I need to give you this."

His brows drew together in puzzlement, his eyes glittered with wariness. "Why?"

She took a deep breath and then let it out slowly, gathering her thoughts and courage at the same time. "In essence, you bought me with a mining permit."

She had taken a bit to work this all out in her head, but though her father had suggested the marriage, she felt as if she had been bartered in a business deal. She needed to redress that before she could share her body with Hakim again.

When he would have protested, she waved him silent.

"When you accept this gold," she said, indicating the heavily weighted headdress, "I am buying you. It makes us even."

She prayed he would understand and not make fun of her or remind her that his own grandfather had provided the dowry.

He did neither. He looked at the gold and then back at her face. "This is important to you? That we are even?"

"Yes."

"And when I accept your dowry, it is so?"

She nodded.

His eyes darkened with comprehension and he put his hand out to receive the gold. "May you find as much contentment with the exchange as I have done."

He meant as he had done before she found out the truth, but she didn't correct him. She wanted this night to be free of the weight of her father's bartered deal or even Hakim's cultural expectations of such a marriage. She wanted to make love on a level playing field.

She released the headdress into his hands.

Then she untied the gold belt around her hips, letting it fall to the woven rug beneath her feet.

Hakim went completely still, his black eyes fixed on her with almost frightening intensity.

She took advantage of his stillness to remove her dress and the garment under it, letting both glide down her body to pool around her feet. She wasn't wearing a bra and the way his gaze locked onto her naked torso told her he appreciated that fact.

Her nipples, which had already peaked in anticipation of her husband's touch, puckered into firmer rigidity under the heat of his look, stinging with the need to have his mouth on them. Her unfettered breasts swelled, making her skin feel tight and sensitive while other intimate tissues became inflamed, pulses of anticipatory pleasure vibrating trough them.

She walked toward him, the tiny silver bells on her necklace and anklets jingling with each step, her breasts swaying in a way that should have made her blush. For the first time, it didn't. It only increased her sense of feminine power because his eyes locked onto that swaying movement and he began to breathe faster.

When she reached her husband, she pushed his *abaya* off his shoulders. "Let me undress you."

He allowed her to remove his head covering and *egal*.

She let her fingers run through his thick, but short curling hair, reveling in the silky feel against her skin. Reveling also in her right to touch him in this way, to see him as no other woman in Jawhar had the right to see him.

He helped her remove his white tunic, the muscles of his chest rippling as he stretched to take it off.

The flat brown disks of his male nipples drew her attention and her desire. She brushed her fingers over them, feeling her own pleasure as they responded immediately to her touch.

"Yes. Touch me. Show me you desire me as I desire you."

His words sent excitement arcing through her and a determination to do as he said, to show her desire. She leaned forward and licked each nipple, then swirled her tongue around them, tasting the saltiness of his skin, smelling the masculine scent of his body.

His hands clamped on either side of her head. "The sultry air of the desert has turned you into a temptress."

She smiled and took the small, hard nipple into her mouth, sucking on it until he crushed her body to his with an agonized groan. She wiggled against him until her fingers could reach the drawstring on his loose fitting white pants. She tugged at it and it came undone so that the only thing holding them up was the way her body was pressed so tightly against his.

Tilting her head back, her eyes met his. "Take them off."

"You think because you have bought me, you can order me like a slave?" The warm humor in his eyes told her he was joking and not offended.

She gave him her best haughty look. "Of course."

His brows rose, but then they lowered and his look became predatory. "Then you are my slave also."

She found herself swallowing nervously. The game was taking a turn she hadn't expected. "Yes."

He said nothing, but he let her go to step back and push his pants down his thighs. Sleek satin hardness sprang up to greet her.

Remembering the pleasure she felt when he was inside her was exciting her.

"Take off your last covering." The way he said it sent shivers of desire and trepidation down her limbs.

All of a sudden it felt as if the small bit of lace was indeed her last covering, or protection, against him.

But she didn't need protection against him. Not now. She wanted what was about to happen. Very much.

She pushed the scrap of fabric down her thighs, exposing damp blonde curls.

"Come to me."

She took the step forward that separated them, stopping so close to him that the tip of his manhood brushed the soft skin of her stomach.

He reached down, grabbed her hand and led it to the rigid shaft between them. "Touch me."

She allowed her trembling fingers to curl around him. The hardness encased in warm satin fascinated her and she stroked him to the base. He made an incoherent sound of need and his head tipped back, his hands clenched at his sides.

She reversed her stroking and allowed her thumb to flick over the end of him.

His entire body racked in a giant shudder. *"More."* Both demand and plea, she found it impossible to deny him.

She did not want to deny him.

Touching him with gentle then firm strokes, she gave him more...and more...and more.

His entire body had drawn taut when he grabbed her wrist to still her hand. "Enough."

He took several deep breaths, his body shuddering. "Now it is your turn."

For him to touch her?

"To command," he clarified and she smiled.

They were still playing their game.

She didn't think she had the temerity to tell him to touch her. "Carry me to bed." It was where she wanted to be.

He didn't hesitate. He lifted her in strong arms and carried her to the bed in the center of the room. He knelt on the coverlet with her still in his arms and then released her legs so they knelt facing each other, his arms locked around her waist. He lowered his head and kissed her.

The kiss seared her lips with heat and touched something deep inside of her.

He was her husband and she wanted him, would always want him.

His lips broke away from hers to trail down her neck.

"I need you, Hakim."

His head came up, ebony eyes blazing into her own. "I have ached for you."

"You have me."

Triumph flared in his features. "Yes. I have you. I will never let you go."

She didn't want to think about the future. She wanted to concentrate on the present. She pulled his head down and kissed him, opening her mouth in invitation against his lips. The warmth of his tongue invaded her and soon the kiss was devouring and carnal.

Their game forgotten, Hakim made love to her with his hands, his mouth and ultimately, his body. When he exploded inside of her, she almost fainted as her own orgasm joined his.

Afterward, they lay entwined, their bodies sweat soaked.

He disengaged himself from her clinging arms and she moaned in protest, too wasted to actually form words with her mouth.

"Shh, little kitten. I want only to make you comfortable."

Soon, she found herself tucked under a silk quilt, surrounded by Hakim and pillows. He had extinguished the lights and released the chord on the bed hangings so it fell in a circular tent around them, an extra layer of privacy.

She snuggled into his side.

"Little kitten suits you well. You cuddle like a small cat, content to warm yourself with my flesh."

"You make me feel small."

"It is only in your mind that you are some Amazon creature."

She kissed the warm brown skin of his chest. "I know, but I like how you make me feel just the same." Because he didn't just make her feel small. He made her feel cherished.

"I am pleased this is so."

Playing idly with the black curling hair on his chest, she asked, "How long are we staying here?"

"We can go to our home in Kadar as soon as you like."

"Will it offend your grandfather if we do not stay longer?" Their short stay in King Asim's palace had been planned as part of their journey, but they had originally discussed staying among his grandfather's people for a few days.

"He would prefer we stayed long enough for me to race his favorite camel."

"When are the races?"

"In two days' time. Two other encampments will participate."

"I don't mind staying if you don't." She liked his sister and found the Bedouin way of life fascinating.

He hugged her to him in blatant approval. "It would please me to stay."

"Will you teach me to ride a camel?"

"Are you sure you want to learn? You looked very nervous today as you rode in the bride's coach."

"The box swayed. I thought it might fall off."

"I would never allow you to be at such risk."

For the first time, it struck her that this stranger he'd become was no stranger at all. He was Hakim. A complex man with many facets to himself. At once hard and unbending and then tender and protective, but always at the core the man she had fallen in love with, her sheikh.

Catherine enjoyed the next two days very much.

Latifah was a wonderful companion and she laughingly taught Catherine the rudimentary moves of Eastern dance while Hakim spent time with his grandfather. The second lesson was a little more difficult than the first as it came after Catherine's first lesson riding a camel. She was sore from the exercise, but the dance limbered up her muscles and Hakim's sensual massage that night completed her recuperation.

Dancing and camel riding weren't the only things she was learning while staying in the encampment. Hakim took great pains to teach her the extent of pleasure her body was capable of experiencing each night. When they were making love, she found it easy to forget the real reasons for their marriage.

As she watched her husband and Ahmed vie for first place in the camel race, ulterior motives for her marriage were the furthest thing from her mind. She was too terrified to think of anything else.

"I didn't know camels could move that fast."

Latifah laughed. "They are magnificent, are they not?"

"But what if the camel stumbles? What if Hakim is thrown?"

More laughter met her questions. "Hakim?" Latifah asked with clear disbelief.

"He's a man like any other, made of flesh and blood, bones that can break." Okay, maybe he wasn't like any other man, but he was still breakable.

Latifah became serious. "You care very much for my brother, do you not?"

"Yes," Catherine admitted, without tearing her gaze from the racing camels. "I love him. It's why I married him."

"I am glad. He deserves this love, I think."

Catherine sucked in a terrified breath as Hakim made a move with his camel that looked incredibly risky.

"He is an excellent rider," Latifah tried to reassure her. "He often wins the race, much to my husband's chagrin. It is good for Ahmed not to win every time."

It was Catherine's turn to laugh at Latifah's complacent statement.

Latifah laughed with her. "I am not disloyal, but my husband has been known to be insufferable after winning a race."

"Arrogance runs in the family, does it?" She'd learned that Ahmed and Hakim were cousins.

The other woman's eyes twinkled. "Yes."

"So, you're wishing the insufferable winner syndrome on me instead?"

"I believe my brother already considers himself the winner. He is well pleased with you for his wife."

Two hours later, Catherine and the winner of the camel races boarded another black helicopter. Again, there was little opportunity for communication as the helicopter flew through the sky, but unlike before, Hakim took Catherine's hand firmly in his, keeping it captive for the entire flight.

Her first view of Hakim's palace was an aerial one. Nowhere near as huge as the Palace of Jawhar, it was nevertheless an impressive structure. Domed roofs and tinted sandstone gave the hilltop structure a distinctively Middle Eastern look.

The helicopter landed in a flat valley several hundred feet from the palace. Men wearing the distinct black of King Asad's private guard were there to meet them along with an SUV to drive them and their luggage to the palace.

Hakim insisted on giving her a tour of the palace right off. She was right that it wasn't nearly as big as his uncle's palace, but she was still overwhelmed by the time he led her up a winding staircase. It seemed to go on forever before it ended at the entrance to a glass domed room.

It was an observatory, obviously built many years ago. Books on stargazing lined one wall. Some were in English, some French and some Arabic.

However, the books could not hold her attention long, not when in the center of the room sat a table and on that table resided a vintage George Lee and Sons telescope in perfect condition. She walked toward it as if drawn by a force greater than herself, her hand outstretched to touch.

Her fingertips brushed along the barrel. "It's beautiful."

"I believed you would like it."

She spun around to face him. "I thought, you know, that you faked your interest in ancient stargazing so we'd have something in common."

His mouth twisted in a grimace. "The telescope was my father's as was the passion for this hobby, but I soon found myself interested beyond pursuing it merely as a means to get to know you."

Why they met was taking on less and less significance the longer she stayed with him. She was sure that had been his plan when he kidnapped her. "Will you continue to attend meetings for the Antique Telescope Society with me?"

"I would enjoy the opportunity to do so."

She smiled.

"I meant to present the telescope to you as a gift before our wedding in the desert. It would have pleased my father for a true devotee of his favorite hobby to have it, particularly his daughter by marriage."

"I don't know what to say."

He took her hands in his, his eyes compelling her agreement. "Say you will accept it."

She sensed that in accepting it, she was tacitly accepting the permanence of that marriage. Was she ready to do that?

No matter what he felt for her, ultimately, it came down to life with Hakim and life without him. The possibility that she might carry his child weighed heavily against life without him. It was much too soon to tell, but she could not shake the feeling she was pregnant.

But even without a baby, the last few days had shown her the richness of life with him. Did she really want to return to the colorless life she had without him in it?

"You've fought very hard to keep this marriage," she said.

"I will never let you go."

"I have a say in it, Hakim."

He spun around and pounded one fist into the other palm. "When will you cease to fight me on this? You are my wife," he raged, shocking her into stillness with his unexpected anger. "I will not let you go. You are the mother of my children. Even now, you could carry my baby. Do you consider this when you make your plans to leave me?"

"I haven't *made* any plans." At least not since the first attempt to leave Jawhar on her own.

She laid her hand over her belly, a warm feeling suffusing her, even in the face of her husband's anger. "Do you think I might truly be pregnant?"

He spun around to face her. "If not, it is not for lack of trying on my part."

The admission stunned her. "You'd do anything to keep our marriage."

"Believe it."

He'd promised her fidelity, honesty and that she would come first in his consideration. It was a better recipe for marriage than many she'd seen and according to Latifah, love came later. Even so, there was no guarantee he would ever come to love her.

And if he had loved her, what was the guarantee he would always do so? In Hakim she had a husband who would always keep his promises.

"I don't want to end our marriage. I don't want to leave you."

His smile sent her pulses racing. In that moment of her capitulation, he looked marvelously happy. He could not be so happy if she personally meant nothing to him.

She put her hand out. "Let's get a little more practice in at starting a family."

Rich, deep laughter reverberated around her as Hakim led her to their room and a night of loving unlike any they had yet shared.

CHAPTER TWELVE

A LITTLE over three weeks later, they flew back into Sea-Tac, greeted by the typical gray skies and wet weather of a Seattle winter. Catherine mourned the loss of the warm sunshine of Hakim's desert home. Her husband clearly reveled in his Kadar lifestyle. Being honest with herself, she had to admit she had as well.

A great deal of it had been Hakim. He'd been so attentive and wanted to share every aspect of his life as a sheikh with her. She'd visited the settlements in his region, learned the only library available was at the palace and discovered an instant rapport with the people they came into contact with.

She had enjoyed their warmth and unreserved welcome for their sheikh's wife. The only downside had been the many requests the people made for Hakim's return. His political responsibilities were being seen to by a cousin from his father's side of the family, but his people wanted the Sheikh of Kadar to come home permanently.

She didn't understand his refusal to even discuss it. Could King Asad truly be cruel enough to expect Hakim to give up his homeland to oversee business interests? It didn't fit with the man she'd observed on their second visit to the capital.

Hakim drove them home from the airport in his Jaguar.

"We will have to arrange a visit with your parents now that we are back in Washington."

She noticed he never called Seattle home.

She swallowed a sigh. She'd have to face her father sometime. "Does Mom know? About Dad's deal with your uncle I mean."

Hakim's jaw clenched and he shook his head once in negation. "He did not think she would understand."

Just as Catherine had not *understood*, but she was glad her mom had not known. It would hurt that much more to think both her parents had been so willing to barter her life away.

"I'll call Mom and schedule something in a couple of weeks."

"Your father is scheduled to travel to Kadar the week after next to investigate the most likely mining sites."

He certainly wasn't letting any grass grow under his feet. "I guess we'll have to wait to see him until after he gets back."

With a little luck, it would take him several weeks to choose a site. By then she might have her emotions under control enough to see him without going totally ballistic.

"Why not before he goes? Surely this can be arranged."

She sighed. "I'm not sure I want it arranged."

"I thought you had reconciled yourself to our marriage."

Her gaze snapped to him. His jaw was taut, his expression unreadable.

"I am."

"Then why do you not want to see your father?"

"Because he betrayed me."

"As you believed I betrayed you."

She couldn't deny it. "Yes." She hated this. Everything had been fine until he brought up her father.

"And you cannot forgive."

That stopped her. She'd forgiven Hakim because forgiveness had been necessary to the healing of the wound in their marriage. But she'd never told him, assuming he knew because she'd stayed with him.

Apparently he didn't.

"I do forgive you."

"And your father? He wants only what is best for you."

"He made my marriage into a business deal."

"I have only met him a few times, but this seems to be his way. To do what he knows. To believe he knows best."

It was an accurate summation of her father's take-no-prisoners approach to business and life. And no doubt about it, he understood business better than people.

"Catherine?"

What could she say? She could not regret having Hakim in her life. Her heart had been shredded by the men's deceit, but it had not ended with the pain and the past few weeks had given her hope that perhaps one day her marriage would truly be one of love, not a business deal. "I'll call Mom and get something scheduled. I want to see Felicity too."

"You and your sister are very close."

"She's always been there for me."

"This is a good thing. Latifah is very important to me, but after the attempted coup we were no longer raised in the same household. We are not close."

It always surprised her when he opened up with something like this. He kept his deeper emotions under guard so much of the time, except in bed. Then his passion was as volatile as a live volcano.

"What about your cousins?" He'd been raised with them. Had they taken the role of brothers?

"It was determined early on that I would accept the role of diplomat and so I was educated abroad from the age of twelve."

"It must have been lonely growing up being part of a family, but having a destiny that placed you on the outside in many ways."

He shrugged, his powerful shoulders shifting with the movement. "I am no longer alone. With you, I am very much on the inside."

The sexual innuendo made her blush, but at the same time, her eyes filled with unaccountable tears. She'd been extremely emotional the past week and couldn't help wondering if the fact her menses were two weeks late had something to do with it. Had all Hakim's concentrated efforts paid off?

She blinked away the moisture and went for an expression of amusement. "I'll say." She gave him her best version of a lascivious wink and squeezed his thigh.

Deep, masculine laughter erupted around her as he caught her hand in his. "Behave, wife."

"I thought I was behaving, *husband*." She drew the word out in a long, slow, intimate breath of sound.

His fingers laced with hers. "We are fully reconciled, are we not?"

"Yes."

He was silent for a couple of miles. "You are no longer considering divorce?"

She was surprised he felt the need to ask. "No. I told you I was committed to our marriage."

"And you do not think I am lower than the underside of a lizard in the desert?"

That shocked a giggle from her. "No. I don't think that."

"Then why have you not repeated your avowal of love since the day after our wedding?"

Tension seeped into her body, making her muscles contract. "You didn't marry me for love."

"Does this negate your love for me?"

What difference could it possibly make to him?

She pulled her hand from Hakim's and turned to look out the window. Gray sky and wet concrete made an uninspiring view. "What do you want me to say?"

"I want you to tell me you love me."

The blatant request buffeted nerves that she thought had settled. She could make her own demand for the same thing and did not doubt he would comply. It was his duty to come to love her, so he would will himself to do so, but she didn't want a duty vow. She wanted the same hot cauldron of emotions that seethed inside her to churn in him.

When she didn't answer he brushed her cheek. "Is it so hard, little kitten?"

"I'm not sure this is the best place for this discussion."

She could see him return his hand to the steering wheel out of the corner of her eye. His jaw clenched for the second time in twenty minutes. "Perhaps you are right."

She hated feeling like all the rapport they had shared for the past few weeks was going up in smoke.

How could she explain that telling him she loved him made her feel vulnerable? That somehow keeping the words locked inside protected her heart from his indifference.

Only he *wasn't* indifferent.

He wanted to hear her words of love. Could it be that he was coming to love her? Did he feel just as vulnerable as she did because she hadn't told him she loved him since learning of the real reasons behind their marriage? Perhaps by trying to protect her own feelings, she was not leaving room for him to express his, or at least to allow his to grow into something stronger than dutiful affection.

She turned to look at his tense profile. "I do love you." Her voice was low, almost a whisper, but he heard her.

His grip on the steering wheel tightened until his knuckles showed white. "You are right. This is not the place for such declarations."

Hurt by the apparent rejection of her words, she demanded, "Why?"

"Because I now want to make love to you with painful fervor and it will be at least fifteen minutes before we reach our home."

Catherine called her father's office the next day. They needed to talk. But he had flown to South America on business and wasn't expected back for several days. Catherine made an appointment to see him before he left the country again, this time to the Kadar Province in Jawhar.

The day before her appointment with her father, Catherine was in the living room of her and Hakim's penthouse, curled up on the sofa, a book on ancient astronomy in her lap. She traced a picture of a telescope very similar to the one Hakim had given her after their wedding and remembered their days in Kadar.

Hakim had spent the first ten years of his childhood

in that palace. She could imagine him as a small boy, learning to ride a camel, teasing his little sister as boys do, climbing into his mother's lap for a cuddle when he was tired.

Catherine gently touched her stomach and pictured the same things with her own child. Only she was having a really hard time picturing them here in Seattle. The palace in Kadar had felt like a home, a grand one, but a home nonetheless. Their penthouse felt like a yuppie launching pad. It wasn't just the difference between Hakim's penthouse apartment and the palace in Kadar, either.

It was more. It was millennia of tradition, family and political responsibilities, an entirely different way of life to the one her child would know here.

A way of life she thought she could embrace. A way of life she knew her husband missed.

"Hello, little kitten. Did you have a good day at the library?"

She'd been so lost in her thoughts, she hadn't heard him come in.

She looked up and smiled. "Hi. It's been a wonderful day. Come and sit by me and I'll tell you all about it."

He shrugged off his suit jacket and loosened his tie before tugging it off. By the time he joined her on the couch, the top two buttons on his dress shirt were undone. Dark hair peeked out of the opening.

She reached out and brushed a fingertip along the open V. "You're a sinfully sexy man, Hakim."

Ebony eyes burned with instant desire. "It pleases me you find it so."

Her own eyes fluttered shut as he lowered his head to kiss her, his customary greeting when they'd been apart for longer than a few minutes. There was something desperate in his lips she didn't understand and she automatically sought to sooth with her response, surrendering completely to his touch.

Ten minutes later, she was lying across his lap, the small pearl buttons on her sweater undone along with the front clasp on her bra. His hand gently cupped her breast, one thumb brushing over an already hardened nipple.

"To come home to such a greeting makes up for a lot." His words whispered against her neck between small, biting kisses.

"And what am I making up for, the lousy traffic in downtown Seattle?" she asked, breathless with rapidly spiraling desire.

He husked a laugh and hugged her tightly to him.

She leaned back a little, wanting to see his eyes. "I've got news."

His brows rose. "Do not hesitate to tell me."

Her lips tilted in a smile. She loved it when he talked all sheikhlike. "As of Monday, I'll be part-time at the library and I've explained that if you need to travel for business I am going with you."

She wasn't sure how black eyes could darken, but his did…with pleasure. "I like this news very much."

"I thought you would." She also hoped he would feel free to make more trips to Jawhar if he knew she could go with him on short notice.

She snuggled more firmly into his lap, reveling in the feel of his hardened flesh under her bottom. "There's more."

He groaned and the hand on her breast contracted. "Perhaps it can wait."

She wiggled again for good measure, but shook her head. "I want to tell you now."

His hands locked on her hips to stop their movement. "Then tell me before I ravish you here on the sofa."

"There's a reason I wanted to go part-time."

His head had fallen back and his eyes were closed, his nostrils dilated with arousal. "What is that?"

"All your effort paid off."

His eyes flew open and he looked at her with reproach. "I did not demand you cut your hours at work."

"I didn't go part-time because you wanted me to," she assured him.

The twist of his lips said her answer had not reassured.

"I altered my work schedule to accommodate an upcoming change in our family." She leaned forward and kissed his lips very softly, then with their mouths only separated by a breath, she said, "I'm going to have your baby."

If she had not known better, she would have thought a spasm of pain crossed his face, but it was gone in a flash to be replaced by unadulterated joy.

"Thank you," he whispered against her lips and then he kissed her.

It was the most tender expression of affection he had ever shown her. Then he broke into speech in Arabic, his hand moving to cover her belly, his mouth kissing her all over her face, neck and chest.

He cupped her breast. "My baby will suckle here," he said with awe.

Tears filled her eyes. "Yes."

He pressed a gentle kiss to one rigid peak and then the other. He moved until he had her laid out on the couch before him; somewhere along the way, their clothes had disappeared. He paid homage to her breasts again, then moved his mouth to press a ring of kisses around her navel. "My child is nourished and protected here in the warmth of your body."

Her fingers tangled in the thick black hair on his head and tears of love, joy, and pleasure swam in her eyes.

His mouth rested over the blond curls at the apex of her thighs. When his tongue darted out to part the folds of her femininity and seek her pleasure spot, she arched up off the couch. "Hakim!"

He pressed her thighs apart and continued to make love to her with his mouth until she was shuddering in exquisite release. He moved up her body, taking possession of her with one sure thrust. "From this pleasure we made life between us."

"Oh, darling…Hakim. My love."

His lips cut off any more endearments, but her heart continued to utter them, beating out a rhythm of her love that he had to have felt.

He established a pace that soon had her arching in renewed tension, but this time when she went soaring among the stars, he was with her.

Afterward he collapsed on top of her and she brushed her hands down his back, petting him, loving him. "I love you."

His head came up and his face wore the most serious expression she had ever seen. "Do not stop loving me, I beg of you."

"Never," she promised fiercely. "I will always love you."

The warmth of his desert home was in his smile. "Then all is worth it, jewel of my heart. For the gift of your love, the gift of our child makes every sacrifice of no consequence."

"What sacrifice?"

But he was kissing her again and any thought of conversation melted under the fire of his physical love.

Catherine dressed for success for her meeting with Harold Benning. Her straight black skirt, short-sleeved black sweater and hip-length hound's-tooth jacket gave her badly needed confidence. She hadn't had a heart-to-heart talk with her parents since before puberty.

He looked up from his desk, a telephone pressed to his ear, when she walked in. Wariness chased shock across his features.

He said something into the phone and then hung it up. "Catherine."

Now that she was here, Catherine didn't know where to start.

"Would you like a cup of coffee, something to drink?"

She shook her head. "Not really. I want to talk to you."

"About your marriage." It was a statement, not a question.

"How did you know?"

Her dad leaned back in his leather executive chair, his pose relaxed, but his expression watchful. "Hakim called from Jawhar to tell me you knew about the mining deal."

Her hands clenched at her sides. "It isn't exactly your average mining deal, though is it? Instead of paying for the privilege to mine in Jawhar, you bartered your daughter like some medieval tyrant."

Her dad's brown eyes snapped with reproach. "It wasn't like that."

She sat down in one of the chairs in front of his desk and crossed her legs, trying to project an air of casualness she did not feel. "Why don't you tell me what it was like?"

"You know your mother and I have been worried about your lack of a social life for years. When this business with King Asad came up, I saw a way to kill two birds with one stone is all. I didn't do a damn thing to hurt you."

She shot to her feet and leaned across his desk until their faces were inches apart. "You didn't do anything to hurt me? Just how do you think I felt when I discovered the man I loved didn't love me, that he married me as part of a business deal? Let me tell you. It hurt! It hurt a lot."

Her dad sank back into his chair like a puppet whose strings had been cut, but he didn't say anything.

She didn't need him to.

She was in full throttle now. "Let me tell you about hurting. I found out that both my husband and my father had lied to me. I knew I wasn't as important to you as Felicity, but I never thought you saw me as an expendable possession!"

He flinched and passed his hands across his face. "You aren't expendable to me. I didn't sell you into slavery in a third-world country, Catherine. I fixed you up with a business associate."

"Without telling me."

His expression turned belligerent at that. "Hell no, I didn't tell you. You would have run a mile in the opposite direction."

"So you told Hakim how to manage an *accidental* meeting."

He shrugged. "It seemed the best way to get you to give him a chance. Listen to me, Catherine. The laser treatment got rid of the scars on your face, but that wasn't enough. Your mom and I thought once the scars were gone, everything would be okay, you'd date like your sister, get married one day. Have a life.''

She looked away, not wanting to see the years-old pity burning in his eyes.

''It didn't work that way, though. You don't trust people, especially men. Hell, maybe that's my fault. I ignored you because I couldn't fix your problem. And you felt rejected because of it. I was wrong, but I can't change it now. Maybe you were afraid of being rejected again. I don't know, but until Hakim, you kept your emotions locked up tighter than the Denver Mint.''

''I trusted Hakim.''

''You fell in love with him. Don't hold the arrangement against him, Catherine. The kind of deal we made is pretty common in his part of the world.''

''I figured that out. The fact that I am a means to an end for him doesn't lessen my value in his eyes.''

''Well, as to that, I'm sure you've heard there won't be any need for long-term living visas.''

''What?''

''Didn't Hakim tell you? His uncle's intelligence sprang a trap on the leaders for the dissidents. They're in jail awaiting trial for treason right now.''

Why hadn't Hakim said something? ''When did this happen?''

Looking relieved by the change in topic, her dad said, ''I got word yesterday.''

Yesterday. She remembered the desperation in Hakim's kiss, his mention of sacrifices and there was that initial flash of pain in his eyes when she told him she was pregnant.

She stumbled to her feet. She needed to think. ''I've

got to go." She walked quickly toward the door of his office.

"Are you okay?" She hadn't heard her dad get up from his chair, but his hand was on her shoulder.

"I'm fine. Why wouldn't I be?"

"I'm sorry, Catherine. If I could change the way things happened, I would."

She believed him.

Walking into the penthouse fifteen minutes later, she was still trying to make sense of what her father's revelations meant for her and Hakim. She couldn't forget that small flash of pain. What had it meant?

There was no longer any need for long-term living visas. Did he regret their marriage now that the personal benefit to him was gone?

The blinking light on the answering machine caught her attention as she tossed her purse on the table. She couldn't listen to the recording, not yet.

So many thoughts were crowding her mind, she didn't think she could take another one in. Not even a phone message.

She sat down and started dealing with the kaleidoscope of impressions one by one. The foremost was the very first time she and Hakim had shared passion. They hadn't made love, but he'd wanted to, had been aching with the need to have her.

The next image she examined was his reaction to her demand for a divorce. He hadn't just been angry. He'd been furious on a very personal level. And he'd done everything in his power to change her mind. The fact that he'd been successful considering how betrayed she had felt meant something.

Then she thought of her life together with him over

the past weeks. Happy. Content. Pleased with one another's company. Sexually insatiable. In harmony.

They fit together.

She didn't know what that small flash of pain meant, but she was absolutely positive it had not resulted from his discovery he was stuck with her. The fact that he hadn't told her about the capture of the rebels yet indicated that in his mind, that aspect of their marriage was incidental to their relationship.

With that tantalizing thought swirling through her mind, she got up to push the play button on the answering machine.

Hearing the voice of the King of Jawhar was a little unsettling, but hearing his request that she, not Hakim, return his call was enough to make her knees go weak.

CHAPTER THIRTEEN

AFTER taking several deep breaths, she picked up the phone to call the King. Her nervousness only increased when Abdul-Malik insisted on sending her call straight through even though the King was in a meeting.

Their greetings were a little stilted, but it didn't take King Asad long to come to the point. "You have heard the dissidents have been arrested?"

"Yes." She didn't bother to tell him her father, rather than Hakim, had told her the news.

"There is no longer a need for long-term visas."

"I gathered that, yes."

"Another could oversee our business interests abroad. Hakim could come home."

Catherine felt her mouth curve into a smile at the wonderful news and then the King's wording struck her and the smile slipped a little. "Why are you telling me rather than Hakim?"

"I have told my nephew." She could hear the royal impatience clearly across the phone line. "It is my will and the will of his people that he return to rule the Kadar province."

"He didn't mention it." Why hadn't he?

"He refuses to return."

"*What?*" She couldn't believe it. Then she realized she'd just shouted into the ear of a king. "I'm sorry, Your Excellency, but I cannot understand this refusal. My husband wants to return to Jawhar, I know he does."

175

"I am certain of this too, jewel of his heart."

What in the world? Why had he called her that? "Then…"

A heavy sigh and then, "He is convinced you would be unhappy living in Kadar."

"That's ridiculous. I loved our time there. He knows I did."

"I think, perhaps I should tell you a confidence."

She wanted to hear anything that would make sense of this bizarre situation. "Please do."

"It is not something I would share with the wife of my nephew in the usual circumstances, but his stubbornness leaves me no choice."

"I understand," she said with a fair bit of her own impatience.

"Very well. When he was at university, Hakim had a relationship with a woman he believed he loved. A woman he believed loved him."

Maybe Catherine didn't want to hear about this.

"Hakim asked this woman to marry him, to return to Jawhar and live as his sheikha. This was before it was decided he would oversee our business holdings in America."

"She turned him down. He told me."

"She told my nephew that no matter how much she loved him, no western woman would willingly give up her career, her lifestyle and her country to move to a backwater like Kadar." The King's voice dripped acid. "This woman told Hakim he had to choose between his position as a Sheikh of Kadar with life in Jawhar and her."

"He chose his position," Catherine said, stating the obvious. After all, the two had not married.

"But with you, he has found the true jewel of his heart. He chose you over his duty to his people."

"What do you mean?"

"He believes your happiness lies in Seattle, therefore he has refused to return to his homeland and his people."

Catherine's body started shaking and she had to sit down. "But I didn't ask that of him. He never said anything."

"He does not wish to distress you. He told me that he thought you might sacrifice your happiness for his, but he would not allow you to do so."

"But I'd be happier in Kadar. I want to raise our babies in his palace. I like the sunshine. The people are wonderful. I could learn to race camels." She was babbling, but so stunned from the news that Hakim had chosen her over his duty that she couldn't control her tongue.

"Babies?" the King inquired with meaning.

"Oh... I..."

"Perhaps you will have good news to share when you and my nephew return to Jawhar?"

"But Hakim said he doesn't want to come."

"No, Catherine, he said you do not wish to come and therefore he will not."

She bit her lip. What was the King thinking now? "Are you angry with me?"

"No. I spoke to Lila and many whom you had contact with on your visit to Jawhar. I am convinced this problem my nephew believes exists is in his head, not your heart."

"You're right, but what should I do?"

"Tell him your feelings." The King sounded a bit exasperated with her dull thinking.

She smiled. "I want to do more." Hakim deserved a gesture that showed how much she loved him, how much she wanted to live in Jawhar with him. "Maybe you could help me out…"

Hakim opened the door to the penthouse with a sense of anticipation he had never had prior to his marriage. She would be waiting. His Catherine. His little kitten.

Perhaps she would be curled up on the sofa as she had been yesterday. He smiled at the thought. Such a welcome did indeed make up for a lot. It made up for everything. He could live the rest of his life in this damp climate if it meant basking in the warmth of her love.

There would be children. Sooner than later. His heart pounded at the thought. She already carried his child, perhaps a son, the next Sheikh of Kadar. A son who would be an outsider to his people like he had been in the Palace of Jawhar after his parent's death. But the child would belong in their family. He would fit with Catherine and Hakim. It was enough. It had to be enough.

The sound of soft music from the bedroom drew him, but he found the room empty. Eastern music played from the built-in sound system and the door to the lavish en suite bathroom stood open. He walked in to find his wife lounging in the deep sunken bath, the fragrance of jasmine surrounding her, a subtle lure to his senses.

"It would take a man very secure in his masculinity to share his wife's bath when the water has been scented with the oil of fragrant flowers."

Her beautiful head turned, the cupid bow of her mouth tilted in a beguiling smile. "It's lucky for me I'm married to a very macho guy then isn't it?"

His fingers were already at work on the buttons of

his shirt. "It is I who am blessed, my jewel." She glittered like the most precious stone with beauty and fire. "To have such a wife is all any man could ask."

Soft pink colored her cheeks and she averted her eyes. "I never know how to respond when you say stuff like that."

He finished undressing and slipped into the hot water with her. His legs brushed the silken smooth skin of hers. "It is my hope you will accept my words with the flowering of joy in your heart."

She peeked at him through her eyelashes, her expression coquettish, the feel of her foot insinuating itself between his thighs not. "I am very happy with you, Hakim."

And it was true. She radiated with the same glowing joy she had on their wedding day. What had wrought this change? Was it her pregnancy?

Her small, feminine toes caressed his male flesh and he felt an immediate and overwhelming response.

She reached out and brushed the tip of his shaft. "Mmm... Very masculine."

He laughed and launched himself at her.

Later, she snuggled in front of him, her breathing still a little ragged. "I think you drowned me."

"You offered an invitation too appealing to pass up."

"Are you sure it was an invitation? Maybe I was just trying to unwind in a nice, relaxing bath."

He laughed. She often gave him the gift of laughter. "It was a shameless invitation and you know it." He tweaked a still rigid nipple.

She squealed and batted his hand away. "All right. I admit it. Sexy invitation all the way."

"You are that."

"What?" she asked, cuddling more snuggly against him.

"You are incredibly sexy."

"You make me feel like it. You make me feel beautiful." She said it with such surprise.

"Your beauty surpasses that of any other woman."

She sighed and laced her fingers with his across her stomach.

Would she accept his avowal of love now? He had wanted to tell her of his feelings, but although she had admitted she still loved him, she held something back. Her trust. When he told her of his love, he wanted her to believe him, to trust him. If she believed his words of love were insincere, it would hurt her and he could not bear for her to be hurt anymore.

Her kiss surprised him and her lips were gone before he could take advantage of it.

"Your uncle called today."

Tension filled him. "What did he have to say?"

"One of your cousins just got engaged."

This he knew. His uncle had told him that along with the news about the dissidents being captured. "She is not technically my cousin. She is my uncle's niece through his wife."

"He still wants us to come to Jawhar for the betrothal celebration."

His heart ached as it always did when he thought of his home. "Do you wish to go?" They had just gotten back. It was a long journey to take again so soon.

"Oh, yes."

"Then we shall go."

Her smile was all woman and somehow mysterious.

He gave up wondering what it meant when her lips once again covered his own. This time he was ready to take the advantage.

A week later they boarded the same jet that had taken them to Jawhar the first time. Hakim was very attentive on the journey, asking Catherine repeatedly how she felt and if she needed anything. Thankfully, she had experienced only the slightest form of morning sickness with her pregnancy and the flight was no problem at all. Which was a relief considering the plans she had for when they reached the airport.

Hakim led her to the helo pad, believing they were taking a short helicopter ride to his cousin's home province. Catherine kept him occupied with a totally inappropriate display of affection he did not seem to mind in the least and it was an hour before Hakim realized they were headed in the wrong direction.

He tapped the guard seated next to the pilot and yelled something in Arabic. The guard answered and Hakim turned to her, his expression furious.

"What the hell is going on?"

The smug smile she'd meant to greet him with withered in the face of his wrath, but she kept her cool. He couldn't go totally ballistic. After all, being pregnant did have its uses.

"I'm kidnapping you," she shouted above the sound of the helicopter's blades.

His eyes snapped black retribution, but he didn't say another word until they had landed near the Kadar Palace. The same SUV was there to transport them, even the same guards. Catherine smiled at them, trying to ignore the glowering man by her side.

Hakim kept his silence until they had reached the privacy of their bedroom in the palace.

Then he turned to her, menace written in every line of his body. "What is happening?"

"I kidnapped you."

"So you said."

She clasped her hands together in front of her to stop their shaking. This was supposed to be easy. Tell him how she felt about living here, he would be pleased and everything would be fine. Only he was mad, really mad.

"Why are you so angry?"

"You usurp my authority among my people and you have to ask this?"

She hadn't considered that angle. "You have to stop taking yourself so seriously. Your consequence hasn't suddenly taken a nosedive, if that's what you're worried about. As far as everyone else knows, everything has been done according to the will and authority of King Asad. It's no big deal."

Hakim did not look particularly reassured. "And what exactly is this *no big deal*?"

She was getting a little frustrated with his anger. "You had no right to refuse to return to Jawhar without consulting me. I'm your wife, not a mindless bed warmer who has no say in the decisions that affect me. And I'm definitely not that stupid woman you lived with. My thoughts and my feelings are my own. You should have found out what they were before refusing your duty to your family and your country."

She crossed her arms over her chest and glared at him, a little of her own anger coming to the surface as she remembered how he'd made such a major decision without her input.

Hakim rubbed the back of his neck, his expression turning resigned. "My uncle convinced you to sacrifice yourself for me, for the good of my country." It wasn't a question, but she treated it like one anyway.

"No, he did not. He simply told me that you had refused to come home when the capture of the dissidents made it possible."

"We will not be staying." He spun as if to leave the room.

He made her so mad sometimes she wanted to spit. "Hakim!"

He stopped.

"I know you can ride a camel. Heck, you can order a helicopter faster than I can order dinner."

His body tensed. "What is the point of this?"

"I can't hold you here against your will. I can't stop you from leaving by dropping you in a desert encampment from which you have no easy escape."

He turned to face her, his expression not so much unreadable as full of conflicting emotions. "So?"

"I have only one thing to hold you here." If he loved her, it would be enough.

"What?"

"Myself."

He shook his head and she squelched the tiny doubt that tried to intrude on her certainty that he loved her. He had to love her to have chosen her over his duty. A man with his strong sense of responsibility would only make such a decision under a powerful influence of emotion.

"This is not about you." He swung his arm out indicating the room, the palace, Kadar. "This is about my uncle manipulating you into sacrificing your happiness for my duty. I won't allow it."

"How do you know what would make me happy?" she demanded. "You never asked."

"I made a promise to you, to put you first from the point of our marriage forward. I will keep that promise."

"Are you saying it's a promise holding you here in this room with me?"

He stared at her, his expression that of a man trying very hard to hold onto his temper. "I did not say that."

"Good. Am I enough to hold you?" She wanted the words. She deserved the words.

"There is no binding that could be stronger." He started toward her, his intent very clear in the obsidian eyes she loved so much.

Her feet started moving of their own volition, taking her to him. They met in the middle of the room. He pulled her into his arms, his hold so tight she could barely breathe.

"I want to raise my children here," she said breathlessly, "I want them to know the tradition of their father's people, to know the warmth of the desert, the love of a family so big I'll probably never learn everybody's name."

He cupped the back of her nape under her hair. She'd left it down and it was wind-blown from the helicopter ride. "But your job..."

She smiled reassuringly. "I'll expand the library in the palace and make it available to the people."

His groan was that of a man who knew his peaceful existence was in danger of extinction. "There are no cities here, no malls, no movie cinemas—"

She interrupted his litany of Kadar's supposed shortcomings. "I told you I'm not that other woman. I don't like shopping. I don't care for city traffic. I was living in a small town by choice when we met. I love this place. I love the people. How could you not see that when we were here?''

He kissed her and she melted into him. Somehow they ended up on the bed amidst a pile of tasseled pillows.

He leaned above her and brushed the hair from her temple. "I want you to be happy, *aziz*."

Her heart constricted with hope and then certainty. ''Because you love me.''

"Of course I love you. Have I not said this a hundred times?''

She could not recall him saying it once. "No."

"I have."

"When?" she challenged him.

"Do you not know the meaning of *aziz*? I would have thought you would ask my sister or Lila. You had their confidence in every other matter.''

She licked her lips, her heart thrilling when his gaze zeroed in on the movement with feral intent. "What does it mean?''

"Beloved. Cherished. How could I not love you? You are all that a woman should be, the jewel of my heart.''

Joy suffused her until she was almost sick with it. She grinned. "When did you realize it?''

Hakim hugged her to him. "I was pretty stupid. I did not realize these feelings I have for you were love until the day I gave you the telescope and I thought you were still thinking of leaving me. Before that I knew I did not want to let you go, but in that moment, I realized that if you did go, you would take my heart, my soul, with you.''

She started unbuttoning his shirt, wanting to get to

the man beneath. "Why didn't you tell me you loved me then?"

"I was afraid you would not believe me, that my avowal would cause you more pain than pleasure."

She stared at him in disbelief. "How could you think telling me you loved me would hurt me? I was dying inside thinking I was nothing more than a means to an end."

"Forgive me, *aziz*, for my many mistakes, but you are and will always be the ultimate means to my end, for I need you to be happy and without you my life would be as arid as the desert and as empty as a dry well."

The words brought tears to her eyes and finally she knew what to do when he said stuff like that.

Later, their naked limbs entwined on the bed, she smiled at him, her heart a melted puddle of feeling from the many words of love he'd spoken during their love-making. "I love you, Hakim."

He kissed her softly. "I love you, Catherine. It will always be so until the stars fall from the heavens and even beyond."

After a lifetime of not fitting in, she had finally found her place. In his arms. Next to his heart.

It would always be.

Sheikh's Honour

ALEXANDRA SELLERS

Alexandra Sellers is the author of over twenty-five novels and a feline language text published in 1997 and still selling.

Born and raised in Canada, Alexandra first came to London as a drama student. Now she lives near Hampstead Heath with her husband, Nick. They share housekeeping with Monsieur, who jumped through the window one day and announced, as cats do, that he was moving in.

What she would miss most on a desert island is shared laughter.

Readers can write to Alexandra at PO Box 9449, London NW3 2WH, England.

For my sister
Donna.
She knows why.

One

The green-and-white seaplane skimmed the tops of the trees, the drone of its engine loud as it headed for a landing on the next lake. Clio Blake, guiding the powerboat in hard jolts across the wake of a cruiser that had just emerged from the channel ahead of her, heard the sound first. As the plane roared over her head, she flicked a glance skyward and wished that her gaze held some magic that could make it disappear.

She did not want him here. He should not be coming. It wasn't right.

She cut her speed sharply and guided the boat into the narrow channel that led between two lakes, where signs posting the speed limit warned boaters of the danger of their wake eroding the shoreline. Some of the cottages were still boarded up, but most showed signs of having been opened for the season. At one cottage two men were working to take down the shutters, and Clio exchanged a wave with them as she passed.

Once through the channel and emerging into the larger lake, she reluctantly booted up her speed again and headed across the water towards the airline dock. The Twin Otter was already skimming along the surface, preparing to take off again.

So he was here. No hope left that something would prevent his arrival…. Seeing where her thoughts led, Clio grimaced self-consciously. Had she been unconsciously hoping for the plane to crash, then? Well, it only went to show how deep her opposition went.

But her parents had simply refused to listen. Her sister Zara had asked, and what Zara asked for, she still got. So Prince Jalal ibn Aziz ibn Daud ibn Hassan al Quraishi, the newly found nephew of the rulers of the Barakat Emirates, was here. For the entire summer.

She wondered if Prince Jalal was remembering their last meeting right now. *It is dangerous to call a man your enemy when you do not know his strength,* he had said then.

She had disdained to notice the threat, opening her eyes wide as if to say, *You and whose army?* But that had been a lie. She felt threatened in his presence, and who would not? He was the man who had taken her sister hostage to force his point on the princes of the Barakat Emirates.

Anything could have happened. They were all incredibly lucky that it had been resolved without bloodshed. It was enough to make him her enemy forever. That was what she had told him, that day at the fabulous, fairy-tale weddings, including Zara and Prince Rafi's. For her the celebrations had been deeply marred by the presence of such a man…even if, in the most outrageous turnaround of all time, he did have the title *prince* instead of *bandit* now.

It is dangerous to call a man your enemy when you do not know his strength.

Clio shivered. No doubt she would get to know his strengths—and weaknesses—over this coming, terrible summer. But one thing was certain—she would never forgive him for what he had done to them, the hell he had put them through, the risk he had run.

Whatever Jalal the bandit's strength was, he would never be anything to her but enemy.

Clio had always half-worshipped her older sister, though there were scarcely three years separating them. *Zary* was what Clio called her, right from her earliest speech. It was her own special nickname, and as a child she got ferociously jealous when anyone else tried to use the name.

Both girls took after their mother. Both had the black hair, the dark brown eyes, the beautiful bones...but Clio knew full well that she had always been a poor man's version of her perfect sister. Zara's hair fell in massed perfect curls, Clio's own hair was thick but dead straight. Zara was a fairy princess, with her exotically slanted eyes, delicate features, and her porcelain doll body. Clio's eyes were set straight under dark eyebrows that were wide, strong and level, giving her face a serious cast. Her eyelashes were not long, though lushly thick, and she had inherited their father's wide, full mouth rather than the cupid's bow that Zara had from their mother.

By the age of eleven Clio was already taller and bigger than her older sister. And in spite of being younger, she had begun to feel protective of Zara. She had always felt the urge to fight Zara's battles for her, even though Zara was perfectly capable of fighting her own. Half the time they weren't even battles Zara thought worth fighting.

Like now. Zara had forgiven and forgotten what Jalal had done to her. Clio knew *she* never could. It was Zara who had asked her family to have him for the summer, so that he could practise his spoken English before going on to a postgrad course somewhere…Clio, meanwhile, had been aghast. She had fought the idea with everything she had.

But she had lost the argument. And now here she was, picking up Jalal the bandit from his flight to the Ontario heartland, deep in the most beautiful part of cottage country, where the family lived and worked on the shore of Love Lake.

He was standing on the dock by two canvas holdalls. He had shaved off his neat beard since she last saw him. Perhaps he thought it would help him blend in, but if so, he hoped in vain. The set of his shoulders, the tilt of his chin as he took in his surroundings were indefinably different, set him apart from the men she knew.

He came out of his reverie when she hailed him, the boat sidling up to the concrete dock. The water level on the lakes was low this year, and he was above her.

"Clio!" he cried, ready to be friendly. So he was going to pretend to forget. Her jaw tightened. Well, she was not.

"Prince Jalal," she acknowledged with a brief, cool nod. "Can you jump in? Toss your bags down first."

He threw her one assessing look and then nodded, as if marking something to himself. She knew that the offer of friendship had been withdrawn, and was glad of it. It was good that he was so quick on the uptake. It would be best if they understood each other from the beginning.

"Thank you," he said, and picked up his bags to toss them, one after the other, into the well of the boat.

Then he stood for a moment, frowning down at the boat riding the swell of its own wake, as if trying to work out some obscure alien art. Clio realized with a jolt that he had probably never before performed the, to her, simple action of jumping into an unmoored boat.

And this was the man who was going to be so useful to her father at the marina! That was the argument her parents had made when she protested: with Jude gone off to the city, they needed someone...

"Take my hand," she said coolly, and, as she would with any green tourist, straightened and turned, keeping one hand steady on the wheel, while she reached her other up for his. "Step down onto the seat first."

She half expected him to refuse the help of a mere woman, but he bent over and reached for her hand. As his fingers brushed hers, Clio gasped, feeling as if his touch delivered an electric shock, and snatched her hand away.

Jalal tried to regain his balance on the dock and failed, but now he had lost his timing. The boat sank away from him just as his weight came down. He landed awkwardly on the seat with one foot, crashed down onto the floor of the boat with the other, skidded and involuntarily reached for Clio.

Her hands automatically clasped him, too, and then there they were—Jalal down on one knee before her, with his arms around her, his cheek pressed against the rich swell of her breasts, Clio with her arms wrapped around his sun-heated back and shoulders.

It was as if they were lovers. The heat of him burned her palms. She felt the brush of his breath at her throat.

For a moment the sun sparkled on the water with a brightness that hurt her eyes.

Clio stiffened. She was suddenly flooded with electric rage, her nerves buzzing and spitting like an overloaded circuit.

"Take your hands off me," she said.

Jalal straightened, glaring at her. He was seething with anger. She could feel the wave of it hit her.

"What is it you hope to prove?" he asked through his teeth.

Flushing under the impact of his gaze, Clio cried, "It wasn't deliberate! What do you think I am?"

He stood gazing at her. "I think you are a woman who sees things her own way. You choose to be my enemy, but you do not know what that means. If you try to make a fool of me again, you will learn what it means."

Nervous fear zinged through her at his words, at the look in his eyes. But she was damned if she would let him see it.

"I think I know, thank you." She had learned what it meant to be his enemy the day he had kidnapped Zara.

He shook his head once, in almost contemptuous denial, still eyeing her levelly. "If you knew, you would not play the games of a child."

"And what does *that* mean?"

"You are a woman, Clio. I am a man. When a woman sets herself to be the enemy of a man, there is always another reason than she imagines."

She opened her mouth, gasping at the implication. "Well, first prize for patriarchal, chauvinistic arrogance! And you from the modern, secular Barakat Emirates, too! You don't seem to have—"

He smiled and lifted his palm, and she broke off. "I am of the desert," he reminded her through his teeth.

"So I gathered!"

Three fingers gracefully folded down to his thumb, leaving the forefinger to admonish her. "In the desert a man will let a woman do much, because he is strong, and she is weak. He makes allowances."

Her blood seemed to be rushing through her brain and body at speeds never previously attained. "Of all the—!"

"In return, Clio, a woman never speaks to a man in such a tone of voice as this that you use to me. Women have sharp tongues, men have strong bodies. We respect each other by not using our strengths against the other."

"Are you threatening me?" she demanded.

"I only explain to you how men and women get along in a civilized country," he told her, and though now she was sure he was laughing at her, she couldn't stop the fury that buzzed in her.

"Well, that isn't how it is here!" she exploded. "And maybe you haven't noticed that, civilized or not, you aren't in the desert now!"

His lips were twitching. "I do know. We are going to hit the boat behind us, and this is a thing that would never happen in the desert."

Two

Clio whirled, diving instinctively for the wheel. She put the engine in gear, barely in time, and drew away from the small yacht moored at the next dock. What a racket there would have been from the anguished owner if she had collided with that expanse of perfectly polished whiteness!

It wasn't like her to forget herself like that when she was in charge of a boat. Clio had had water safety drummed into her with her earliest memories. It just showed what a negative effect *he* had on her.

But the sudden change of focus had the effect of calming her wild emotions. As she guided the boat over the sparkling lake, she understood that he had been deliberately baiting her, and was annoyed with herself for reacting so violently. She needed better control than that if she was going to get through the summer in one piece.

Jalal gazed at the scene around him. "This is the first

time I have seen such a landscape." He had an expression of such deep appreciation on his face that Clio had to resist softening. She loved this land. "It is beautiful."

She certainly would always think so. "But I guess you feel more at home in the desert," she suggested. She had not liked what she saw of the desert when she was in the Emirates. No wonder if an environment like that produced violent men.

"I am at home nowhere."

She stared at him. "Really? Why?"

He shook his head. "My grandfather Selim never meant me to follow in his own footsteps. When I was a little boy he told me always that something great was in store for me. I learned to feel that where I was born was not my true home. I belonged somewhere else, but I did not know where. Then my mother took me to the capital...."

"Zara told me that the palace organized your education from an early age," she said, interested in his story in spite of herself. He had a deep, pleasant voice. He engaged her interest against her will.

"Yes, but I did not know it then. Curious things happened, but I was too young to demand an explanation. Only when I approached university, and my mother gave me a list of courses to follow in my studies. Then some suspicion I had felt became clearer. I demanded to know who controlled my life, and why. But she would tell me nothing."

"And did you take the recommended degree?"

He laughed lightly at himself. He never told his story to strangers, and he did not understand why he was telling Clio. She had made it clear she was no friend.

"I never knew! I tore up the list, like a hothead. I said, now I am a man, I choose for myself!"

"And then?"

He shook his head, shrugging. "I graduated, I enlisted in the armed forces—and then again I felt the invisible hand of my protector. They put me into officer training. I rose more quickly than individual merit could deserve...still my mother was mute."

She could hear the memory of frustration in his voice.

"But you did eventually find out." Clio wondered if this story was designed to disarm her hostility by justifying his treatment of her sister. Well, let him hope. He would find out soon enough that what she said, she meant.

"Yes, I found out. It was on the day the princes came of age according to their father's will. The Kingdom of Barakat would be no more, and in its place there would be three Emirates. There was a great coronation ceremony, televised for all the country to see. Television sets were put in the squares of the villages—a spectacle for the people, to reassure them of the power, the mystery, the majesty of their new princes."

She was half-smiling without being aware of it, falling under his spell.

"I watched in my mother's house. Never will I forget the moment when the camera rested on the faces of the princes, one after the other, coming last to Prince Rafi.

"Of course I knew we were alike—whenever his picture was in the paper everyone who knew me commented. But what is a photograph? True resemblance requires more than the face. That day...that day I saw Prince Rafi move, and speak, and smile, as if...as if I looked in a mirror instead of a television set."

She murmured something.

"And then it fell into place. The mystery of my life—I knew it had some connection with my resemblance to

Prince Rafi. I knew that the old man I had called my father was not my father.

"'Who am I?' I cried to my mother, trembling, jumping to my feet. 'Who is Prince Rafi to me?'"

"Did she tell you?"

He nodded. "My mother could no longer refuse, in spite of the shame of what she confessed. She was disappointed that the great future that they had promised for me for so many years had not arrived on this momentous day. 'He is your uncle,' she told me. 'The half brother of your father, the great Prince Aziz. You could be standing there today instead of them.'"

Jalal paused, a man hovering between present and past. "Of course I knew—every citizen knew—who Prince Aziz was, although it was over twenty-five years since he and his brother had so tragically died. Singers sang the song of King Daud's great heartbreak."

His eyes rested on her, but he hardly saw her. He was looking at the past.

"And this noble prince, this hero dead so young...was my father."

Clio breathed deeply. She had been holding her breath without knowing it. "What a terrible shock it must have been."

It would be something, a discovery like that. In a young man it might motivate...seeing where her thoughts were leading her, Clio mentally braked.

He nodded. "I was a lost man. As if I stood alone in a desert after a sandstorm. Every familiar landmark obliterated. All that I had known and believed about myself was false. I was someone else—the illegitimate son of a dead prince, grandson of the old king...how could this be? Why had I not been told?"

"What a terrible shock it must have been."

"A shock, yes. But very soon I felt a great rage. If they did not wish to recognize me because of the illegitimacy of my birth, why had they taken me from my ordinary life, for what had they educated me…? Why had I never met my grandfather, the king, and my grandmother, his most beloved wife, in all those years when my future was being directed—and to what purpose was it all? My grandfather was dead, and I was left with no explanation of anything."

He paused. The boat sped over the lake, and he blinked at the sun dancing off the water.

"What did you do?"

He glanced towards her, then back to the past again. "I made approaches to these new princes, my uncles. I demanded to know what my grandfather's plans for me had been."

"And they didn't tell you?"

He shook his head. "Nothing. They would not speak to their own nephew. I had been taken from my mother's home, but those who had done this thing would not let me enter my father's."

He turned to gaze intently at her. "Was this not injustice? Was I not right to be angered?"

"Zara told me they never knew. Your uncles, Rafi and Omar and Karim—they didn't know who you were. Isn't that right?"

"It is true that they themselves had never been told. They said afterwards that my letters, even, did not make the point clear. They thought me only a bandit. But someone had known, from the beginning. My grandfather himself…but he had made no provision for me in his will. No mention."

"Isn't that kind of weird?" It struck her as the least credible part of the whole equation.

His eyes searched her face with uncomfortable intensity.

"You would say that my uncles knew the truth, and only pretended ignorance until they were forced to admit it? Do you know this? Has your sister said something?"

She shook her head, not trusting the feelings of empathy that his story was—probably deliberately—stirring in her.

"No, I don't know any more than you've told me. It's just very hard for me to accept that a woman wouldn't insist on meeting her only grandchild, the son of her own dead son."

His face grew shadowed. "Perhaps—perhaps my illegitimate birth was too great a stain."

"And so they never even met you?" Clio tried to put herself in such a position, and failed. She herself would move heaven and earth to have her grandchild near her, part of the family, whatever sin of love his parents had committed.

"Nothing. Not even a letter to be given to me after their death."

No wonder he felt at home nowhere.

He was silent as they skimmed across the endless stretch of water, that seemed as vast as any desert.

"What did you do when your uncles refused your requests?"

He had made his way back to his "home," the desert of his childhood. But the bonds had been severed.

"The desert could never be home to me. The tribe—so ignorant, living in another century, afraid of everything new—could not be my family." So his determination to force his real family to recognize him grew. He had collected followers to his standard—and eventually...he had taken a hostage.

"And the rest you know," he said, in an ironic tone.

"The rest I know," she agreed. "And now your life has changed all over again. Thanks to Zara, you've proven your bloodline, you have your father's titles and property...and you're so trusted by your uncles they've made you Grand Vizier and now you're on a mission to—"

His head snapped around, and if his dark eyes had searched her before, they now raked her ruthlessly.

"Mission? Who has told you I had a mission?"

She returned his look with surprise. "I thought the reason you were coming here was to get a better command of English so you could study political science or whatever at Harvard in the autumn. I thought a summer with the rowdy Blake family was supposed to be the perfect way to do it."

The guarded look slowly left his eyes. "Yes," he said. "It is true."

Clio turned back to the water ahead of her, her mind buzzing with speculation. What on earth was that about? Did it mean he wasn't really here to learn English at all? That it was some kind of blind? But for what? What other reason could Prince Jalal possibly have for coming here to the middle of nowhere?

Three

Jalal stood and moved towards the stern, gazing around him as they passed into yet another lake. He lifted both arms, stretching out his hands in powerful adoration. "It is magnificent! So much water!" He breathed deeply. "Smell the freshness of the water! This water is not salt! Is it?"

A loud horn startled her, and Clio whirled to discover that she had turned onto a collision course with another boat. She waved an apology to the indignant pilot as she hastily and not very gracefully adjusted her course. Jalal half lost his balance and recovered.

"Dammit, don't distract me when I'm driving!" she cried. She had been staring over her shoulder at him. He had a huge physical charisma, but she would get over that. "No, of course it's not salt," she said when the danger was past. "All Canada's lakes are freshwater."

"*Barakallah!* It is a miracle. And you drink this water!'' He spoke it as a fact, but still he looked for confirmation from her.

"Yes, we drink it.'' She smiled, and then, realizing how much she had already let her guard down with him, steeled her heart against the tug she felt. "For now. It may end up polluted in the future, like everything else.''

But his joy would admit no contaminants. "It must be protected from pollution,'' he said, as though he himself might fix this by princely decree. "This must not be allowed, to destroy such rich bounty.''

"Yes, really,'' Clio agreed dryly.

"Why do they pollute such beauty?''

"Because it is cheaper to dump than to treat waste.''

Prince Jalal nodded, taking it in. Was it his grandmother's blood in him that so called to this place?

"My mother's mother was raised in a country of lakes and forests.'' He spoke almost absently, as if to himself, and he blinked when she responded.

"Really? How did she happen to marry a desert bandit, then?''

"On a journey across the desert, she was abducted by my grandfather, Selim. She spent the rest of her life in the desert, but she never forgot her beloved land of lakes.''

The result of that union had been only one daughter, his mother. Desert-born Nusaybah had heard many longing tales of her mother's homeland as a child, and later she had passed them on to her son. She had also passed on the information that his grandmother was a princess in her own country.

That had seemed unlikely, until the DNA tests showed that he was more closely related to Prince Rafi than to Rafi's two half brothers. Then a search of the family tree showed that Rafi's mother, the Princess Nargis, was the daughter of a prince whose sister had been abducted and never spoken of again.

For centuries the family had spent every summer in the highlands, just as Jalal's grandmother had always said. So it was deep in his blood, the longing for lake and forest, though he had not felt its force until he saw these sights.

Clio frowned. "She spent the rest of her life in the desert? She was never rescued?"

He shook his head. "In those days no one would have troubled. She had no choice but to marry her abductor."

"You mean her family knew where she was but *left* her there?"

"I cannot say what they knew, only what was the tradition. A woman captured by a man in this way...her family would have ignored her existence from that moment."

She threw a look over her shoulder at him. "And you accept that?" she demanded incredulously.

"There is nothing for me to reject, Clio. It was finished, many years ago. I am here because of it. My mother Nusaybah was the child of that union. What shall I say? *Maktoub*. It is written."

"So that's in your blood too, is it—abducting women? I suppose that makes it all right! Were you expecting my family and Prince Rafi to leave my sister Zara to her fate?"

He shook his head impatiently, but did not reply.

"But no," she supplied for him. "That wouldn't have served your purpose! You knew Rafi had to get her back—world opinion would dictate that. You probably thought he'd refuse to marry her, but that wouldn't have bothered you. If you spoiled their love, it would be just their bad luck, wouldn't it? So long as you got what you wanted."

"I did not reason in this way," he said levelly. "I believed that he would want her back and would make her his wife when I released her unharmed."

She had succeeded in talking herself into deep anger. She could not trust herself to make an answer.

So he was a chip off the old block. Did her parents know this about Jalal's genes? But she didn't suppose it would have made any difference. If they weren't concerned about what *he* had done to Zara, they'd hardly worry about what his grandfather had done to a nameless princess fifty years ago.

A few minutes later they arrived at a large, rambling brick house. It was on the shore of a very pretty lake, smaller than those they had crossed to get here. There were tree-covered hills rising high around one end of the lake, as if some spirit brooded protectively over the water. Fewer houses dotted the shore.

As they approached their destination, he saw a marina clustered with boats on one side, and a pretty painted sign high on one wall of the house that advertised homemade ice cream, a crafts shop and an art gallery.

Clio guided the powerboat in, cut the engine and expertly brought it up beside the dock. Meanwhile, the door of the house exploded outward, and at least half a dozen children of all ages, four dogs and a couple of cats erupted into the morning to cries of "Is he here? Did the prince come? What does he look like?" and loud excited barks.

Everybody raced down to the dock, except for the cats, who dashed up the trunk of a large, leafy tree that overhung the water so picturesquely he felt he was in some dream, and clung there indignantly, staring at the scene.

"Calm down, yes, he's here and he doesn't want to be deafened on day one! Here, Jonah, grab this," Clio com-

manded lazily, tossing the mooring rope as a tall boy ran
to the bow. The dock beside the boat was stuffed with
children and canines, all gaping at him and all more or
less panting with excitement.

"Is that him? Is that the prince?" In the babble he
could pick out some sentences, but most of what they
were saying was lost, as always when too many people
talked at once in English.

"He isn't weawing a cwown!" one tiny creature cried
piercingly, her woebegone eyes locking onto Jalal's with
heartfelt grief.

Clio and Jalal exchanged glances. She resisted the impulse to laugh with him.

"The natives are restless," he observed.

Then she did laugh; she couldn't help it.

"I should have realized what the result of an hour's
wait would be. They were excited enough about you when
I left. Out of the way, everybody! Prince Jalal wants to
get onto the dock. He isn't ready to go swimming yet!"

One of the dogs was, however, and leapt off into the
water with a loud splash.

Meanwhile, Jalal braved the natives to step onto the
dock.

"Are you Prince Jalal?" "Are you a real prince?"
"Where's—"

"Cool it!" Clio cried beside him. "What did I tell
you?" Getting a general reduction in the babel, she reeled
off their names. "Rosalie, Benjamin, Sandor, Alissa, Jonah, Jeremiah, Arwen and Donnelly. Everybody, this is
Prince Jalal."

"Welcome to Canada, Your Highness," said several
voices in ragged unison, and the welcome was echoed as
the laggards caught up. And then Jalal watched transfixed

as, to his utter astonishment, they all bowed. From the waist.

He couldn't restrain the bursting laughter that rose up in him. Their heads tilted at him in surprise. "Thank you!" he exclaimed, when he could speak. "I am very glad to be here. But I am not used to such bowing, or this name, Your High-ness!"

"But Clio said people have to bow to princes."

"Clio said we had to call you Your Highness."

He flicked her a glance, as if to an awkward child. She returned the look impassively, then bent to the task of tying the stern rope.

"Clio did not know. She thought I was a tall man," he said, his lips twitching, and she thought, *He thinks I'm not a worthy enemy, but he'll find out.*

"You *are* tall. You're as tall as Daddy."

"What will we call you, then?"

"Why not call me—Jalal? That is my name, and it will make me feel very welcome if you use it. Then I will think we are friends. Shall we be friends?"

"Oh, yeah!" "Cool." "Sure."

"I'm your fwiend, Jalal," said Donnelly confidingly, reaching up to put her hand in his. She had clearly taken one of her instant likes to him.

His smile down at the child would have melted Clio on the spot, if she hadn't steeled herself.

"Don't people bow to princes?" Arwen asked, her head cocked on one side.

"Yes, people bow to princes, unless," he said, raising a forefinger, "unless they are given special dispensation. And since we are going to be friends, I give you all special dispensation."

"But you are a real pwince, aren't you?" It was the

little curly-haired darling again. Jalal squatted down to face her.

"My father was the son of a king. My mother's mother was a princess. Am I a prince?"

Her eyes were wide. "Ye-es," she said, half asking, half telling. She looked around her, then up at that fount of wisdom, seventeen-year-old Benjamin.

"Of course he's a prince, Donnelly, that's how you get to be a prince—your father was one," Ben said knowledgeably.

"But you don't have a cwown," she reminded Jalal. "You don't look like the picture."

"Do you have a picture of a prince?" he asked.

Donnelly nodded mutely. Jalal lifted his arm, and she snuggled in against him as confidingly as a kitten. "Well, I have a crown, my father's crown, but princes don't go swimming in crowns, do they?"

"They don't?" Donnelly sounded disappointed, as if she had been hoping to see just that sight.

"No." Jalal, smiling, shook his head firmly. All the children had fallen silent, listening to him, almost entranced. "Do you wear your swimsuit to school?"

Donnelly, who did not go to school, gazed at him wide-eyed, and shook her head with mute solemnity.

"Princes only wear crowns in their palaces. There is no palace here. So I left my crown at home."

"Ohhhh."

"But one day, I hope you'll come and visit me in my home, and then I'll show you my crown."

"Oh, neat! Can I come, too?" "Do you have a palace?" "Can I come, can I come?" "Is your home in the desert?" "Is it an Arab's tent or is it a real palace?" "Do you have camels, Jalal?" "What's it like in the desert?" "Were you a bandit before you were a prince, Jalal?"

And then somehow, in a circle of fascinated children, the two oldest boys carrying his cases, Jalal was being led up to the house, into the kitchen. Clio stood on the dock watching the progress of the little party.

No doubt she should have realized that a man capable of drawing as many followers to his cause as Jalal was said to have had would have powerful charisma. She didn't like the way they were all falling all over him, but there wasn't much she could do about it.

Not right now, anyway.

Four

"Uncle Brandon dropped the guys back and went out again. He said not to save lunch for him," Rosalie reported, when Clio entered the kitchen.

That wasn't unusual in the run-up to the season. He had probably had to go for more creosote or something, and would grab a hamburger in the plaza. But Clio would rather her father had been here to meet Jalal.

"You've got lunch going already?" she asked, sniffing the air. "That's terrific, Rosalie."

Whenever her mother was absent on one of her buying trips among the First Nation artists she represented in the gallery, as she was this week, Clio was in charge. This year Rosalie, who had arrived in tears shortly after Christmas declaring that she hated her new stepmother, was proving to be a big help in filling the gap left by Romany. Romany was on a visit to Zara and Rafi.

"What's cooking?"

Rosalie told her, and the two cousins began to organize the meal.

Jalal was at the table, surrounded by kids. Everyone had something to show him, a question to ask....

"You have to choose a plaque." Sandor was informing him gravely about one of the house rituals. Sandor himself had moved in only a month ago, so he knew all about it. "It's for the duty roster."

They had spread the available plaques out in front of him, and Jalal was considering his choice, though she doubted if he was making sense of the garbled explanation he heard, from several sources.

"Okay, everybody, the table needs to be set!" Clio announced, not sorry to break up the group. "Sorry, your fan club has work to do," she added dryly to Jalal.

Jalal nodded impassively, recognizing the jealousy in that.

"He has to choose a plaque first!" someone exclaimed indignantly, and of course Clio had to give in.

"What is Clio's plaque?" Jalal asked, as he browsed among the little squares of plastic, each with a different image on it, that were reserved for the use of visitors. For the length of his stay, this plaque would represent him.

"Clio's the pussycat," Donnelly articulated carefully. She pointed to the duty roster on the wall. "The black-and-white one. I'm the butterfly."

"All right. I will take this one," Jalal said, choosing a plaque with his finger and drawing it out of the spread.

"The tiger!" they chorused.

"He's a very *wild* tiger!" Donnelly informed him impressively.

Clio tried, but she could not keep her eyes away.

He was watching her gravely, and something unspoken

passed between them. Something that made her deeply nervous.

"Right, then! He's chosen a plaque! Let's clear the table!" she cried, and the children all moved to their usual mealtime tasks.

"And I," Jalal said. "What shall I do to assist?"

She had been hoping that he would expect to be served. She had been anticipating telling him that in this kitchen, everyone did their share, male and female, bandit and *nouveau* prince alike. She flicked him a glance, and saw that he was watching her face as if he could read her thoughts there. He gave her an ironically amused look, and she blushed.

"You can help me, Jalal," an adoring voice said. "I have to fold the serviettes."

One of the boys snorted. "Princes don't fold serviettes, Donnelly!" he began, but Jalal held up a hand.

"No job worth doing is beneath any man." And it infuriated Clio even more to see Ben nodding in respectful agreement, as if he had just learned something profound.

Jalal smiled down at Donnelly. "I would like very much to help you," he said. "Will you teach me to fold them just right?"

It wasn't often that Donnelly got to pass on her wisdom to anyone; she was usually on the receiving end. At Jalal's words, her chest expanded with a delighted intake of air.

"It's very important to match the edges!" she informed him.

A few minutes later they all sat down, amid the usual mealtime babble. When their parents were at the table, a certain amount of order was imposed, keeping it, as their father Brandon said, to a dull roar. But when Clio was in charge, she didn't usually bother. It didn't hurt anyone if once in a while bedlam reigned.

But the first time someone said, "Is that true, Jalal?" and the prince replied quietly, "I am sorry, I didn't understand. When everyone talks at the same time, I can't follow," a respectful hush fell on them.

After that, it was, "Shhh! Jalal can't follow!" when anyone tried to interrupt the current speaker.

Then lunch was over, and there was the usual competition to be first to get their plates into the dishwasher. Donnelly explained the task to Jalal, and again he performed it without apparently feeling that it was any assault on his masculinity or his princely status.

Clio was almost certain that he was doing all this just to spike her guns, because he had guessed that she was waiting to tell him how unimportant his princely status was here in the democratic confines of the Blake family, or to explain that male superiority had been superseded in the West. She was even more convinced of it when, straightening from having set his utensils in just the right place under Donnelly's tutelage, he threw her another of those glances.

"Round one to you," she bit out, feeling driven.

"Only round one? I have counted three," he observed mildly. "How many before we stop the match, Clio?"

The match went on, under cover of surface friendliness, for several days. Brandon showed Jalal the ropes at the marina for a couple of days, and on the following day Jalal and Ben started creosoting the marina dock while Jeremiah went with Brandon to work on one of the cottages, taking their lunch with them. Teaching at the high school had stopped, and the next three weeks was exams, but the younger children were still at school full-time.

It was a beautiful day, and when they broke at lunch the first coat was done.

"That's the fastest I've ever seen the first coat go on," Ben said. "You really know how to swing a brush."

The youthful admiration in his tone made Clio grit her teeth.

"I've had a lot of practice," Jalal said.

"Paint the palace a lot, do you?" Clio interjected.

Jalal gazed at her for a long moment, as if he was bored with her childish taunts.

"We've got another hour till the second coat can go on," Ben said. "Want to take a boat out? I could show you around."

"Thank you, Ben, another day. Just now, I would like to talk alone with your sister Clio."

The hair stood up on the back of her neck, but there was nothing she could say. Within a couple of minutes, she found herself alone with him in the big friendly kitchen. Tense, and angry because she was, Clio determinedly started her usual tasks.

"You dislike me very much, Clio," Jalal said. "Tell me why."

Taken aback by his directness, she shook her head and bent to scoop some dishwashing powder into the dishwasher.

He caught her arm, forcing her to straighten, and the touch shivered all through her. She did not want this. She was not at all prepared to start defending her attitude to him. And he had no right to demand it.

"I thought you weren't allowed to touch a woman not related to you," she said coldly, staring down at where his hand clasped her bare arm, just above the elbow. She felt under threat. She did not want to have this conversation.

He ignored her comment. "Tell me," he said. "I want to know why you alone are unwilling to be my friend."

She wrenched her arm out of his grasp, using far more effort than was necessary for such a light hold, and staggered.

"I told you at the wedding. We will never be friends."

"Why not?"

She was silent.

"Your sister has forgiven what I did. Your parents, too. Why cannot you?"

She turned her back on him deliberately, closed the dishwasher and set it going. He was silent, too, behind her, and her nerves didn't seem up to the strain. Her skin shivered with awareness of him.

"Do you believe it impossible that your sister took no hurt while she was my hostage? Do you suspect me of hurting her, or allowing her to be hurt?" he asked, finally.

She was silent. Was that what she feared? She hardly knew. All she knew was that Jalal was a threat, and she wished he had never come.

"Look at me, Clio."

His voice was seductive, almost hypnotic, though he did not seem to be doing that deliberately. Feeling driven, she turned to face him. He was too close. She thought dimly, *Middle Eastern people have a smaller body territory or something—they always stand too close for Westerners' comfort.* Her heart kicked uncomfortably.

"Can you imagine that Princess Zara would have encouraged me to come here, into the home of her own family, if such a dreadful thing had happened?"

"If she was pretending to herself it hadn't happened, she might," she felt driven to point out. It wasn't that she believed it, necessarily, but it was possible. He had to see that.

He stared at her, honestly startled. "Pretending to herself? How could a woman pretend such a thing? Why would she?''

Clio felt anxiety creeping up in her. ''It does happen, you know! Women take the blame on themselves, or they don't want to face what happened to them! Denial does happen!''

He was silent, watching her. Then he said softly, ''Does it, Clio? Are you sure?''

''If you understood anything about psychology you wouldn't have to ask.''

''Do you deny something? Has someone hurt you, so that it is easier to imagine I hurt your sister than to accept what happened to yourself?'' he asked, proving that he understood more than somewhat about psychology.

She gasped in indignant fury and clenched her fists. Never had she so wanted to hit someone. But she looked at Jalal and saw the warning in his eyes. Gentle as he was with the children, his look warned her that he would not be gentle with her if she attacked him.

''Nothing has ever happened to me!'' she exploded, her rage escaping in words. ''Let's get one thing straight, Jalal—whatever did or did not happen in your camp, we're enemies, and it's because of what you yourself did.''

He shook his head in flat contradiction. ''We are not enemies. That is not what is between us,'' he said softly.

Five

Clio opened her mouth soundlessly as shivers like a flood ran over her body.

"You make your sister an excuse to avoid what frightens you. That is all, is it not?"

He stepped closer, and she backed up against the counter. In the pit of her stomach a hard ball of fire suddenly revealed itself.

"I am not afraid!" she protested hotly.

"Good," he whispered, and when she lifted a hand in protest his hand wrapped her wrist. Every nerve leapt at the touch. Fury seemed to come from nowhere and whip against her like wild wind.

Slowly he bent closer. He was going to kiss her.

She couldn't allow it. She wanted to hit him. Something like a scream was in her throat and she wanted desperately to beat him off. But she couldn't seem to work her muscles.

"Do you always just do what you want without asking?" she demanded.

"I want to kiss you," he murmured thoughtfully, his mouth only inches from her own. "In this country, do men ask permission for such a thing?"

She tried to swallow. "Yes," she said defiantly. Her mouth felt as dry as the desert he came from, where the rules between men and women were so different. She wanted to push him away, to get to a place where the air was clear. But the unfamiliar lassitude would not let her go.

"Then they understand nothing." He drew closer, and she felt the heat of his arm encircle her back, his firm hand at her waist. His breath touched her cheek as his eyes challenged hers. She felt the look deep inside her, stirring the depths of her self.

He stroked the skin that she had so foolishly left bare between her short top and low-cut shorts. Sensation skittered down her body to her toes. Under the thin top, her breasts shivered.

Suddenly she was angry with *herself*. This was the man she had sworn only days ago would be always her enemy!

"What do men do in the desert?" she demanded cynically. "Grab whatever they see? Well, of course they do!" she told herself brightly. "You proved—"

"In the desert we first make sure that a woman longs for the kiss, and then we kiss her without asking."

The sheer male arrogance of such a statement caused angry fire to leap in her chest and abdomen. She clamped her teeth together, because she could hardly prevent herself from shouting at him that he was an arrogant barbarian. But he had warned her....

His hand was moving against her spine. His other hand touched her neck, and his thumb traced her jawline.

Her mouth felt swollen—not that she wanted any kiss from him! But he was as mesmerizing as a snake, he really was. She flicked her eyes up to his.

The naked desire she saw there shook her to the core. She had thought him attracted, but not as powerfully as this! He looked at her like a starving man. Clio's heart tripped into an unsteady rhythm. Feeling she didn't recognize roared through her.

"Then you will never kiss me," she said, finding her voice.

His hands stilled their motion. The heat was too much. She felt burned.

"Do you challenge me, Clio? When a woman challenges a man, she must beware. He may accept her challenge."

She had no idea why his words created such sudden torment in her, or what that torment was. Her whole body churned with feeling. She felt faint, almost sick. She wished he would get away from her, so she could breathe.

"Why doesn't it surprise me that you hear the word *no* as a challenge?" she asked defiantly.

His thumb tilted her chin, bringing her face closer to his full mouth, and her heart responded with nervous, quickened pulse. He smiled quizzically at her.

"But I have not heard the word *no*, Clio. Did you say it?"

Bee-bee-bee, bee-bee-bee.

They were both jolted by the high, piercing sound. Jalal frowned and looked around, and Clio tried to gather her wits.

"Is it a fire alarm?" he asked.

She finally identified the noise. "Oh, my God, it's an

intruder alarm!'' Clio cried, and as he released her she ran to the monitor panel above her father's desk in an alcove. A dozen lights glowed steady; one was flashing its urgent beacon. She bent down to read the tag.

"Solitaire!'' she breathed. ''It can't be Dad, he wasn't going there today.''

He watched as she opened a small cupboard and snatched up a set of keys, then stood back out of her way as she whirled and lightly ran to the screen door of the kitchen and opened it.

''Ben!'' she called.

Jalal followed her as she ran along the wooden porch and down onto the dock. When she reached the boat, he was right behind her. She quickly untied the stern rope, and when Jalal bent to the bow, Clio clambered aboard and started the motor. Meanwhile Rosalie and Donnelly raced towards the dock from further along the beach.

"The intruder alarm has gone off at Solitaire! It's probably a raccoon!'' she cried, as Jalal came aboard with more grace and expertise than his first effort. Clio swung the boat in a wide arc, and as they passed the end of the dock, she continued to Ben and Rosalie, ''You'd better call Dad! Tell him I'm on my way there and I'll call him if there's a problem.''

Rosalie stood holding Donnelly's hand, and all three were nodding. ''Be careful!'' And then Clio booted up the motor and the boat obediently climbed up out of the waves and planed across the surface at top speed.

"What is Solitaire?'' Jalal asked, settling beside her.

She blinked and seemed to see him for the first time. ''Oh, hi!'' she said. It had seemed so natural for Jalal to be there that it was only now she actively registered his presence.

"One of the rental cottages," she said. "It's kind of isolated."

He knew the family owned and rented cottages on the lakes. He had visited a couple with Brandon, doing repairs. "Will your father meet us there?"

Clio shrugged. "He might not bother unless I call to say it's something really bad. It depends where he is, I guess. Ben will tell him you're with me."

"What weapons are on this boat?"

Clio blinked. "What, you mean like a shotgun?" She shook her head. "Nothing that you could call a weapon. We aren't going to kill the raccoon, just open the door and scare him out. The point is to get there before he tears the place to ribbons."

Jalal eyed her calmly. "You are certain that it is a raccoon?"

"Well, unless a deer got frightened and jumped through the picture window. That's been known to happen. More likely a window got broken somehow and a raccoon got the screen off. Solitaire is empty this week."

He had a vision of a mysterious little animal with a black mask over its eyes. Take a screen off a window? Well, he would like to see that.

"And what if it is not a raccoon?"

"Well?"

"You are setting out to challenge intruders in a remote place, not knowing their numbers, without weapons of any kind?"

Clio blinked.

"And you were surprised to see that I was aboard," he continued ruthlessly. "If I were not here, you would have gone alone on this mission?"

How to explain that she *had* known he was with her, but half unconsciously? How to say that, maybe because she had felt safe with him there, she forgot to stop and consider?

She hardly noticed the curious fact that her unconscious mind was so very far from considering Jalal the enemy.

"Why not?" she said, since that confession was impossible.

He was angry, she could see.

"I'm sure it's a raccoon," she said, half placatingly. "We have to get there fast before he wrecks the place. Raccoons can be worse than thieves half the time." He nodded, unconvinced. "Are you afraid? People around here aren't usually violent, they just rob."

He shook his head. "How many times have you challenged people who are just robbing a cottage?"

She was abashed. She really had acted too quickly, but that was probably Jalal's fault. If he hadn't had her in such a confused state to begin with, she probably wouldn't have been so hasty. He was right—what if it wasn't a raccoon? She looked at the powerful shoulders under the snug-fitting polo shirt and unconsciously relaxed.

"I think Dad surprised some guys once, but they heard the boat and got away before he landed."

He didn't make any comment, instead began looking around him at the boat. "Where is the storage?"

"Some in lockers below, and some under the bench seat at the stern."

He stepped to the stern, and she noticed, not for the first time, how lightly he moved. His body was muscled and well-knit, and when he shifted from one position to another all his muscles seemed to regroup and rebalance. A hunting cat, a panther, she thought, with the promise of power in every economical movement. The tiger had been an appropriate choice of plaque, though she knew he had chosen it only to irritate her.

Meanwhile he moved around, opening lockers. He found a paddle, and his fist closed around it and he hefted it testingly. Satisfied, he returned to the cockpit and slipped into the seat beside her.

No wasted effort. She felt no anxiety from him, just watchfulness. Waiting, like a cat, till the moment when effort would be needed. Then the muscles would bunch and flex, but for now they were long and easy.

She was sure she was completely safe with Jalal, whatever they might find.

"What is the position of Solitaire?" he asked.

She described it to him: an island in a narrow, shallow river, surrounded by forest. At the top end, beyond the island, the river narrowed and became an impassable creek. There was only one way out by water, the way they would go in. A picturesque wooden footbridge led over the water on one side, but only to a footpath that went for miles through the forest before you reached even another cottage.

He took it in in silence, and she could see him building a picture in his mind. She did her best to fill in the details, describing the dock, the approach, the land around the house, even though she was almost sure he was overreacting. There was something about his air of readiness that communicated the more serious possibilities.

"Here's the river mouth," she said at last, and he nodded. His mouth was set, his jaw firm but not clenched.

"You will stay in the boat until I make a check," he said. "You will keep the motor running. If there is danger, you will turn the boat immediately when I tell you, and go to find your father, or the police. Do you understand?"

Clio stiffened. "You aren't in your rebel camp now, Prince Jalal! And I am not one of your followers!"

"No," he agreed calmly. "None of my followers would act so stupidly as this. Nevertheless, you must obey me. If someone captured you, I could do nothing. I would have to surrender if they threatened to hurt you."

Six

It was called Bent Needle River because of its shape. A long ribbon of water looped around an island that formed the eye of the needle. The river twisted at the bottom end of the island, so that from the air its shape was like a darning needle bent sharply just before the eye. Beyond it, a few hundred yards of creek stretched like a short thread trailing from the eye of the needle.

The cottage was on the far side of the island, and the sound of their approach, she knew, would be well muffled by the trees and thick foliage until they were around the bend and almost at the dock. She approached at low speed. The channel was not marked and there were shallows on both sides.

A small motorboat bobbed against the dock, secured only by the stern rope. Goods were stacked on the dock. Clio saw the television set, the video player, a cardboard box. The front door of the wide-windowed cottage gaped open, broken on its hinges. There was more loot collected on the porch.

Not a raccoon, then. She thought of her danger if she had come here alone, and threw Jalal a look as she guided the powerboat quietly around the bend and coasted up to the dock. Just then a man stepped out onto the porch, carrying the vacuum cleaner.

Jalal seemed to take in the whole scene with one comprehensive glance and make up his mind. "Stay in the boat, keep the engine running, and be ready to go if I give you the signal," he commanded quietly. He leapt lightly off the boat onto the dock and stood there, leaning casually on the paddle he had taken with him.

She saw the man break stride for a second, then make up his mind to brazen it out. He kept walking down towards the dock. Thin and wiry, with shoulder-length dirty brown hair, in his forties, she thought. His clothes were grubby but not really dirty—a light grey T-shirt with some kind of logo, black denims.

"Hello there! Can I help you?" he called casually, but too loudly, and she hoped Jalal had picked up the information that there was someone else in the cottage.

"Are you moving out?" she heard Jalal ask, with easy interest.

"Oh, I wish, eh?" The man was grinning self-deprecatingly when she looked again. He clearly did not want to arrive on the dock, but had no choice. He set down the vacuum cleaner and straightened warily.

In the doorway of the house a shadow moved. "Naw, I'm just the hired moving man, eh?"

Jalal nodded. "I understand. But you have the wrong

address. No one is moving from this house. So why don't you get in the boat and go?''

The man feigned indignation. "Hey, buddy, who ya think you're talking to, eh?'' But Clio could hear his essential weakness in his voice and breathed a sigh of relief. He would bluster and then obey.

Already he was inching towards where his boat was moored.

"I know very well who I am talking to. Now I tell you, you are making a mistake, and you can get in your boat and leave, and your friends, too.''

He raised his voice. "Why don't you come out? Your friend is leaving and you may go with him.''

A figure appeared in the doorway. "What the frig's goin' on?'' he said, and Clio's breath hissed in between suddenly clenched teeth. This man was very different from his partner. He was big and muscled, his head shaved, his lower jaw protuberant with low intelligence and aggression. His white singlet and camouflage pants were cleaner than his partner's clothes. He wore a wide belt and hard boots, several metal studs in one ear.

He clumped deliberately down the broad steps from the porch and strode down to the dock with a threatening swagger. Jalal's posture, negligently leaning on the paddle, did not change. The thug stopped a few feet away from him and spat deliberately on the ground.

"Hey, a Ay-rab!'' His eyes swept past Jalal and over Clio with a look that turned her stomach. "And a skirt!'' But he did not say *skirt*. She shuddered with revulsion. He turned to Jalal again. "Thanks for bringing my dessert, Saddam! You can go now, less you wanna be the main course.

"Ooooffff!'' The breath seemed to explode out of his body as, almost faster than she could see, Jalal drove the paddle into his solar plexus. The thug seemed to leap into the air and fold in the middle simultaneously.

"Behind you!" Clio screamed, as the smaller man leapt for him, and somehow, instead of connecting, the thin man seemed to sail over Jalal's shoulder as Jalal dropped the paddle, grabbed his arm and assisted his forward motion.

He landed sprawling on the big man, and screamed like an animal, a sound that sent a rush of horror over her skin. His partner threw him impatiently aside, and the reason for the scream was suddenly evident as blood spattered the thug's hands. The thin man had landed skidding on the knife that the thug had pulled from somewhere, and his chest was sliced from shoulder to waist. His T-shirt gaped. Blood poured from the wound.

The wounded man cursed violently. "I'm hurt, man, I'm hurt!"

The thug ignored him and got to his feet. He was sweating. "Okay, Saddam, you shouldna done that. You shouldna made me mad."

Jalal stood with his arms loose at his sides. "Your friend needs a doctor," he said. "Get in your boat and go."

"Jeez, man, I'm hurt bad! Let's do what he says!"

"Drop the boat keys on the dock, Saddam, leave the skirt, get in my boat and take off, and nobody'll get hurt," said the thug to Jalal, as if he hadn't heard his friend's cry.

Jalal said nothing. She could not see his face, but from the back he looked so lightly poised he almost seemed to move with the breeze.

"You hear me, Ay-rab?" The thug began to toss the bloody knife between his two hands, bouncing his weight from foot to foot. He was inches taller than Jalal, and thirty pounds heavier. And clearly he made it his business to be menacing.

Still Jalal made no reply.

"I'm not gonna hurt her, don't you worry none about that. I'm gonna treat her real nice. Whereas you, I'm gonna hurt you bad, if you don't—"

As if he were dancing, Jalal stepped to the side, and his foot arced up, connecting with the thug's right hand as it was in the act of catching the knife. The man cried out with a shriek of pain, and Clio saw with ugly shock that his forearm now bent where it should not. Stumbling forward off balance as he clutched at it with his other hand, he suddenly felt Jalal's hand close on his wrist and his scream changed note. Jalal's other hand fell ruthlessly on his shoulder, and, tripping over the television set, the thug was propelled forward off the dock and down into his boat with a crash.

He screamed in wild, almost demented agony, clutching his shoulder, his arm, his shoulder again, as a stream of curses spewed out of his mouth. His face was cut, his eye already swelling.

"My shoulder!" he screamed, with such a terrible cry that Clio's stomach started to heave again. "My arm!"

Jalal turned back to the other man, who was with difficulty scrambling to his feet, trying to stop the bleeding from his chest with his hands. His eyes widened at whatever he saw in Jalal's face.

"I'm wounded, man! Don't hit me!"

"Get in the boat and take your friend out of here."

Clio gasped at the deadly menace in his voice.

"I can't, man! I can't drive a boat! Man, I'm all cut! You gotta get me to a doctor."

"Get out," Jalal said softly.

The man choked off his protest and stumbled to the

edge of the dock, then let go of his bleeding chest to clamber into the boat. His friend was still screaming in agony. Somehow, the thin man got the motor started on the second try.

"Jeez, the rope! Untie the rope, will ya?" he cried.

Jalal bent to pick up the bloody knife, and with one powerful stroke he chopped down against the wooden dock, severing the rope that tied the boat, as if only now he let his anger escape.

The thin man swore in fear, dragging in the remnant of the rope, and clumsily steered around the powerboat and back down the river. Clio cut her own motor, and they stood listening to the sound retreating in the distance.

Silence fell over them, the silence of wind amongst leaves and of chittering birds. With painfully sweet normality water lapped against the hull of the boat.

"Should we follow them to make sure?" she asked.

Jalal shook his head. "No need."

Her boat was drifting, and almost without conscious thought she started her engines and brought it in to the dock. She threw him the rope and he made it fast, then helped her to come ashore. She accepted his hand, although of course she needed no help. She had been getting in and out of boats all her life.

At the touch of his warm, living flesh, though, she began to tremble.

"Are you all right, Jalal? Were you hurt?" she whispered. "Did he cut you?"

"No. I was not hurt," he said firmly.

"Oh, thank God! Oh, when I saw that knife!"

Jalal took her wordlessly in his arms, and suddenly sensation swept up and engulfed her.

"Jalal!" she breathed hoarsely. "Oh, Jalal!" And she

lifted her face up for the touch of his, wanting to know that he was alive, that he was real.

The tiniest, tenderest smile pulled at his lips, and then he bent and obliged her seeking lips with a gentle kiss. Only then did she remember that barely an hour ago she had sworn she would never want his kiss...but it didn't matter to her. The sweetest relief swept her body at the touch, and she wrapped her arms around him and wished he would kiss her harder....

Then, as if this touch was what she had needed to release the pent-up tension, Clio suddenly began to shake. She was seeing again how the man had looked at her. When Jalal lifted his lips she drew back, squeezing her eyes shut.

"Oh, Jalal, thank God you were here! My God, if I'd come alone!"

"*Alhamdolillah* you didn't come alone. You came with me," he said steadily.

She was shaking all over. He put his arm around her and led her to a bench by the water. "Sit down," he commanded gently, and when she obeyed, he smiled.

"Now I know you are not yourself, when you obey me without protest!"

She smiled, but in spite of herself she felt sick. "I can't stop shaking!" she said.

Jalal sank down beside her and took her in his arms to hold her against his chest. She felt the hot tears prickle her eyes, and let them have their way. She found without surprise that she could cry in front of Jalal. An hour ago she would have said he was the last man on earth she would show weakness to.

He held her while she wept out the tension, the fear, the horror—and maybe something else, which she didn't want to face. "Thank you," she murmured, between sobs. "I'm sorry I have to do this. I can't seem to stop."

He merely held her more tightly.

At last, with a watery smile, she asked, "Do you by any chance have a tissue?" and Jalal let go of her with one arm and searched the pocket of his pants. He found some clean but crushed tissues and handed them to her.

"Are you better now?"

"Much better! Thank you," she said, wiping her eyes. She shuddered. "You could have been killed!"

He smiled grimly. "Not by one like him."

"Oh, God! Wasn't he horrible!"

Jalal's face tightened, but he did not reply.

"I guess we'd better radio the police," she said. "Tell them what to look out for."

"Yes." He nodded. "Radio the police while I look around. Please stay by the boat till I tell you it is clear."

He straightened and moved quickly up towards the cottage.

Clio climbed back aboard the boat, punched up the police channel and made a report, then radioed home. The radio wasn't always on at home, but it would be on now, with the kids nearby, waiting for news. When Ben answered, Clio told him what had happened and then kept him on the line till Jalal reappeared and signalled her that everything was clear.

"Okay, Ben, I'll call you again when we're on our way back," she said, and put the radio on standby.

"How bad is it?" she asked, meeting Jalal on the dock.

"Not bad," he said. "They did not deliberately vandalize the place." She sighed her relief.

They began to restore order, carrying the looted items back inside the cottage, plugging things in. An observer might have noticed how coordinated their work was, how easily each seemed to understand the other's intentions and assist, but Clio didn't consciously notice. When Jalal began to lift chunks of broken mirror from the bedroom wardrobe door, it was natural to her to bring in the big garbage can so he could drop the pieces straight in. And when the job was finished and she swept up the remnants of glass, she found him bending with the dustpan when she needed it, without surprise.

That night they had to recount their adventures over the dinner table, to a fascinated audience. Brandon had eaten quickly and returned to Solitaire with Jonah for repairs. All the remaining children sat around the table.

The police had come and dusted for fingerprints, and had gone away with the bloody knife. Tonight Brandon would board it up, tomorrow a new front door would be installed, and the mirror, ready for the renters on the weekend.

So it was only a thrilling story, and the kids were enthralled by it. It went without saying the part they were most enthralled by was Jalal's "kung fu magic," as they insisted on calling it.

"Did you study self-defence, Jalal?" Ben asked. He was more than halfway down the road to hero worship, Clio could see. She wanted to resent it, but how could she? After this afternoon, how could she say anything to dim their admiration? If Jalal had not been here, would she have gone to Solitaire alone when the alarm went? Or maybe with only Ben for company?

She was a mess of conflicting feelings and ideas. He had kidnapped Zara and held her hostage, but he had also saved Clio from an experience so awful she could not bear to think of it. These two images of Jalal couldn't be reconciled. She could only leap back and forth between them, in a dizzying contradiction that made her brain hurt.

When she tuned in to the conversation again, Jalal was agreeing to teach Ben the rudiments of the art of self-defence, and all the others were chiming in with pleas not to be excluded.

"I can teach one or teach all," Jalal said pacifyingly. "We can do it, but—!" His forefinger went up, and they all gazed at him intently, as if every word out of his mouth held magic. "Everyone comes to every class, unless for a very good reason. If you want to do this, then we do it. But it involves discipline."

They all nodded solemnly at this expression of author-ity, and abruptly Clio was angry. Was the man going to start recruiting followers right in the family?

"Did you teach your supporters self-defence?" she asked, after the kids rushed off in a body to clear out a room and find some mattresses.

He heard the hostility under her tone and frowned thoughtfully as he looked across the table at her. They were alone in the big kitchen. Sunset was slanting through the windows. She could hear crickets screeching, and a boat went past far out on the lake. They sat in shadows, watching each other.

"Yes, many of them learned."

"What a pity Zara never took a course in self-defence."

"Your sister is a brave and resourceful woman, but self-defence would have been of little use to her in such a situation."

"You admired her, then. How deep did the admiration go?"

"Too deep to do to her what that thug would have done to you today. Do you equate me with him in your mind?"

Clio closed her eyes. Did she? Why was she baiting him, after what he had done today?

"Is what you did so different?" she asked. Her feelings were deeply confused. She didn't understand herself at all.

His jaw tight, Jalal got to his feet. "If you do not trust me, Clio, it is because you do not trust yourself. In your heart you know the truth. It is not me, but your own heart that you do not trust. Ask yourself why."

She heard his quiet tread up the stairs, heard the children call out to him, heard a door close.

Clio sat alone in the deepening shadows for a long while, and then one of the dogs, sensing her distress and confusion, pushed a cold, wet, sympathetic nose into her hand.

Everyone had forgotten their table-clearing duties in the excitement, but for once she would let it go. She was grateful for the activity, as well as the solitude. She stacked the dishwasher without putting the lights on, cleared the table, tidied the kitchen. She spent a few minutes liberally dousing herself with insect repellent and pulled on a light jacket. Then she picked up the dogs' leashes and pushed open the screen door onto the evening.

They tumbled out ahead of her, and set off along her usual path, following the line of the shore away from the town, climbing. After a while, she came out onto her favourite vantage point, a clearing on a hillside overlooking the lake, where the dogs immediately began to chase and play. She sat on her favourite rock, watching as the lights came on in the town of Love's Point and in cottages all around the lake.

Ask yourself why.

Seven

Madeleine Donnelly and Brandon Blake had come separately to Love's Point in the sixties, when it had been a centre for hippie culture. They had met and fallen in love during their first summer there, when Maddy was painting chalk portraits for tourists, and Brandon played the guitar.

A few years later, in a wild venture, they decided to buy the ramshackle, almost derelict old Love house with a mortgage their parents gave them, and restore it. The Love house had been built by the family who had come here in the nineteenth century and given their name to the point. Once a summer playground for Toronto's old money, Love's Point had fallen on hard times with the Depression, and the big Victorian house had been for a while a cheap hotel. By the late sixties it had been virtually abandoned.

Now, thirty years on, the place was a landmark again, and the Blakes, like the Loves before them, "owned half the lake.'' A marina, an ice cream parlour, rental cottages around the area, a pioneer cabin museum with a barn turned into an artisans' studio and craft shop where you could go to watch craftspeople working in the old ways, and Maddy's special baby, an increasingly important art gallery showing mostly First Nation art, were all part of the casual, sprawling Blake empire.

When the house was about half finished, Maddy and Brandon had decided the time had come for children, and once they started there just didn't seem to be any reason to stop. There was always another bedroom to fill. Now there were nine Blakes, of whom the two eldest had departed for the city—but that was never the end of the story. For the Blake brood had an endless supply of cousins and friends, and somehow or other there was always a reason why someone was moving in for a while.

At twenty-two, Clio was third oldest. Zara and Jude had both left home for the bright lights, and Clio knew people were thinking her turn was next. But Clio wasn't going anywhere. Love Lake and the area around it was her spiritual home. She was one of the lucky ones. She had been born right where she belonged.

While her sister Zara had dreamed of foreign travel, of seeing all the strange places they read about in books, Clio had dreamed of being married, of having lots of babies, like her mother. Her dreams of career reached no further than someday managing her mother's art gallery as she now managed the ice cream store. She always loved meeting the dark-eyed artists who spoke familiarly of their spirit guides and spirit places, and whose paintings were not ordinary landscapes, or distant places, but different ways of seeing what was right under your nose.

For Clio, now, as for the artists, nature was alive with

the spirits of Bear, Wolf, Coyote, Beaver, and a dozen others.

The bright lights held little attraction for her. She could understand the yearnings that Zara and Jude felt, but she did not share them. Everything she wanted had always been within her reach.

Everything but one thing.

She had first seen Peter Clifford on her first day of high school, and she had fallen in love with him the same moment. Peter was in his final year. He was handsome, with thick dark blond hair and wicked hazel eyes, and a body to die for.

It didn't take her long to find out that every day after school he went down to his father's car dealership…. It didn't take her long, either, to work out that the bus route from the high school to Love's Point went right by Clif*Ford*'s. After that, several times a week after school, Clio walked three bus stops down the road, past the car dealership, before catching her bus. She was almost always rewarded with the sight of Peter in the forecourt or through the window.

He often seemed to notice her, almost as if he was looking out for her. When he waved to her, Clio's day was made.

When Peter and Zara started dating, Clio almost didn't mind. No one in the family knew how she felt about Peter, so it wasn't as though Zara was poaching. And it seemed only fair that her fabulous sister should get the handsomest boy around. Anyway, Clio had always known that she was too young and ordinary to really interest Peter.

Zara's relationship with him was very casual. The last thing Zara wanted, she told Clio, was to get involved with a local boy without any ambition of his own, who would want to tie her down.

Clio was fifteen when her adored older sister went off to university. And then the magic she had dreamed of happened. Within two weeks of Zara's departure, Clio, walking as usual past the car dealership, stopped in on an impulse to say hi...and Peter suddenly seemed to *see* her for the first time.

"Hey, Clio, you're all grown up all of a sudden," he said, with a smile on his face that melted her where she stood.

"You just noticed?" she returned flippantly, over a heartbeat that was drowning out the world.

"You're almost as beautiful as your sister," he said, and, fool that she was, she had taken it as a compliment.

He asked her out on a date, and that night, in his fabulous sporty convertible, tickling her cheek and ear with one lazy hand while he expertly drove with the other, he told her again how gorgeous she was, now that she was all grown up.

They dated all that fall, more and more often, and with more and more intensity in the passionate kisses they exchanged. She thrilled to his touch, as crazy to be near him as he was to be near her.

When she looked back on that time now, those wild, wild responses, it felt like a dream. Had she really felt like that, or had she imagined it, because that was the way she thought it should be?

He always stopped short of actual lovemaking. "Not yet, sweetheart," he would whisper, because Clio was so young, so innocent, so crazy for him she couldn't have denied him anything he wanted.

She knew Peter really cared for her, because he was so determined to wait. She knew from her friends that not every guy was so unselfish, not by a long chalk.

She imagined—she was almost certain—that he was

waiting till they could become engaged. They were too young now, of course, nineteen and fifteen! But twenty and sixteen...oh, Clio thought, what a world of difference there would be when Peter was twenty and she was sixteen!

When her mother started worrying that Clio was getting in deep with a guy too old for her, she assured Maddy that Peter had serious intentions, and was waiting. He wasn't trying to pressure her into early sex at all....

He turned twenty in November. Clio's own birthday was in December.

On her sixteenth birthday Peter took Clio out to a special restaurant, in a neighbouring town, wining and dining her like the grown-up woman she now was, and she smiled into his melting look and knew that Peter had made up his mind that it would be tonight. Tonight... She wondered if he had already bought the ring....

They went straight to a motel from the restaurant. Her body had been melting for miles. And when he closed the door and locked it behind them, and took her into his arms, she heard his passionate indrawn breath and chills of excitement poured over her....

It was when he was at last lying beside her, his eyes closed, kissing her, fondling her breasts, when heart and body were melting and singing with love and desire, that she heard it.

"Zara," he whispered. Like a drunk man, although he wasn't drunk. Slurring the word. "Zara."

"Peter!" She had tugged at his chin, making him look at her. "Peter, what did you say?" She smiled frowningly at him.

"Oh, baby! Oh, baby! I'm sorry, but you always knew, didn't you?"

She would never forget how her heart started beating

in that moment. She knew that she would never be able
to wipe it from her memory, not if she lived to be a hundred, like the old medicine woman on the reserve....

"Knew?"

"I've been dying for you, sweetheart, she never let
me!"

She did not resist what happened next. Now, when she
thought of the strange passivity that had invaded her at
his words, she supposed she had been in a kind of shock.

Whatever caused it, she hadn't fought him, and it
wasn't rape. She had felt invaded, used...but it wasn't
rape, she knew that, even if it was the worst thing she'd
ever experienced in her life....

Afterwards, lying there, she had wept. *I thought it was
what you wanted,* he had said sulkily. And she responded,
helpless in the face of such blank ignorance, *Not like this.*

There was worse to come. When he drove her home,
just as if she could possibly be interested, he told her how
deeply he loved Zara. "As crazy for her as you've always
been for me," he said.

With a new cynicism, she asked, "Why did you wait?
If all you wanted was a second-class Zara, why wait so
long?" He had to know she would have given him whatever he asked for weeks ago.

He smiled at her naivete.

"Baby, you were jailbait, remember? I knew you were
crazy for it, but hey! Fifteen years old! Tonight you became a consenting adult."

Clio sat up. The moon was climbing up the darkening
sky, and the dogs were snuffling at something interesting
in the bushes. They never seemed to learn that such an
interest almost always resulted in a scratched nose...or
worse.

"Come on, Buddy, Frowner!" she called, not at all wanting to have to deal with skunked dog tonight.

Was there something wrong with her, that she was attracted to such men as Peter and Jalal? Men who could use a woman entirely for their own purposes, without stopping to consider her feelings?

Still, Jalal was wrong when he accused her of blaming him because she couldn't face what Peter had done to her. Peter had hurt her, all right, but he hadn't raped her, and she had never hidden from the memory. She'd never told anyone, but she hadn't pretended it hadn't happened or anything like that.

She was wary of Jalal because of what he himself had done. She wasn't loading him with Peter's—or anyone else's—sins. He had his own, whether he wanted to face it or not

Anyway, she wasn't attracted to Jalal. It was hardly a statement of undying love if in her relief this afternoon she had wanted to kiss him! That was just an automatic human response, wanting to reaffirm life when death had seemed so close. Everybody knew sex and death were like two sides of the same coin.

Her mind slipped to the thug at Solitaire, and with a shiver of sick dread she remembered the way his eyes had travelled over her. She might still be his prisoner, subjected to whatever horror he could think of...if Jalal hadn't been with her.

She had seen in Jalal's eyes how much he despised the man. The involuntary escape of rage that she had seen, when the knife came down and severed the rope, had made her gasp, had terrified the little man in the boat.

Was it a form of self-hatred? Had he seen himself in another form?

Clio shook her head, but that didn't clear it. The moon

was high, the mosquitoes ravenous, and at home they would be wondering where she was. She stood and whistled to the dogs, and set off on the path home.

"*Assalaamu aleikum.*" The voice crackled in his ear.

Jalal hesitated, glancing around the darkened hallway. "*Waleikum assalaam.*"

"You know my voice, I think."

He relaxed at this use of the code. "There is news?"

"A rumour has surfaced."

He was silent, waiting. The window at the end of the hall stood wide open onto the night, but his voice would not carry so far.

"A rumour that says you have been secretly sent into exile by the princes, your uncles, and that your silence on the subject is the price of your life."

Jalal stood silent in the shadows as the soft wind caressed the trees.

"It may mean danger."

He smiled. "What is the reason given for my banishment?"

Soft laughter. "What else? That you were intriguing for the throne of Barakat."

"Ah."

"Be on your guard. *Ma'assalaam.*"

"*Ma'assalaam,*" Jalal repeated, and quietly replaced the receiver.

As she came out of the trees the dogs rushed to the verandah in the darkness, waggling their backsides as if they wanted to break their spines in two, making happy whines in their throats. Clio stiffened. Her skin shivered to attention. She knew it was him.

"Dad?" she queried anyway, as she came up the steps.

Jalal's voice came out of the darkness. "He has taken everyone out for a ride on the lake."

"You didn't go?" Another shiver coursed through her.

"As you see."

He sounded harsh. Usually his voice stroked her. The verandah was deep in gloom, out of reach of the moonlight. With one foot on the top step, she paused, almost afraid to enter the darkness where he waited.

If he tried to make love to her now, what would she do?

She was outlined in moonlight as she hesitated there, nervous, as if at the entrance to the cave of some wild animal. Jalal's blood leapt angrily. Why did she persist in thinking of him as she did? He was not a man of violence. Had he not proven his worth to her today? In just such a way would he have dealt with any of his own followers who had tried to harm her sister. The episode should have shown her what a gulf existed between himself and the sort of filthy infidel he had protected her from.

She had asked for his kiss afterwards, as reassurance. Could she be unaware of the meaning of her own actions?

Her legs were long and their shape was revealed by the fine cloth of the striped *shalwar* she wore, pants that ended below the knee. The old Mughal paintings showed women of the harem in such pants, inviting a man to start at the delicate, jewelled feet, the naked ankles and calves, and work his way up....

Jalal's jaw clenched. She stood there quivering, thinking her response due to fear, but he knew it was at the promise of delight.

"What do you fear?" he asked roughly.

She started, listening alertly, like a wild deer that instinctively feels the sights of the hunter's gun.

"Wh-what?" she whispered.

"I kissed you today," he continued, his voice harsh. "Do you fear me because of it?"

"Yes...no," she murmured helplessly, still frozen there in moonlight.

Her stomach was bare, exactly as in those antique erotic paintings. Only the jewel in the navel was missing. He could imagine the texture of the underside of her breasts behind the little top, so near to a seeking hand....

"Do you fear that we will feel more pleasure than you can bear, Clio?"

Her breath hissed audibly. As her eyes became accustomed to the gloom of the verandah, she could see the faint outline of him. He sat on the battered old rattan settee, his arms spread along the back, his knees wide apart. Even in the darkness she felt the impact of this offering of his sex to her. His presence was unmistakably male, as if some masculine perfume enveloped her, which she could not quite smell....

"No," she said. She could almost have laughed at the idea. But somehow she couldn't laugh, couldn't tell him how far from correct his assessment of her sexual capacity was.

"The promise of overwhelming pleasure between a man and a woman is rare," he whispered, as if she hadn't answered. "I, too, almost fear it. This is natural, perhaps, but the old poets swear that to lose the self in the moment of union is a gift. Shall we prove together that it is so?"

She watched the shadow of his arm detach itself from the gloom and reach out to her. She licked her lips, unable to speak.

"Clio," he commanded softly, almost irresistibly. "Let me show you the root of your fear of me."

A door opened in the distance and a few faint bars of music reached them before being abruptly cut off again.

In the dying lilacs a sleepy bird briefly queried whether it was morning.

Caught in the beam of his masculinity, she could hardly breathe.

"I know what it is I fear," she said. But her voice was hoarse when she had meant it to be strong. Her body was coursing with icy sensation, yet she knew the air around her was still warm.

"And convince you that it is not to be feared," Jalal murmured. A greedy beam of moonlight caught and caressed a dark curl as he moved his head. She felt a sudden pain, as if one could be jealous of a moonbeam.

She shook her head, to clear it of such insanity.

"It's not pleasure I fear!"

The rattan creaked. She stiffened in alarm, but he had merely withdrawn his arm and replaced it on the back of the settee.

"What, then?"

"How arrogant you are!" she marvelled, as fury released her from the need to recognize something that had almost surfaced.

He could feel his own impatient anger vying with the desire that burned in his heart and loins.

"First kiss me, and then tell me that I am wrong," he growled.

As if this were a direct physical threat, she leapt up the last step and quickly crossed the verandah to the screen door. In the kitchen a night-light gave quiet promise of refuge.

She half expected that he would get up and challenge her, but when she dragged open the screen and slipped through, Prince Jalal did not move from his seat.

Eight

The next day, Maddy Blake returned from her buying trip with a vanload of paintings, carvings, dream catchers, jewellery, beadwork and deerskin items of all kinds. Everyone helped unload and unpack, oohing and aahing as the season's catch was revealed.

"I'm starting a new line—deerskin clothes," Maddy announced, displaying several items that had the girls gasping with delight.

"I'm trying that on!" "Oh, and that!" "Me, too!" Clio and Rosalie and Arwen exclaimed at a rate of about once every two minutes.

"I'm twying that on!" Donnelly exclaimed in her turn, as an adorable little fringed skirt and vest in soft white deerskin with delicate turquoise and red beading came out of the wrappings.

Maddy smiled. "I'm glad you like it, darling, because I bought it just for you!" Everyone laughed at the face of exaggerated surprise and pleasure Donnelly made, her eyes big, her mouth a perfect O.

"Look at this! Oh, this is so sexy!" cried Rosalie next, pulling out a man's black cowhide cowboy hat with a beautiful beadwork band and a small feather. "Here, Jalal, you try it on!"

And suiting the action to the word, she put it on his head and stepped back to admire him.

"Oh, you're so handsome!" she exclaimed, in a voice that showed she was at least halfway to losing her heart.

Clio clenched her jaw, glancing back and forth between the two. She suddenly saw a danger she hadn't foreseen. She wondered how Jalal was taking that. It was hard enough to guess how even the guy next door would take such adoration from a girl almost of consenting age. Jalal was a total stranger to the culture. His rules would be an impenetrable mystery.

"Oh, all the tourist women are just gonna love you!" Rosalie continued. "You could sell them anything!"

It was a disguised way of saying *I love you,* and Clio's heart thudded. Poor Rosalie! It was impossible to disguise love at that age. She must have been just that obvious with her crush on Peter. Afterwards it had been a source of the deepest humiliation to know that he had always seen right through her.

She had spent a long time awake last night, thinking.

Jalal was wrong when he thought—if he really did think it!—that she wanted him. Or that what frightened her was the potential passion between them. She did not have any passion, potential or actual, in her.

Sometimes she wondered, looking back such a long way, if she had ever really *physically* wanted Peter. Perhaps it had been a kind of dream of wanting?

Certainly after that night she had never felt serious sexual desire for a man again. Nothing again had touched her so deeply. The most she felt had been a kind of detached physical urge and, understanding that that was all she would ever feel, she had learned to believe that it would do.

She had no doubt that other women felt more than she did. Maybe much more. For sure not a single love song or poem could ever have been written and sustained on any passion Clio felt, so there must be more.

Men were annoyed by her coolness under fire, yet she was grateful and polite about the pleasure they gave her— why wasn't it enough?

A boyfriend had said once, "There is another woman in there, Clio, I know there is!" but if so he had never reached her.

Even Peter hadn't been able to reignite the feelings she had once thought she had for him. He had wanted to try, but she couldn't understand why. "But, Peter, what's the point?" she had asked coolly, when he had tried to kiss her. "I'm not Zara. I never will be."

"Clio, you love me!" he had exploded. "And I'm finally coming to realize maybe it was you I loved all along!"

She had smiled, almost laughed, at that.

So she had no fears about Jalal stirring up depths in her she couldn't control. She was a woman without much sex drive, and it was going to take more than a handsome Arab sheikh to change that.

Now Jalal smiled lazily as they all admired him, telling him he looked like one of the *coureurs de bois,* those intrepid explorers of Canada's past.

He really is a wonderful-looking guy, she thought. The sight of him hurt her somehow. *Handsome and strong and much more macho than Peter ever was... Gorgeous! No wonder Rosalie's falling for him!*

Jalal said something and took off the hat, setting it on Rosalie's head. Like one of the family already, except that the look Rosalie gave him wasn't one anyone gave a brother...Clio couldn't be sure what was in Jalal's eyes when he smiled back.

Her heart began to beat with the deep trouble she felt—hard, slow thuds that frightened her. How would Jalal react if Rosalie made it so clear she adored him? He said he wanted Clio...would he take Rosalie as a substitute? Was she watching history about to repeat itself?

On Saturday the ice cream shop, the crafts shop and the art gallery went on full-time summer hours, and within a couple of weeks the season was in full swing.

Generally speaking, the boys helped out Brandon at the marina and the tackle shop, and the girls looked after the ice cream shop, the craft store and the art gallery. They shared duty at the barn. For years, this had made Maddy despair. Her feminist impulses hated to see such clear sex-linked leanings.

"Couldn't *one* of you try for a little cross-gender interest?" she sometimes wailed.

Not that Clio didn't like working on boats and motors, or minded selling bait—on those occasions when her father needed an extra hand, or when business in the boutiques was slow, she enjoyed messing in the marina.

But this year she had certainly been avoiding it.

Blake's Marina sold, repaired and rented boats and tackle. Sometimes inexperienced tourists wanted someone to take them out fishing, and Brandon accommodated them when he could.

For the last few years, Jude had split this job with his

father, and Ben was now in line for it. But Ben was not allowed to take anyone out alone till he was eighteen, and Brandon had given Jalal a crash course so he could fill the vacancy.

Ben always wanted to go along on such fishing trips, and whenever there was a chance, Clio was certain to get a request from a panting Ben for someone to take his place in the marina for a couple of hours....

"Who's taking them?" Clio asked, one wet morning in early July, as she stood behind the ice cream counter facing another such request.

"Dad, I think," Ben said. "Come on, Clio, they only want a short trip, and you won't get much business here till the sun comes out. Anyway, Jalal knows what he's doing, he'll hardly need you."

Clio hesitated as Rosalie came running in from the craft shop.

"Clio, I don't mind doing it!" she said, with a praise-worthy attempt at casualness.

Clio did not want to go and spend two hours with Jalal in a not very busy marina on a day when it was probably going to rain. For a moment she weighed the probable damage to Rosalie of that time alone with Jalal against her own disinclination.

Then she reached behind her and, to Rosalie's evident disappointment, began to untie the white baker's apron that covered her T-shirt and pedal pushers.

"Thanks, Rosalie, but Jalal's really not very experienced yet, and neither are you. You can cover here and leave the craft shop to Isabel. It won't get busy. If you have any problems, send Arwen over to the gallery for Mom, okay?"

Rosalie's chin sank, and she nodded wordlessly. Clio

felt like a heel, but as the old phrase had it, *This is hurting me more than you.* She was doing her cousin a favour.

Her heart anxious, Clio followed Ben along the board-walk that led from the house to the marina.

Two men were standing on the dock above one of the fishing boats, but it was Jalal, not her father, who was aboard, loading the fishing tackle.

Clio blinked and looked again, then stopped a few yards away, catching her breath on an astonished grin.

It was like a scene from a movie. Two dark-haired, swarthy-skinned men in navy *business suits* stood on the dock among the boxes of tackle, looking as out of place as if they had just flown in from Mars.

"Ben, who *are* they?" she asked in a whisper.

But Ben did not stop. He surged ahead, crying, "Oh, great! Jalal's going to take them! Jalal!" he called. "Are you going out with them?"

Jalal, expertly stowing a tackle box aboard, looked up and nodded. "Yes, I'm taking them out." He already seemed totally at home in this environment, Clio realized. Maybe boats were in his genes.

"Great! I can go with you. Clio's going to cover for me," said the boy, jumping aboard and immediately start-ing to help stow the gear.

"*Laa! Laa!*" bleated a guttural voice above him, as one of the men turned to the other in a babble of protest.

"The boy does not come," the other man translated to Jalal, in English. "No one comes. No room."

Jalal glanced impassively from one to the other. "All right," he said. Clio thought admiringly, *No one could guess what you are thinking.*

The customer was always right, but it was certainly the first time any customer had ever rejected the help of a spare, unpaid-for hand. Nodding sadly, Ben helped stow the last couple of items and then climbed out of the boat again.

The two men stepped awkwardly into the boat, as if they had never performed the action before, and under Jalal's instruction put on life vests over their suit jackets. They now looked even more ludicrous.

Heck, they're even wearing dress shoes! Clio noted in amusement. She stood watching while Ben tossed Jalal the ropes and then pushed them off with his foot.

Jalal put the engine in gear and eased away from the dock.

The eyes of the two men suddenly raked Clio in rude assessment, and one said something to the other that made her flesh creep even though she couldn't understand the actual words.

She saw Jalal's jaw tighten, and the boat turned, too sharply and too fast, causing the men to stagger and clutch each other for balance, ruffling their male dignity. Seconds later, the boat was heading out into the lake. Clio stood staring after it, her brain whirling with speculation.

The men and Jalal had all acted as if the only language they had in common was English. But Clio was almost sure that the language the two men were speaking between themselves was Arabic.

She was absolutely certain that, whatever language it was, Jalal understood every word they spoke. And that, for all their careful pretence otherwise, the men knew it.

Who were they? What business could they have with Jalal?

Nine

"**J**alal, I *can't!*"

Clio froze, her ears pricked, not sure what she had heard. Her heart kicked uncomfortably.

She had had a long, hard day. One of the high school girls had not shown for her evening shift in the ice cream shop, and after a full working day, Clio had had to fill in for her. Her parents were out at a meeting. Clio had missed the evening meal, and when she came in she had gone straight upstairs to the attic room where she slept, to relax in a warm bath. Now, in her bathrobe, she was on her way down the back stairs to find something in the fridge to tide her over till morning

Rosalie's voice had come from behind a closed door. Barefoot, Clio crept along the passage, listening intently to locate the room.

"But won't it hurt?"

A man laughed softly. "Only a little," said Jalal, his

voice seductively reassuring. Clio only just caught the words, and her heart clenched spasmodically. She couldn't believe her ears.

This was far worse than anything she had imagined. She had imagined him breaking Rosalie's heart, but not—!

Maybe she should have known. Maybe a man who would take a hostage wasn't above anything.

"But—"

She stopped outside the door. It wasn't Rosalie's room. She wasn't sure whose it might be. The two or three empty rooms on this floor and the next one down were filled by whatever cousin or friend had come to stay temporarily, on a regularly changing rota.

"Think—you will get hurt if you don't. Come, now, Rosalie. Be brave."

Her stomach twisting, her heart beating in her ears like thunder, Clio wrapped her hand around the doorknob and silently turned it. Her heart's thunder was so loud she could barely hear anything else, and her chest was so powerfully constricted she could take only the shallowest breath.

"I *can't!*"

The door moved by quarter inches, while she prayed for strength. When she saw them at last, directly in her line of vision, her heart contracted with almost desperate pain.

They stood on the far side of a mattress that was on the floor between them and the door. Jalal had Rosalie in a firm grip, one arm around her neck, the other hand clasping her arm above the elbow. She had her head tilted up over her shoulder towards him, and he was smiling down at her with seductive encouragement.

They were both too absorbed to notice her.

"Think of Arwen, then!" Jalal urged. "Think what might happen to her if you don't!"

Arwen? This was worse than she could have imagined in a week of black fantasies. Rage electrified her, consumed her, obliterating everything except hatred. Clio launched herself, just as, goaded at last into action, Rosalie moved an arm sharply and dropped to one knee, sending Jalal flying in a graceful arc over her head.

Clio, darting full tilt towards them, screeched with astonished admiration, and on the other side of the mattress Rosalie saw her and stared, mouth open.

"Excellent!" Jalal cried.

He landed on the mattress spread-eagled neatly on his back, in time to receive Clio, who, trying to stop her forward progress, made a misstep, tripped on the mattress's near edge and fell.

Her knees landed between his spread legs, her outstretched hands slammed against his shoulders, then slid down into the mattress. Momentum drove her body down against his. Her face ended up buried beside his neck, where she was conscious of his breath tickling her ear. Her hair lay tousled over his face, the rich turquoise-and-purple fabric of her bathrobe splayed out around them.

Jalal, with the honed, split-second reactions of a trained fighter, instantly wrapped his arms around her.

There was a moment of stunned silence from everyone. Then, covered in foolish confusion, Clio steeled herself for ridicule and lifted her head. She heaved for breath.

Above her Rosalie was still staring at her like a fish. Beneath her, Jalal was smiling broadly, his teeth white against his tanned skin.

"Class dismissed," he said, and her ears were filled with ringing laughter like the peal of church bells.

"What—" she began stupidly. "What on earth—?"

They lay staring into each other's eyes, while his body shook with laughter, and she felt as if something as real and physical as electricity shot into her from him.

His body stirred urgently against hers. Fire seemed to whoosh through her. Jalal's lips lost their smile and parted and his eyes darkened with hunger.

Clio gasped, assailed from too many directions at once, and stupidly turned her head in the direction of the chiming laughter.

Every member of the household save her parents was sitting against one wall of the room. Their sparkling eyes were fixed on her, their mouths open wide, teeth glinting with delight.

"What on earth is going on?" Clio finally managed to mutter weakly, just as her brain finished its interpretation of events and offered the answer.

This was one of his self-defence classes. How stupid could she get?

She was wearing only a short, silky nightdress under the open robe, and he was wearing the white trousers of his judo *gi*. Nothing, not even a zipper, got in the way of the hard, intimate pressure. Nothing disguised the hot, unfamiliar reaction of her own body, either. The touch of his hand was light now, against the curve of her back, and she wanted it to move lower, to press her against him.

"Let me up," she muttered.

She was drowned out by a chorus of voices all demanding to know what she had been trying to do. She shook her head, because of course she could not tell them the truth. She felt like every kind of idiot under the sun, but what story could she possibly invent that would be in the least plausible to cover such bizarre and astonishing behaviour?

"Let me up," she repeated.

He raised a quizzical eyebrow, and of course he wasn't doing anything to prevent her getting up. If she felt trapped there, it was by her own wishes. Clio jerked away from him, kneeling and then getting to her feet, twitched her bathrobe around her, tossed her loose hair back. After the first impossible-to-resist urge to look, her eyes resolutely stayed away from his groin.

With a reluctant, lazy smile of his heavy-lidded eyes that burned her where she stood, Jalal also flung himself to his feet.

"What kind of an attack was that?" the kids were still demanding, and she realized dimly that all those messages between their bodies had been the work of an instant. It had felt like long minutes.

"Never mind," Clio said with dignity. "It didn't work, my timing was off." She thought how impossibly unfair it would be to let the kids get any idea of her momentary suspicion of Jalal. How confused and unhappy it would make them all, to know that Clio had actually believed Jalal was trying to force Rosalie!

She could not do that to them, shake their trust in a friend—in their hero! she told herself. And then, with the clarity that sometimes comes in the wake of such powerful emotion, she saw the truth.

The truth was that Jalal was not her enemy. He was right: she had made it up because of fear. She was afraid of him because she was sexually attracted to him. That was the whole truth.

A weight seemed to drop away from her. And as it did so, just as arms that have unnaturally strained against an immovable weight will rise unbidden when the weight is released, her spirit seemed to lift.

As that happened, she was invaded by a sweet, melting wave of pure sensuality that filled her entire being, so that she seemed to be floating on the sea of her own limitless being.

She gasped with astonished joy. Never had body and spirit been a source of such pure delight.

Meanwhile the kids were all on their feet, chatting and laughing about how Clio's wild, crazy entrance onto the scene had stunned them.

"Next time!" Jalal called, signalling the breakup of the class for this evening, and to Clio's only faint surprise, the children instantly fell into two neat lines totally unlike their usual rowdy indiscipline and in perfect unison made a smart obeisance before calling their good-nights and filing out of the room. Even Donnelly.

"Come on, Donnelly, bedtime," Rosalie called.

"Okay. Good night, Pwince Jalal."

"Good night, Donnelly," he said.

"So they bow to Prince Jalal after all?" she observed, as Ben, the last one out, closed the door.

"To make respectful obeisance to the teacher is part of the discipline of a fighter," he said. "Just so must one submit one's will to doing only right before one uses the powers and abilities that are taught."

"And did you submit to the necessity of doing only right?" she asked, groping for a familiar support in a new world.

"No," Jalal said softly. "No, Clio, do not hide in this way."

The sun was setting; the room was soft with shadows now.

She turned as if to leave, but his hands caught her, drew her into his arms. "Why do you do it?" he murmured. "Why do you tempt me and then call me a monster? Why is your fear so great?"

Oh, this was too soon. She hadn't had time to collect her thoughts yet. She needed to go away and think.

His hands expertly found the opening of her robe, slipped inside. She started shivering uncontrollably. Distractedly Clio hoped the weather wasn't going to turn cold just in time for the weekend.

"What do you want?" he whispered seductively.

"I don't want anything," she said, and even she could hear the lie. The unbearable lightness of her being began to shimmer and coalesce into a new shape.

"No?" He paused, gazing at her eyes, her face, her lips. "You are not polite, you do not ask me what I want, Clio."

She could remain silent, but she would have needed the help of horses to get her out of that room, out of his arms. She mentally ordered herself to go, but it was futile.

"What then? In this culture I must ask for permission to kiss you? I do not like this. A woman knows what she wants, why is it not also for the woman to ask permission of the man? Or to make demands? Why is only the man understood to have desires? In my country we know better than this."

She licked her dry lips, hardly aware of what he said. It was only the vehicle for the sound. His voice was seductively rough, like a kitten's tongue. Her skin leapt with little shivers of delight and anticipation. She knew she should not answer him; he would only confuse her further if she did.

"Women can ask for what they want," she said anyway.

"Ask me to kiss you, then," he commanded, in a voice so indescribably delicious to the senses she instinctively stopped breathing, to better concentrate on the sensations it aroused in her.

Oh, such sensations as she could hardly remember having felt before. As if she had been born only a minute ago, it was all so new—yet she also knew she had been starved of such feelings for a long, barren lifetime.

All this time his arms were around her, intimately warm through the delicate silk slip that served her as nightwear, holding her only lightly, but with the promise of power in every muscle. One hand on her back, the other inescapably across her hips. She felt the agile strength of his fingers, understood with the direct physical knowledge of her body's hunger how easily he could slip the pale turquoise silk up a few inches to expose her naked thighs to his expert touch....

Oh, but shouldn't she take time? This was all so new, shouldn't she go away and think over what it meant? If it turned out she was a highly sexed woman after all, didn't she have to consider what to do about that?

"No," she muttered weakly, in answer to his command.

He showed her his teeth then, drawing her lower body gently against his, pressing oh so lightly against that heat, so that she could learn, if she had doubted it, that he was still hard, and she was still melting, with desire.

Her sudden indrawn breath rasped in her open throat and her eyes widened, unconsciously inviting him into her being. The hungry blackness of his eyes thrust and probed her deepest self, until she understood the necessity of his body also entering hers.

"I think the men of this culture are not such fools as you tell me," Jalal murmured, and then, inevitably, his head moved closer and his mouth covered hers.

Wild, delicious sensation poured over her. His hands

moved against her back under the robe, just enough to make the silk of her own thin shift caress her skin. The silk belonged to her, perhaps, but the heat was all his.

It coursed over and through her system, a sensual brushstroke that clouded her thoughts, made her glow with delight.

His mouth was a whole gallery of artistic expertise, exploding on the tiny canvas of her lips. He stroked, he brushed, he licked, he dabbled, and meanwhile she saw all the colours of the most inventive palette imaginable. Rich blues, haunting turquoises, deep greens, sensual pinks, erotic purples drowned her, and gold and silver burst and shot across her vision while she sank to a place in herself she did not know.

Her spirit soared free. Laughter and delight bubbled in her.

Her arms slipped up around his neck, her fingers touching and tangling with his hair, brushing his ear, his chin. Her hands tingled with the joy of caressing him.

His mouth left hers then, and nibbled up the line of her cheek to her temple, her eyes. His tongue trailed over the thickly curling lashes, to teach her that every tiniest pore was a source of stinging electric charge, with lines that reached over her whole body.

She kissed his neck, breathing in the scent that was only him—masculine, heady, and pungent enough after his labours of the day to cut through every civilised barrier straight to her animal senses, with the urgent message of male potency.

His arms wrapped her safe against his chest, and he dropped backwards with her onto the mattress. She gasped in wild drunkenness, feeling the hard pressure of his body more fiercely now, and when his hand cupped her head

and drew her face remorselessly down to his mouth, she
seemed to melt again and again.

His lips devoured her with kisses. Every nerve in the
world seemed attached to her lips, as if the sunset, the
wind in the trees, the very evening chorus of the birds
derived its inspiration from the movement of his mouth
against her skin.

Her mouth could not get enough of him. Her hands held
his head, her fingers threading and clenching through his
curling black hair, desperate for more than kisses could
give.

He knew it. His hand, caressing her, found the swell of
her breast where it pressed against his chest, and trailed
against it, and down over her back under the soft covering
of her robe to her hips, and then up to press her back with
delighting firmness.

Her body hungrily sought his, in little urgent pressings,
and he lifted her head away from his kiss and smiled,
shaking his head. Then he rolled her over onto her back,
and lay above her on one elbow. His mouth lost its smile
as his hand, free now to wander, ran hard up her outer
thigh from knee to hip, with wild masculine possessiveness, as if defining his own territory.

She melted again with his hungry declaration of ownership, and when his hand pushed the silky slip up over
her hip, as if he would not allow even that to trespass,
she was assailed with such wild, desperate melting that
she groaned.

She was another woman completely than the one she
had been an hour ago. Nothing that she had believed and
known about herself was real now. She hardly knew her
name. All that was real about her was Jalal's hand, Jalal's
body, his mouth, her need.

His mouth was against her breast, his tongue wetting

the silk to rub against her swollen hungry nipple. Shafts of delicious light exploded behind her eyelids, swept as sweet as honey to her skin, poured like celestial water through all her melting limbs.

A spiral of intensely burning fire spun hypnotically between her thighs, and her fingers clenched in his hair as she pulled her mouth from his to cry out. Dimly she realized that his hand was there on her sex, his fingers stroking the fiery spiral into being, stoking its urgency, on and on till her body, with shocking suddenness, began to clench spasmodically...then sensation and sweet delight etched new pathways of pleasure all through her, like water pouring along just-carved channels, bringing liquid delight to a starving, drought-stricken land, in a moment that went on to infinity.

"Oh!" was all she could say when it was over. Her body was flooded with heat and honey, and she lay feeling as lazy as a cat.

He bent and kissed her mouth, then lifted his head.

"We must go to my room now," he said.

She nodded dimly, her consciousness scarcely functioning. When he stood and reached a hand down for her, she obediently followed him to her feet.

He opened the door and glanced up and down the darkened hallway. A radio was playing softly somewhere.

"My room," she whispered. Her legs were like rubber. She had to concentrate to stand straight.

"All right," Jalal said. His mouth covered hers with a hungry, promising kiss. "Go there. I will follow in a moment."

She slipped along the passage and up the stairs to her own lair, amazed that she could still make her legs function. If they were hers. Her entire lower body felt melted. Her head was full of memories of what was just past, and at each one her body was swept with sensation that caused her knees to buckle.

In her attic room she swept clothes from a chair and tossed them into the closet, kicked shoes under the bed, fluffed pillows, straightened the already neat duvet. She turned on the lamp that was in the corner on the far side of the bed, and then stood looking down at the bed, cosily nested under the sloping roof, in its intimate circle of light, and heaved a sigh of anticipation that went all through her.

Ten

She heard light footsteps on the stairs, and chills raced up and down her being. She sat down on the bed, got up again, turned nervously as the door opened.

Jalal came through the door, pushed it silently shut, felt for the lock and turned the key with a grating sound that shot through her like a bolt of sensual lightning. He took a couple of steps towards her, enclosed her in one strong arm, and dropping something onto the bedside table, turned and wrapped her tightly to him, smothering her with the wildest kiss she had ever dreamed of, all her life long.

It went on forever, and it was all the kisses she had never had, it was a lifetime of kisses all in one. It was giving and taking, it was burning and ice, it was melting, utter, delicious delight.

When he lifted his head at last, she could only breathe his name.

"Take this off," he ordered softly, drawing her robe down over her shoulders and tossing it to one side.

She stood there trembling, with only the tiniest covering of silk between his hungry eyes and her body. Two narrow straps traced her perfectly formed shoulders. Thin turquoise silk, still damp from his mouth, caressed her warm, milky breasts, fell over swelling hips to brown, smooth thighs.

He bent his head, and his mouth settled just under her ear and trailed kisses down the side of her neck, while his hands enclosed her thighs with possessive firmness.

Just like that, she melted into flame.

His hand drew up the resistless silk, and with the lightest possible caress his fingers again brushed the warm, melting place where his body would soon demand entry.

Jalal understood that he had never been so lost in his life. Desire like the hot desert wind blasted him. She was every elemental force of nature against his being. He understood that all of nature's wildest forces, creative and destructive, that which brought both life and death, had one source, and that she took him there.

"My rose," he murmured, drowning in passion like a storm-swollen river in spring. He touched the rose and knew with the deepest, most primitive knowledge, that this part of her belonged to him. His to touch, to taste, to tantalize with his tongue and his body until the soft silk of the petals trembled and opened to him and willingly enclosed him.

Lightning streaked out from his fingertips and shot through all the wild hot colours of her being. Clio gasped, deep in her throat, and heard him grunt in response as if she had struck him, felt how his fiercely hard sex pulsed against her, heard the urgent, hungry whisper of his voice.

"*Zahri,*" he whispered. "*Zahri.*"

Zary.

Slowly the word penetrated the fog of pleasure that stupefied her. Clio gasped with shock. Splinters of ice rushed along her passion-swollen senses, cutting and slicing the softest parts of her being with a pain like nothing on earth.

She felt his touch now urging her down on the bed. He was murmuring in Arabic now, words of passion she didn't understand.

But she had understood enough.

"Let go of me!"

Like a drunkard, Jalal lifted his head and held her face between his two hands with bemused concern. "Clio?"

He seemed unaware that he had spoken any name but her own.

"Let *go!*"

He did not need to let go of her. She was already out of his hold, wrapping her arms over her beautiful breasts as if to protect herself from him.

"What is it, beloved?" he asked, frowning, unconsciously reaching for her again.

Stepping out of reach, she stared at him coldly for a moment, not answering. Her eyes were wide and black with such horror as he hoped never to see in a woman's eyes again. He swallowed.

"Clio! What is it? What—" And only then did he realize that he was not speaking English. "What is it?" he said again.

"Don't you ever touch me again," Clio said hoarsely. Blindly she groped for her robe, clutched it to her breasts, hiding herself from him.

"What has happened?" he cried softly. "What have you remembered?"

He stepped carefully towards her, sure that the solution lay within his own arms. "Tell me."

"God, I loathe men!" She stared at him, her chin up, as if it was himself that she hated, but he knew it could not be so. "Get out!"

"Clio," he said more urgently, as if his voice might bring sense to such blank wildness as he saw in her face.

She turned to the door, and under her hand the key scraped in the lock. Flinging open the door, she faced him again, a statue of anguish and fury.

"Get out!" she said again.

"I will go when you have told me what troubles you," he said, not moving from where he stood.

But she was lost in grief, anger, and violent self-loathing. She whirled and was out of the room before Jalal, master of the quick defence, could even engage his feet.

He did not follow her, but waited in the shadowed room, following with his ears as she stumbled down the stairs like a wounded animal.

He did not know, but thought he could guess, what made her run from such wild passion. There could not be more than one reason. Some man had hurt her. He had suspected it before, but now it was clear.

His heart tightened with the hardest, most bitter anger he had ever felt, like stone at the centre of his being, and he knew that if he met the man he would kill him, with one damning blow. There could be no mercy for a man who used his superior strength against a woman, when God had given him such strength to protect them.

He thought of her wild passion, remembered how she had opened her heart to him, then thought of the suddenness of her transformation.

What horror had she suddenly remembered, and why? What was the touch that was unbearable?

He felt that he wanted to heal the wound, to restore her to the full enjoyment of her passionate nature. He felt that he could do so. When he touched her, when she shivered, when she cried her pleasure, it was with a joy that was fresh, was new, and all this told him that other men had not been able to overcome her memories in the way that he had. She had allowed him to take her to unexplored places in herself....

He could teach her body, her spirit, a new memory. He could wipe out the old.

Clio pulled off her shorts and shirt to reveal a fashionable cream two-piece bathing suit, and stuffed them and her sandals into the waterproof bag, where her portable CD player, a novel, her towel and sun cream already were. In a separate bag she carried fresh fruit and a bottle of water.

All the residents of the Blake household, temporary and permanent, were expected to contribute labour according to their age, whether in the running of the house, or in the boutiques and marina. To the younger ones, of course, the "work" of observing how the cash register was operated, or a boat motor was repaired, often seemed more like play, especially when they were allowed to ring up a sale or insert a washer all by themselves.

There was a second iron-clad rule, too—they all took one day off each week. On that day they looked after only their own needs: they helped set the table or cook if they ate with the family, put their dishes in the dishwasher as usual, tidied away after games.

Sometimes in the busiest periods, of course, this rule went by the board for Maddy and Brandon and the older children; there were always rainy days when they could catch up. But today was Clio's scheduled day off, and unless all hell broke loose requiring her instant attendance, she was going to take it.

So after staying in bed late to avoid the family breakfast, and any meeting with Jalal, she had scribbled a note on the kitchen blackboard "Down at the cove, C" and slipped out.

Now, pausing a moment to clip her hair in place, she slipped into the deliciously cool water and, one hand clutching the waterproof bags, struck out for her favourite rock with a half sidestroke.

This small, out-of-the-way cove, only a twenty minute hike from home, had no beach, only a few precarious rocks at the bottom of the cliff. The water was deep right from the shore. At the mouth to the cove, a bed of reeds and a spread of rocks, some of them submerged, discouraged speedboats and jet-skis.

All this meant that in the mornings Clio could be pretty sure of being undisturbed, and, short of taking a boat to a more secluded beach, it was her favourite place to relax. And think.

And she had a lot to think of today, she told herself ironically, as she arrived at the large flat rock in the middle of the cove, dumped her things there, and slipped back into the welcoming water.

Well, what a glutton for punishment you are, she told herself with brutal self-contempt, as she dived deep under the surface into the rich, dark depths. Sunlight shafted down through the water, showing her her own greeny-white arms, and a startled fish made good its escape.

There must be something seriously wrong with her psyche. Twice in her life she'd been wildly attracted to a guy, and both times he just happened to be obsessed with her own sister? Just an unhappy coincidence?

Not very likely.

What weird and twisted mental wiring made her want to punish herself like this? Had she really felt so second-rate beside her gorgeous sister that she could only want a man who really wanted Zara?

Last night, she had looked back over the course of her life since that scarring moment with Peter and realized that many crucial conclusions about herself she had come to in those years were wrong. She was not a woman cursed with faint sexual appetites at all. She was a woman who had put herself in cold storage because of the hurt inflicted on her sexual image of herself at a critical, vulnerable moment—her first full sexual encounter.

Clio snorted, and the air bubbled like laughter through the water, but it was not lightness that she felt. Because what had it taken to show her this simple, obvious fact? How did she know it? Because her body was still running with a river of desperate, hungry sexual passion of a kind she had not felt since that night—had not, she saw now, *allowed* herself to feel since that night....

She surfaced, gasping for air, and floated for a time on her back, staring up at the hot sun.

Oh God, she was going to go out of her mind! How could she resist Jalal now, when the source of what she had been feeling for him, and had hidden under the convenient blankets of suspicion and hostility, was revealed in all its divine simplicity as pure, raw sexual attraction?

Yet how could she give in to it when she was facing another hurt identical to the first one?

Give me another one
Just like the other one...

She couldn't go through that again. Not with Jalal.

Well, at least this time she had had the courage and the sense to resist. She hadn't gone passive with Jalal as she had with Peter. She hadn't let him use her as a substitute for her own sister.

She squeezed her eyes shut, suddenly imagining how it would have been if he had not said her sister's name till later, till it was too late.... That would have been the end of the world.

If Jalal had made love to her wanting Zara, it would have killed her. Peter's betrayal had severed her access to her sex drive, but Jalal's—his would cut the cord to her heart.

She turned away from the thought, not wanting to see why that was so, and struck out in a hard, fast crawl.

But even that could not stop the hungry, coursing, melting desire that swept her body and soul every time she let herself whisper—*think!*—his name.

In the beautiful structure called for centuries past the King's Pavilion, three young men lay on cushioned divans, eating sweetmeats, with princely abandon. The Pavilion's broad walls of glass, at one end of a long, beautifully planned garden, overlooked a scene cool with fountains and serene with greenery.

It was one place of very few in the Barakat Emirates where the men—whose handsome faces would have been instantly recognizable to almost every one of their subjects—could be assured of complete privacy without anyone remarking the fact. By tradition guards prevented anyone entering the grounds that enclosed the Pavilion, whenever the monarch was in his refuge.

They could relax here, sure that no servant would trouble them unless rung for, that no subject would appear seeking a boon. And there was an additional factor that made the Pavilion a desirable place to be today.

It was swept for electronic bugs every day.

Even so, the princes—Karim, Omar and Rafi—took the added precaution of sitting by one of the small inside fountains, for the sound of running water confuses voice-transmitting devices.

They were handsomely negligent, lying in the cool, traditional summer costume of baggy white cotton trousers, their chests bare under open shirts, their feet and dark heads also bare. They appeared totally relaxed. No one could have suspected, seeing their casual postures, that what they discussed now was a heavy matter of state.

"He has been approached," Prince Karim was saying, for the King's Pavilion was in the gardens of his own palace, on the shores of the Gulf of Barakat, and it was he who had received the news.

They were all silent for a moment, absorbing this evidence of the truth of their suspicions.

Prince Omar's eyebrows went up as he thoughtfully took it in. "I suppose that's good," he said at last. Absently he reached for the lid of a polished gold humidor, lifted it and drew out one of his favourite small cigars.

"Any hint yet who by?" Prince Rafi asked.

"None."

They all waited as Omar carefully lit his cigar. Rafi took up two walnuts, cracked one against the other, and dropped the whole one back in the plate.

"And how did he respond?" Omar drawled, absently

watching the end of his cigar, as if the smoke might scribble the truth they sought in the air before his eyes.

"He'd be a fool to show interest so soon," Rafi said, tossing the meat of the walnut into his mouth.

Karim nodded. "And they would scarcely wish to work with a fool."

"They may wish soon enough that he was one," said Omar, with a dry smile. "I wonder why it does not occur to such intriguers that once installed in power he would have no more need of their assistance."

"Perhaps they feel that they will not need *him* for long," Rafi suggested.

"I wonder if you're right. Will they offer guarantees?"

"If they are wise," insisted Omar dryly, "they will *ask* for them."

Eleven

***

"Clio."

Oblivious to any outside sound, she lay stretched on the warm, flat rock, her earphones in her ears, drowning her worries with fem-rock music at a volume just below permanent damage level.

"Clio."

Her skin was smooth, brown, glistening with sweat and sun cream. Her long loose hair fell down over the edge of the low rock, its tips just trailing in the water. A couple of minnows were nipping curiously at them. One arm was stretched languidly out, hanging over the water, the palm half cupped with lazy vulnerability.

If he heaved out of the water and lay between her thighs and kissed her, would she resist?

He suppressed the impulse, staying in the water and watching the long lines of leg and hip, the generous curve of her breasts above the white material of her suit, the full glistening lips, the curl of her eyelashes.

She appealed to him as no other woman had ever done. He would require every ounce of discipline he possessed to control his need and subdue it to her own need, go at her pace.

Rather than try to compete with the angry music blasting into her ears, he lifted an arm from the water and sent a light spray across the neatly muscled expanse of her abdomen.

She blinked and turned her head, after a few moments finding him against the sun. Then one hand groped to the CD player and killed the sound, the other meanwhile drawing the earphones from her ears.

Then they were still for an unmeasured moment, gazing into each other's eyes as the sun beat down and the water lapped and paradise seemed to beckon.

Seeing the note she had left, he had followed her here, where they might be private, and where, away from her family, she might be encouraged to tell him a little of the history that had scarred her. But when he looked at her, those searching dark eyes, that generous mouth—all speech seemed to dry in his throat.

Clio gazed at him, and almost cried out with the surge of conflicting sensations—melting in her body, anguish in her heart. Her entire body seemed turned to liquid sugar, sweet, warm, delicious. Just seeing him, like a seal beside her in the water, his head lifted to stare at her…she sensed the elemental self of him. He was like a creature still more than half-wild, and that knowledge thrilled her.

He was pursuing her for reasons all his own, and that stifled her breath.

He heaved himself half out of the water onto the rock beside her, but there was not enough room for two on her rock, unless he lay so close that lovemaking became inevitable.

It was already intimate enough, his body propped on his elbows, his shoulders above her.... The posture of his body, and her own, invited him to sink down and kiss her.

She rolled and sat up abruptly, turning away from him, dragging her bag over and thrusting the CD player into it. Her back shivered with the nearness of his heat.

"What do you want, Jalal?" she asked coolly over her shoulder as he pulled himself up to a sitting position behind her.

Her skin was so warmly brown against the white of her swimsuit. He knew many Arab men who longed for pale, blonde women, but he had never felt the draw. For him, as for the ancient poets and storytellers, it was dark eyes and hair that caused the heart to beat uncomfortably fast....

"To be with you." He stopped, coughed, and breathed deep.

Suddenly he realized the impossibility of broaching such a subject with words. What could he tell her? *I can be patient while we slay the demons that haunt you?* Would she be angered if he told her to what conclusions he had jumped?

And suppose he was wrong? Perhaps he had merely convinced himself of the truth of his suspicions to hide the hurt another interpretation of last night's events would deliver to his male ego? Suppose it was himself she objected to, and not to the act at all?

No. He had seen her eyes. And it was not him that she had seen when horror gripped her.

"I guess it never occurred to you that you are the last person in the world I want to be with right now," she observed in a conversational tone.

"Yes, it occurred to me. But I thought, too, that if we talked about last night a little, you might change your mind."

Her heart shrivelled. God in Heaven, why didn't he have the sense to shut up? What on earth did he imagine he could possibly say to make anything better?

It didn't help that the incantation *It's Zara you want* was about as effective as sunglasses against a supernova. When she looked at him, felt him there, she still burned to touch him. Her body was on fire and aching for him. No matter what she knew.

Not like Peter at all. When she had seen Peter again, when he had tried to touch her, assuring her that after all he really was attracted to her for herself, her stomach had heaved with disgust.

So, did this constitute progress? Clio asked herself with bitter humour. She let out a choked laugh at the thought.

"Do you know," she informed him brightly, "I really don't want to hear anything at all about last night!"

She had been hurt, and he knew he could heal her. He was as sure as he could be that he could get behind whatever was making her say these things...and maybe she knew it, too, in some part of herself, and wanted to be released....

"Can we not say a little?" She was stonily silent, her back rigid and turned against him.

"I came here because I wanted to be alone."

"Sometimes, is it not better not to be alone, even though in a part of yourself, you wish it?"

"I am not a damsel in distress, Jalal. I am not a kitten up a tree."

He paused. "I do not understand these cultural idioms," he observed, with a tone that forced a laugh from her.

He swallowed and rubbed his chin.

"Such a hot day!" he murmured. "Why did no one warn me that in summer Canada, the land of ice and snow, is as hot as spring in the desert?"

"It's a closely guarded secret," she said, without expression. "Otherwise half the millionaires in the world would want to buy property here and force the prices up."

She knew she was just at the edge of control. She was trembling inwardly, and she could feel the tears threatening from deep in her being.

She began hastily packing up her things, shoving her towel and book into her bag, picking up the bag half filled with strawberries.

"Clio, don't leave," he said.

"Jalal, what happened happened. I think we both have to agree that it will be better if it never happens again."

She sounded angry, but underneath, he knew, she was only hurt. He did not know how he knew it. By some magic between them, that had never happened to him before, telling him her inmost thoughts and feelings.

If he could touch her, take her in his arms, if he could hold and comfort her, she would tell him what past hurt had made her react in this way. But he must be careful. Until he knew more of what had caused her change last night, any physical move on his part might reignite the memories....

"No. I do not agree. I think we should not be put off by what happened."

He knew that it was important to tell her that he had not been angered by her abrupt rejection of him in the heat of the moment. She had to know that he was capable of controlling himself, of accepting with patience whatever she needed.

She almost laughed at the sheer ludicrousness of that. What was he going to say? That he would be happy to accept her as a Zara substitute if she didn't object? That the price for the hottest sexual pleasure she would ever experience was to let him imagine he was with her sister?

Well, fortunately she had been down that road before. She knew the trip wasn't worth it.

"Do you!" she said, with a cynical half laugh. "Well, no doubt I'm turning down an opportunity in a million, but you'll have to excuse me."

"Clio…" he begged.

She should jump into the water and leave him. But she felt bound to him by the cords of electric feeling that swept her body at his nearness. She wanted to reach for him, to touch the source of the pleasure that swept her. Like smelling your favourite, deliciously cooked food, she thought in a ridiculous aside, and wanting a taste….

If she turned to him now she would get more than a taste. She would get the full-course meal, and nothing she could tell herself would stop her wanting it from him. She was on a knife-edge and she knew it. She was shivering with years of pent-up need.

But if she gave in to this crazy desire to throw herself against Jalal's muscled, water-beaded chest, be wrapped in his willing arms—she would risk another deeply soul-destroying experience.

"Jalal, I don't want to hear it!" she said. Then, exerting all her self-discipline, she grabbed up the waterproof bags and slid into the water.

Out of her paranoia, she began to watch him. He would speak on the phone to someone, in Arabic, his voice soft as if he were afraid of being overheard, even here, where no one understood the language. On his time off, he took a boat and disappeared, sometimes for hours.

Once, driving past in a boat, she saw him on a restaurant dock, sitting with two dark men, and she was sure they were the same two who had hired the boat that day, and refused to let Ben go along.

She remembered that moment, on the day he arrived, when he had forgotten his stated reasons for coming here. She had reminded him that he was here to practise his English. ''Yes,'' he'd said, but she remembered that she had wondered, and she began to wonder again now, what his real reasons were.

He knew he was a fool if he blamed her attitude entirely on some other man's actions. He had to look into himself for the cause of Clio's repudiation of him. It was too easy to attribute her behaviour entirely to past trauma.

He had to accept that she also blamed him, believed him capable of the kind of behaviour that had caused her own evil memories.

For the first time, he began seriously to wonder whether more than he understood had happened to Zara while he held her hostage. Always before he had believed that his word was law with his men. Had one of them defied the ban he had imposed?

Surely his mother would have known, even if he himself did not, a part of him argued. And if his mother had known, she would certainly have told him. She, who had always disapproved of his plans in the strongest terms, who had bitterly reviled him when she learned that he had returned to camp with Prince Rafi's intended wife as his captive, had visited Zara twice every day. She could have had no hesitation in telling him if, as a result of his arrogant stupidity, his hostage had been hurt.

Unless... He thought of his mother's history, and his grandmother's. Both of them had suffered because of the archaic attitude that said a woman who lost her virginity before marriage, whether she was at fault or not, could be written out of history, even killed.

Nusaybah, his mother, had escaped death at her own father's hands because, and only because, the illegitimate child she carried in her womb was the grandchild of a king who no longer had an heir. She had been forced into marriage, with a man old enough to be her grandfather, to save her reputation in the tribe.

Jalal gasped, making a connection for the first time. But she must have been still in love with Prince Aziz! In love with a handsome prince, mourning his death, carrying his son, and forced to marry that old man...

And no doubt, Jalal saw suddenly, she had had to put up with whatever her husband exacted from her in return for the favour of his protection.

These were things his mother had never spoken of. But the tribe had never been kind to women. Women were better off in the cities of Barakat, where a secular state imposed its own codes.

His grandmother, Nusaybah's mother, a princess, had also suffered deeply. Abandoned to her fate, with no choice but to marry the bandit who had abducted and raped her—or flee into the desert and die.

She had survived on memories of her old life, its cool water and green trees, until a mercifully early death.

Had these facts surfaced in his mother's mind? Had she moved to protect the hostage by denying that such a thing had ever happened, in order to, as she might well believe, save Zara's life—or at the very least, her marriage to the prince?

If so, and if he knew it, Rafi would by now have killed

the man. Nor would he have allowed Jalal himself to be treated as he was now being treated, trusted as he was now trusted, by his uncles.

So if it had happened, Zara had not told Rafi.

But might she have confided in her sister?

Perhaps even, it had occurred in darkness, so that Zara had not known who it was, had believed he himself was her attacker?

There was more to Clio's abrupt rejection of him than the scars of the past. He must find out his own share of her trouble.

"Are you watched?"

"Of course I am watched! We are undoubtedly under observation at this moment," Jalal said impatiently. "Can you not at least attempt to disguise yourselves in the local costume?"

The men looked down at their own neat suits and pale tailored shirts in surprise. "Is this not—?" one began.

"You are not in the city now! Here the traditional dress is such as you see me wearing."

They looked at his brightly patterned, baggy shorts, his cotton shirt open over a white T-shirt, and nodded. "Your point is noted, Excellency."

"You might also try to look as if you are here to fish."

"Of course," they said, and then glanced uncertainly at each other, wondering how to do it. He almost laughed.

"Here's a worm. Bait the hook."

The worm wriggled. The dark man withdrew his hand. "This worm is alive."

Jalal glanced at him with a coldness in his eyes that made the other feel how close the grave might be. "You involve yourself in plots that will result in the deaths of thousands and you cringe at a worm? Of course the worm is alive," he said. "That is how the fish like them."

Twelve

"Clio, I ask you to tell me something," Jalal began without preamble, grabbing the first opportunity in days. It was pouring with rain outside. The children had been taken by their parents to see a famous visiting circus in a town miles away, leaving the two of them in charge. At lunchtime he had left the hired help alone in the mostly deserted marina and come to the house.

"Even if Zara has sworn you to strict secrecy, you must now find a way to tell me the truth. Who among my men hurt your sister when she was in my..."

"Prison?" Clio supplied brightly. She busied herself with the sandwich she was making, keeping her back to him. She had not conquered her physical reaction to him. Bad enough when they were merely in the same room together. When he focussed his attention on her she could hardly keep her knees from buckling.

"Yes," he agreed softly. "In my prison. Did she suffer more than I knew?"

She turned, summoning her old anger as her shield against present feelings. "You know, it's fascinating," she observed. "You talk as if Zara was the only one who could have suffered anything because of you. Do you have any idea, Jalal, what hell we went through here, knowing some rebel fanatic with a score to settle had taken Zara hostage thousands of miles away? Can you conjure up the glimmer of an idea of what my mother and father went through?"

"Yes, of course, I—"

"No," she contradicted flatly. "No, because if you did, you would never have come here." Oh, how she wished he had not! "You would never have so blithely expected them to play host to you after what you had done to us all. You thought that because Zara survived more or less unscathed and you very kindly didn't let your men have a regular go at her, the way we all feared for days on end, that it was all over and no harm done.

"Let me fill you in—my father was as grey as death from the moment we got the news Zara had been abducted to the moment he heard her voice on the phone telling him she was fine. I thought he was going to have a heart attack, and no doubt he would have, if it had gone on much longer. I was terrified it was going to kill them both.

"And the kids, too. Even Donnelly. We couldn't keep it from the kids. Everyone in the country knew about it— it was on television twenty-four hours a day! They called her the Barakat Hostage, did you know that? It was 'Day Three in the Barakat Hostage Crisis' for the journalists, but for us it was another twenty-four hours, one thousand four hundred and forty minutes, of fear, misery, and feelings so horrible I bet you've never experienced anything like it in your life.''

He was silent, listening.

''All right, I accept that nothing worse than the fact of imprisonment happened to her. But don't think that knowing that wipes away all the scars, Jalal. You don't recover from an experience like that just because it's all over now.''

She was reminding herself as she spoke, and the old feelings now poured up through the well hole she had at last created, and flooded her.

A hundred protests rose to his lips and were quelled as she spoke. He forced himself to listen, not to defend himself in word or thought, but to let what she said find its mark in his heart.

He listened as she ran out of words and began to weep, and he did not make the mistake of trying to touch her when she did. How could he offer himself as her comforter when the wounds she described had been inflicted by himself?

When all the words and all the storm of weeping were finished he sat in silence with her. She wiped her nose and face, letting the sobs subside. Finally she raised her head and looked at him.

''Thank you,'' he said then. ''Thank you for telling me what I did not understand before. I have heard what you said, Clio.''

She had not told him everything. She had not said anything about the fact that he had fallen for her sister and then tried to exorcise his illicit passion for his uncle's wife on her own sister's body. She had not said that she wondered how deep his love for Zara went, and whether he was willing to betray Prince Rafi in order to gain her.

* * *

"Rest assured, your uncles will not be martyrs."

It was a hot, sunny day. Two men sat at a table on the terrace of the rented mansion overlooking the lake. Below, beside a small yacht, Jalal's boat bobbed on the swell caused by a passing speedboat. A serving man silently set tiny cups of strong coffee and a plate of honeyed cakes down in front of them and silently withdrew.

Saifuddin ar Ratib was the name of the man who had spoken. He had replaced Abu Abdullah in the negotiations. He was more intelligent, more powerful, closer to the heart of the conspiracy...more dangerous.

"I have not the pleasure of understanding you," said Jalal.

"Considering the lives they lead, each might easily expire in circumstances that are sure to disgust true believers."

Abruptly Jalal lost interest in the coffee he was stirring. He set the spoon into the saucer and looked up at this latest emissary from whoever it was.

"How so?" he demanded softly.

Saifuddin ar Ratib raised an eyebrow. They had him. He himself had seen the light of greed in the prince's eyes, however Jalal had tried to feign lack of interest.

"A fatal car accident at the moment when a prince is being serviced by a cheap whore—or perhaps two—would leave little for the people to regret in the passing of such a libertine."

"And which of my uncles has a taste for such pursuits?"

The man, whose name meant "The Arranger" and was undoubtedly a pseudonym, shrugged largely and showed his palms.

"This is merely an example of what might possibly

happen to the kind of man who would make a foreign unbeliever queen of an honourable and believing people.''

Jalal lifted an eyebrow. ''Have not all my uncles' brides accepted the faith?''

''Lip service merely. It is a known fact that at least one of them encourages the prince to drink alcohol.''

''If you mean Omar, I doubt if he caught his taste for Scotch from his wife.''

''Nevertheless, if he killed himself and her in an accident caused by his own drunkenness, who would mourn?''

There was a silence broken by the drone of boats, the slap of water against the dock. Jalal got to his feet and walked to the railing. He stood looking out over the water, then turned.

''Do your friends indeed have their plans so carefully constructed already?'' Jalal asked quietly.

Saifuddin ar Ratib's hand went up pacifically. ''Rest assured, Prince, I give you no more than possibilities. Nothing would be firmly planned or executed without your approval.''

''Good.'' Prince Jalal ibn Aziz showed his teeth. ''Take this back to those who sent you—let them not forget that I am bound by my grandfather's deathbed command, and subject to his curse. To send the princes into exile, to reunite the divided country and take the throne in their place—this would be perhaps no more than is my right. Although of course I do not say so.''

''Of course.'' Saifuddin ar Ratib nodded blandly.

''To allow them to be assassinated is so far from possible, that I would be on my honour to hunt down the perpetrators of such crimes, from the lowly doers to the highest planners, to kill them and all their kin without mercy. I would spread their blood on the desert sands and wipe their line from the face of the earth forever.''

Saifuddin smiled, his good humour unabated. ''Prince, do you indeed live in terror of an old man's fantasies?'' He lifted his hands. ''A curse? Are you not an educated man?''

Jalal inclined his head. ''But my people—my uncles' people,'' Jalal corrected himself quickly, ''are not. If I did not obey King Daud's injunctions, the entire country would expect to see me dethroned, and every petty sheikh in the desert would think it worth his while to challenge my rule.''

Saifuddin nodded. ''I take your point. But—is it not worth the risk? In exile, would not the three princes form an even more potent rallying point for the disaffected?''

Jalal stood and looked arrogantly down as if Saifuddin ar Ratib were an insect he might crush.

''I am Jalal ibn Aziz ibn Daud ibn Hassan al Qura-ishi,'' he said. ''That will be enough for the people.''

She was a strong woman.

He thought of the woman named Nusaybah—his mother's namesake—one of the Prophet's earliest disciples. At the battle of Uhud, when it had gone so badly for his army, the Prophet had been under direct attack with only a small group to defend him. Nusaybah had been one of that group. She was armed, with the Prophet's express permission, and she stood in front of the Prophet that day and defended his life.

''The Prophet himself allowed women to be different,'' Jalal's mother had said, when she recited this story to him. ''He was a great warrior himself, but he allowed a woman to defend his life. You also, my son, be a man who is not afraid when a woman is strong.''

Like his mother, much of Clio's strength was in her moral judgements. Sometimes a woman's moral strength was harder to accept than the physical. He could no longer reject her condemnation of him.

He had to face the fact that, like any criminal, he had used his superior strength against a woman, for his own ends. He had held himself above such men, believing that because his own ends were political, he remained morally unstained by his actions.

He was wrong. But how to tell her what he had learned?

Clio wandered through the days in a haze of dullness, punctuated by sharp spear thrusts of humiliating memory.

Now she could understand so much that she had never understood before. Now she could see the long line of underground motivation that had been driving her ever since that long-ago night with Peter Clifford, and had led her straight to this situation with Jalal.

When Peter had gone on to make love to her that night, after calling Zara's name—her body had responded. That was what she had wanted to forget. That was what she couldn't bear to face. In spite of what she knew, she had thrilled when he stroked her. She had moaned when he moved in her, in spite of the first-time pain, had arced her body hungrily to meet the thrust of his....

And she had despised herself afterwards. How could she have let him do that to her, when in his imagination he was with Zara?

It had been the rape of her own soul. And she had acquiesced in it.

From that moment, Clio saw, she had considered her body the enemy. Something that had to be ruthlessly controlled. She had suppressed her sexual nature ruthlessly, without even being aware that she did so. She had not allowed any man to create more than the mildest response in her. She was always in control.

Jalal had threatened that facade. Because her sexual and emotional response to him was more powerful than anything she had experienced before, she had unconsciously realized that he was a profound threat to her self-control.

She thought of the moment when he had stepped into the boat and fallen, remembered how strong her reaction had been, how swiftly her defences had moved to deny it…. That had set the pattern for everything that had happened since.

She had pretended to herself that what she felt was righteous anger, and because she had a long history of suppressing and disguising her sexual nature, she had been pretty successful at the deception—until the day she had stood outside the door listening to him with Rosalie. As though it was only by plumbing the deepest well of suspicion that she could let go of everything else…like a door that you have to push further shut in order to unhook the latch and open it.

How richly tangled the human psyche was! Clio found time to marvel detachedly.

But turning the microscope of real understanding on herself was not an easy task. She was alternately burning and freezing with self-condemnation and contempt. Because even if she had invented the brutality of his nature…she had not invented his attraction to Zara.

She must have unconsciously picked that up from him right at the beginning. The messages must have been there. It was nothing but more self-deception if she tried to pretend now that she could not have known it, that it was merely coincidence that she had fallen for yet another man who wanted not her but Zara.

What horrid little twist of her psychological makeup dictated that she could be deeply sexually aroused only by men who really wanted Zara?

God, she needed a shrink! What had driven her to repeat that horrific experience, the worst and most crippling encounter of her life? What was wrong with her?

Every Friday night in the season, Maddy Blake drew up a duty roster for the coming week. Mostly this was for the sake of the younger children, who enjoyed the whole process of negotiation, and were learning something about duty and responsibility. Even Donnelly knew that when she was scheduled for half an hour in the ice cream shop she had to be there, and felt her importance in the scheme of things.

Each of the Blake children had learned to consult the schedule for their own "plaque" from a time before they could read.

Donnelly's sign, carefully chosen by herself, was a butterfly. In the same way, nearly twenty years ago, Clio had chosen the picture of a black-and-white cat. The boys usually went for something more macho—Ben was a Jedi knight, Jonah a shark.

Part of the ritual that introduced any new member, however temporary, to this household was the choosing of the plaque that would, for the length of their stay, be used to signify them on the duty roster.

"Okay, Harry is going to be staying for a while, I take it?" Brandon would ask at the family breakfast.

The prospective tenant would nod eagerly.

"Has someone explained the house rules?"

More nods.

"Do you agree to abide by the rules as outlined to you, Harry?" Brandon would pursue gravely.

"Yes, Uncle Brandon." One of the rules was that you called Brandon *Uncle* and Maddy *Aunt,* unless you preferred to call them *sir* and *ma'am.*

"All right, and have you chosen a plaque, Harry?"

"I picked the Chief on the horse."

Clio rarely needed to consult the roster—which took the form of a board on the kitchen wall full of little metal cup hooks on which the plaques were hung in rows—because these days her duties were nearly always the same. She generally supervised between the craft boutique and the ice cream shop, while her mother ran the gallery and supervised "The Barn."

Clio's schedule was different on Saturdays, when she and Ben together made the rounds of all the rental cottages, changing sheets and towels and checking to see that everything had been left clean and in order before the new renters came in the afternoon.

So she didn't even eyeball the roster until Saturday morning at ten, when she was in the kitchen with all the linens, waiting for Ben to make his appearance. Absently spooning yogurt into her mouth, she paused in front of the big board with its display of plaques that had been a part of her summers all her life long.

Her father's plaque, a guitar because he still often played while they sang together on long winter evenings, almost always had the picture of the sailboat under it, which of course signified the marina. What was under her mother's rose, though, had changed over the years. When Clio was tiny, there had been first only an ice cream, and then a paintbrush, but now there were added to the repertoire a tiny Mountie, to signify the crafts boutique, and a farmer with a pitchfork, who symbolized the pioneer barn.

The arrangement was a source of security to them all.

Even those too young to read need only consult this chart to learn exactly where their parents were.

Cottage duty was signified by a tiny house with a smoking chimney, and there it was as usual under Clio's cat. She blinked absently, swallowing another spoonful. Under the Jedi there was no matching house. Ben was apparently on marina duty this morning.

Then who was coming to do the cottages with her?

Frowning over this little mystery, Clio searched the board for another house plaque. And then she found it...under the tiger.

Thirteen

He's a very wild tiger!

Chills rushed all over her skin. *Jalal* was coming on the cottage run with her? Why on earth would her mother have arranged this?

Jalal stage-managed it! she told herself fiercely and, setting the yogurt container on the counter so hurriedly that it slipped and fell, spilling its contents on the floor, turned and ran. Out of the kitchen and down the hall to the front door, out and along the pretty, tree-lined street under the picturesquely lowering sky, over the bridge, till she arrived panting at the art gallery, in a beautiful century-old red brick building.

"Mother!" she cried, storming in. In spite of the heavily overcast sky, two middle-aged women in poplin shorts and blouses were in the main gallery, standing in front of a massive canvas of a mountain disguised as a sleeping woman. They turned to gaze at her.

Behind the desk, her mother put down her pen and looked up.

"What's wrong, Clio?" she asked impassively. Clio was dramatic by nature, and the stormy entry made less impression on Maddy than on the tourists.

Embarrassed by the two women's attention, she rushed over to the desk. "Why is Jalal down for cottage duty this morning?" she hissed.

"Weren't you there? Oh no, that's right, you were out last night." Clio had been to a friend's birthday party, where they had driven her crazy demanding to know what it was like living with a prince....

She couldn't escape him.

"The people in Solitaire called to say the generator had practically given up altogether. Jalal agreed to go this morning and see if it could be fixed."

"What does *Jalal* know about fixing generators?" Clio demanded in stagey disbelief.

Maddy gave her the benefit of raised eyebrows. "Quite a bit, apparently. He did after all run that camp of his on wind and a prayer most of the time, you know."

"I'll just bet! Well, I don't want him along! Can't Dad come?"

"Your father wants to be in the marina this morning. He asked Jalal to do it. Why is it a problem, Clio?" Maddy regarded her severely over the top of her reading glasses. "Apart from the fact that you refuse to overcome your dislike of him."

"Because I—" Where to start? Clio wondered hopelessly. "I just don't want to spend the day with him. He'll probably leave me to make the beds by myself in some kind of macho—"

Her mother gazed at her with disapproval. "I think you know that's unjust. However, if you feel that strongly about it, I don't see why Rosalie can't take your place.''

''Rosalie!''

''If you think she knows the ropes sufficiently.''

''But I—Rosalie can't...''

''Clio, I have customers here. Please sort it out your-self. Whatever you think is best,'' said Maddy.

She turned away to speak to one of the tourist women who had approached the desk. ''Yes, sorry, do you have a question?''

''That's all right,'' said the woman comfortably. ''Would you have any inexpensive prints by Jerry Eagle Feather?''

''I have a couple of limited edition prints—oh, excuse me a moment! Clio!'' her mother cried as she got to the door.

She turned.

''If Rosalie does go, remind her to keep an eye out for the Williamses' cat at Solitaire.''

Nodding, Clio went back out onto the street. That was how important it all was to her mother. Either she or Ros-alie had to spend the next few hours alone with Jalal, and uppermost in her mother's mind was the Williamses' missing cat!

Clio jogged back to the house. In the kitchen she found Jalal standing by the back door, a cup of coffee in his hand, staring out at the darkly brooding sky that only en-hanced her mood.

''There is going to be a storm, I think,'' he said.

She laughed nervously. ''Yeah, probably.''

''The boat is loaded. Are you ready to go?''

She stood uncertainly in the middle of the room, gazing blindly at him, feeling her skin already twitching with awareness. ''Ummm...yeah,'' she said, trying to think. Should she ask Rosalie to do it? ''Yeah, I guess so.''

She glanced up at the duty board, found Rosalie's

plaque. Working in the Barn this morning. Rosalie loved it there, being with all the artisans...still, she would happily trade that in for a day spent with Jalal.

What if Rosalie used the opportunity to make a sexual move on Jalal? What if he made love to *her* and called Zara's name? Did he understand that fifteen-year-olds were jailbait in this country?

Jalal moved to the sink, putting down his empty coffee cup. Someone had cleaned up the yogurt she had dropped.

"Shall we go?" he asked, holding open the screen door.

His face was a tight mask of anger, as if he knew exactly what she was thinking about.

Feeling that her brain still wasn't working, Clio followed him out.

"Is the line completely secure?" asked Rafi.

Karim, bent over the keyboard, nodded. "Yes, we have the highest security encryption. Wait a minute, here we go."

A tense silence fell as the three princes bent to the computer monitor. With slow stripes down the screen an image was forming.

"Pretty good," Omar observed. "How far away was the camera?"

"This is from Ramiz. He was positioned in a fishing boat perhaps a few hundred yards away."

There was silence as the princes waited. Suddenly the image gelled. "That is Jalal?" said Omar, his finger pointing to a man whose back was to the camera. Over his shoulder another man's face gazed almost directly into the camera.

"That is Jalal," Rafi agreed. "Who is the other?"

They were silent, frowning with concentration. "I have seen this face before," Omar said.

"Yes," Karim breathed. "So have I. But who is it?"

"What name does he use?"

"Saifuddin ar Ratib."

Rafi shook his head. *"Sword of the Faith, The Arranger."* He murmured the translation thoughtfully. "A nom de guerre, obviously."

"Perhaps Akram got some better shots. Pull up some more."

Karim punched the keyboard. "But the face is clear enough. It is just that—the circumstances are missing."

"The man's head is bare," Omar said suddenly. "It could be we are more used to seeing him with a *keffiyeh.*"

"Yes," said Karim slowly, as another photo began to form. "Yes."

Jalal slowed the engine and guided the boat into Bent Needle River.

Renters had to vacate the cottages by ten on Saturday morning, and the incoming ones couldn't take possession till five in the afternoon. That arrangement usually gave Clio more than enough time to do what was needed to put the cottages in shape for the new arrivals.

But a faulty generator was an unknown quantity. Maybe it could be fixed on site, with the tools he brought with him, or maybe not. It might need a new part, which would mean a trip back to the marina and out again, in which case he would probably still be working on it when the renters arrived.

Clio and Jalal had gone through the work at all the other cottages as fast as possible, leaving Solitaire till last. They had hardly spoken all morning, except for what was absolutely required to get the work done.

She was nervous and jittery in his company, and it was harder to disguise than she would have guessed. Making the beds was the worst trial. Even with the space of a bed between them, his powerful aura seemed to affect her with longing and anguish. Or maybe it was *because* it was the space of a bed between them...

She knew he knew. But he said nothing. If she stiffened when his hand came too close, he did not make it obvious that he knew, but nevertheless withdrew his hand instantly.

He was careful not to brush up against her, always waiting till she left any room first....

After a while the embarrassment she felt at making her uncontrollable sexual awareness so obvious was adding acutely to her discomfort. Thank God he would have something else to do at Solitaire!

She glanced at her watch as they rounded the bend and the dock came in sight.

"Oh!" she remembered suddenly. "Will you keep your eye out for a cat while we're here?"

"A cat?" he repeated.

"A couple of weeks ago the Williamses were here with their cat, and it went missing. They had to leave without it. We've been leaving dry food out, which gets eaten— but that could be raccoons, of course. The Williamses are very upset. They call every second day, but none of the renters have seen anything so far."

"What colour is the cat?" he asked with a lazy smile.

"Black and white." She laughed at a sudden thought. "For goodness' sake, Jalal, don't go grabbing any skunks! If it's sporting a wide white stripe down the middle of its back, you leave it alone!"

He looked at her. "I don't intend to grab any black-

and-white cat, either. It will have to come to me of its own accord.''

She suspected him of double meaning, and her cheeks got hot. What was he suggesting? That if she wanted him she would have to make the first move?

That was just fine with her. She had no intention of exploring her newfound sexual self with him, one way or the other. She wouldn't be making any moves on him, and it was a relief to hear this declaration that he wouldn't be making any on her.

She wasn't naive enough to think that just because Jalal was maybe in love with Zara he wasn't actually attracted to Clio for her own sake, too. At sixteen, she had believed that kind of thing, but now she knew better. For men sexual attraction was a pretty random response. Of course he was capable of making love to Clio even if his heart was elsewhere. Men did that all the time, didn't they? Even men who could have the one woman they loved cheated.

And one thing had to be said in his behalf—at least the woman he really wanted was absolutely forbidden to him. He could hardly be expected to swear himself to chastity for the sake of another man's wife.

Looking at it rationally, Jalal really hadn't done anything *criminal*. It was just their mutual bad luck that the woman whose name he had murmured was Clio's sister, and that the incident held such deep and distressing memories for her.

Probably, like Peter, he would never figure out why a little slip like the wrong name in the heat of the moment bothered her so much. If he even realized it had escaped him. If he didn't, he probably figured she was a complete neurotic.

It was a huge relief to know he wouldn't be trying anything.

Thunder rumbled threateningly as he guided the boat in, and a sudden wind warned them that the rain was on top of them. Clio jumped onto the dock with the bow line. Heavy drops began to fall as Jalal off-loaded the plastic bag of linens and the toolbag.

On the verandah, she fished the keys out of her pocket. "I'll do the housework by myself, Jalal, if you want to get started on the generator."

He nodded as she pushed the door open. "Will you be all right on your own?"

He meant, because of what had happened last time they were here together. But she had been back every Saturday since that incident, and Solitaire was too lovely for bad associations to cling.

Still, on those other occasions, she hadn't gone inside alone. Ben had been with her.

"Would you mind just coming in with me first?" she asked.

Leaving his toolbag on the verandah, he stepped inside after her, and together they walked through the place. He was careful not to follow her through a doorway too closely.

But that only drew attention to the fact that they were completely isolated here.

Solitaire wasn't very big, only two bedrooms, but it was in a beautiful location. This cottage always got repeat customers.

Honeymooners in particular loved it. Several couples, having come for the first time on their honeymoon, came back year after year. The site was both sunny and secluded, with lots of mature deciduous trees. And you couldn't get more private.

The big L-shaped dining/sitting room was filled with dappled light throughout the day, though not on a day like today. Today it felt cosy and protected from the coming storm.

The master bedroom was beautifully decorated, and had a king-size bed....

When they had walked through the place together and found everything in order, Jalal picked up his tools again and went off through the rain to the small shed among the trees.

From one of the bedroom windows Clio watched him go, her heart thumping. He was so gorgeous. The way he moved, as if he'd been walking these forests for centuries! It appealed to something in her so deep it seemed to hurt her heart.

She noticed he didn't duck his head, or run, to avoid the rain. He seemed to like walking through rainfall. No, it wasn't quite that. He *accepted* the rain—in the same way as he accepted the earth under his feet, the tree branches that brushed his shoulders.

She watched, sighing, till he was out of sight among the trees.

She worked at an easy pace, while wind and rain began to slap at the windows. After absent-mindedly flicking the sitting-room lamp a few times, she realized she couldn't put the lights on with the generator down, and she worked in the grey half-light, dusting and polishing, stripping the beds and making them with fresh sheets, cleaning the bathroom and kitchen, laying out fresh towels.

And thought of Jalal.

I don't intend to grab any black-and-white cat. It will have to come to me of its own accord.

She supposed she would be forever grateful to him, once she got over the agony of repeating trauma. Whatever else he had done, he had shown her that she was a woman with a normal sex drive, and had given her back the promise of a fulfilled life.

Not with him, of course. And probably never again with the powerful passion she felt right now. Her feelings and emotions were so deeply aroused that she felt they could kill her. When she even thought of his name she was tortured, mentally and physically, by a mixture of pain and desire that brought her close to desperation.

She wanted him, with deep emotional and sensual passion. She was burning alive. And when she thought that she would never fulfill this yearning it was like being under torture. When she forced herself to remember the moment that he had whispered Zara's name, she was torn on a rack of fire and electricity.

She finished her work and wandered through the rooms, looking out at the storm. Now that she had nothing to do, the fury in her heart was no longer kept at bay. It began to swamp her.

She wanted him, passionately, desperately. What difference did it make if he preferred her sister? What did it matter, in the scheme of things? *Jalal* was not to blame for the horrific experience of her past. It wasn't his fault if she had an unconscious inferiority complex that was looking to be reinforced....

She wanted him. She hadn't wanted a man for years, and now she wanted Jalal like someone who'd been starving in a desert and come on a feast of champagne and lobster served on gold plate.

He was a mirage. She knew that. He wasn't a man who would love her for her own sake. No good could come of it. Nothing would come of this...except sexual pleasure.

She was as sure of getting that as if she had a written guarantee.

For the first time since the age of sixteen she had a chance to experience true sexual passion. What if it was also the last time? What if she was destined never to feel such powerful desire for anyone again? What if she slipped back into that grey, featureless, sexless inner self again when he was gone?

The cat must come to me....

The storm increased in fury all around the little cottage, but it was no worse than the storm in Clio's heart.

Fourteen

She stood gazing blindly out the broad window at the crashing storm, drowning in whirlpools of thought. Then, against the cloudy darkness behind the glass, she saw a sudden flicker of light.

She whirled to stare at the lamp behind her, on the little table. The one she had tried to put on a while ago. Clio gazed at it, almost hypnotized, as it flickered twice more and then settled to its normal steady glow.

The generator was fixed, then.

He would be coming in.

She was raging with anguish, indecision and desire. She couldn't face Jalal, not feeling the way she was at this moment. She couldn't be locked up with him here, miles from nowhere, in a storm!

Oh, if only she had understood what she was thinking before! She had believed it was cut-and-dried, that she had all the strength necessary to resist her feelings for him.

If she had had any inkling, she would never have risked coming out with him today, not for anything! Too late she realized she should have told her mother, should have confided the whole story, rather than be forced into this situation.

She whirled and rushed into the kitchen, turning on lights as she went, filled the kettle and plugged it in. She was busily setting out cups and the jar of instant coffee and powdered creamer when he opened the kitchen door and stepped inside.

There was a simultaneous flash of lightning and deep roll of thunder. As if he were produced by the storm. A storm devil...

She lifted her head as he closed the door, and they stood for an immeasurable moment, staring at each other while the thunder rolled away into silence.

Then he said, "I have never seen so much rain in all my life as comes down in this country in five minutes."

It broke the mood, and Clio jerked into action. He was soaked to the skin, absolutely dripping.

"Stay right there!" she cried. "Don't move or you'll drip water everywhere!"

She opened the bag of dirty linen and dragged out a towel at random, tossing it on the floor at his feet. "Stand on that while I get you a fresh towel!"

She ran into the bathroom and dragged one of the towels from the stack of fresh ones she had placed there. When she returned to the kitchen, Jalal had stripped off his jacket.

"What will you do for clean towels, if I use that?" he asked, hesitating, as she offered him the towel across the kitchen counter.

"We can give them fresh ones at the house when they pick up the keys," she said with a shrug.

But he shook his head. "It isn't necessary. This will serve."

He was rubbing his hair with a dry corner of his jacket. His polo shirt was also well soaked over the shoulders and chest.

"You'd better take that off, and I'll throw it in the dryer," she said.

He threw her a look. "I am fine."

"Jalal, you're soaked!" It was her mother's voice in her. "You'll catch your death if you wander around like that!"

He smiled. "My death is not so easily caught as that."

"I mean, you'll get a cold."

"No," he said quietly. She gazed at him, half hypnotized, and got the message. She swallowed with difficulty.

The cat must come to me....

The kettle began to hiss, and she used the sound as an excuse to turn away and fuss with the tray.

Thunder rumbled overhead, then there was another huge, bright flash of lightning and a crack of thunder like a bomb exploding over the roof.

"Well, we won't be getting out of here for a while!" she said with false brightness, as if it hardly mattered.

He stiffened. "We can drive the boat in the rain, can't we?" Spying a row of hooks by the door, he flung his jacket onto one. "I have done it with your father."

"Not when it's as heavy as this, and not when there's lightning. Visibility's nil out on the lake in a deluge like this, and a boat on the water attracts lightning."

His jaw tightened as if that was the last thing he wanted

to hear, but he made no comment beyond a murmured "I see."

She had chills racing up and down her back, along her arms and legs. Was he thinking about how easy sex would be right now? She was. So easy. A moment out of time. Madness that would be a thing apart. She was melting with her own heat.

She swallowed and lifted the boiling kettle to pour water on the coffee in the carafe. The aroma caught her nostrils with another temptation of the senses, teasing her with one sensual stimulus into thinking of others....

She picked up the tray and moved into the sitting room, and after a pause while he kicked off his muddy deck shoes, Jalal followed. Thunder and lightning were now almost continuous in the heavens, and the sitting-room windows gave them a front-row seat on the magnificent drama.

It was a real downpour, coming in sheets. It thundered on the roof, made the water in the river leap and dance, turned paths into channels of mud.

Jalal sat in an armchair, nodding when she had poured his coffee, and picking it up off the tray she had set on the table before the sofa.

"Is so much rain usual? Is this why people come here?"

She smiled. "They usually come for the sun. But it's been a wet season so far. A storm like this happens every five years or so, I guess."

There was a fireplace. How pleasant it would be to light a fire, Clio dreamed, and sit here on the sofa with someone you loved...it really was a perfect cottage for honeymooners.

The main front windows looked out on the river, but the window also turned the corner of the house, so that a narrow strip, beside the fireplace, looked out over the forest. In the dangerous silence that fell between them, Clio sipped her coffee and nervously turned her head to watch the rain bucketing down on the trees....

"My God, the *cat!*" she cried. On automatic reflex she slapped her cup down on the table and jumped to her feet, staring.

Out there, just on this side of the bridge over the part of the river that ran behind the house, sat a half-drowned black-and-white cat, its pink mouth piteously open in a cry that was drowned by the storm.

"Wousky!" She cried its name, though of course the cat couldn't hear her. "Wousky!"

She rushed to the front door and tore it open, while behind her Jalal was getting to his feet. "Are you going to—" he began, but Clio was already out in the deluge.

Good grief, it was even worse than it looked! This was like standing under Niagara Falls! She was drenched to the skin in a second, her shoes turned to pails of water. She put up her hands to protect her eyes and stared at where she had last seen the cat.

It had crossed the damn bridge, she saw, and was sitting under a leafy plant, soaked and bedraggled to the last degree. Muttering curses, Clio splashed across the grassy clearing, over the picturesque little footbridge, calling its name.

"Wousky, Wousky! Kitty, kitty, kitty!"

The cat sat as if waiting for her, but as she got closer, suddenly got to its feet and shot away again.

She answers to her name, Clio remembered the Williamses assuring her. Dammit, why did no cat on earth ever answer to its name, and why did owners persist in imagining that they did?

"No!" Clio wailed, and her foot slipped and she fell

headlong, landing full length in thick sloppy mud. "Oh, damn you, Wousky!" she cried. She struggled to her feet, covered in mud, just as Jalal arrived beside her.

Lightning illuminated the scene, and there the cat was, a few yards away, its pink mouth open, repeating the cry. Directly overhead the thunder cracked and rattled and applauded as if this were all a game.

"Wousky!" She tried again, taking another few steps. The cat waited as if wanting to be caught; then again, as she got close, dashed away.

"What are you doing? The cat will not let you catch her!" Jalal shouted.

"Yes," she contradicted him, pushing her mud-caked hair out of her face. "She's trying to tell us something. She's trying to lead us somewhere. Okay, Wousky, what is it?"

It wasn't unknown for an animal to lead humans to other humans or animals in trouble, and her heart was now kicking uncomfortably.

Wousky led them on into the forest, turning every few feet to check that they were following. Under the thick cover of the forest at least the rain was not so drowningly heavy, but wet leaves slapped them unmercifully, and Clio was starting to shiver.

"Can we find our way back?" Jalal asked.

Clio turned to glance back. Through the trees there was a tiny glow of light. "If she doesn't take us too much further we'll be okay."

Just then the cat stopped, beside a tree, wailing now in a voice that could be heard. "What *is* it?" Clio wondered, drawing close.

Then she saw. "Oh, my! Oh, *Wousky!*" she crooned.

In a hollow under a raised root, the cat had formed a nest. It must have seemed perfect when she built it, but the rain had turned it into a mudhole. She had done her best, dragging her tiny kittens up the slope of the hollow, but it had clearly filled deeper and deeper with water, and the kittens were now so far out they were exposed to the rain.

"Oh, Wousky, what a clever cat you are!" Clio told the anxious mother. She smiled at Jalal, who had squatted beside her. "Isn't that amazing? She must have realized we were there when the lights went on and come to get us!"

"This one is half drowned already," Jalal said, reaching carefully to pick up a kitten lying half in the puddle.

The mother moved anxiously to his side, watching as he examined the muddy kitten on his strong, safe palm. He stroked it with one finger, until he was rewarded with a pink-mouthed complaint.

Clio laughed in delighted relief. "Okay, we're going to fix this little problem, Wousky, don't you worry!" she cried.

One by one, she began to pick up the tiny bedraggled lumps of fur and, lifting her mud-stained T-shirt at the waist, she laid them carefully inside the little hammock that was formed.

"Four altogether," she said. "Is that all of them?"

Jalal was still carrying the one he had rescued. He bent over and ran his free hand through the puddle, dredging for bodies, then looked all around the area.

"I think we have them all," he said.

The cat made no complaint as they got to their feet and turned to leave, so they searched no further. With half-agitated, half-approving cries, Wousky rushed along the path and back to them, as if urging them to hurry.

They followed the light through the trees and came out at the bridge again. The rain was still torrential. In a few more minutes they were stepping inside the kitchen door. After such drama, it was almost strange to feel the peace of the cottage enclose them again.

Clio rinsed the mud from the kittens under the warm tap, making sure noses and mouths were clean and in working order, and then made a nest of some of last week's used towels beside the fireplace, where Wousky, after scoffing a huge amount of dinner, immediately settled down with the kittens and started to purr and lick.

Jalal meanwhile had lit a fire. Clio plugged in the space heater and drew it to the other side of the kittens' nest to give them more immediate warmth.

Then she got to her feet and stood looking down at herself. She was mud from head to foot. Jalal was almost as bad.

"Okay, I think we're next," she said.

Clio emerged from the shower wrapped in a huge towel, another one wrapping her hair. Jalal was where she had left him, in the kitchen, leaning against the counter, his arms across his chest, coffee cup in his hand.

She couldn't look directly at him as she moved past him to the washing machine.

"Your turn," she said, busily stuffing her muddy garments into it. "If you toss your things out, I'll put everything in the washer together."

Behind her she heard him set down his cup and move towards the bathroom. When the door closed, she heaved a massive sigh, trying to let go of the tension that gripped her.

A moment later, he did as she suggested, tossing his clothes out the bathroom door. Clio bent to pick them up, and heard the shower start again, and suddenly her mind was a jumble of erotic images of Jalal naked.

She gasped, leaning against the wall, while a sensual flood assailed her body and mind. She thought of the water hitting his body, saw the curling black hair on his chest, his hand stroking soap into it, the water drumming it into bubbles, the suds caressing his muscles, rinsing down his chest, his arms, his thighs, knees, ankles...those strong bare feet.

She heard the soft sound of him blowing water out, and knew that he was standing with his head under the stream, saw the water in his dark eyelashes, squeezed shut, on his lips....

The sound of the shower stopped suddenly, and she leapt guiltily, as though he might open the door the next second and catch her there, melting with passion for him.

She grabbed up his things and moved over to the washer, and, stuffing them in, added detergent and turned the dial. Water gushed into the machine and she held it, feeling the vibration under her hands.

She needed strength. She needed to think. But she was incapable of thinking, with him naked in the next room....

She could hear him moving around, and thought, *No wonder this place is popular with honeymooners!* The air seemed to have an erotic charge, as if the memory of passion had soaked into the fabric of the place, steeping the beams themselves with sensuality.

She fled into the sitting room, where Wousky, half-asleep, was purring in her nest, all her little ones glued to her teats, throbbing with the sensual pleasure of warm milk and the closeness of their mother's body.

Outside the rain still hammered down.

Clio went back to the kitchen and called up the main house on the CB radio. Her mother answered.

"Everything has ground to a halt here," Maddy said, after a few moments' chat. "We're just waiting for it to stop. I imagine people have stopped on the road to do the same. Stupid to try to drive in rain like this.''

"We'll be back when it's over," Clio said, and a moment later they signed off.

The thunder and lightning had passed over, and now it had settled down to a steady downpour. Clio stood in the sitting room staring out. She could see her own reflection in the glass, superimposed on the river and the rain.

She saw Jalal, a huge towel wrapped around his waist, a smaller one slung over his shoulders and naked chest, enter the room behind her.

Fifteen

____

She stayed where she was, staring into the glass, watching as he stepped slowly across the room towards her. When he was still several feet away she could feel his presence against her skin. Her body, already pumping with heat, leapt into sensual awareness as if his hand stroked her.

He stopped close behind her, and she saw how his head tilted as he looked down at her. Still she could not look at him directly.

Slowly his hand came up and cupped her naked shoulder. She twitched with the electricity that jolted through her, and swallowed, her lips pressed tight.

"Clio," he said softly. His other hand came up, and he gently, inexorably, turned her to face him.

"Look at me."

Her heart was leaping all over her body with fear, nerves, need. She raised her eyes and felt another powerful connection as their gaze met.

"Are you afraid?"

She looked away and gasped for air, sighing it tremblingly out. "A little, I guess," she admitted.

"Do not be afraid. We will go no further than you wish, now or any time. There will not come a point when I push you beyond what you can accept."

She was silent, staring out at the storm. The contented sound of the mother cat singing the song of security to her kittens purred on the air.

"Can you trust me to keep my word in this?"

"Look…" She licked her lips. "I'll be all right, it's just—if you could just…not say her name. I know you—"

Jalal moved one hand to lift her chin, making her eyes meet his. He was frowning. "What does this mean? 'Not say her name'?"

"A long time ago there was a guy who loved Zara and took me as second best, and it was—I was young, Jalal, it wasn't a good experience, it kind of—left me…raw." Her voice was trembling, though she was fighting to speak calmly. She swallowed against the huge lump of feeling in her throat and wondered if she could go any further with this.

He was listening closely. "He forced you against your will, wanting your sister?" he asked gently, masking his outrage.

"No…" she sighed on a sad, long outbreath. "No, he didn't force anything. It was just that…I didn't know till it was too late—almost too late—" she corrected herself ruthlessly "—that he was pretending I was Zara." She looked up at him, trying to smile matter-of-factly. "He said her name, and then I knew."

He was silent for long moments, so still as he watched

her that she imagined he understood and she wouldn't have to explain further.

"And what do you fear now? Are you afraid that I, too, will say the name of some other woman? I will speak no name but yours. I think no name but yours. Clio," he whispered urgently.

Desire and anguish in equal measure clutched at her.

"It's just—when you said her name last time, it just cut through me, I'm sorry. And if you did it ag—"

She realized, with a suddenly sinking heart, that she could not go through with it. She could not do this, no matter how desperately she wanted him. She couldn't do it to herself, knowingly make love with a man who loved someone else, fearing all the time that he might whisper her name.

"Whose name?" he demanded, frowning.

"I'm sorry," she said after a moment. "I can't do this after all."

"I said no one's name."

If he didn't even remember the moment, how could she hope that he would be able to control the impulse?

"Jalal, it doesn't really matter—"

"If you think I spoke another woman's name while making love to you, it matters very much! Whose name do you believe you heard me say?"

His certainty was so convincing. But she *had* heard it—she hadn't imagined it.

"Zara's. Maybe you didn't realize—"

"*Zara's!*" He was completely surprised, incredulous. "Why should I say your sister's name in such a moment? It is ridiculous! Do you believe that I desire my uncle's wife? I do not. What could you have heard? What did you imagine?"

She stared at the strong pulse in the top of his throat, the thick red terry cloth of the towel around his neck.

She took a deep breath, the better to stand her ground. "I didn't imagine it. I heard it. You said, *Zary*. As plain as day." She cleared her throat. "Funny, Zary is what I called her when we were kids. I didn't think anyone else ever used it."

"Zarie," he repeated, testing the word. He began to shake his head, but stopped. His eyes narrowed with concentration.

"*Zahri,*" he said, in another voice, as light dawned. "I called you *zahri,* is this what you heard?"

"Yes!" she said, suddenly hearing it again, the little explosion of breath on the vowel. "Yes, that was it! You said it."

"I said it, yes." He nodded. "This word means *my flower* in Arabic." His hand encircled her throat and gently tilted her chin. "I was not speaking of your sister, but of you. Of the flower of your beautiful body, that I wanted so much to open for me."

A storm of sensation coursed through her, blowing her flat. Clio's head fell back. She sighed out all her pent-up tension and anguish on a long moan of surrender.

"And this is all there is to fear?" he demanded in a harsh whisper. "There is no other torment in your past— only this one word?"

She took a deep breath, trying to cope with the sensations that were rushing up and down and over her skin in a thousand directions at once. Suddenly she felt she wanted to weep.

She sniffed, and a breath of air escaped from her throat on a half sob. "That's it!" she said brightly. "That's all she wrote!"

Without another word Jalal bent and slipped an arm

under her knees and, lifting her high in his strong arms, turned towards the bedroom.

Beside the bed he set her on her feet, and as he did so the towel around her body began to slip from its moorings. She clutched at it, but he caught her wrist.

"Let me see you," he ordered.

At the tone of sheer possessiveness in his voice, she melted into fainting stillness. He clasped her other wrist and held both hands helplessly away from her body, his eyes burning into her as the towel slipped and spiralled around her breasts and hips like a lover's hands, and fell to the floor.

He stood gazing at her.

Intensely dark brown eyes under strong brows such as the poets loved, questioning, nervous, and watching him with such a strength of wanting his heart kicked brutally with answering hunger. Her wide, mobile lips alternately smiling and pressing against each other, wet and shining where she licked them, a pink that matched the dark pink nipples shivering to awareness under his gaze as it travelled down to those high, heavy breasts. A long, slender waist curving into sloping hips that invited a hand's caress...long smooth legs...

"You are a beautiful woman," he breathed hoarsely. "Poems have been written about you for a thousand years, and I did not know."

"About me?" She smiled.

He nodded. "They called you *Asheeq.*"

Her wide mouth moved, tremulous with feeling. "What does it mean?"

"Beloved," he murmured. "*Asheeq* is Beloved. *Anti asheeqi.*"

He lifted his other hand to the bright towel that wrapped

her hair, and pulled it free. Her wet hair fell heavily over one shoulder and down her back. She shivered as its weight pulled her scalp, caressed her skin. She trembled at the look in his eyes.

Passionate desire such as she had never experienced flowered and blossomed in her in bright bursts, as if a rich, thick garden burst into ripe fullness in the space of seconds. Perfume, colour, the silky touch of new petals crowded her senses all at once, stroking her into wild anticipation....

And he had scarcely touched her save with his eyes. Clio was almost frightened for what would happen when he touched her with his hands.

Slowly, still watching her, he pulled the towel from around his own neck and dropped it to the floor. Then his hands carefully, irresistibly, cupped her shoulders, drew her against his body, made her breasts press his warm naked chest, her thighs brush the thick terry that covered his muscled thighs. His head bent and his mouth tasted hers...and then devoured it with a suddenness that made her gasp.

His hunger for her melted her into wildest need. When his hand clasped her head to pull her lips more urgently against his, when his arm encircled her back to drag her tight against him, her body sensed his deep hunger and sent thrilling heat through her. When his fingers squeezed and his palms pressed her back, thighs, arms, urgent messages zipped along her nerves, igniting fire beacons everywhere to signal her hunger to her whole body.

After an eternity of kisses, gentle and passionate, teasing, tasting, urgent...his lips left hers.

"Lie down," he said.

She turned in his hold to the high mattress and drew off the spread, tossing it down to the foot, hiked one knee up, then the other, and slipped on all fours towards the centre of the wide bed.

She heard a gasp of indrawn breath, and his hands enclosed her hips in firm command, stopping her where she was.

And then, before she knew what was happening, his mouth came at her from behind, directed with unerring suddenness between her legs, its damp heat thrusting sharp pleasure against the nerve centre of her being.

She cried out uncontrollably. And again. She tried to move, for the pleasure was unfamiliarly shocking her system, but his hands grasped her thighs, irresistibly, pulling them apart to give him better access. She was pinned to the place, by his grip and by the pleasure that poured through her, raising her desire to a pitch she hadn't known existed.

She could do nothing except wait, her thighs opening uncontrollably to his mouth, her knees spreading further, her whole body listening to the buildup of nearly intolerable sweet need as his tongue stroked, rasped, caressed, pushed the pleasured anticipation along her nerves.

She had expected nothing like this. So quick, so overwhelming, a need so desperate it was almost rage. She began to whimper her urgent need for release from his tongue's hungry stroking, his mouth's hot embrace, from the savage yearning they made her feel.

He went on with that wild, rough, relentless caress, building the torment till it could hardly be borne. Her mind reeled and she lost herself—to a primitive, barbarian, all-consuming need that she had hidden from herself for too long.

She pressed her upper body down, clutching a pillow and burying her face in it, moaning, arching her body to his mouth without shame—totally, utterly dedicated to her own pleasure.

Then at last it happened: hot, sweet release began a slow spiral out from under his mouth and poured over all her skin and muscles, to every fingernail, to each single hair tip. As the throbbing pleasure reached her throat Clio cried aloud, a long, haunting cry of gratitude and release.

When it had passed, she collapsed flat on the bed, and six and a half years of pent-up need flowed and flowered and was satisfied in her.

"Oh, thank you! Oh, Jalal, that was so sweet!" she murmured to the pillow in a husky, sensual voice that made his eyes narrow as he looked at her. "Oh, so delicious! Oh, was there ever anything like that since the dawn of history! Will there ever be anything like it again!"

Behind her, dropping his own towel to the floor, he smiled.

"I think I can promise that there will be," Jalal said softly.

Languidly she rolled over and lay with her head curved at an angle to look at him. His body was so beautiful. As he stretched out on the bed beside her, she admired the flexing and contracting of his whole musculature, the gorgeous shape of him, the hard, hungry, long, strong sex.

She looked away to catch her breath, and he came down beside her, one hand carefully enclosing her breast, the other tangling in her damp hair.

She stroked his cheek, smiling lazily, brushed the generous lips. He drew her finger into his mouth and sucked it, and as pleasure contracted in her abdomen the spiral of tension started again. She grunted softly.

His hand strayed again to the mat of pleasure-dampened hair between her thighs, and his thumb toyed there, watching while her eyelids fluttered. Her hands sought out his body, and stroked him, feeling with delighted curiosity where he was smooth and where hair roughened his skin, how muscle curved into muscle....

When she touched his engorged sex his eyes narrowed and his lips parted in a deeply erotic smile, his teeth flashing white. She explored the smooth hardness with a joy she could hardly contain, swept with a wanton, hungry flood of feeling she had believed herself incapable of.

"Oh, I love this!" she cried, her hand tightening possessively on him.

Then, as his hand stroked her to a sudden second release, she arched her back, thrusting her hips up, and as the pleasure peaked and sank away he was suddenly above her, moving his legs between hers as she willingly opened herself to him.

Her pleasure had barely ebbed when he pushed into the hot pulsing rose. It enclosed him with hungry gratitude, and he thrust further and further in, till he had reached his length in her. He heard her cry of satisfaction then, and knew he had waited all his life for such a cry.

He wrested himself from the rose's loving embrace, and wildly thrust home again, and she grunted with such deep surprise he gasped in a fierce, almost uncontrolled response.

He pounded into her over and over, each thrust causing a savage pulse of pleasure through her system. Helplessly she cried his name, and then she wordlessly moaned, and then, losing her knowledge of time, of place, of self, she sank into a wordless thirst for the pleasure he gave her, drinking it in with choking, desperate sighs.

Only pleasure mattered now, pleasure that shimmered out beyond her own body, so that she felt her joy as far as she could reach, and in the air that surrounded them.

With crazy, unbelieving joy she stroked the marvellous body, felt how the strong back, the clenching buttocks, the powerful shoulders and thighs moved under her hands, felt how the hard masculine sex moved within her.

He bent his head, murmuring, and smothered her mouth with a hungry kiss, thrusting as wildly with his tongue as with his body, to drive them both beyond the reach of everything they knew, deep into the unknown.

She heard his wild cry and felt the pulsing throb of his sex in her, in the same moment, and at last more pleasure than her system could hold burst through her. She arched up to meet his body's desperate thrust, and again, and again, and then wild pleasure coursed through them, seeking and finding that timeless place they sought, in the Other.

Sixteen

They lay in each other's embrace, listening to their heart-beats reflected in the rain. His arm was around her, Clio's head nesting in the curve of his shoulder, her arm lying across his chest, her hand lazily stroking his shoulder and arm.

She was humming a tuneless hum, just on the breath, without knowing it. He lay listening, a smile pulling at his lips.

"You are like the cat," Jalal murmured.

"Mmm? I am?"

"You are purring."

Suddenly hearing her own song for the first time, she laughed. "I suppose I am."

"Do you always purr at such moments?" he asked. It was a jealous question. He would not have voiced it if he had known what he was going to say.

"I've never had such a moment before, so I wouldn't know," Clio replied in a matter-of-fact tone.

His fingers, stroking her flank lazily, stilled.

"Never had—what do you mean? Do you tell me that no man has before known how to please a woman of such passion as you? What sort of men does this culture produce?"

"Oh, plenty of dedicated ones, really." She lifted herself on an elbow and smiled down at him. "I've been in a cage. Some very nice guys tried, but no one before you could find the key."

It shook Jalal to the core. He kissed her with an abrupt surge of passion, rolled her over on her back, and thrust his way inside again. She gasped and melted with the suddenness of it, and, her body still swollen with fulfilled desire, accepted his wild thrusting with mews of delight. Almost at once she was driven up to the peak again, and over, crying wildly, feeling how his hands, wrapped in her hair and around her wrist, clenched with his own joy.

"Mmm," she sighed appreciatively, when they had become calm again, and he found that that sound in her throat stirred him to his core. It was necessary to him now, like water, and he suddenly felt it would be so forever. He had been seeking something all his life, but had only known that it was so when he found what he sought.

Jalal kissed her lightly on her sweat-damp shoulder, loving her passionate openness and responsiveness. That such a woman had found so little joy in a body made for pleasure was almost unbelievable.

"You have—what do you say?—some catching up to do."

"Years," she agreed with a smile at once satisfied and longing.

"Perhaps it can be condensed."

She glinted at him with a glance of such sensually charged abandon that he felt it like a blow.

But as he reached for her again she sat up, her damp hair tousled all around her shoulders, smiling down at him with lazy, pleasure-sated eyes.

"I wish we could stay here all night," she said. "But people will be arriving as soon as the rain lets up."

She slipped off the bed and padded into the kitchen, where she quickly transferred their clothes from washer to dryer. She returned to the bedroom and bent to pick up the scattered towels, then hesitated. He was just getting to his feet.

"Do you want another shower?"

He looked at her, sex on his mind. "Yes," he said. "Let us go to the shower."

She melted where she stood, dropping the towels again, and let him lead her into the bathroom. The stone-tiled floor was cool underfoot, adding another sensual input to her already overloaded nerve pathways. When the soft flow of water came down over them, she sighed with delight.

He caught her under the buttocks. "Put your legs around me," he muttered, and she could only moan in anticipation and obey, wrapping herself around his hips, opening her thighs to the magnificent body, ready for her again.

He set her back against the shower wall, grasped her thighs, and slipped hungrily between the soft petals of the rose again.

Water and pleasure simultaneously flowed over and through their bodies, soft and delicious, combining into a sweet rosewater that their senses could taste. He thrust a little, then paused and, supporting her with one hand, lifted the other to the bud of the rose, and caressed it till her tears of joy mingled with the water that poured so luxuriously over them, and her clenching, spasmodic submission to the pleasure brought him his own release.

The rain abated. They tidied the cottage, laundered the sheets and remade the bed, leaving the towels they had used still whirling in the dryer, and a note on the table for the renters. Then they carefully set the kittens into a small cardboard box and Jalal carried it down to the boat, with Wousky anxiously watching from a supervisory position over Clio's shoulder.

The sky was clearing, the sun breaking through to make an appearance over a wet world. She stood within the circle of his arm as he steered the boat for home, and felt a closeness she hadn't felt for a man since that night with Peter, and a lightness of spirit she had hardly imagined possible.

"I want to know about this man who hurt you," he said. "Will you tell me the story?"

"I've never told anyone," Clio murmured, half to herself. No wonder the incident had had such a hold over her imagination. She had never known how to tell even her mother about such deep humiliation, and of course she had never told Zara, but she could tell Jalal.

"He was kind of what you'd call my high school crush," she began. "I was thirteen and just starting, and he was in his final year. I thought he was so gorgeous...."

She took him through it, step by step, and as they sped across the lake, the clouds dispersed completely and the sun glowed over the scene, all so clean and fresh after such thorough washing, and it really seemed like a metaphor for her own soul. All the anguish, all the dust of the past, washed away by Jalal's passion.

His face hardened when she described that night when

she had lost so much more than her innocence, but he didn't interrupt.

"What does that mean, jailbait?" he asked when she had arrived at the bitter end.

"For a guy of nineteen or twenty to make love with a girl under sixteen is illegal here, even if she consents," she explained. "He could have gone to prison if he hadn't waited till I was at the legal age of consent."

He was silent as they headed under a picturesque bridge. "Oh, someone's in the MacAllister place," Clio observed absently when they came out the other side.

Jalal looked startled. "Pardon?"

She pointed through the plastic window of the rain hood. "See them up there on the deck?"

He glanced up as they passed the mansion-sized summer house, but didn't answer.

"What has happened to Peter?" he went on after a moment.

"Happened?"

"Has he married?"

"Married? Golly, no, he's only twenty-five or six! He still runs his father's car dealership, last time I looked. I guess he dates, but I have no idea who. I saw him once in the street a couple of years ago. He was driving yet another splashy sports car. I don't suppose he'll want to trade that in for a station wagon for a long time yet."

"He is a fool," Jalal said with an amused smile, as if Peter were about as important as last week's newspaper.

Clio laughed, light and free. "The sun's out, let's take the rain hood down!" she said, and he stopped the boat and they quickly did so.

"Now," he said, as if he understood more than she had

said. "Now the wind will blow tangles into your hair. And tonight...tonight I want to lie in the tangles again."

"Of course he is interested," Saifuddin ar Ratib said carefully. "He would not wish to commit himself until he sees exactly what we have to offer."

"He must be made to commit himself," said the voice at the other end of the phone.

"Of course, Excellency."

"If I made myself known to him too soon, he might be tempted to expose me to his uncles in exchange for a return to their good favour. We must have him compromised first."

"Can he possibly have any loyalty to them? Do you fear it? A man who has been sent into exile?"

"Did you not tell me you sensed that he had some sentimental attachment to them?"

"I did, Excellency. Partly perhaps because he feels he owes the course of his life, his education, to the care of his grandfather the king."

At the other end of the wire there was a thoughtful pause. "You are right, as always, Saifuddin. Now is the time to tell him. Call me again when it is done."

Jalal was late for dinner. He had taken a boat out, no one knew where, shortly after he and Clio brought the cat and kittens back from Solitaire. It wasn't usual for Jalal to miss a family meal without warning, and everybody was wondering what had happened.

Clio's worries now had more, not less potency. What if she had to choose between loyalties? If Jalal was conspiring against the princes—

It was the evening of their regular self-defence class, which made the children even more anxious. "He always says discipline is important, so he wouldn't just miss the class," Ben said.

"Well, then, he'll be back in time for the class," Maddy said. "Will you all please stop worrying? Someone phoned for Jalal and I gave him the message when he got in. He probably went to see someone and just got delayed."

Did he have an accent? The question arose in her mind completely against her will, but Clio gritted her teeth and managed not to speak it aloud.

"Where *is* Jalal?" Donnelly asked in a hopeless voice, for the third time, and Clio smiled at her with deep fellow feeling. Donnelly was right—the family group was not complete without him.

The sound of a boat engine made them all stop talking to listen. It came closer, making all the familiar noises of drawing up at the family dock, and the kids began to smile and sigh with relief.

Clio bit her tongue to stop herself smiling too much, but when Jalal's light footstep was heard on the verandah and he came through the door, she was grinning as broadly even as Donnelly.

"Jalal, Jalal!" the child cried in her sweet, piercing voice, as if the end of the world had been averted at the last minute.

He came in smiling, picked up his plate from the table in a way that had become totally familiar, and went to the stove to pluck a cob of corn from the pot there.

Everyone was chatting, relaxed, happy. Jalal sat down at the table and flicked Clio a glance so loaded her heart started jumping like a sheep caught in a fence. Her father said something, her mother replied, and the river of life flowed on in the big friendly kitchen as it had always done.

Clio marvelled that she could sit in the middle of all the usual family row, and connect to Jalal as intimately as if they were alone on an island...and know that, in the last couple of hours, wherever he had gone, something had happened to worry him.

When supper was over and the dishwasher stacked, it was time for the self-defence class. Surrounded by kids, Jalal flicked Clio a glance. She nodded with her eyelashes, swallowed convulsively, and felt her cheeks go hot. When she risked another look at him his jaw was tight with brutally imposed self-control.

They all rushed out, leaving Clio with her parents in the kitchen. A part of her had wanted him to cancel the class, but she knew he couldn't. You couldn't teach self-discipline without practising it.

So she helped her mother as usual in the kitchen, and then, turning down a TV film, went upstairs, to while away the time in luscious anticipation and sybaritic preparation till he could come to her.

She bathed in her sexiest perfumed bath oil, an expensive Christmas present she had never used before, and conditioned her hair, and gave herself a manicure and a pedicure, painting her nails a creamy bronze that matched her tan. She rubbed body satin everywhere.

She sprayed perfume into her hair, blew it dry and left it to spread freely over her shoulders and back.

But when it came time to dress, she discovered a gap in her wardrobe that she had never noticed before: she did not have one lacy, sexy nightgown or piece of underwear anywhere in her drawers. There was the little turquoise silk slip and matching robe her parents had given her for her last birthday, and that was the closest thing she had to a garment deliberately designed to ignite a man's desire.

In the end, she slipped on one of Jude's cast-off shirts in peach oxford cotton. It was worn and a little frayed, but blissfully soft.

And underneath...only her own brown body, already melting at the thought that he would soon be here, leaping with excitement when, a few moments later, she heard the soft footfall on the stairs, igniting into ready flame when the tap on the door was followed by her dark lover....

Clio was lying on one elbow on the bed, with a book that she hadn't been able to read a word of, the room softly lighted, the window of her tiny balcony open on a magical night. Soft blues wafted from the speakers of her CD player. Outside the lake glinted with the reflected light of moon and stars and the lamps of the houses around its shores. A fresh breeze stirred the open curtains, caught his robe as he turned to shut the bedroom door behind him.

He stood for a moment looking down at her. Jalal dressed like a Westerner during the day, but at night, when relaxing, he sometimes reverted to the clothes of his homeland. Tonight he was wearing an oriental-print green-and-gold dressing gown in flowing cotton, open over a bare chest and loose trousers tied at the waist. He looked like a fantasy sheikh.

The sight of him, so dark and exotic in the strong colours, made her heart beat even faster. She tilted her chin to smile at him, and he bent over her and kissed her.

She lifted her arms around his neck as he sank down on the bed over her. She felt his hands busy with the buttons on her shirt, and then he pushed the soft fabric aside and he lifted his head and his eyes and his hand stroked her bare shoulder, her breast, her stomach. Then he drew her naked breasts against his warm chest and devoured her lips with another kiss.

She was already on fire with need, with the memory of the pleasure he could give her, with deep anticipation. She moaned against his mouth and felt his body leap in response.

"I hunger for you, Clio," he murmured against her lips, with a fierce desperation that thrilled her with longing. "Kiss me, kiss me."

Shivers of electric feeling burnt over her body, making her womb melt into readiness, lifting her rosebud nipples to his attention. She felt with hungry, yearning abruptness that she could never get enough of him, that until their bodies and souls fused forever into one being she would not have what she sought from him.

He rolled over onto his back, drawing her onto his chest, cupping her head and kissing her again. She lifted her head and gazed down into his eyes with hungry urgency.

"I love you," she whispered, and gasped as she heard her own words, understanding their truth only as she heard them.

"I love you, Clio," Jalal said, and her heart beat with such crazy wildness she couldn't find breath.

Seventeen

His two hands came up to encircle her head as if she were both precious and fragile, a perfect rose, and his dark eyes gazed into hers.

"You looked at me at the wedding, do you remember? And you said, *We will never be friends....*"

"I remember," she murmured, ashamed.

"I knew then. I knew that you were right—not friends, we were not destined to be friends, you and I, but much more. I knew then that I would not rest until you called me Lover."

She smiled, though tears were burning her eyes. "Lover," she whispered.

His mouth trailed sweet fire along the underside of her chin, her ear, and down her throat to the pulse that beat there.

"*Asheeqi,*" he murmured there, and monitored with his lips the pulse's leap into wild disarray.

Under her shirt his hands caressed her back, her waist, her thighs, with a firm, hungry possessiveness that thrilled and burned her. His eyes were like doorways into the black depths of the universe, and he gazed at her, drinking her in.

His fingers slipped between her thighs and began to toy with the rose with a touch like the brush of silk. He smiled and watched her response, watched her eyes lose focus, her eyelids droop, her mouth purse and swell with sensuous swooning.

When her hips began to press against him, he rolled her over onto her back and lay above her, one arm under her head, his other hand trailing in the mat of hair that hid the petals of the rose. He cupped one thigh and drew it aside, to give his hand and his eyes better access. And then his fingers began a sweet, slow torment of stroking amongst the damp petals, and around the pulsing bud, over and over and over, with the utmost patience.

Unbelievably delicious sensations began to uncurl in her at this urging, an intensely burning fire without flame followed the trail that his finger drew on her flesh, a heat that was almost unbearable, a sweetness sweeter than the sweetest sugar....

He was in no hurry. He did not try to rush her, though at any time he could have brought the pleasure on her just by applying a more concentrated pressure...he just went on, slowly and deliberately, drawing lines of fire over her skin that reached deep inside her body.

When the pleasure slowly spiralled out in her at last, needing no effort from her, nothing but to lie and accept it, it was so intense that she did not know whether it was pleasure or pain that she felt. All she knew was how her whole body drank it in, like a starved desert in a flood.

Only when it was over could she make a sound, so

intently had she been listening to the physical joy he gave her. Then she gasped, and sighed, and told him her gratitude with words and smiles and wordless moans.

They kissed and toyed, and laughed with total joy. And then Jalal stripped off his robe and his trousers and lay down again beside her, and her breath hissed between her teeth as she admired his handsome body, the instrument of her pleasure.

"Come over me," he said. He suited the action to the word by drawing her thigh over his, till she was above him on her knees, her hair falling down her back, her thighs parted over his.

He drew her hips down and fitted their bodies together, and pulled her firmly down against him, and together they grunted their satisfaction at this union.

He reached up to strip off the shirt that still swathed her shoulders, dragged it down her arms, and tossed it aside, and then his hands cupped and caressed her shoulders, ran along her upper arms, trailed across her midriff and slipped up to curl over the full, heavy breasts.

At the same time he moved in her, hard, and she gasped and fell forward onto her hands, so that her breasts were pressed into his hold, and her hips began involuntarily writhing against the pleasure of him inside her.

He thrust in her, watching how the concentration of pleasure was mirrored in her face, and when her body began to push and seek, he grasped her hips, pulling her body against his, so that the joy fountained up and gave her the release she sought.

She sank down against him, her breasts pressing his chest, her mouth against his ear, sighing the little noises of gratitude that made his flesh leap. He pulled her face over his and kissed her, knowing that never before had he taken such pleasure in the giving of pleasure. Feeling for the first time that to give one woman pleasure could be enough for a man, all his life long.

She was moving against him in a search for more, and he gripped her thighs and moved her against him till her body's clenching response relaxed.

"Now," he murmured, and rolled over with her again, and this time he rose above her, their bodies still joined. His thighs pushed her thighs wide apart, and he began to thrust with hard, purposeful thrusts, deep within.

She grunted in hunger, and she knew that what he had given her had merely ignited her whole body, to prepare it for this. Each thrust was a whole new world of intense physical sensation, as if he reached inside her soul....

She tossed her head as her cries became wilder and wilder, and she lost her awareness of the room, the light—she was aware only of pleasure. Even self was gone, even Jalal was lost in the cloudy haze of physical and mental sensation, the deepest, maddest pleasure she could possibly imagine, and more.

Still he drove into her, on and on, until time also had no meaning, until for both of them there was only the depths of darkness, where the jewel they sought lay hidden, but sending out shafts of fire....

They entered the utter darkness, then, and clasped the jewel, and its light shimmered through their united selves until they cried out in helpless gratitude with the perfect joy, perfect knowledge the jewel contained, and its blinding light.

"What has worried you tonight?" she asked, lying with him in the still night, with music playing softly.

He was silent. Then, "It is nothing to do with anything here. Nothing to do with your fam—"

Then he remembered Zara, and broke off.

Her heart began to beat in hard, anxious thuds. "Is it something to do with Barakat?"

He sighed. "If I tell you, Clio, it will be to put a burden on you that you can share with no one. You can mention it to no other living soul. Do you wish for such a burden?"

"Oh, God," she whispered. "I'm not sure I can stand this. How—what kind of a burden?" If it was the burden of choosing between his happiness and Zara's...how could she bear it?

He wound a hand in her hair. "It would be very dangerous if you spoke of it. You must understand that lives will be in danger. Do you accept to know?"

"Is one of the lives yours?"

He was silent, merely gazing at her from his dark eyes, but she knew.

"Is—is one Zara's?"

Jalal took a breath and stroked her hair, down over her scalp and where it lay across her shoulder. "I am doing my best to see that this is not a danger."

"Oh, my God!" Clio closed her eyes painfully. "I don't think I want to know."

They were silent for a moment, while she wondered if she had made the coward's choice. Could he be the man he was, the man she knew him to be, and be plotting a horror? And yet—if he *was* conspiring with someone—shouldn't she try to find out?

But she was afraid to hear something that would destroy her newfound joy. One day? Was that all that was allotted to her? No, she couldn't face that. What would it hurt if she lived in ignorance a few more days?

"I may have to return soon to Barakat," Jalal said suddenly. His hand grasped hers, and he kissed it. "If I go, Clio—will you go with me?"

Her heart kicked painfully. The change was too quick for her. "What?"

"If circumstances call me home—come with me, Clio."

"To the Emirates?" she almost wailed. "For how long? It's right in the busiest part of the season!"

"For how long? Forever! Will you marry me? I love you, Clio. I want you to come home with me. Please be my wife."

She gazed into his face, her heart racing and kicking. Warmth seemed to pulse through her system, as if love had its own pathways that also came from the heart. But—

"Oh, Jalal."

"Say yes."

"Go away from here? Forever?"

He reached for her, and drew her into his arms. She clung to him. Her eyes moved around her room, pausing at the curtains billowing on the night breeze, and she listened to the magic cry of the lake.

Owl, and Bear, and Wolf seemed to cry out to her from the distant hills. She would not hear their voices anymore, in the desert.

"We will visit," he said.

"I can't!" she breathed. "Jalal, it's my home!"

"I will give you a new home. A palace, with fountains and beautiful things. We will not be far from the mountains…."

"I can't go and live in another country! I belong here!"

His eyes darkened. It was her early reaction. Women softened in such matters where they loved…if she loved. It was a woman's role to follow her husband.

Abruptly he thought of his grandmother, her broken-hearted yearning for the high country of her youth. If he took Clio back to Barakat, would she also tell her children stories of the land she loved and longed for? But if he did not, how would he survive?

"Clio, I have found you now. You are everything to me. Do not you love me?"

Tears burned her eyes. "I love you! I love you, I want to be with you! But—oh, Jalal, please don't ask me this!"

He had no answer. He drew her down and kissed her with urgent passion, covering her body with his own, seeking solace for his tormented soul within.

The morning was bright after the previous day's torrential rain; it was going to be a scorcher.

"You're going to be swamped in the ice cream shop today, and last night's delivery didn't get through," Maddy commented over breakfast.

Clio was grateful for the necessity to concentrate on everyday things. She had awakened depressed and didn't want to think about the choice facing her. Why was love so full of pain? It was supposed to be wonderful.

In the small hours of the morning, Jalal had left her, and she had fallen asleep before he returned. When she awoke this morning, she was alone, but the light had been turned out, so she supposed he had found her asleep and gone to his own room.

It seemed like a portent of the future.

This morning, they had sat in their usual places, about as far apart as two people could be at the Blakes' big table. She had arranged that herself, how long ago? In the dark ages when she had believed she hated Jalal.

And now she loved him, but it was still a dark age....

"...probably a good idea to call," she surfaced to hear her mother saying.

He had smiled at her as he left with her father for the

marina a few minutes ago, but his smile, too, was dark with torment.

She thought of Zara, making the choice so easily, as if it were nothing more than a new dress—a new country, a new people, a new family...how could she have faced it so easily?

"Clio, where on earth are you this morning?"

"What?" She blinked, trying to replay the mental tape of what her mother had said, but she had been too deeply lost in her own thoughts even to record it. "Sorry, Mom, what did you say?"

"What is it, Clio? You look as though a Bearwalker is after you."

A little choke of laughter escaped her, and then suddenly she was weeping. "Oh, Mom, I don't want to leave here! I don't want to spend the rest of my life in a place where no one understands what a Bearwalker is!"

Maddy Blake jumped to her feet. "What? Darling, why should you? Leave?" Then her face lost all expression. "No!" she breathed. "Not Jalal? Not you and Jalal?"

"He asked me to marry him last night."

"Oh, darling! Not you, too! Oh, Lord, why didn't I listen when you said not to let him come? Oh, no, not you, too, thousands of miles away! Oh, will all my daughters leave me?"

"Mom, I didn't say yes. I love him, but how can I leave here? I *know* this is my home! If it were somewhere like Quebec or something—but so far away?" She buried her face in her hands. "Tell me what to do!" she whispered.

Her mother slipped into the chair beside her, put an arm around her daughter's shoulders.

"I wish I could just say, no I can't do it, and that would be the end of it. Why does love have to be so hard? I thought it was supposed to be wonderful—we didn't even get one day of real...real happiness.''

Her mother blew out a troubled breath. ''What a fool I was. Bring a man like him here...''

''What do you think, Mom? Could I be happy? Would I learn to love the country, would loving him make up for...everything?''

Maddy's eyes fell. ''I don't know, Clio,'' she said. She took a deep breath and tried to forget her own feelings. ''Don't forget, you'd have Zara close by. You wouldn't be...''

''Zara is in East Barakat. Jalal told me last night that his place is in the capital. That's miles away from Zara.''

The ice cream shop doorbell rang, and both women, instinctively responding to duty, looked up. ''That must be Willa with the ice cream,'' said Maddy.

''I'll go.'' Clio got up and bent to kiss her mother's cheek before dashing out to open the shop door for the delivery woman.

''Oh, boy, what a day that was!'' said Willa cheerfully. ''All that rain totally ruined my schedule!'' Willa was practically a one-woman band, making and delivering her ice cream, and even growing some of the fruit she used in it.

She and Clio had been friendly for years, just another of the pleasant strands of Clio's life that bound her here to Love Lake. She wasn't a close friend. If Clio moved to Barakat Willa was one of the many people she would probably never see again. A single thread in the tapestry of her life, perhaps, but still there would be a hole if it were plucked out.

''You feeling okay?'' Willa asked, as the two women unloaded the tubs of ice cream and carried them into the freezer.

"Yeah, just fine," Clio lied. "I had a bit of a headache yesterday, but it's going now."

A few minutes later she waved goodbye to Willa and began to prepare the shop for opening.

She stood for a moment looking around the shop. She had never wanted more than this. Zara had always had her ears tuned to a different drummer, but not Clio. She had never wanted a palace, she scarcely even hankered after one of the mansions on the lake. A few years ago her father had taken a vote on whether they wanted him to buy one of the big places that had come up for sale...they had all, in the end, preferred to stay where they were.

Wife of the Grand Vizier of the Barakat Emirates.

Arwen came in. "Gosh, what a fabulous day!" She suddenly looked at Clio. "Clio, what's the matter?"

"Nothing. I had a headache yesterday. I didn't sleep very well."

Arwen stood straight. "I can look after the shop if you want to go and take a swim or something."

"Thanks, honey, but there's actually quite a bit to do. The ice cream only came in this morning and we have to get all the tubs changed."

"Oh, boy, does the butter pecan need to be scraped out? Can I do it?"

The small joy of a sister who loved butter pecan ice cream. Clio stood looking at Arwen and knew that, one way or the other, this decision was going to kill her.

Eighteen

─────

They made love that night with a passion that took them both to a country of wildest pleasure, and beyond its borders to a place of naked pain. To reach together that place of total union was to know that they were not truly united, and that night she wept with joy and sorrow intermingled.

Afterwards, they lay entangled in each other's arms, their bodies wet with their exertions in the hot night.

They chatted of uncontroversial things, like ordinary lovers, but in the back of her mind worry nibbled like a mouse at the cheese of her happiness.

"You said—" she began suddenly, almost without meaning to, then pressed her lips together and heaved a sigh. "Jalal, last night you said there was danger."

He nodded. "You wish me to tell you about it?"

"I think I have to know."

He paused, as if searching for the words. "There are

men who wish to overthrow the reign of my uncles. They wish to reunite the Barakat Emirates into the Kingdom of Barakat, under one king. A puppet king, whom they will control because they have put him in power.''

Her horrified breath hissed in her throat.

"You?"

His chin moved. "I am of inestimable value to such a conspiracy. Because my father was Aziz, there are many in the country who believe, or will be convinced, that I have a valid right to the throne. And if these people are taught that the division of the kingdom has been a bad thing, if they are brought to anger because their frivolous rulers have all married foreign women—then they will accept it when they are told that the answer is to put another king on the old throne...."

"Is all this propagandizing going on now?" she asked.

"There are rumours, articles in certain papers. My uncles knew—suspected that it was not chance. But how to find those who instigate the unrest?

"So publicly they sent me abroad to study...but the rumour escaped that I had been banished for conspiring against them.''

In the warm night air, Clio suddenly began to shiver. She leaned over Jalal to pluck her nightshirt from the floor, then sat up cross-legged on the bed, slipped her arms into the sleeves and wrapped it around her, her arms tight across her breasts.

"What do you mean? Is it—I don't understand.''

"They hoped that this would make those who plotted believe that I would be vulnerable to an approach.''

Clio drew in a trembling breath. "Oh, Jalal, you mean—you're part of their investigation?" And all at once she realized how stupid her suspicions of him had been. Born of paranoia and fear. He was not a man built for betrayal.

"What else?" he said matter-of-factly, and she bit her lip in self-condemnation.

"But how dangerous! What if someone finds out you're playing a double game!"

He stroked her strong smooth thigh with a lazy hand. "That is why you must not speak of this to anyone. Now you have my life in your hands twice over."

She wished her heart would calm down. What a lousy conspirator she would make—her heart rate would give her away every time.

"Go on," she said.

"My uncles were right. I was approached."

"And—who is it?"

He shook his head. "Still I have no names. But last night they asked for another meeting. They have said they have something...they believe it will convince me to throw in with them."

"Do you mean they might think they have something they could blackmail you with?"

He shook his head helplessly. "It seems obvious, but I cannot imagine what this could be. The evil I have done is a matter of public record. Everyone knows I kidnapped Princess Zara. What else is there?"

Jalal shrugged. "So, they will show me this—whatever it is. If they also reveal who is their ringleader, as we hope, my job is done. But if not—I have discovered nothing, Clio! I have not learned anything of real value. And it may be impossible for me to go along with them any further. I may be faced with a choice that...something to which I must say no. And then it will be all for nothing."

She was frightened suddenly, shivering with nerves. "When is the meeting?"

"Tomorrow. It is possible that afterwards I will have to return to the Emirates." He paused, stroking her head, and her hair all down her back. "Clio, beloved, I ask you again to go with me."

She dropped her head in helpless misery. "Jalal, you don't know what you're asking. You told me once that you aren't at home anywhere. I am at home. This is my home. Please don't ask me to go to the desert to spend my life, when you yourself don't even feel it's home. Please don't."

"I should not have said this. Of course it is my home."

"But what would I *do* there?"

He said, "We could spend every summer here. In Barakat everyone who can leaves the city for the summer. We can do the same."

She tried to think of it as a solution that would make her happy.

"What would I do the other nine months of the year? Be your wife at social events?"

"And be a mother to our children."

"And what of our children—what if we have a son?" she demanded.

He arched up to kiss her. "I hope we have many sons."

She turned and looked down at him lying against her pillows in the soft pool of light. Was light ever so sweetly gentle in the desert?

"To provide more temptation for future conspirators?" she suggested. "This is an endless thing, isn't it? There will always be someone, won't there, looking for a figurehead, a puppet, to front for their ambitions? I don't want that for my children."

"People forget," he murmured half-heartedly, not wishing to see the truth of what she said. "They will forget I was anything but Grand Vizier."

"And that's another thing. I couldn't be a political wife, Jalal. I couldn't learn to take it all seriously, all that...I mean, Zara enjoys it. And anyway, she has a career. She's an archaeologist. Whether she's on a dig or building a museum, she takes that part of her with her.

"But that part of me is just what I can't take with me. For me that's the ice cream shop, it's working with my mother, it's all the little things. It's having home and work so smoothly entangled it's practically seamless.

"Why don't you stay here? You like it here, you said it's in your blood."

He shook his head, as she knew he would, and her heart clenched with pain. She could foresee no unblemished happiness for herself now.

She said miserably, "You know—Zara avoided getting serious with Peter Clifford, because he was a small-town guy, with small-town ambitions. She knew if she got involved with him, one of them would be unhappy. I didn't have that problem with Peter—his lifestyle would have suited me down to the ground. That was exactly the kind of marriage I wanted."

"I am sorry I am not this man," Jalal said stiffly.

"I'm sorry, I'm not explaining it well, but don't you see what I'm saying? Zara avoided getting mixed up with anyone who couldn't understand what sort of a future she had in mind, or wouldn't want to share it. And I—I tried to do the same.

"Only you came here, and—oh, it's not fair!" she cried. "I didn't ask for this! I didn't ask for a foreign prince to come here and sweep me off my feet!"

Out of the torment of indecision and anguish, she wept, but for once he did not understand. His own pain was too powerful in him. To love at last, to understand the great mystery of the other half—and to be rejected in this way…it was one rejection too many in his life.

Jalal stood up, pulled on his clothes. "The foreign prince will go away again," he said.

She suddenly understood that she had hurt him. "Why can't you understand?" she cried. "Why should it automatically be me who gives everything up? Why can't you move here? Why do you think I should just jump at giving up everything I ever wanted, and you don't even have to look at the possibility?"

"What will I do in this country? My home is Barakat," Jalal said with stiff formality. "Let me advise you to go to your first lover Peter and invite him into your bed again. After one hour with you he will forget he ever knew your sister's name. Then you will have everything you want."

"I do not love Peter Clifford, I love you!" she said stonily, not sounding at all like a woman who meant love.

"But somehow you do not stop dreaming of him."

He opened the door and went out. She let him go.

Saifuddin ar Ratib lifted a briefcase onto the table. "You asked," he began, "for some proof that my principals have sufficient influence to carry their plans into successful action."

"I also asked," Jalal put in dryly, "for some evidence as to who they are."

"The time is not yet ripe for that, but the evidence I bring you will show you how close to the heart of the monarchy and the reins of power my principal has always been."

He removed a file folder from the case, snapped it shut and set it to one side. He sat with the file under his hands for a moment, regarding Jalal thoughtfully. Then, pushing the entire folder across the table to him, he said softly, "Read this."

Jalal smiled at the neat orchestration of the moment. His appetite whetted, of course he was now expected to grab it open. He leaned back casually in his chair, his legs spread, so that The Arranger should detect no impatience in him, find no weak spot of eagerness, and threaded his fingers together over his stomach.

"And what is this that you would have me read?" He indicated the folder with an arrogant tilt of his nose. "Tell me why it should interest me."

"Merely some documents that you will find enlightening as to my principal's long-term intentions and convictions, and his ability to put his plans into action."

"I will need more than a sheaf of documentation to convince me that he can successfully overthrow the present monarchy and reinstate a unified Barakat."

The Arranger smiled. "Nevertheless, he believes you will find these papers of supreme interest."

Still in no hurry, Jalal nodded and sipped his mint tea. At last he reached a lazy hand for the folder.

The first thing that met his eyes was his own signature. "Jalal ibn Aziz ibn Daud al Quraishi." He flicked a glance at Saifuddin and then his eyes fell irresistibly back to the document. He frowned.

"I am Jalal, the son of your brother, Prince Aziz. You know my history. I now request the right to take my place…"

Jalal murmured the words aloud as the tendrils of memory reached out to claim him. He remembered the shape of the pen in his hands, the smell of his mother's cooking, remembered even the hot wind that had blown through the garden as he sat composing this first letter to his uncles, long years ago.

He looked up. "This is no more than the letter all the world knows I have written, to my uncles."

Saifuddin ar Ratib watched him steadily. "Note that it is the original letter," he said.

Jalal stroked the paper between finger and thumb, felt the tell-tale ridging. "How did you get this?"

The Arranger merely smiled and shook his head, lifting a casual finger to encourage Jalal to read on.

He turned to the next document.

"From Jalal ibn Aziz ibn Daud to his uncles the Princes: I am astonished to have received no reply to my letter…"

He was surprised, now, to see how clearly he had set out his parentage. Over time he had forgotten. How could his uncles have pretended, after reading these, that they did not know of his existence?

"From Jalal ibn Aziz…why do you call me grandson of a bandit? Was King Daud a bandit? Are his sons?"

And yet they had seemed so convincing when they at last understood and accepted him….

Was this how these people intended to convince him to commit himself? By proving that his uncles had lied and betrayed him from the beginning?

"From Jalal ibn Aziz to his uncles who ignore their father's deathbed behest, know that I am determined…"

He looked at the letters, both sides. "There is no palace stamp on any," he said, frowning.

With a stroke like lightning through his brain, he understood. His eyes lifted to meet the steady, assessing gaze of Saifuddin ar Ratib. Jalal struggled to control his emotions. He must allow this man no window onto his soul.

"My uncles never received these letters," he said slowly.

Saifuddin ar Ratib inclined his head in acknowledgement of the truth of this.

"That is the reason they did not know who I was. How was it done?" Jalal asked, struggling to maintain an appearance of calm. "How was it effected? My own letters were intercepted, and others substituted as if from me, omitting all mention of my claim to my birthright? A letter from Jalal the grandson of Selim, demanding land only because his grandfather had been a bandit with de facto ownership of the desert...."

He faded into silence, thinking of those months in which he had believed himself spurned by his family, his father's half brothers, feeling again the anguish and its transmogrification into fury.

"That is how you were presented to the princes, yes."

His eyes dropped back to the file. There were many more documents than these letters. He turned to the next.

A photocopy of an assessment from a commanding officer during his military training, the name of the recipient obliterated with the censor's wide black stroke, but the terms of respect in the body of the letter making it clear he wrote to someone with position in the palace, to whom he described Jalal's abilities and progress....

Half a dozen similar letters, charting his progress in the military. Then his graduating marks from university. Respectful letters to an unknown recipient describing various details and incidents of his university career. *"In extra-curricular activities, too, he excels, his particular interests self-defence and swimming...."*

Letters from his schoolteachers, even. Everything.

His entire life, from the moment his mother, alone and desperate, had approached the palace, till he had returned to the desert and set up his camp. All here. All fully documented.

All that was missing were the letters he had sent after he abducted Zara.

"They never knew," Jalal said slowly, staring into the distant past. "My grandfather King Daud never knew of my existence. My grandmother...no one knew."

The dark head was graciously inclined. "That is true."

"My mother never learned the identity of the man she spoke to the day she went to the palace to reveal my existence. My uncles guessed that it was the late Nizam al Mulk, then the king's Grand Vizier. It was not Nizam al Mulk."

"It was not."

"It was not, as my mother believed, at the king's bidding that we moved to the city, that I was educated, that I was sent into officer training. It was this man. The man you call your principal."

The Arranger nodded. "May I say I admire the quickness of your grasp of the situation."

Jalal flicked him a look.

"What could his purpose have been in so great a deception lasting so many years? Revenge on my grandfather for some slight? Disdain for the illegitimacy of my birth?"

Saifuddin ar Ratib smiled. "Nothing so petty. He is a man of infinite patience and far-reaching command. When your mother arrived at the palace to tell her story, he saw at once the potential that might lie in your existence. The future he envisaged then for you required you to be carefully prepared, and he undertook to provide that preparation."

He sat as if listening to a distant voice.

"The preparation to be an outcast," Jalal murmured. "A man without roots. He tore me from the desert, from every subsequent certainty. All my life my mother spoke to me of a future different from what I was living…and that future never arrived. He knew my mother would break her silence eventually. It did not matter when. And when I made my representations to my uncles, he prevented their knowing me, as the final step in making me a rebel, the more easily to manipulate me," he added.

Saifuddin inclined his head. "You surprised him, however. Let it comfort you that he did not expect your return to the desert, nor the setting up of your camp. Nor the successful taking of a hostage, and forcing your uncles to recognize…"

Jalal showed his teeth. "You neither comfort me nor disturb my comfort with anything that you can say," he said with level contempt.

"And this fool—" he indicated the file with a flick of his hands and tossed it onto the table "—who has spent his life with this nonsense! Is such a man to be respected? This is not a fairy tale of lost heirs!"

He got to his feet. "Was it your intention to convince me that this man is a worthy partner in my endeavours? He is no more than a daydreaming old man. He mistakes plots for deeds," said Prince Jalal ibn Aziz ibn Daud al Quraishi, and he turned and went with contemptuous ease down the steps of the terrace to his boat.

Nineteen

The light shone under her door, showing that she was awake, and perhaps waiting for him.

Jalal knocked, and at her murmur, entered. She was sitting propped up by her pillows under a thin sheet, a magazine neglected in her lap.

"I heard your boat," she said. "Have you found out anything?"

"Yes." He came and sat on the bed. "He has exposed himself without realizing it. If I were not in contact with my uncles, there would be little risk to him in letting me know what I learned tonight. But my uncles will be able to guess, from what I tell them, who was in a position to do the things that he has done."

"So it's all over?"

"As to that—yes, one way or another, he is finished. Though it may take time to discover the full extent of the conspiracy."

She was silent, looking gravely into his eyes. "Then what is the bad news? What has so distressed you to-night?"

He stared at her. "How do you know it?"

She leaned close and smiled into his dark eyes. "You told me. When you came up the stairs I could hear it in your footsteps. I see it now, in your face."

His hand cupped her head, holding her there. His eyes searched her face for a moment.

"It is said in the stories that even so did my grandmother understand my grandfather...without words. And he could read her mind also. My uncles say this is no more than the truth.

"They knew my grandfather and grandmother intimately, as father and beloved stepmother...I knew them only as king and queen of the country."

"Yes," she murmured sadly.

"This was always a mystery to me. From the moment I learned my true birthright I struggled to understand why my grandfather and grandmother had never wished to see me. You, too, said it. The son of their own beloved son. The single product of their great love. Yet they were satisfied to educate me from a distance. Why? My grandfather lived more than a dozen years after my existence and parentage were discovered to him...so many days and years when we could have enjoyed each other's company."

"He was an old man," she whispered.

"Something like this I have always told myself. I made many excuses for them—that the pain of meeting me would revive their old grief in the loss of their only sons. That my grandfather perhaps did not entirely believe my mother—her case could not then be proved, as it is now, with DNA tests. Or that the stain of my birth was an impossible barrier.

"Or perhaps he did not want to be faced with the choice of disinheriting his three younger sons or dividing the kingdom into four.... I told myself he avoided being tempted into these things by never meeting me, never loving me."

He paused, and she sat with him in silence and soft lamplight, waiting for his thoughts to form. Outside the soft circle of light, the world was dark and still. The water brushed the shore, a boat squeaked against a dock, wind murmured in the branches.

When he shook his head and heaved a breath, she reached both hands to clasp his head. "And what have you learned tonight that changes all that?" she asked gently.

"They never knew of my existence," he told her baldly. "My grandfather, my grandmother—they were robbed of the knowledge that one of their dead sons had left a son behind him. That is why they never summoned me to the palace. They did not know I was alive in the world. They died without knowing."

His pain was palpable in the room. Her heart clenched with sorrowing feeling.

"Oh, Jalal!" Clio whispered. "But then—your education, your whole life...who did they think you were when they did all that?"

"They knew nothing of these things. I have been, from the moment my mother went to the palace, a toy...a pawn in the hands of a man, a despicable man...."

"What?" she breathed, horrified.

Absently he stroked the delicate, precious line of her collarbone. "This man pretended to my mother that he told the king her secret. He acted as if on the king's orders, and passed on 'his' messages and instructions.''

"But why didn't she insist on your meeting your own grandparents?''

He shook his head at her. "No, Clio, you do not understand—what did she know? She was an ignorant woman from the desert. She could not read. She had committed a grave sin with her princely lover, which she had to confess in order to tell the king of my existence. What could she understand of her value to the king? Or of mine? How could she insist that her illegitimate son meet his grandfather?''

"But even so—''

He touched her lips.

"Clio, you cannot understand such a woman as my mother. It is so far from anything you know. You are a free woman, knowing your importance in the world. Your father values you, your mother is a woman of influence, and you hope to be like her. You are the equal of your brothers. Even this ugliness with this man, Peter—he was one man who made you feel of less value than your sister. My mother has struggled against the opinion of all society, for the simple belief that she is a human being with value in God's eyes!''

His voice was choked with feeling. She made no reply, but waited for him to say what he needed to say.

"She was deeply and always grateful to her father—to her own father, Clio!—because he did not kill her and me with her in the womb! He did not deliver her to the tribe for stoning, but instead gave her into slavery with an old husband—when she had been the beloved of a prince!''

She whispered his name.

"When this man in the palace told her the king would never see her, but would support her and her son...this

was much more than in her heart she expected. Can you
see the huge bravery that she had, to go to the palace at
all? And there to insist on seeing someone of importance!
Perhaps the king would kill her for bearing his illegitimate
grandson. Perhaps she would be accused of lies, of trick-
ery…. How was she to know?

"The Prophet said, 'Women are the twin-halves of
men,' Clio, but he spoke to an ignorant desert people who
lived by the sword, who valued nothing but a man's sword
arm, and who would not learn the lesson. And still we go
on refusing to learn it, turning our backs on what he said,
the knowledge he brought fourteen hundred years ago.

He turned to her, lifting his hands to her face. Strong,
sure, they cupped her head, and he stared deep into her
dark eyes.

"They told me all this tonight for a purpose. They said
it was to convince me that the man behind all this is
powerful and can deliver on his promise. Close enough to
the throne to… But I know that it was psychological ma-
nipulation—they wanted to deliver such a blow at last
that, doubting everything, I would commit myself to them
finally and completely."

"And—did it work?"

"It has shaken me to my soul to know that my life is
so different from what I believed. To think that I have
been a pawn—deliberately frustrated so that my anger
could be used by this man for his own purposes. He created such an existence for me so that I would hate, because hatred can be twisted into useful shapes. And he
thought to make me a weapon in his own hands."

"Oh Jalal, what a monster he must be!" she said, feeling deeply helpless. What could be said to comfort such
appalling pain?

"Yes, a monster." He lifted a hand. "And a fool. A

fool. To spend twenty-five years on a plan that has no end, no goal, but destruction. Destruction of my uncles, of the whole structure of the Emirates...not one positive, one good, to anyone, nothing but backward ignorance and evil.

"And as long as I am in Barakat, Clio, I will be a focus for such madmen. Always I will be the nearest puppet prince for fools who cannot remember that the Prophet said also that a state survives without religion, but not without justice."

"*Did* he?" she interjected, amazed.

"Yes, and many other wise things that fools ignore."

He heaved a sigh and held her head between his hands. "You were right. How can I take you to that, to such a life of politics and conspiracy as would always surround us and our children?"

She was silent, breathless with hope, with shock, with love, with compassion.

"I have no life there now. Everything is severed. I am free from what I believed, from all that I wanted and fought for—free from the burden of my past and my history.

"If you accept me as your husband, Clio, I will stay here with you, and build a life amongst the lakes and forest. I will see that my grandmother's descendants return to the kind of land she loved, and our children will inherit what we build for them, and nothing more.

"Do you accept, my beloved? Will this please you as it pleases me?"

She was weeping too hard to answer.

In the King's Pavilion, four men lounged around the fountain, drinking mint tea, eating the rich powdered sweetmeats that lay on small silver trays.

"As long as I remain here, how can I fail to be a focus for every sect that is disenchanted with the state of the monarchy or the country?" Jalal asked. "It's too obvious, too easy. I don't want to spend my life being tempted, by one manipulator after another, to overthrow your joint rule, against my grandfather's clear wishes."

"Father might have had other wishes, if he had been privileged to know of your existence," Omar said. "It's possible that you would even have been seen as a way out of his dilemma. He could have favoured you over all three of us, with the country's blessing, and none of his wives could have complained. And the kingdom would have remained undivided."

Jalal nodded. It was true. Perhaps it would always remain a tormenting mystery, what course his life would have followed if Selim had taken his pregnant daughter immediately to the palace, instead of playing a deeper game, or if, when his mother at last went, she had not fallen into ambitious hands....

At the very least, perhaps, his uncles would have seemed like cousins, or brothers, rather than the virtual strangers they now were. And he might have felt at home in his father's grand palace.

"Perhaps. In that case, however, I would have been raised to the task of rule. But I was not. You were, and you do it well. All of you." He looked around. "The people love you, and they love your beautiful, foreign wives. If I am not here to be always pointed to as an alternative...the little discontents will seep into the ground and be lost."

"What are you saying, Jalal?" Rafi asked.

Rafi's near twin set down the tiny gold-etched teacup, and waited till the eyes of all three princes were on him.

"I want to leave Barakat. I will renounce my father's titles and go abroad to live. I want to be done with the quest for power and recognition, and for family."

There was silence as they took it in, each in his own particular way. Omar gazed absently at the sparkling fountain, stroking his beard, listening intently; Karim raised his eyebrows, nodding; Rafi looked at his all-but-twin with a level, assessing gaze.

The silence stretched and stretched.

"Where will you go?" Karim asked.

And Rafi suggested softly, "Clio?"

Jalal's head bent in a quick nod. "Yes, Clio. I will buy a house on a lake where she has lived all her life. I have spoken to her father about the business. We think of me investing in it, perhaps…or I would like to invest in water purification, industrial waste treatment, to keep the lakes free from pollution."

"Jalal, are you sure about all this?"

Jalal ibn Aziz ibn Daud ibn Hassan al Quraishi nodded. "Yes, I am sure," he said. "Sure."

The old church at Love's Point had not seen such a crowd for a very long time. The congregation glowed as they spilled into the quiet, tree-lined streets, everyone dressed in the most beautiful outfits in their wardrobe, young and old, rich and poor, prince and commoner alike.

The marriage between Clio Blake and Jalal al Quraishi had taken place in the 150-year-old church, and the reception had followed in the beautiful gardens, with their flowered lawns rolling down to the banks of the quiet, pretty river.

The bride was beautiful in traditional white, her elegant, long-sleeved matte satin dress smoothly fitted from breast to hip, and billowing into folds down to her feet, her train as gauzy and romantic over her long flowing hair as any of her young bridesmaids could have wished.

They all wore white, with tiny seed pearl and flower wreaths in their hair, and as they crowded around Clio now, they looked like vestal virgins accompanying their goddess.

In the street a white limousine, now sporting a massive Just Married sign and strings trailing numerous tin cans, bore witness to the labours of some among the congregation during the past hour. A long line of cars behind proved that many of the guests intended to accompany the bridal couple on the first leg of their journey, to the airport, where they would board a flight for an unknown destination.

The late-September sun was smiling and warm as the congregation stood in happy groups, and a small breeze obligingly lifted the bride's veil and blew it picturesquely around her.

There were still pictures being taken, but these were all by friends, the media long since having taken their photos of the bride and groom, as well as Prince Rafi and the prettily pregnant Princess Zara of East Barakat, and departed to meet their deadlines.

Everyone stood around chatting, unwilling to leave, or bring an end to a lovely day. The bride and groom stood in the church path smiling and talking to well-wishers, until someone looked at his watch and said, "Well, time to get started, if you want to catch that plane."

Clio and Jalal smiled wickedly into each other's eyes, and then clasped each other's hand and started…not towards the car, but along the curving paved pathway that led down under willow trees to the river.

They turned back, giving the startled congregation one

last chance for a photo, smiled and waved, and then set off lightly running down to the river.

Before anyone could seriously get it together to realize what was going on, they were seen climbing into a large powerboat that was moored by the bank, and by the time anyone had arrived at the river, the engine was running smoothly and the groom was guiding the boat out into the narrow river.

"Bye!" they called, laughing as the congregation spilled down the banks and, mouths open with smiling surprise, stood waving at the disappearing couple, Clio standing within the embrace of Jalal's arm as he drove, her veil streaming wildly out behind.

After a moment they were out of sight, under the bridge, heading out into the lake.

Clio unpinned her veil and tossed it lightly down into the cabin, then shook her long hair and stretched luxuriously up towards the sun, tilting her head to smile at her new husband.

"Hello," she said softly.

He flicked a glance around for any approaching boat, and seeing none, took his eyes off the water long enough to cup her head in one powerful hand and kiss her willing mouth with contained passion.

"Hello," he said, with proud possessiveness.

"Oh, what a beautiful day!" she exclaimed, happiness shimmering through her voice. "Wasn't it fabulous?"

"Fabulous," he agreed, with a look at her that melted her so that she had to close her eyes.

"Do you think they'll guess where we're going?"

"Maybe. Your friends maybe. But let's hope they won't tell anyone who really wants to know."

"Maybe the press will be happy with pictures of Zara and Rafi for the next week."

"We don't have to worry. Today they want our photographs, but we will soon be very ordinary people."

She kissed him. "Yes, to think I could have married a prince!" She lifted a haughty shoulder. "I'll always be able to tell our children that a prince once proposed to me!"

"And I will always be able to tell them that you turned the prince down for a commoner," he said.

They took the familiar route, across the lake, through a channel, into another lake, and at last making their way up Bent Needle River towards Solitaire. A few minutes later the boat drew up by the dock, and Clio stepped out, still in her gracefully beautiful dress, with the bow line.

She stood on the dock in the late sun while Jalal made the boat fast, sighing in happiness as she took in the rich reds and yellows of the turning leaves. And then they caught each other's hand again and started up the path to their honeymoon cottage and a new life.

* * * * *

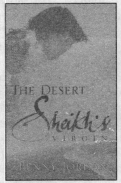